CHAOS

CHAOS

BY

CM FENN

Chaos
By
CM Fenn

Published by CM Fenn
Copyright © 2017 CM Fenn
All rights reserved.

Editor: Sharon Honeycutt
Cover art: Damonza.com

ISBN: 0-9903864-3-0
ISBN-13: 978-0-9903864-3-8

For Jensen Adam

*"It turns out that an errie type of chaos can lurk
just behind a façade of order – and yet, deep inside
the chaos lurks an even errier type of order."*

–Douglass Hofstadter
American Novelist, & Pulitzer Prize Winner

CHAPTER 1

FALLING. I'M FALLING. Again. I'm always falling when my dreams bring me to this place. This time it's a vast and empty desert that stretches out below me. Last time, it was a dark, angry ocean. There's no sound but my desperate, uneven gasps while I fight to breathe against the wind rushing past me as I fall out of the sky. I can't hear the wind, even though it's so strong that it whips my hair and clothing around violently. I can't hear the fabric snap and ruffle as it threatens to tear from my body. I can hear only my breath and it's louder in my ears than it should be.

Color is also absent from this place. Though my eyes sting and tear, I'm able to see that everything is a blurred and muted black and white. As I fall, the details of the desert are at the center of my vision, but the edges of the scene are fuzzy, out of focus. I'm able to view it calmly at first. I've experienced this dream so many times that I'm able to push past the initial feeling of terror and take in as much detail as possible. I'm not sure why it's important for me to do this.

I've never experienced this level of clarity in any of my

other dreams. In this dream, I know that I am dreaming. I know that I'll wake up soon and it will all be over. This helps me past the panic.

That is, until the very end.

Right before I am about to slam into the hard earth, the terror rises. My heart hammers in my chest against my ribs. Harder. Faster. My mind tells me it's only a dream but my body screams. My arms and legs flail, trying to push back against the air. My head and neck arch backward and turn away in an attempt to further distance myself from the solid ground that's rushing up to meet me all too quickly now.

I gasp for breath desperately. It's so loud in my ears. I squeeze my eyes closed as tight as I can to hide the sight of the jagged rocks and shrubs littering the hard earth. My mind tries one last desperate attempt to convince myself there is no impending impact.

Stop. Stop! Wake up! It's too real! I can almost feel the heat from the desert air. Maybe it IS real this time! Maybe I won't wake up soon enough! I fight the scream climbing up my throat but it's tearing its way through, up and out and I open my eyes and the ground is—

∾

"Adelaide. Addy! Stop screaming!"

Someone's shaking me. It's so dark. Is it over? Is it over now?

"Sheesh, Addy, you scared the crap outta me! You probably woke the neighbors. I wouldn't be surprised if they call the cops." Jana reaches above me and snaps on the bedside lamp. It takes a second for my eyes to adjust to the sudden brightness, but when they do, I see my older sister sitting on the bed in front of me looking very annoyed. My anxious mother suddenly appears in my doorway. She's in her lavender pajamas and wielding a... pumice stone?

"What is it? Jana? What's the matter? I heard a scream! Addy? Is everything all right?" I've never seen Mom so wild-eyed and panicked. She clutches the neck of her pajama shirt as she tiptoes into the room, eyes darting to the darkened corners.

"Mom, it's okay, we're okay. It was just another bad dream. Sorry," I apologize sheepishly.

Jana explodes with laughter. "Gee Mom, let's hope there aren't any bad guys around with really rough skin. You'd show them who's boss, wouldn't you!"

Mom sticks her chin out and frowns. "Well, it was the most threatening thing I could grab in a hurry."

"Oooooo, calluses beware! Bunions cower in fear!"

"It was either this or my loofa!" she says as she turns a shade of pink. Poor Mom, she does her best.

I shove Jana. "Hey, it's more productive than sitting there shaking me and yelling." I realize I'm dripping in sweat. Ugh, even my sheets are soaked. The disgusted look on Jana's face tells me she's noticed it too.

"Next time you decide to wake up screaming bloody murder at the crack of dawn, make sure it's on a day I'm not visiting. A girl's gotta get her beauty sleep, you know." She pats me on the head as she gets up to leave. "Anyway, stop reading those books of yours before bed. They give you nightmares," she says as she walks back down the hall to her room. I glance guiltily at my favorite suspense author's latest novel on my bedside table, dog-eared two-thirds of the way through.

Mom takes Jana's place on the bed. She looks really concerned. "Another falling dream?"

Mom and I talk a lot about my dreams lately since they've gotten worse and more frequent. The lack of sleep has begun to take its toll. She thinks stress at school is causing the dreams. I'm in my last semester of my senior year and I'm swamped, prepping for finals.

"This one was worse than all the others. It felt so real, Mom. I was almost convinced it was, right there at the end. I keep waking up later and later, or in other words, closer to becoming a pancake." I can't fight the shiver that runs through me. "This time I must have been just feet from hitting the ground. Maybe inches."

She notices I'm shaking and motions for me to scoot over so she can sit next to me. She puts an arm around me and pulls me close. I try to shrug away. "No Mom. I'm sweaty and gross."

"Nonsense. Now tell me about this one, if it helps."

"Thanks," I mumble. Telling her about the dreams does help, as if voicing them makes them less real and almost silly.

"Well, it started out normal, like always. We were at Gram's. Jana and I were younger and we kept asking her if we could swim in her pool, which is weird because Gram doesn't have a pool. Anyway, she made us wait until you were in your bathing suit. Then I was on the diving board and Jana kept saying, 'Belly flop! Belly flop!' I jumped up and shouted, 'Cannon ball!' but then there was no water. Instead, I was alone above a desert. You know the rest."

Mom sighs heavily. She wants so bad to help me, but what can you do when it comes to nightmares? "Maybe there's some truth to what Jana said. Maybe the book you're reading is getting to you. Or maybe you're worried about your physics final and it's seeping through your subconscious into your dreams."

Now it's my turn to sigh. While physics is a difficult class for me, I put in plenty of study time for the final and I know I'm ready for it. I'm too tired to argue the point so I concede. "Maybe Mom. Anyway, I'm already wide awake so I might as well shower and get ready for school. I can even use the extra time to go over my physics stuff again before the final today." I grin at her, hoping to dispel some of her worry. While she's not completely fooled, she does seem mollified a little.

"All right, sounds like a good idea. I'll make your favorite this morning while you're showering. Maybe blueberry pancakes can chase away any bad feelings the dream left behind. Only... let's let Jana think it's because she's visiting!" She giggles a bit deviously at me.

"Ooo good plan!" I hug her tightly. "Thanks Momma, you're the best."

"I love you, sweetie." She gets up and kisses me on the cheek before she leaves.

I know Mom babies me. I know it can appear quite nauseating. Not fighting it is the least I can do for her after everything she's gone through. Jana and I are all she has now and she holds us that much closer because of it.

The rest of the morning is typical of the Shepherd home. Jana and I tease each other mercilessly all through breakfast, as is our routine. No one understands our relationship. Fighting is how we get along. It's when we aren't giving each other a hard time that you need to worry something's wrong. I really have missed her. This was her first year away from home. She's only a few hours north of us, at college in Flagstaff, so she's still comes home every few weeks.

Home is Queen Creek, Arizona, a desert land much like the one from last night's dream, only some farmers have tamed the land here enough to raise corn and cotton. Some of my neighbors raise horses, and there's even a dairy farm a few miles up the road, close enough for a strong wind to remind you it's there.

Queen Creek is a quiet place, filled with good, humble, salt-of-the-earth people. Everything is slower here. But travel twenty minutes north and you find yourself in the middle of the bustling, busy, metropolis of Phoenix, Arizona. Jana comes into the bathroom to do her makeup while I'm brushing my teeth. I watch her put on her eyeliner. She's concentrating so hard on the task that I'm tempted to bump her, but I think better of it.

She's focused on what she's doing, so I take the chance to examine her. We don't really look like sisters. She got Mom's petite, girly features: a small, delicate frame; light brown hair; crystal-clear blue eyes. And here she is, flawlessly putting on makeup like a supermodel—like she even needs it!

Then there's me: I can't tell my eyeliner from lip liner. I never got the whole makeup thing. Heaven knows Jana's tried to teach me time and time again, but after that last mascara massacre, I feel like she's finally given up on me.

No, I didn't inherit my mother's natural beauty and grace. I follow more after my father. I loved his face so much that, while I'm not a "conventional" beauty, I can't help but be proud of what I see of him in me. I have his thick, dark brown hair that halfheartedly curls like it can't make up its mind—curly or straight? We have the same smile and our eyes are the same shape, only different colors. His were a light cucumber green, while mine are a very light golden brown. "Honey eyes" my parents would call them.

I finish getting ready, kiss Mom goodbye, and run out to "Old Blue," Dad's old pickup. She really was blue at one time, but the hood is so rusted over it's hard to tell anymore. Mom's offered to trade it in for something younger and "cuter," but I love this old hunk of metal. Even after all this time, I swear the cab still smells like my father's cologne. The memories that smell stirs up are priceless. I sit there this morning in the pre-dawn light and think of him. It's been four years since he died. My mind takes me back to that night.

It was mid-August, which for Queen Creek and the surrounding areas is monsoon season. You wouldn't think a desert could get so much rain. But when it rains here during the monsoons, it pours. For hours. Sometimes for days. I used to love the rain. In the sweltering heat of the desert, rainy days were holidays. But now they're depressing, like they are to the rest of America.

I was thirteen that August. Dad had picked me up from my friend's birthday party and we were on our way home. It was dark out and the rain pounded the windshield. Dad was asking me about the party and which friends were there and if I had a good time. He was that kind of dad, one that knew the names of all my friends and how I felt about each of them. He wasn't only my dad, he was my friend. I remember his favorite country station was playing quietly in the cab of the truck. He was driving slowly because the rain had collected and pooled in the streets, making it difficult to drive. While the rhythmic thumping of the windshield wipers was soothing, they were useless against the constant downpour. Visibility was at a minimum.

Up ahead blurred red and yellow lights blinked on the side of the road. As we got closer, Dad recognized the small black car. It belonged to Patricia Greenwood.

Patty is an older lady, a widow, who lives four houses down from us. Dad never questioned why she decided to go out into a storm. He didn't call her a crazy old lady, or even hesitate at all. He pulled over behind her, turned on "Old Blue's" hazards, and told me to stay in the truck—he'd only be a minute. I remember those green eyes as he smiled at me that last time. So clear, so kind.

RAP RAP RAP! The sharp noise startles me and I jump and look out the window. Mom's waving a brown sack next to her grinning face. I crank the window down and she says, "I didn't mean to scare you. You were really in the zone, you know? Going over equations in your head?"

"Oh… yeah. Just some last-minute stuff to make sure

I have it all down," I lie as I shake the fog from my mind. I can't tell Mom what I was thinking. I can't bear to see the heartbreak that's still so plain on her face whenever she thinks of Dad.

"Well, I'm glad I caught you before you left. I got you a little something for lunch today. For extra good luck! Do your best today, okay sweetie?" She hands me the sack lunch.

I peek in the bag and see my favorite chicken salad sandwich wrapped in cellophane tucked next to a square of last night's homemade brownies. I smile and thank her. She winks and wishes me good luck as I back out of the driveway.

Instantly I'm back in the land of teenager, where my biggest worries are the test in third hour, and getting the library set up for the end-of-the-year art exhibit, and whether or not I'll get up the nerve to speak to Kevin Ludlow in fifth hour.

If only I can shake this feeling that my nightmare has left behind. Like something big is coming. That gnawing sensation that something awful is on the way twists my stomach into sour knots. My gut tells me there's a storm on the horizon, my only question – can I make it through unscathed?

CHAPTER 2

I PULL INTO my usual parking space in the south lot on campus. It's one of the farthest spots from the buildings but it's also under a large tree. Parking in the shade at this time of year can mean the difference between getting into a 120-degree car at the end of the day and getting into a 150-degree car.

It's still pretty early and there are only one or two other students around, so I find a bench next to the lockers and begin studying for the umpteenth time. I submerge myself in my notes, and before I know it campus buzzes with the chatter of students. I look up and scan the crowd for familiar faces. Everyone seems more upbeat than normal. The school year is almost over and the anticipation for lazy summer days is palpable. It doesn't hurt either that tomorrow is Friday, and for most of the students here, the last day of finals.

I see Kevin about ten yards off and heading in my direction. It's no coincidence I'm sitting on the bench closest to his locker. His adorable, floppy brown hair bounces in his eyes as he walks. He brushes it away and looks up.

All right, Addy, smile. Just smile at him. It isn't hard. His eyes travel toward where I'm sitting and my heart does a quick double-beat. There's a funny fluttering feeling in the pit of my stomach. I'm deciding how big my smile should be, and what type of smile I should give, and how long I should maintain eye contact, when Kevin's best friend Josh runs up to him and puts his arm across his shoulders, commanding all his attention.

Damn.

A shrill voice pierces through the crowd noise. "What… in the hell… are you wearing?"

I clench my jaw and sigh inwardly. Tori. My best friend. As she stomps over to where I'm sitting, her stilettos clack-clack-clack angrily on the concrete and her earrings and wrist bangles jingle frantically.

"Good morning, Tor!" I smile up at her, hoping to dispel the coming rebuke, but to no avail.

"My gosh, Addy. Why do you do this to me?" She gestures somewhat hysterically at my clothing. "I know you own nice clothes! I bought them for you!" Her voice gets louder and higher in pitch as she goes on. "You've had that shirt since the fifth grade, for crying out loud!"

People are beginning to stare. I glance toward Kevin's locker and find to my horror that he and Josh are watching the scene. I look down into my physics notes on my lap to avoid seeing Kevin's face. I can't bear to see if he's laughing. My cheeks are hot and I know I'm blushing.

"It isn't that bad, Tor." I say defensively as I examine my clothing. I'm in a pair of slightly torn and faded jeans and my old black *Felix the Cat* shirt. They're both worn thin and as a result have become soft and light and are the most comfortable clothing I own.

"I wanted to be comfy for finals," I explain.

She rolls her eyes and heaves a sigh as she plops down next to me. She begins rummaging through her over-sized designer purse. "Whatever, Addy. You need to keep in mind you're almost done with your high school career and you're going to have to grow up sometime."

Tori and I have a bizarre relationship. We have absolutely nothing in common and I don't believe that either of us particularly likes the other. But we continue to call each other friends. We met in third grade and were instantly best friends. We spent every weekend through the school year together playing, and every day in the summertime. Then in the seventh grade, her estranged grandfather died quite suddenly and left an obscene amount of money to her father. It might sound like something straight out of the movies, but it really happened.

At first, I was ecstatic for Tori. They immediately sold their old double-wide trailer and moved into a sprawling, three-story mansion surrounded by acres of horse property. Her parents bought nicer cars for themselves and a thoroughbred for Tori.

They started traveling a lot and went on cruises to exotic places every other month. I hardly saw her anymore. When we were together, we were either bored out of our minds because we couldn't find a shared interest, or we were at each other's throats arguing. Suddenly, we couldn't relate to each other anymore. I couldn't compete with her expensive toys and exciting new lifestyle. We were on the verge of going our separate ways. Then came that awful night in August when I found myself fatherless and in desperate need of comfort and friendship.

Tori had been my best friend for years, and even though we'd drifted apart, she knew me better than anyone. I really needed her during that difficult time and she was there for me. Even though we would probably both be happier apart, I believe we're still friends because of a mutual sense of guilt: She would feel guilty ditching me because Dad died, and I would feel guilty ditching her because she was there for me through the hardest time of my life.

So now we're "besties" who are nearly complete opposites. She's a blonde (from a bottle), who has blue eyes (thanks to colored contacts), a figure to die for (yes, she paid for that too), and wears expensive designer clothes and accessories.

I, on the other hand, value comfort over couture, practicality over pretty. And I still have only my natural God-given body parts to work with. I decide not to let the minor public humiliation of her critique on my appearance ruin my day.

"So are you ready for third hour?" I ask, as she perfects her lip gloss in her compact mirror's reflection.

"I think so. My tutor gave me a practice test yesterday and I aced it. I'm feeling pretty good."

"This is your last final, isn't it?" I ask.

She nods her head as she puts her makeup back into her

purse. A devious grin on her face. "Daddy says if I ace all my finals I can trade in Trixie for next year's model!"

Trixie is Tori's cute little red convertible.

"I thought that was going to be your graduation present."

Her expression gets even more devious, if that's at all possible. "Nope! My mom finally convinced him to let me go to Paris!" She grabs my shoulders and shakes me. "Avec Jordan!" she squeaks.

"Whoa," is all I can manage. Jordan is Tori's older boyfriend. He's twenty-two and attends the local community college. He doesn't have a job, or any motivation to get one. Why would he? He still lives at home and his parents pay for his car and schooling and endless partying. He's frequently drunk and reeks of cigarette smoke. Tori's father hates him.

"I know. I can't believe it! My mom is an angel."

I'm thinking to myself how I'm not certain what kind of angel would send their teenage daughter on a trip halfway around the world with someone like Jordan. Since their increase in wealth, Tori's mother Candice has done everything in her power to regain her youth, which includes being the "cool" mom and allowing her daughter to do basically whatever she wants. I do a mental eye roll and wonder how "Candi" thinks this couldn't possibly come back to haunt her.

Tori glows, however, looking rather like the cat that caught the canary. Before I get a chance to discuss the matter more with her, the first bell rings. I cram my notes into my bag and glance up in the direction of my first-hour AP government class, which happens to be located across the hall from Kevin Ludlow's first-hour Spanish 3 class. I see him ahead of me talking with Josh and watch the back of his head as Tori and I walk. While she rambles on about her plan of attack on the tourist attractions in and around Paris, Kevin looks back over his shoulder and our eyes lock.

He is looking right at me. Blatantly and openly. He smiles. I smile. We hold eye contact for a second before he turns around and disappears through his classroom doorway.

Did that just happen? I'm light-headed and giddy and not even hearing Tori anymore. Her chatter is a distant buzz in the background. Did Kevin really turn and look at me? I can't stop my smile from turning into a huge grin that takes over my whole face.

He is so adorable with his sweet brown eyes and crooked smile. But why would he smile at me? I've never even talked to him, except to lend him a pencil one time in class. Was my infatuation with him so obvious that he had caught on? That would be so embarrassing! But still, if he didn't like me, why smile at me?

Then it hits me like a runaway train and my smile disappears. Of course he wasn't looking at me. I'm walking with Tori, one of the prettiest girls in school. It's nearly impossible to get noticed in her company. How could I have thought that smile was meant for me? I try not to resent Tori for this. I already have enough of that to fight off.

"So, I was hoping I could get them to let me stay two weeks instead of one but that is going to take some serious charming on my part," Tori's still talking away, oblivious to the fact that I've not listened to a word she's said.

"Well, good luck. Knowing your dad, he'll probably cave," I say as we reach my class door. "Hey, have a good morning, Tor. I'll see you third hour."

"Yeah, see ya," she says as she waves over her shoulder and heads off to AP chem.

I duck into class before the warning bell can ring. Today's an easy day in government. We took the written part of our final on Monday; every day since we've spent giving and listening to the oral presentations that make up the other half of our final. Mine isn't scheduled until tomorrow, so today I sit back and listen. I take notes and try to focus on what the other kids are saying so my mind doesn't wander back to Kevin and his smile.

Second hour is intermediate art—my favorite class. We've been meeting in the library this week trying to set up for the end-of-the-year exhibit. Each year three students are chosen throughout the art departments (performing and applied) to be showcased as "Tomorrow's Stars." They get an entire section of the exhibit for their work. My art teacher, Mrs. McCowen, nominated me this year and I found out last week that I was chosen!

It's a huge honor and one that I'm sure will look good on my college application – if and when I decide to apply. With money being tight, and mom already paying for Jana's tuition, I haven't decided if I'll even make it to college.

When class starts, I still haven't made up my mind on which works to display, but by the end of the hour, and with the help of Mrs. McCowen, I've finally decided on a lineup for my section of the exhibit.

My third-hour physics final takes almost the whole hour, but when I'm finished I know I'll earn at least a "B" on it. When class ends, Tori and I walk to our lockers together to drop our stuff off before we go to lunch.

"How do you think you did?" I ask.

"How, you say? Magnifique!" she says in a flawless French accent. She throws her head back and her hands up and shouts, "Oh, no more finals! Paris, here I come!"

The rest of the school day goes pretty well. I don't get up the nerve to speak to Kevin in my fifth-hour class and he doesn't flash his smile at me, which only confirms my previous suspicions—he'd been smiling at Tori.

I meet her at the lockers when school's out. She's talking with some of the other "high-maintenance" girls, so I hang back and wait for her. The sun's beating down and there's no breeze today. I'm dreading getting into my truck. The air conditioning usually doesn't start to kick in until I'm pulling into my driveway. Tori looks like she has news to share when she makes it over my way.

"I got a text from Jordan last hour. He says he's throwing a party tomorrow night. I was just telling Emily to invite everyone she knows. You should come by. There's gonna be a ton of college boys there!" She smiles and winks at me. I have a moment of complete panic as I search for some valid-sounding excuse not to be there. Then with relief, I remember Jana's in town and we're supposed to have a girls' night out tomorrow, just the two of us.

"Oh shoot. I can't." I put on my best bummed-out look. "Jana's here this weekend and I promised to go shopping with her." As we walk out to the parking lot, I realize I'm actually looking forward to spending time with Jana.

I say good-bye to Tori and head home. Sure enough, I'm sweating buckets by the time I get there so I take a quick shower. When I'm finished and getting dressed in my room, I hear dishes clinking in the kitchen. Mom must be home from her part-time job at the post office. I head to the kitchen to help her unload the dishwasher.

"Hey!" she greets me with a smile. "Sooooo? How did you do?"

I laugh because I know she's been wondering all day how my test went. "Great, I think. There were only a few questions I wasn't positive about. It was multiple-choice answers, though, so I still have a decent chance of getting those right." I can tell she's relieved. We talk about her day and she tells me a funny story about a friend of hers at work. As she laughs, her blue eyes sparkle and the lines at the corners of her eyes crinkle up. I can't help but be so grateful I have her in my life.

Losing a parent can put life into perspective, forcing you to view everything so differently. You cherish and love the ones that remain with you. You recognize moments like this as precious. You study every detail and commit it to your memory so you have it with you always. Hopefully, someday I'll have enough of these types of memories to fill up the empty space inside.

Jana gets home from visiting a friend and Mom orders

delivery pizza. We all sit around the television and watch the news as we eat. Stories about Hurricane Ilsa and all the devastation it's left behind are everywhere. Rich Bennet, the lead anchor from Channel 5 news, is on site and stands in front of a pile of rubble that used to be a church. He wears a solemn expression as he tells how the estimated death toll has climbed to over three hundred.

I look out our back window and see the sun glaring in the sky. I can almost feel it sucking all the moisture from the dirt and plants and air, and I marvel at the thought that a handful of states east of here, entire towns have been torn apart by storms and floods.

After dinner, I practice my presentation for government a few times with Mom and Jana as my audience. My topic is on creating stricter laws and punishments for repeat domestic abuse offenders. I take their suggestions and tweak a few things until I'm satisfied with it. By the time I finish, it's only early evening, but last night's lack of sleep is really kicking in. I get ready for bed, kiss Mom good night, stick my tongue out at Jana, and head to my room. I climb into my queen-sized bed and stare at the shapes that the fading light from my window makes on my ceiling. I put a slow song on my iPhone on repeat. Before it can play through even once, I'm asleep.

᪐

Tori and I are at Jordan's parents' house. Teenagers and college students are everywhere. Some are talking and laughing; others dance to the booming music. Jordan finds us in the entryway.

"There ya are, babe!" He shoves a cup filled to the brim in each of our hands, sloshing beer all over.

"Ugh, Jordan! Can't you be more careful!" Tori turns to me, "I've got to wash this out of my shirt. Come with me to the bathroom to cleanup." She pulls me toward the staircase.

I've been here before, so I know there's a closer bathroom than the one upstairs.

"Wait. Let's use this one. It's right here." I start to head to the door at the back of the hall and off the side of the kitchen. Tori jerks me back the other direction, spilling more beer.

"No, the only bathroom is upstairs. Let's go!"

Her insistence confuses me. "Tori, I've been here before, and I know there's a bathroom right down there. I can see the door." I point right at it. She follows my gaze then shakes her head. Her grip on my arm tightens and she looks angry.

"I think I should know where the bathroom is, Addy. It's my boyfriend's house after all." She starts dragging me toward the stairs.

My stomach rolls uneasily. For some reason Tori doesn't want me to go into that bathroom. Why? Is there something in there she doesn't want me to see? All I know is that the farther away she pulls me, the more desperate I am to get through that door. It's as if something inside is calling to me.

"I don't want to go upstairs. I want to go in there!" I'm yelling at her now because the music keeps getting louder, making it harder for me to be heard. I don't know what's going on with Tori, but I know I have to get to that door.

I think my life depends on it. I steel myself and prepare to jerk away from Tori's grasp, but she must have known my thoughts because she whips her head around to face me.

Her face is distorted and she growls at me viciously, reminding me of a pack of wolves fighting over a kill. She digs her nails into my flesh until I see blood running down my arm and dripping off my elbow onto the white tile floor. Her eyes glow a dull, rusty red, and her face fluctuates between the distorted mask it's become and something veiled in shadows. I can't see through the shadows, but somehow I know that underneath them is a face so horrific and evil that seeing it would drive me mad.

All the while the music is getting louder and the room is getting darker and everything seems to be spinning. I look around at the people standing nearby, hoping someone will help me, and I'm horrified. The party guests are faceless, but they watch us with eyeless malevolence. I can sense them laughing; some are pointing. They are gleeful spectators to this frightening ordeal, mocking me, feeding off my terror. I'll receive no aid from anyone here. I have never felt so helpless and alone.

"Stay away from that door!" the thing that used to be Tori roars at me. Reflexively, I throw the cup of beer I'm holding with my free hand into its face. There's a loud hiss, like water hitting a burning skillet, and its skin begins to bubble and melt away. It shrieks in agony and lets go of my arm to cradle its wounded face.

I turn and run.

I'm running as fast as I can but I'm hardly getting

anywhere. The world is in slow motion. My legs are heavy, like I'm running underwater.

I can hear the thing behind me, snarling in rage. I make it to the hall. I can see the door at the end. It's cracked open and a bright light shines through. If I can only make it into that light, I know I'll be safe. The thing's frantic breathing is right behind me as I run. It's getting closer. The heat from its breath is on my neck as I reach for the door knob. I won't make it in time. Any second it will tear into my back with burning razor claws. I get my hand around the knob and pray my sweaty grip will hold as I throw open the door.

CHAPTER 3

EVERYTHING IS FLOODED with brilliant white light. I hear a distant and muffled keen of defeat in the background and know that it must be the thing that used to be Tori. I step into the blinding whiteness, not knowing what awaits. As I bring my foot down into the room, it meets only air. I try to grab the door frame as I'm slipping downward but it's too late. I'm falling.

I'm tumbling head over feet into the white void. As I try to stabilize myself, I have a moment of clarity. I realize with relief that I'm dreaming. Tori is still Tori. She is not a demonic creature bent on my destruction. It's difficult to relax, however, while hurtling at full speed toward the ground. My heart pounds loudly in my ears. The only other sound is my gasps as I fight to breathe against the silent wind. I scan the black-and-white world beneath me, trying to figure out where I am.

As I get closer, I see I am plummeting toward a suburban neighborhood. Cookie-cutter houses dot streets in perfect parallel lines. A few cars are parked outside some of the residences. There are no cars in motion, though, or people walking about. Everything is still—like a black-and-white aerial photograph of an empty town.

As I descend even more, the houses and lawns become clearer and I start to feel that familiar choking sensation of panic. I'm breathing faster and fighting the urge to scream. Down and down I go, nearing the point where it will be too much for me.

I know it's a dream—it's always a dream. I can't get hurt. But how can I feel the wind whipping my hair around my face? I shouldn't be able to feel anything if I'm really dreaming. That's what they say, isn't it? That you can't feel anything in dreams? Then why are my eyes stinging? No, it's not a dream. Somehow, I'm really falling and when I slam into the street below me, I'll really die!

I'm fighting with everything I have now. I kick my legs, flail my arms, grunt with effort. My grunts turn into whimpers as I realize there's nothing I can do. This is the end of everything. I squeeze my eyes shut so I can't see the last few seconds of my descent and the hard black street that will claim my life. The last word screaming through my mind is *Dad!*

And then, it stops. I'm not falling. I'm lying perfectly still and it's as though I have fallen onto a giant cushion of air. It isn't painful. My breaths come easier than when I was falling. I peek through squinted eyelids, expecting to see my own bed beneath me and my dark room all around, but I can't make sense of what I see.

I open my eyes wide and turn my head from side to side,

taking in everything. I'm hovering in the air over the neighborhood street, suspended about ten feet off the ground.

Well, this is new.

I've never had a falling dream like this before. Everything is still bleached of color and there is still no sound but my breathing.

Before I can contemplate my situation further, I begin to feel a light pressure on my back as though a gentle wind is blowing downwards against me. It steadily picks up strength, and as it grows stronger, the cushion of air below me starts to push up. The competition between the two is uncomfortable, and my hair whips around against the opposing forces of wind. I get the distinct feeling that something or someone is trying to force me through an unseen barrier surrounding this neighborhood. Meanwhile, something or someone on the other side is trying to keep me out.

The pressure builds and I'm having a hard time getting air into my lungs. If this continues much longer, I'll be squished flat. And what happens if I do make it through the barrier? There will be nothing to catch my fall but the street below me. I'm sure I can survive a drop this high but not without some scrapes and bruises.

I'm in pain now. Everything hurts. I swear I can feel my ribs cracking inside me. Right when I'm certain I can't take another second of this excruciating pain, something beneath me breaks. I'm through! Only the rushing wind behind me doesn't let up and I find myself being hurled with extreme force onto the pavement of the street below. I barely manage to get my hands in front of me to break my fall before I slam into the ground.

Pain.

Searing, red-hot pain. Sharp as a knife and as real as it comes. I can't breathe. The wind must have been knocked out of me. My lungs ache for oxygen as I gasp for air, and I try to stave off the panic that feeling brings. I force myself to relax and settle for the short breaths I'm able to take now.

As I lie in the street waiting for my lungs to regain their functionality, I take note of other painful areas. My head hurts and I'm dizzy. My hands and knees sting. I can tell without looking that my palms are shredded and bleeding. They must have taken the brunt of the impact. Given everything, I think I've survived surprisingly well.

My left cheek is resting on the warm road, so I'm able to feel it when the first vibrations start—soft little vibrations, almost soothing, like someone tapping their fingers on a table. Over and over.

My lungs have loosened up so I try for a deeper breath. As I breathe in, a sharp pain shoots through the left side of my rib cage. Something's broken there.

The scent of tar fills my nostrils. I slowly lift my face off the pavement as far as I comfortably can and feel blood trickle down my cheek and neck. The skin on that side of my face burns when a light breeze touches it. I'm lying directly in the middle of the road. My feet face a driveway and my head faces another one across the street. I consider calling out for help, but this neighborhood looks completely deserted. I don't see a single soul. I don't hear anything—nearby or in the distance. No hum from car engines, no dogs barking. Nothing except for dead leaves scraping crisply down the street in the breeze.

It takes me a second to realize that the scene around me is no longer devoid of color. Instead it looks as though the color had been washed out of the surroundings. Where the trees and grass should be a brilliant green, it's pale green instead. A faded maroon Volkswagen is parked to the left of the driveway behind me, though it otherwise looks brand new. The house in front of me is pale tan. Even the sky is a weak pastel blue.

I try to sit up using only the sides of my hands, but my arms quiver and balk when I try to support the weight of my upper body on them. I decide to rest another minute and then try again. I lay my face back down on the street and concentrate on breathing. I can feel the vibrations again. They're stronger than before and I wonder what's causing them. It suggests there's someone in this place other than myself. I feel the rhythmic beating through my chest as the vibrations get stronger. Bits of gravel in the street in front of my eyes begin to tremble in time with the vibrations. Soon they are shaking and dancing around.

Something in the distance, beyond the dancing gravel bits, catches my eye. There! At the end of the street is movement. I pick my head up and squint in that direction. Whatever it is, it's big, and it's moving this way fast.

The vibrations intensify to a steady thump-thump, thump-thump. It reminds me of the cadence of galloping horses, but the thing at the end of the street doesn't resemble a horse in any way. Its shape is vaguely human, only it's at least ten feet tall—far too tall to be any person I've ever seen. Its legs and arms are impossibly long and it glides too smoothly—almost fluidly—to be human. As it gets closer, it looks as if it's wearing a helmet on its stretched out head and are those… rollerblades on its feet? That would explain the way it moves as well as its speed.

The pounding is so strong now that I begin to shake on the street the way the gravel had only seconds before. Most importantly though, it's so strong and loud that I realize the rhythm doesn't match the gait of the stretchy figure heading my way. If this impossible rollerblading creature isn't responsible for shaking the earth, what is?

I continue to watch Stretch-thing approach and it seems to be gesturing frantically at me. I can't figure out what it's trying to say, but I watch in fascination as it puts its head down and pounds the pavement harder to speed up. Just then, an unbelievably loud roar comes from the other direction. The hairs on my arms lift as I turn my head around to see where it's coming from.

At the other end of the street, running toward me full tilt, is an incredibly large, unrecognizable beast. It looks like the offspring of a rhinoceros and a bear. It's as big as a semi truck and pitch black—a black darker than the deepest shadows on the darkest night. Looking at it makes my flesh crawl and the word *abomination* screams through my mind.

The beast is closing in fast. It grunts and growls as it pushes down the street, shouldering entire cars off the road and into the houses. I think it wants nothing more than to trample the life out of me.

I whip my head around as I start to get up to run, my previous pains forgotten in my desperation to survive. The stretchy creature has nearly reached me and yells something but I can't make it out. It motions with its too-long arms for me to lie back down. Frantically I turn my head back and forth, trying to see who will reach me first. I pray it isn't the beast. As they are both nearly on me, the beast leaps up in the air bellowing victory. In mere seconds, it will crash down on me.

"Get down!" I hear as I turn toward the elongated thing. It dives and crashes into me. We tumble on the pavement, rolling out from under the dark monster. We roll maybe five or six times and the Stretch-thing maneuvers all the while, taking the brunt of each impact. We are up just as fast and I'm in its arms and it's carrying me as it glides down the street and away from the beast at breakneck speed.

Clinging desperately to my rescuer, I glance over its shoulder. Through wisps of the creature's blonde hair whipping around behind us I see the monster skid to a stop as it realizes it's missed its target. It ricochets off the side of a house and U-turns in our direction. I'm in awe of its agility.

"Hang in there, mate! We're nearly there!" This thing was talking to me! It was trying to reassure me! It sounded female and oddly enough, Australian? Whatever it is, I am grateful it saved me. I only hope it's as benign as it seems. I hold on as tightly as I can.

I'm amazed at how easily this being can carry me and still move so swiftly. The houses and cars around us are a blur. I look ahead and see the street ends at a big white house. Behind us, the monster is gaining and will reach us in a matter of seconds. As we get closer to the house at the end of the street, she doesn't seem to be slowing at all. She's going to crash right into the garage door!

I bury my face in her neck and wait for the impact—the impact that doesn't come. She stops moving. Is she crazy? The beast is right behind us! I look up and am shocked to see we're inside a huge garage-like room, but this garage is way bigger than the one we almost crashed into should have been.

What just happened?

I look up into the face of the stretchy girl. She's panting slightly but grinning down at me. As I watch her, she slowly begins to shrink. She sets me down gently on the concrete floor and steadies me so I don't collapse. All the while, she continues to get smaller and smaller.

"Well, that wasn't so bad, was it? Could've gone a lot worse really. It was lucky for you, being dropped so close to a Calm, wasn't it?"

She is now a perfectly proportioned girl about my age and height. She sees me glance nervously at the garage door and says, "Oh, no worries, mate, she'll be apples. Nothing can get in here but us Realmwalkers. I'm Melissa by the way. Mel if ya like." She tips an imaginary hat. "And let me be the first to say, welcome to Chaos."

CHAPTER 4

I STARE WIDE-EYED, mouth agape, at a perfectly normal-looking, five-foot-five-inch, tan girl with dirty blonde hair and hazel eyes. Her grin falters slightly as I continue to stare blankly at her.

"Ahh, are you all right there? Did you knock your noggin a bit too hard?" She examines me critically while walking a slow circle around me. When she makes it back in front of me, she smiles encouragingly and says, "Nothing too serious that I can see. You did well out there."

I'm still trying to formulate some kind of intelligent response when I hear an electronic chirp and then a man's gruff voice that sounds like it's coming through a radio.

"Mel, give me a status report."

I notice Mel's wearing something that looks like a Bluetooth device in her ear. She presses the outside of the small black unit and says, "Mel here. I got her. We're in Minor Calm now. Just arrived."

As she sits down on a stool nearby and starts to take off her rollerblades and safety gear, I gaze around the garage.

It's so large I could drive "Old Blue" in figure eights in here without hitting any walls. Power tools sit on a few workbenches. On the shelves lining the walls are all sorts of knickknacks and doo-dads that you would expect to find in a well-equipped garage.

A couple strange vehicles are parked nearby. They look like huge motorcycles, only wider and much longer. They have broad tires and large, shiny exhaust pipes on each side. There are buttons and strange gadgets all over the handlebars. Each is a different, vivid color and they sport unique designs on them. The one closest to me is black and adorned with bright blue waves. On the rim over the rear wheel, in decorative blue writing, is the word "Crank." The man's voice coming through Mel's earpiece says, "Good work. Are there any injuries?"

"Nothing too serious. There was only one brute out there, but we gave him the flick. She may have sustained a small concussion. I'm taking her upstairs now to get looked at." Mel says as she stands and offers me her hand.

I look down at my palms and am almost sick at the sight of them. They're torn up worse than I had thought. The blood has begun to dry, but every time I move my hands the wounds split and reopen. They hurt.

Mel slaps her forehead. Instead of grabbing my hand, she puts one arm around my back and a hand under my elbow closest to her. As she guides me to a nearby stairway leading up, the man's voice comes through again. "Make sure you get her information right away so we can make contact top-side."

"Sure thing, Boss. It'll be up in the system here in no time."

We get to the base of the stairs and I hesitate. If my knees are as bad as my hands, this is going to be hell.

"Easy does it now," she says in a kind voice. "Take your time. If it's too much, I can carry you."

I'm determined not to be carried.

I breathe in slowly and deeply, grit my teeth, and take the first step. I wince as the wounds on my knees reopen and fresh blood flows again. I'm shaking from the pain. I'm still weak, so I lean on Mel for stability. She's solid as a rock and must be incredibly strong.

"I know you're frightened and confused. Maybe if we chat it will take your mind off the pain. So what's your name?" Mel asks gently.

"Adelaide." It's all I can manage right now.

"You sound American."

I nod my head in confirmation.

"Thought so. Angel said you would be. She guessed Southwestern too. Is that right?"

I nod.

"That's wonderful. We have two other Americans here. You look about my age. Are you eighteen?"

"Seventeen." I pause for breath. We are almost halfway up the stairs. "How are we alive?"

She chuckles and shakes her head, "Oh, one little Lesser Shade is nothing to fret about."

Little! I would hate to come across a large Lesser Shade, whatever that is.

"Why didn't it..." I stop climbing and breathe. My ribs are really killing me. "... smash through the... garage door?"

"Shades can't enter the Calms, not as long as the wards are up anyway." She looks at me sideways and sees my puzzled expression. "Don't worry love, you'll understand soon."

I start climbing again and take a break at the top. I peek inside and see a large, fully furnished, comfortable-looking living room. On one of the oversized sofas, lies a boy who looks about fifteen. He has light brown skin and neat dark hair. He has earbuds in his ears and his eyes are closed. He's tapping his foot and waving his hands in the air like he's holding a baton and directing a symphony.

"CRANK!" Mel shouts at the top of her lungs.

"Ay-eee!" Crank squeals and almost falls off the couch. He spouts off a rapid stream of something that sounds like angry Spanish. He stops short, however, when he sees me. With a look of surprised excitement, he jumps off the couch and rushes over. Now that he's up I can see he's very thin and very short.

"Oh, I'm so sorry! I didn't know! I didn't even hear the alarm. Did she just get here? Oh, is she hurt?" He turns to me. "Are you all right? I'm Oscar Torres by the way. Everyone calls me Crank, though, but not because I'm cranky. I'm delighted to meet you. What's your name?" His accent is so strong and he's speaking so fast that I can hardly understand him. He's bouncing up and down where he stands and looks like he's about to burst with excitement.

Mel puts a hand up and he stops immediately. "Crank, help me get her to the couch. She's hurting."

"Of course, of course. Right over here." He takes my other elbow and together they get me to the sofa. I sit down slowly as Crank grabs a throw pillow and places it on the big mahogany coffee table in front of me. He gently picks up my feet and props them up on top of it.

"How is this? Good, yes?" He grins warmly at me. His dark eyes smile with the rest of his face. Out of all of this confusion, one thing is clear: I'm safe with these people. In fact, now that I think about it, all my fear and apprehension have completely faded away. Something about this place, "Minor Calm" Mel had called it, feels familiar even though I've never dreamt about it before. The room is rich with color—a stark contrast to the outside world. I'm overwhelmingly comfortable.

A warmth spreads through my chest. I feel like I'm home—safer than I've ever felt before. I never want to leave. I look to Mel and Crank and am surprised to find I'm seeing them through a curtain of tears brimming on my lower lids.

I blink them away, laughing, and exclaim, "This is the strangest dream I have ever had! And I've had some real doozies."

Crank and Mel exchange a significant glance. Mel looks at me and places a hand on my forearm.

"Let's have a look at those hands and see what can be done about them." She examines my palms gently and then looks over my knees through my tattered pajama bottoms. Pajama bottoms? Whoa. I check the rest of me—I'm wearing the pajamas I went to sleep in. They're dirty and torn in places and stained with blood, but they are definitely the clothes I wore to bed.

"It's a good thing I don't sleep naked," I mutter under

my breath. Mel and Crank look at each other and burst with laughter. Mel laughs so hard her eyes tear up and Crank clutches his sides. It takes a while for them to stop laughing enough to talk.

Through her giggles, Mel manages to say, "That's how Timothy showed up. Butt naked! Oh it was the funniest thing you ever saw."

"No no, let me tell it!" Crank interrupts her. "So there he is, in the middle of a wooded forest, running for his life from a herd of Shades. He's screaming in his Scottish voice, yes? He goes 'Help! Someone help me!'" Crank butchers what I can only imagine is his version of a Scottish brogue and waves his arms over his head hysterically.

"So Boss, he comes riding in on his Big-Bike, and to find what? A pasty white, orange-haired, *completely naked* man!" He laughs so hard now that Mel has to take over telling the story for him.

"And that isn't even the best part!" she exclaims. "The best part is that Boss has to scoop him up and ride all the way back to Major Calm with Timothy's skinny white arse right behind him, holding on for dear life!"

Their laughter is contagious and even though I have no idea who Boss or Timothy is, I can't help but laugh along with them.

"And that's why," Mel pauses and looks at Crank, "YOU NEVER SLEEP IN THE NUDE!" they both shout together.

They sigh with joy as Mel continues examining my injuries.

"Well, Miss Adelaide, you're really not that bad off. I'm

not much of a healer but I can at least stop the bleeding for now. Our Doc's over at Major Calm at the moment, so you won't get a full heal until tomorrow night. I suggest you take it as easy as you can tomorrow. You'll be in a right amount of pain but you'll live." She gently places a hand on each knee, closes her eyes, and furrows her brow.

"So your name is Adelaide? That's very beautiful! Are you an Ameri—"

"Ssshhhh! Crank! How can I do this with your constant earbashing? I need to concentrate."

Crank gets a sheepish look on his face and mouths "sorry" to no one in particular. I smile at him and he doesn't seem so wounded anymore.

A strange thing begins to happen as we sit quietly. I begin to feel warmth grow on my knees under Mel's hands. The flesh there begins to tingle and itch.

"What's that feeling? What are you doing?" I ask worriedly.

"Shh. I'm almost finished," Mel whispers. She's holding her breath and her face is scrunched up in concentration.

I watch her hands, almost expecting them to glow or do something spectacular, but they appear normal. She suddenly exhales and slouches forward.

"That's all I can do for your knees. I'm not a natural healer, but I know a trick or two to encourage the body to speed things up. Let me try your hands now."

When she removes her hands from my knees, I gasp. Through the torn holes in my pajamas, I'm able to see that both knees are completely scabbed over. Around the edges of the scabs is the fresh pink of newly healed skin. I'm amazed at first, but then I remember this is a dream and so anything is possible.

She's working on my hands now and that warm, tingly feeling begins again. When she's finished, I see it's had the same effect as it did on my knees. She turns my face from side to side until she finds a cut above my left eyebrow. When she's finished healing it, she places her hands on my rib cage and concentrates, relieving much of the pain there.

"That was amazing. Thank you, Mel, I feel much better now." She beams with pride but I can see she's worn out from the effort.

I nod to the sofa cushion next to me, motioning Mel to sit. She sits carefully and lays her head back, closing her eyes. She sighs deeply, "Haven't had to do that in a while. I really should practice more. Anyway, Boss will kill me if I don't get your information before you go top-side."

"What do you mean 'top-side'?" I ask. So much has happened and so much has been said that I don't understand.

"Top-side, Earth-side, call it what you like. When you wake back up, leave Chaos, and go back to your Earth-side existence. It could happen anytime, and Boss wants to be sure we know who you are and where to find you." She pinches the bridge of her nose.

"You're one of us now, a Realmwalker. Welcome to the family. Anyway, Crank and I can spend all night explaining everything to you, but it's all moot if we don't know how to find you top-side. You'll continue to believe you're having wild dreams, and that can really hinder the training process."

Training process? Earth-side existence? My head is spinning. Mel sees my perplexed expression and smirks knowingly.

Crank tries to reassure me. "It's confusing, yes. It will be this way for the first few nights, but trust me, it will get easier." He cocks his head to the side.

"Where are you from, Adelaide? I mean, we're pretty sure we've got it narrowed down. Angel has sensed you getting closer to us this last week, but it's always hard for her to nail it down exactly. She was guessing Southwest America. Oh, and what's your last name? We'll need your address too, and phone number." His leg starts bouncing up and down as he talks faster. "We'll probably want to know who you live with too. And where you work. Do you own a car? What's your favorite color? That's not something we have to know—I'm only curious."

"Slow down, Crank! Give the girl a chance to answer." Mel gives me an apologetic smile. "You'll have to forgive him, he's… hyper. He's like a Chihuahua on crack sometimes."

I laugh out loud at the mental image, but I stop quickly when I see Crank's injured expression.

"I'm sorry, Crank. I'm not laughing at you, just at the image of a Chihuahua on crack," I explain. This seems to pacify him.

It's bizarre to me that I feel protective of Crank's feelings. I mean, I know this is only a dream but I feel so invested in these two people. I've only just met them but I feel inextricably tied to them. It's similar to the way this place, Minor Calm, feels so much like home. These people feel dear to me in a way I've never felt before—not even for

Tori or any of my other friends, for that matter. I know I'll miss Mel and Crank when I wake up. Though this definitely started out as a nightmare, it's turned into something beautiful and amazing and I'm sad to think of it ending.

"My name is Adelaide Shepherd—Addy for short. I'm from America. I live in a town called Queen Creek in the state of Arizona." I tell them my address, home phone number, and the number to my cell.

"I'm seventeen years old. I'm a senior in high school, at least for the next two weeks. I live with my Mom. I have an older sister, Jana, who lives in Flagstaff, Arizona. She's going to college there but she visits often. I drive an old, beat-up truck. It's light blue and there's rust on the hood. I don't have a job, and my favorite color is light green." I take a second to breathe. "Did I cover everything?"

Crank gets up and walks over to what looks like a large flat-screen television on one of the walls. It lights up when he taps the screen.

"Let's see…" he says as he pulls up an image of planet Earth. He spins it around to the Western Hemisphere with his finger then touches the North American continent. The image zooms in drastically until a very realistic looking satellite image of North America fills the screen. He mutters under his breath, "United States… Arizona…" Each time he touches the map it zooms in further. When he finds Queen Creek, Arizona, I'm able to see tiny lights all over the city. It's an image of my town at night. Even though it's dark, I recognize certain structures.

"Hey look, there's my school!" I've seen programs on the

Internet that let you view satellite pictures of your town, but this is different. The picture is so clear and detailed. As I try to find my house, I notice a few lights in the streets are moving. Are those cars? That's when I realize this image wasn't taken sometime in the past. I'm viewing my hometown as it is, right now.

"Whoa! How are we seeing this? Wouldn't you have to have access to a satellite? I didn't think just anyone could do that. Don't you have to be part of the government or something like that?"

Crank grins at me and winks conspiratorially. "We can access any satellite at any time. We're cool like that." He brushes some pretend dust off his shoulders. Pointing to some data along the bottom of the screen, he says, "It says here that in your hometown, right now, as we are speaking, it's 5:46 a.m." He pulls up an input bar and types in my address. The map zooms in once more and I see an aerial view of my home. From the glow of a street lamp, I can see my truck parked in the driveway next to Mom's white compact sedan. If it really is 5:46 in the morning, my alarm clock is due to go off in less than an hour.

"So, I'm supposed to be sleeping in there? Right now?" I ask dubiously.

"Unless you sleep walk." Mel says next to me. "Hey, Crank, can you start a new file for Addy while you're in the system? And could you input all her data?"

"Would you like me to repeat it? Or write it down somewhere?" I ask Crank.

He shakes his head no and taps his forehead. "Eidetic

memory. It's one of the beautiful things about Chaos. We all have it."

"Is that like a photographic memory?" I ask.

He explains as he types my data into a file on the screen. "Even better than that. Photographic memory means you can remember images with exact detail. We, however, can not only perfectly recall images, but also sounds, smells, tastes, and feelings. It comes in pretty handy." He's typing rapidly, and I can't help but be impressed at his ability to multi-task.

I'm beginning to grow frustrated with how much I don't understand about this dream, so I turn to Mel. "What is Chaos exactly? And what are Calms?"

Mel rubs her temples as she thinks. "I'm not sure how much to tell you now. You're still convinced you're having a dream, which means you won't take anything I tell you as the truth. I'm tempted to not tell you anything until you accept you aren't dreaming."

I'm floored by this. "You're saying I'm not asleep? But you just showed me my house and told me I was sleeping."

"Your body Earth-side is sleeping. Your body here, in Chaos, is very much awake. You must be asleep there to be awake here. For us, sleep is the gateway to Chaos," she explains, as if it's common knowledge and not confusing at all.

"So… you're telling me I have *two* bodies?" I ask her.

"I'm telling you," she pauses and looks me in the eyes, "you have one body that resides in two realms of existence. Hence the term 'Realmwalker.'"

I stare back at her, waiting for her to start laughing and

tell me she's kidding. She really expects me to believe this? I must have a very active imagination to dream all this up.

"I can see you still doubt what I'm telling you. You can't believe there is any other existence but the one you have known all your life. And why should you? It sounds too incredible to believe. It took days to convince me when I was first called to Chaos. But consider this." She reaches over and gently pokes my injured knee.

I feel a sharp pain and jerk reflexively.

"If you're dreaming, Addy, then why does that hurt?" She waits for me to consider what she's said.

Goosebumps rise on my arms. For a second I'm at a loss for words, completely dumbfounded, then I find my answer. "Maybe I'm not really feeling pain. Maybe my dream is activating that area of my brain that simulates pain, and it seems so real that I've convinced myself I'm hurting."

"Clever girl!" Crank laughs over his shoulder. "She's a stubborn one, Mel. Give up. She'll know soon enough, maybe even tomorrow."

"I hope so. That would be great. I'm pretty sure Boss is already out that way. And Crank and I'll be here to say, 'Told ya so'!" She grins at the thought.

"Oh, no." I inhale sharply. "Please don't tell me I have to go through all of this again tomorrow night. That beast out there was the scariest thing I've ever encountered! And before I was falling, that evil demon-Tori thing with its claws and eyes and its shadow face! I can't do that again!" I start to panic as I imagine that twisted face and the unfathomable horror hiding just beneath the shadows.

That was its true face, I realize now. The one behind the shadows was there all along, hiding in the illusion of Tori. I was able to glimpse it only as its rage caused its control of the illusion to slip away. I'm shaking just thinking of it.

Mel puts her hand reassuringly on my arm. "No, Addy. You won't have to go through that ever again. You're here now in Chaos. Every time you nod off top-side, you'll wake up here and find you're right where you left yourself. And the next time you have to face darkness, you'll be better prepared."

"And protected by us," Crank interjects as he jabs a thumb at his puffed-up chest. I can't help but wonder what such a little guy like Crank can do to protect me from beasts the size of the one I encountered earlier.

"That's right," Mel says adamantly. "You're one of the family now, and we protect our own." She gives my arm a gentle squeeze.

I do feel like they're family. My chest fills up with that warm feeling again and my eyes get misty. It's difficult to talk through the swell of emotion.

"What is this I'm feeling? About this place… about the two of you?" I'm almost embarrassed, having such tender feelings for Mel and Crank.

Crank finishes working at the big screen and comes to sit on the coffee table by my feet. He smiles endearingly and says, "Do you mean the warm, squishy feelings? Like Mel and I are your most favorite people in the world and that you never want to leave Minor Calm as long as you live?"

I laugh through the embarrassment and wipe away tears. "Yes! That's exactly what I mean!"

Mel explains it further. "We all feel that way about each other. And about being in the Calms. I know it can be overwhelming at first, but you get used to it. We share a connection. We're among the chosen few who are called to Chaos, and coming here physically changes us. We feel that change in each other and it connects us. It helps us band together more tightly, and to be protective of one another. It helps us survive."

"Survive?" I ask. "What happens when you don't survive? Do you just wake up…" I fumble over the new term, "…'top-side'?"

Mel shakes her head and says, "That's a lesson for another day. Anyway, it's certainly not something you have to worry about now." Her tone is reassuring but I don't miss the meaningful glance she and Oscar exchange. "As for the Calms, I believe the reason we feel so happy and comfortable here is to provide us with some relief from what we have to face outside."

I wager a guess. "And outside of the Calms… where we were before… that's Chaos?"

"She's catching on. I said she was clever, didn't I?" Crank looks smug.

"Of course she's clever, Crank. We're all clever here. Not just anyone is called to Chaos," Mel says matter-of-factly.

"Called? You mean like, we were summoned here? By what?" I ask through a yawn. The trauma of the dream must have worn me out. I'm sleepy.

"She's yawning," Mel says abruptly to Crank who jumps up and returns to the screen on the wall. He pulls up the satellite image of my house again and it's obvious it's gotten lighter out.

"It's 6:28. What time do you normally wake up?" He asks me quickly.

My eyes are drooping as I open my mouth to answer, "My alarm is set to go off at-"

EEERRRR-EEERRRR-EEERRRR-EEERRRR!

I reach over and hit the snooze button on my alarm clock. It reads six thirty in bright red digits. Just ten more minutes. I'm not ready to wake up yet. I smile sleepily. I was having the nicest dream.

CHAPTER 5

I LIE STILL and try to hold on to the memory of the dream. I know it'll only be a matter of time before the details begin to fade. Dreams are like that. They're fresh in your mind the moment you wake, but later in the day when you try to remember them, they're fragmented. They come back to you only in bits and pieces. I don't want that to happen.

I think of Mel and Crank and am happy to find that I can still see them in my mind's eye so clearly. I can still feel that warmth in my heart when I think of Minor Calm. I think of our fascinating conversation. What a wild dream! I can't wait to tell this one to Mom.

Then I remember the rest of the dream: the pitch black beast that almost crushed me, the Tori-demon that tried to keep me from answering the call to Chaos.

Even though there's a little morning light seeping in through my blinds, my room is still dark enough to leave the corners steeped in shadows. My eyes are automatically drawn to the darkest parts. I squint and study them to see if there's anything there. My mind imagines rusty red eyes glowing out of the darkness. I know I'm being ridiculous but I can't seem to shake the fear away. I decide it may be a good idea to get up and turn the lights on.

As I reach up and turn on the lamp next to my bed, a sharp pain shoots through my chest. The pain makes me cough, which makes my chest hurt even more. I force myself to relax and steady my breathing. I must have slept on my side wrong.

With the light on I can see there are no shadow demons hiding in the corners. Relieved, I pull back my covers and sit up slowly so I don't hurt my chest too badly. I freeze. I can't believe what I see. This can't be right.

My cream-colored sheets are marred with dark patches of red. I blink repeatedly, trying to make it go away. The knees of my pajama bottoms are intact but they're clearly blood soaked. I reach out to touch the fabric but I see something on my hand that stops me. Slowly, I turn my hand over and inhale reflexively as I stare, wide eyed, at my palms. They're completely scabbed over and covered with dried blood.

What's going on?

My hand starts to shake visibly. Am I losing it? How could this have happened? I need someone to help me understand this.

I get out of bed as quickly as I can without causing myself too much pain and walk down the hall to Mom's room. Her door is open a crack, so I push it farther and peek inside. She's lying in bed and though she's facing away, her heavy breathing tells me she's still asleep. I walk softly across her room, carefully climb into bed, and lie facing her.

She looks so pretty and peaceful that I'm almost

tempted to let her sleep. But I think of the blood-covered sheets and my hands and knees and change my mind. I need my mother now. I need her to tell me everything is okay. I start to cry quietly. I pray she has an answer for me, something that explains everything.

She starts to stir. I force myself to stop crying so I don't frighten her too much when she opens her eyes and sees me. "Momma?" I say softly, the way I did when I was young.

She looks at me sleepily and smiles. "Good morning, sweetie," she says as she stretches.

"Mom, I need your help," I say quietly.

She rubs her face and really looks at me, concern instantly apparent in her eyes. She puts her hand on the side of my face. "Honey, what is it? What's the matter?"

"Something's happened, Mom. I'm confused and I'm scared."

She sits up in bed and faces me. "Addy?"

I hold my hands out for her to see. She stares at them for a few seconds before saying anything.

"Addy! What did you do to your poor hands?" She looks me over. "My gosh, child, your clothes! What happened?"

"I don't know how it happened. I woke up this way. There's blood all over my bed too. And my chest hurts." I'm worried she won't believe me. I wouldn't blame her.

She gets out of bed without saying anything, walks over to the phone on her dresser, and grabs her address book off the shelf next to her door. She thumbs through it quickly until she finds what she's looking for. Punching a number into the phone, she looks up at me and says, "I'm going to have Ronnie come over and look at you."

Ronald Mack is our next-door neighbor. He's a paramedic and he and Dad were good friends.

"Ronnie? Hi, it's Margaret. Listen, Addy's been hurt. I don't think it's too serious, but I was hoping you could come have a look at her just in case." She pauses a second, then, "Oh, thank you. You're wonderful. I'll see you soon." She comes and sits on the bed next to me, smoothing my hair back out of my face. "You really don't have any idea what happened to you?" she asks.

"Not really. I mean, I went to sleep fine and woke up like this." I hesitate a second, trying to decide if I should tell her about my dream. I'm afraid she'll really start to worry about my sanity. Maybe she'll even make me see a shrink.

"Addy, I can tell there's more you're not saying. Are you afraid I'll be mad?"

"No. It's not that. It's just… it sounds so crazy I'm worried you'll think I'm losing it."

She smiles warmly at me. "Addy, I know you better than that. Tell me and we can work it out together."

I recount my dream from start to finish. I tell her about Jordan's party and the Tori-imposter. I describe how I fell through the bathroom door and plummeted toward the neighborhood. I try my best to explain getting pushed through the barrier. I tell her how I cut up my hands and knees on the street and hurt my ribs. I explain how Mel rescued me and how she and Crank insisted I wasn't dreaming but actually in another realm of existence. By the time I finish saying it aloud, I realize how impossible it all sounds.

"Well that is definitely strange, Addy, but you shouldn't have been afraid to tell me. I'm sure there's a logical explanation for this." She chews on her bottom lip. "In fact, I'm pretty sure I know what happened."

Already I'm relieved. I knew I could count on Mom to bring me back to reality, so I wait eagerly for her theory.

"A few years before Dad died, there was an awful leak in our bathroom sink." She points to the open door leading into her bathroom. "It would drip, drip, drip all night and drive us crazy. The night before I finally made your dad fix it, I was listening to it drip as I was falling asleep. That night I had all kinds of dreams that had that noise in it. In one dream, I remember I was trying to finish a résumé for an interview. The interviewer was standing over me, waiting and tapping her foot with impatience. The beat of her heel was the sound of the sink dripping. In another dream it was the turn signal in my car."

I look at her confused. "I'm not sure I understand. How does that explain my hands and knees?"

"Well, I've never known you to sleepwalk, but what if all this mess with finals and graduation has stressed you out enough to change your sleeping habits? What if last night you went sleepwalking?"

I give her a disbelieving look. "I don't know, Mom. That's kind of a stretch. I mean, you're saying I hurt myself in my sleep, and instead of waking up, my mind worked it into a dream?"

"It's not unheard of, sweetie. There are all kinds of sleep disorders. I saw a news show a few years back where they covered a story of a man who murdered someone while he was asleep."

"Oh, get out of here!" I exclaim. "You've got to be kidding me! Killed someone? And didn't wake up?"

"Yes, I'm serious! They proved it scientifically and he was found innocent. Since then there have been all kinds of studies done to see how much a person can do in their sleep without knowing it. One woman would get up every night and eat food out of her refrigerator, not knowing why she couldn't lose weight. Think about it, Addy. You've always been a heavy sleeper. It's the only explanation that makes any sense. You must have tripped over something and hurt yourself."

Just then, the doorbell chimes, so Mom goes to let Ronnie in. I get up carefully and check myself in her mirror to make sure I'm decent before following her down the hall. As I sit at the kitchen table, I look around for any signs that I might have been out here last night. Nothing appears unusual or out of place. How violent an accident would I have had to have to hurt myself badly enough to shred the flesh on my hands? And how could that not wake me up?

"Good morning, Maggie, you're radiant as usual." Ronnie kisses Mom on the cheek.

"Oh nonsense, I just woke up. Anyway, please come take a look at Addy." They come into the kitchen and Ronnie sets down a bag he brought with him on the counter behind me.

Ronnie's a middle-aged man of average height and

average weight. In fact, he's pretty much average in every way. He's the most average person I know. He's kind and was a good friend to Dad, but place him in a crowd of people and he would be the last person to get noticed—though I bet the people whose lives he saves don't think he's average. That's what's so neat about Ronnie. He's a quiet hero. I really like him.

"So, Missy, what have you gotten yourself into?" He asks with a smile and a wink. He pulls a chair over so he can sit and face me. Noticing my bloodstained pajamas, he whistles. "How'd ya do that?"

"I'm not really sure…." I show him my palms. He takes my hands in his and examines them closely.

Mom is leaning on the wall behind Ronnie chewing her thumbnail. "We think maybe she went sleepwalking last night and hurt herself somehow. When she went to bed, she was all in one piece, but this is how she woke up this morning."

"I think I would call that sleep-adventuring," Ronnie chuckles. He examines my wounds and determines that my ribs are only bruised, not cracked. He wraps my hands and knees in simple bandages. "I suggest you take Tylenol or Ibuprofen for the pain. If you find that's not enough, then you'll have to go see a doctor for a stronger prescription. I also recommend you rest. Stay in bed today. Be lazy."

Mom is nodding her head, but I speak up before she can agree. "Mom, I have to go today. I have my oral presentation."

"I'm sure your teacher will understand if you explain it to him. If you like, I can call and leave him a message.

You can stay home and rest the whole weekend and then do your report first thing on Monday."

I consider this while Ronnie packs up his bag. Mom gives him a hug and thanks him. He waves and tells me to take it easy as he leaves. When Mom comes back, I've made up my mind.

"Mom, I'm really not hurting that bad. Honestly. This is nothing that Tylenol can't fix. Let me go and give my report. I'm pretty sure that I'm one of the first to go. If I'm feeling yuck after that, I'll come home. Okay?"

I know she would much rather have me home for the day, so I'm surprised when she says, "All right, Addy. If you're certain you'll be okay, then you can go. But I want you to let me or Jana drive you there and pick you up afterwards. If you feel it's too much for you, call and we'll come get you. Understand?"

"It's a deal," I say.

I take the pain relievers Mom hands me and head back to my room to get ready for school. I look for something to put on my hands to cover the bandages. I don't want people asking me what happened. It'll get to over one hundred degrees by lunchtime, so mittens won't fly. I can't find anything and I'm running out of time when Mom calls me for breakfast. Jana is sitting at the table, talking with Mom.

"Well, I always knew you were a world-class klutz, but this really takes the cake!" Jana laughs. I make a face at her as Mom reaches over and swats the back of her head with the morning paper. By the time I finish eating, I only have time to grab my stuff and go. Jana gets her keys, so I gather she's taking me, which worries me a little. Jana doesn't have the best driving record—and that's putting it nicely.

"Try to get me to school in one piece please," I quip.

"You're not worried I'll hurt you, are you? You seem to be handling that pretty well yourself."

"Hardy-har-har," I say lamely.

As we back out of the driveway in Jana's little car, she nearly backs into a dark truck driving past. It was such a close call I'm surprised when the driver doesn't honk or give us the finger. They do, however, slow down a little to check us out through their tinted windows. I'm unable to see who's behind the wheel, but the license plate is from California.

That makes me think of Dad's mom, Gram, who lives in Glendale, California. Summer is almost here, which means it's almost time for my annual trip to see her. I'm really close to Gram, and I look forward to my visits with her all year.

Jana is surprisingly quiet the entire trip to school. As we pull into the parking lot, she stops next to the curb and gets out of the car. I'm shocked as she opens the door for me. I gather my stuff and climb out of my seat. I'm about to deliver some witty remark about her managing not to kill me when she spontaneously hugs me. She's gentle so she doesn't hurt my ribs.

"Please try to be careful with yourself. You're my only sister, and even though you can be a twerp, I kinda like ya," she grumbles.

A show of affection like this from Jana is rare. "Thanks, Jana. You're not so bad yourself."

"Have a good day, sis." She gets back in her car and

pulls out to leave, narrowly missing another car driving by. It's so typically Jana that I can't help but laugh.

I make it to first hour without anyone asking what happened to my hands. Once I'm called to give my presentation, I grab my visuals and charts and head to the front of class.

Mr. Perry immediately notices my bandaged palms and says, "Good gracious, Addy, what did you do to yourself?"

Because I'm not even sure what did happen, I decide to stick close to the version of events in my dream.

"I fell in the street last night and skinned up my palms," I mumble, hoping to avoid further questions.

"Bummer. All right, well, good luck." He smiles and motions for me to begin.

My presentation goes off without a hitch, and when I'm finished, I feel pretty good about it. Technically, I could go home now and sleep the rest of the day, but as I take inventory of my injuries, I find they really don't hurt so much. The medicine must be doing its job. I use Mr. Perry's phone after class to call Mom and tell her I'm doing fine and that I'm going to stay and get a ride home from Tori.

I'm a little apprehensive about seeing Tori after last night's dream with the *fake* Tori. But when I see her in third hour, it's reassuring to find my worries are unfounded. Tori is still her normal, shallow self—the first thing she says upon seeing me is how much my bandages make me look like a leper. She doesn't even ask why I'm wearing them. Some things never change.

"Let's go out for lunch today," she says as we walk

to our lockers after class. "I'm in the mood for a big, fat juicy burger."

"Did you and Jordan get in a fight again?" Tori always craves junky food when she's upset with her boyfriend.

"He tells me," she puts a finger in the air, "that I'm supposed to stay here in this dumpy dairy town and wait for him to decide what he wants to do with his life. I told him, hell no! I'm leaving for college as soon as I can. I'm not going to get stuck here waiting for him while he wastes his life away and miss my chance at a real college experience."

"If you go to ASU, you'll only be in Tempe. That's a twenty-minute drive. What's his deal?" I ask.

"His deal is he doesn't want me going to a real college filled with smart guys getting a good education and doing something with their lives. That's his problem," she snaps.

I let her vent at me as we drive to a nearby burger joint. It's the kind of place where you park, order out your window, and they bring the food out to your car. There are a few picnic tables on an island in between the parking areas and shaded by a large awning with misters around the edges of it. We see a few other students sitting at one of the tables, so we sit at a table next to them. We use the intercom on the order box by our table to order some food.

As we're waiting for our meal to arrive, Tori says, "Oh my gosh, that guy is totally checking me out. Can he be any more obvious?"

I follow the direction of her gaze. She's looking at a guy sitting behind the wheel of a black pickup. The driver's window is down, so we can see he's looking in our direction.

He's wearing sunglasses, so we can't see his eyes, but he's clearly watching the two of us. I half expect him to turn away now that we've caught him, but his gaze never falters. Something about his intensity is a little off-putting. It's very direct, as if he doesn't care that we know he's staring.

"He's certainly not shy, is he?" I mutter and turn back to the table. There's nothing new about a guy checking Tori out.

"Well, I don't mind. He's actually really cute. I wonder how old he is?" she says thoughtfully. She starts twirling her hair around her finger and flashing coy smiles in his direction.

"Oh, never mind," she says as a waitress on roller skates brings us our food. "He's not even from here. I wonder if he's moving here or only visiting," she muses. "Hey, maybe he'll take me back with him! I wouldn't mind some California weather about now."

"California?" I ask, puzzled. I turn and look at the guy in the truck again.

"Yeah, his license plate."

Sure enough, the plate on the front of his truck says California.

"Whoa, that's creepy," I mutter under my breath. "What is?" Tori asks around a bite of hamburger.

I study the truck closer. It has to be the truck Jana almost backed into this morning. Same dark color, same make and model. It's too much of a coincidence not to be. And here he is, sitting here, staring at Tori and me.

I'm beginning to think that maybe it's not Tori he's

been checking out. I try to decipher his expression. Is he angry? I wouldn't be so bothered by him if I hadn't noticed he's not eating anything. Well, maybe he ordered something and it hasn't come out yet.

"What's creepy?" Tori demands impatiently.

"Oh, nothing really. It's just, Jana almost crashed into that guy this morning. And here he is. A weird coincidence, I guess."

"There's nothing weird about that at all," she says. "The way your sister drives, we probably come across her victims more often than we know—there are so many of them. Besides, a guy's gotta eat."

Tori's right. I try not to think about it as I finish my lunch, but I can't keep my eyes from flicking in his direction every few minutes or so. He never takes his eyes off us, and the whole time we're eating, no one brings him any food. Maybe he finished before we got here, but I don't remember seeing his truck when we parked.

"This is so awesome!" Tori's thumbing through some bills the waitress brought back as change. "I paid with a twenty, and that idiot brings back my change, *and* the twenty. Guess it's my lucky day!"

I snatch the twenty from her hand as she's waving it around like she won the lottery and start to get up.

"What are you doing? That's mine!" she says, sounding a little too much like a bratty three-year-old for my liking. "Come on, Tor. That waitress could get in trouble for this. Besides, it's not like you need the money." I head up to the order window at the front of the restaurant, tell the girl there what happened, and give the twenty back. She seems a little surprised that I actually returned it, but she's really grateful. When I get back to the table, Tori's sitting with her arms crossed, pouting.

"If it really bothers you that much, I'll give you a twenty myself," I say as I dig into my pants pocket.

"Forget it. I'm not upset about the money," she says grumpily.

"So, what did I do?"

I can tell she's having a hard time getting the words out.

"When you went up to the counter, I was watching 'Mr. Hottie' over there." She pauses, reluctant to go on. I look at her expectantly and wait.

"When you got up and left, he watched you the whole way there and back. All this time I thought he was into me, and it's you he's been watching." She seems so offended that someone might show interest in me rather than her.

"Lucky you," she says.

Only I don't feel so lucky. I'm worried that this guy is some kind of psycho who wants revenge for this morning's near accident. He's obviously trying to intimidate me. What other reason would he have for staring at me like this? The more I think about it, the angrier I get. I wasn't even the one driving Jana's car.

Tori and I gather our trash and toss it into a nearby bin. We head back to her car, which is parked about ten spaces away from the truck, and his gaze follows us all the way there.

I wonder if he plans on keeping this up all day. Will he

follow us? Will he be there in the parking lot after school? Will he follow me home? All of a sudden I'm furious. I didn't do anything to this guy, and I won't put up with him harassing me.

"You know what?" I say angrily when we get to the car. "This is ridiculous. If he thinks he can frighten me, he's got another thing coming." I slam my bag down on the passenger seat and turn around.

"What are you doing? Addy! Are you crazy?"

I ignore her and march purposefully toward the truck. I'm thinking of some very choice words to say to this guy when he surprises me by unbuckling his seat belt and getting out of the truck. He shuts the door, turns around, and leans on it, arms crossed. He stares at me expectantly. My steps falter and my resolve begins to fade.

This guy is scary! He has a definite militaristic air about him. His posture displays that rare kind of quiet confidence, the kind you get only after years of being in charge. He looks about six feet tall with short brown hair and is obviously in great shape.

Though his posture is relaxed, I get the feeling that underneath he's coiled like a snake, ready to strike in an instant. Something about the set of his face tells me he isn't someone to be messed with. His eyes still hide behind the shades.

By the time I'm ten feet away, I've lost all my confidence and am questioning my own sanity. At least we're in public. Maybe the threat of witnesses is enough to protect me from anything dangerous he's planned.

I stop walking and find myself staring at him stupidly as I try to remember the angry retort I had planned on saying only a few moments ago. We just stand there, silently watching each other. As much as I would love to turn around and run back to Tori's car, I can't do that. It would show him that I am, in fact, scared. If he really is a psycho, that would only encourage him.

I fidget with the bottom hem of my shirt as I think of how to salvage this. I decide to take the high road and hope that kindness can defuse him.

"Um, hi," I say rather pathetically. He raises an eyebrow at me but says nothing. I walk a few steps closer, stand up tall, and clear my throat. "If you're upset about this morning-"

"Are you Adelaide Shepherd?" he asks quietly. His tone is surprisingly calm and absent of hostility.

"What did you say?" I take a step closer.

"Are you Adelaide Shepherd?" he asks again. There's something vaguely familiar about his voice. His whole demeanor drips with authority, and I choke down the urge to answer "Yes, sir."

"I'm sorry, do I know you?" I ask him.

He reaches up and removes his sunglasses and I'm suddenly speechless. His eyes are a startling iceberg blue. I'm figuring him to be around twenty-five or so. Tori was right—this guy is seriously good-looking, but I'm uncertain if it's his physical appearance or the confident way he carries himself that makes me think so.

He examines me critically from head to toe and manages to do it without a hint of sexuality. I feel almost as if he's measuring my worth. Even though a few seconds ago I wanted to tell him off and never see him again, I oddly find myself hoping he finds me acceptable.

"We've never met." He shakes his head.

I stand there looking confused, waiting for an explanation. Just then Tori lays on her horn and shouts, "Come on, Addy! We'll be late!"

I close my eyes and grit my teeth. Thank you, Tori, for telling this potential lunatic who I am. I open my eyes to find the stranger watching me with a crooked smirk on his face.

"You better go," he says. He doesn't get back in his truck but continues to look at me.

I want to stay. I want to ask him a million questions. Who are you? How do you know my name? Why are you following me and why does your voice sound so familiar? Instead, I awkwardly walk backwards a few steps before turning around to jog to Tori's car. Once I'm in the passenger seat, I turn to look at him again. He's on his cell phone.

"What was that all about? I thought you were going to tell him off, but then you just stood there like a dummy. What happened? Did he talk to you? Do you know him?" Tori fires questions off as we head back to school.

I stare out the window and try to understand what just happened. I murmur to myself, "Today has easily been the strangest day of my life."

"What's that supposed to mean?" Tori asks in a not-so-nice tone.

I sigh. I know she's still mad that the stranger wasn't "checking her out," but I don't get why. She has a boyfriend anyway, so it's not like she could have pursued him. If I don't think of something to make her feel better, she'll pout all day.

"He thought I looked like a friend of his he hadn't seen in a while. That's why he was staring. He was trying to decide if I was her or not. When I got close enough for him to see I wasn't her, he apologized. That's all."

"Oh… well, then. That makes perfect sense now." And like that she's completely happy. Now that she thinks he didn't actually choose me over her, all is right with the world. If anything, Tori's always consistent. Even if she's consistently shallow.

Back at school, it's hard to focus on anything. I can't stop thinking about the guy from lunch. I try not to, but when I'm not thinking about him, I'm thinking about my dream. What's odd is that as I try to remember the first part, all the details are fuzzy. But from the point in my dream where I fall through the barrier into the street to the point when I wake up, everything is crystal clear.

I remember every tiny detail and marvel that I'm able to recall the conversation exactly. If I tried, I'm sure I could write down everything that was said word-for-word. I can still see Mel and Crank perfectly. I can hear Mel's Aussie accent and feel her reassuring hand on my arm.

In fifth hour, Kevin makes my day by asking me what happened to my hands. I suddenly wish I had a much more exciting story than falling down in the street. I'm embarrassed when I tell him, but he looks really concerned and tells me he hopes I get better soon. This puts me on cloud nine and I actually forget about all the other stuff for a while. That is at least, until it's time to go home.

As Tori and I head out to her car, I scan the parking lot for the black truck. I don't see it anywhere. I study the rearview mirrors the whole way home but there's no sign of it. I thank Tori and remember to tell her to have a good time at Jordan's party. She's still upset at him but I know she'll get over it soon. She always forgives him for acting like a jerk.

When I get home and open my front door, the mouthwatering smell of pot roast immediately strikes me, and I know Mom's making it for me. It's my favorite comfort food, and knowing her, she thinks I need it after this morning. Jana's on the couch watching a rerun of some reality show where strangers have to live together on an island and survive off nature. I join her and she tells me she wants to postpone our girls' night out and instead have a girls' night in.

She points to the coffee table where there are some chick flicks she must have rented earlier and a huge pile of assorted candy and junk food. I know she'd probably rather be shopping and that she changed her plans so I wouldn't have to walk around a mall for hours feeling as crappy as I do. I feel a little guilty but mostly I'm thrilled. I've never enjoyed shopping.

I watch TV with Jana for about an hour until Mom tells me my bed sheets were unsalvageable and that she bought me a new set and washed them for me. I find them in the dryer and head back to my room to make my bed. Before I can finish, I hear the doorbell ring.

I wonder if maybe Jana invited one of her gal pals over to watch movies with us, but Mom hollers down the hall, "Addy, your friends are here to see you!"

My friends? Basically everyone I know should be over at Jordan's party by now. As I make my way to the front door, I cross my fingers and hope it isn't Tori trying one last attempt to get me to go. When I open the door, I'm completely surprised to come face-to-face with a girl I've never seen before.

She's shorter than I am but looks about my age. She's pretty. She's thin and pale with deep emerald eyes. The most distinguishable thing about her, however, is her unnaturally bright red-orange hair. I try not to imagine her head on fire as she grins at me and says, "So you're Adelaide! Wow! You're bright. And adorable! Happy to meet you." She holds out her hand and waits.

"Um… hi." Unsure what to do, but not wanting to appear rude, I show her my bandaged hands so she understands why I can't shake.

"Oh, of course! Sorry. Here." She balls her hand up and gives me a fist bump. "I'm Ember! I'm pretty sure I'm your new BFF. I'm a great judge of character and from what I can see of you so far, we're gonna get along great!"

The sound of someone clearing their throat a little ways behind Ember startles me. I look out and standing on the lawn with his hands in his pockets is none other than the burger-joint guy—Tori's "Mr. Hottie."

Ember turns in his direction and says, "I know! I'm getting to it. I'm only trying to be polite. So much rides on first impressions you know." She turns back to me. "So Adelaide, you wanna come for a walk? We've got lots to talk about."

CHAPTER 6

My curiosity is piqued. I should be concerned, maybe a little frightened, that there are strangers at my door who seem to know an awful lot about me. Either I've taken complete leave of my senses, or my instincts are telling me these two are no threat.

"I think I would like that very much. I've got a lot of questions," I tell her.

"And we've got your answers." She grins at me like we're old friends. I glance meaningfully behind her. She understands right away. "You don't have to worry about Sam. He's a great guy—one of the best. You'll see."

I have to take her at her word. "Give me a minute please," I say to her. She nods her head and goes to stand by Sam. I find Mom in the kitchen, checking the pot roast in the slow cooker.

"Those are some nice-looking kids. I've never met them before, have I?" she asks me.

"No, Mom. You've never met them." *And neither have I,*

I think to myself. "Listen, do you mind if we go for a walk? I won't go far."

"Sure honey, just take it easy, okay? Remember Ronnie suggested you rest today, so don't overdo it."

"I won't. Thanks, Mom." I turn to leave.

"Oh hey! Dinner should be ready in about half an hour. Try not to be late. And your friends are more than welcome to join us. We have plenty."

"Sounds good. Thanks."

I find Ember and Sam on the lawn where I left them. Ember smiles warmly and asks, "Is there a shady place nearby we can sit and talk?"

I look up and down the street, thinking. The Morgans have some good shade trees on their property, and they won't mind us hanging around.

"There's some horse property right up the street there. They've got lots of trees."

"Perfect!" Ember crows. "I love horses."

We head down the street. Ember walks next to me while Sam hangs back a few paces. "Have you lived here long?" she asks me cheerfully.

"All my life."

"I'm from Omaha. Not for long though. As soon as I graduate, I'm moving to L.A. I can't wait! Are you a senior too?" she asks.

"Yeah, I graduate in two weeks." My mind races with questions and I wonder when she'll cut the small talk and explain what's going on.

We get to the edge of the horse field and the section

of fence that's shaded by a big leafy tree. The wooden fence isn't too high, so I carefully pull myself up to sit on it. Ember does the same and sits next to me while Sam leans on the side of the tree trunk facing us.

Ember looks me in the eyes. I get the same feeling I did when Sam was sizing me up in the parking lot at lunch. She smiles, so I must not be a total disappointment.

"You have pretty eyes," she tells me. I don't know what I was expecting, but it wasn't this. "They shine like your aura – which is very bright by the way. You have one of the brightest auras I've ever seen. It's a pretty, sunny yellow. I'm getting major good vibes from you, Adelaide, and I'm excited to get to know you."

What she's saying is kind, I guess, but it's only confusing me more. Auras? Vibes? Was she some kind of hippie into "mojo" and stuff like that?

She laughs. "I can tell from your face that I'm not helping things. All right then, first things first. What I'm about to tell you, Adelaide, is difficult to accept. But try to remember that we've gone through this and that we're here for you. Don't forget that." She places her hand on the back of mine.

Before continuing, she looks at Sam, and he gives her a small nod. She takes a deep breath.

"Adelaide. Sam drove out here from Los Angeles to find you. And I flew all the way from Omaha to meet you and tell you the dream you had last night wasn't a dream. You entered Chaos last night for the first time. When you fall back asleep tonight, you will find yourself in Chaos again, at Minor Calm."

I stare at her blankly. Did I hear her right? In my head I go over everything she just said. Then I understand what's going on and I'm suddenly angry.

"This isn't funny," I tell her. She immediately starts shaking her head.

"No, I'm not-"

"Seriously," I cut her off before she can say more, "I don't know who told you. It must be someone my mom told, but I really don't find this amusing." I slide off the fence, intending to go straight home, but I bump into Sam as he blocks my path. He puts his hands up in front of him in a "wait" gesture.

"Give us five minutes," he says softly. "And in five minutes, if you still aren't convinced, we'll leave you alone." He's looking down into my face, but my attention is on his upraised hands. I'm frozen in place at the sight of them. I start to shake and find my legs aren't strong enough to support me. Sam reaches out to stabilize me before I collapse. I feel lightheaded and dizzy. This can't be real.

He sets me on the ground gently and sits next to me, one arm still on my back for support.

Ember is there in a flash, sitting on my other side, looking concerned. "What is it? Are you all right?" she asks anxiously. I'm shaking my head back and forth, refusing to accept what I just saw.

Maybe I'm wrong. Maybe it was a trick of light. I see Sam's hand, the one that's not supporting me, resting on his leg. I reach for it, take it in my own, and slowly turn it over. No, it wasn't a trick of light. His palm is scarred.

I lightly run my fingers over it. His hands are warm and

rough and nearly twice as big as mine. I can feel the scar tissue and I know it's real. Resigned, I take off my bandages. It takes me a second but once they're off, I hold my open hand next to Sam's to compare. My injury is nearly identical to his. As I'm looking between our two hands, Ember places hers next to ours. She has the same scars.

"We keep the scars," Ember explains quietly, "the ones we get from falling. It's a personal choice. We can choose to have Doc heal the wounds with or without leaving scars. I guess it's sort of a rite of passage, a badge of honor. It's something we all have in common and we wear them proudly."

I can't deny what they're telling me anymore. If my dream wasn't a dream, and Chaos is real, then everything Mel and Crank said was real too. I was summoned to Chaos. Something, or someone, some grand unseen power, plucked me from this world and quite literally thrust me into a horrifying dimension where giant evil beasts roam free.

"Why?" I ask aloud.

"Because you are needed, Adelaide," Sam says to me.

"Me?" I erupt with laughter but it sounds more hysterical than amused, and that frightens me so I abruptly stop. "Yes, you," Ember insists. "Everyone who is chosen to come to Chaos has a purpose there. We each have some unique, much-needed quality that we bring to the fight."

"Fight? What fight are you talking about?" I'm starting to feel sick thinking about what she may say next.

"Before you can understand that, you first have to understand what Chaos is. Are you well enough for me to continue?"

I nod.

She takes a deep breath and continues. "Chaos is another realm of existence. Some would call it a parallel dimension. We aren't really sure how many different realms exist, but we do know of three for sure. First, there is Earth realm, where we are right now. Some Realmwalkers call it 'Top-side' or 'Earth-side.' Then there's the realm of Chaos."

"Where I was last night."

"That's right. Chaos alone isn't an evil place. It simply acts as a bridge-realm between here and the third realm I'm going to tell you about."

"But if Chaos isn't an evil place, why are there Calms to protect you? And what are Calms exactly?" I interrupt.

"Good question. Mel and Crank mentioned them to you," she confirms.

"Yeah. Mel said we were in Minor Calm and that we were safe from that creature there."

"That's right." She nods. "A Calm is a space created by the Realmwalkers within Chaos. It's easiest to think of it as a room within a room. There are currently two Calms in Chaos. Major Calm is our main base. It's basically our headquarters.

"Minor Calm is more like a way-station for Realmwalkers who need a safe place in a hurry and are too far from Major Calm. The Calms are the only places in Chaos that we can be safe all the time with no fear of Shades. There's only one entrance into a Calm, and it's protected by wardings."

"Do you mean, like, magic spells and stuff?"

She smiles. "Not exactly. What we do in Chaos can

easily look like magic to an outsider, but it's really not. You'll learn all about that soon." She looks at Sam. "Am I doing this right?"

He nods approvingly. "You're doing well. Now tell her about the third realm and the reason the Realmwalkers are needed."

"Right. The third realm that we know of is referred to as the Nether Realm. This is the realm of the Shades. It's where they come from. All of us Realmwalkers have our own ideas and theories of what it actually is. Some say it's a prison for damned souls, some think it's a negative version of our Earth Realm, and some say it's Hell. Just like some people from Earth Realm are able to enter Chaos, so can some of the Shades from the Nether Realm."

I stop her again. "So that creature that tried to kill me, that was a shade from the Nether Realm?"

Sam answers my question. "Yes. The shade that attacked you last night is what we call a Lesser Shade."

"There's more than one kind?"

"Yes," he answers again. "There are two kinds that we know of. The Lesser Shades, like the one you came across, and the Greater Shades."

Despite the heat, I can't stop the shiver that runs down my spine. The fact that there are shades referred to as "Greater" seems to suggest that they are somehow more dangerous than the one I saw. How can there be anything in existence more dangerous than that horrible beast?

Ember scoots closer to me and leans into my side. It's comforting feeling her there as she continues to explain.

"You'll learn all about Shades in the nights to come. For now, there is only one thing you need to know about them. Some of them have the ability to tear holes in the fabric of Chaos. Through those holes, they are able to enter THIS realm. Once a tear has been made, it's then possible for entire hordes of Shades to pass through. Once they're here, they wreak havoc, causing death and destruction everywhere they go."

"Those things come here? Why haven't I heard of them before? Why doesn't everyone know about them?"

"They can only be seen by Realmwalkers, those who have been touched by Chaos." She's quiet for a moment, then, "Okay, so for example, you know Hurricane Ilsa? The one that recently tore up the East Coast?"

I nod my head. "Are you saying Shades caused that? Wasn't that a natural disaster?"

"The Shades are creatures of pure evil. They don't belong over here. The Lesser Shades' presence has a terrible effect on this realm. They tend to bring out the ugliest and most hateful traits in people. They stir up emotions and adrenaline, causing mass riots, or if their numbers are large enough, even wars. They can focus their energy on the elements causing fires, storms, tornados, and earthquakes."

Sam explains further, "There was a tear in Chaos last week, and we weren't able to close it fast enough. An entire herd of Lesser Shades escaped through before we could seal it. Hurricane Ilsa is an example of what these things can do when they get over here."

"But why? I mean, what's their purpose?"

"We used to think it was just in their nature to be evil," Sam says. "But in the last couple hundred years we've come to understand that these Lesser Shades are driven by an intense and unquenchable hunger. They literally feed off of the misery of men. The pain and agony of mankind is what sustains them. That's why they create horrific events of mass destruction everywhere they go."

I cringe as I think of a herd of those things romping over the land unseen by others as they thrive off the turmoil and misery of humans.

"You said 'Lesser Shades,'" I point out. "What do the Greater Shades do once they get here?"

Sam's face is etched with disgust. "They are drawn to the worst of us, individuals who are destined to do evil. Like parasites, the Greater Shades tie themselves to these people, feeding off the horror and pain they cause. They follow them throughout their lives, whispering dark deeds into their subconscious, encouraging and inspiring them to commit even greater acts of evil."

Ember nods. "Stalin, Hitler, Pol Pot. Even men in our own backyard—Manson, Bundy, Dahmer—all tromping throughout history with their own personal Greater Shade."

My heart goes cold at hearing this.

Ember continues, "It is our sole purpose, as Realmwalkers, to make sure these things don't happen. There is a war going on, Adelaide. It's good versus evil and human lives are at stake. It's we who must protect them. We are the guardians of Earth Realm."

CHAPTER 7

THIS IS TOO much for me to take. I don't understand why I was called. I'm not special. I'm not a warrior. I wouldn't even say I'm particularly brave.

I think of the giant black monster charging down the street at me. I'm supposed to fight those things? And the Greater Shades? I'm embarrassed to find tears standing in my eyes. I'm not cut out for this. I wish so badly that I could make it all go away. I look at Ember, then Sam. Did they feel like this in the beginning? Were they as scared as I am now? It's hard to imagine Sam afraid of anything. What do I do?

I close my eyes and see my father. I'm entirely overwhelmed by the feeling that he's here with me. I think of how he lived his life and how he would have wanted me to live mine. I want more than anything to make him proud.

"Okay," I whisper. I open my eyes. Looking from Ember to Sam I say, "I'm a Realmwalker now. I'm scared, and I don't have any idea what I can possibly do to help, but I promise you both I'll do everything I can. I'll try my hardest." I'm surprised at the conviction I hear in my own voice and how certain I feel as I say those words. It's as if my whole life has been leading me here, to this very moment, to say those exact words and accept this calling.

I look at both of them. Sam is smiling for the first time since I've seen him, and Ember is grinning as big as she can.

Ember squeals and throws her arms around me. "Welcome to the family!" I wince as she squeezes my sore ribs but I can't help but laugh. I feel some relief now that I've accepted my fate. At least I know I won't be alone. I look at Sam over Ember's shoulder and he nods his head in approval at me. I'm filled with the familiar swell of emotion that I had in Mel's and Crank's presence. I just met these two people, Ember and Sam, but already they are two of the most important people in my life.

It's beginning to get dark out, so I look at my watch and see that it's been over half an hour since we left my house. Mom will start to worry if I don't head back soon. At first, I'm sad I have to leave them. I still have so many questions. Then I remember Mom's offer.

I smile at both of them. "Are you guys hungry? My mom made pot roast and it should be ready by now."

Ember gets a dreamy look on her face. "Mmm, that's what I smelled when she opened the door! It had my stomach growling. What do you think, Boss? Wanna stay and eat?"

"I don't know. We may get asked questions that we don't have answers to right now." He looks to me for my opinion. "Do you plan on telling your mother about Chaos?"

I haven't even considered this. "Would she even believe me?"

"Well," Ember smirks, "we have ways of proving ourselves." She glances around, checking to see that we're alone. Holding a fist out in front of us, she opens up her hand. At the same time, a spark and then a small ball of fire ignites and hovers over her palm. I jump back reflexively, but she's already closed her fist and the fire is gone as quickly as it appeared.

"They don't call me Ember for nothing," she says with a wink.

"That. Was. Awesome," I say. This opens a whole new set of possibilities. I could share all of this with Mom, even Jana. I wouldn't have to hold it all in like some terrible secret. But then, how would she feel about it? After losing Dad, Jana and I are all she has left. She's already so protective of me. She may beg me not to fight. The constant worry about my safety may drive her crazy. I don't know if she can handle it.

"I don't want to tell her anything yet. She'll worry herself to death," I decide.

"Well, then, if we're going to meet your family, we're going to need a good cover story. How do you know us?" Sam asks me. I get the feeling he's testing me. I'm reminded of something and turn to Ember.

"Did you call Sam 'Boss' a minute ago?"

"Yeah, he's the boss. Well, reluctant boss really. He's the oldest Realmwalker we have right now. Not by age—he's been in Chaos the longest of all of us, so that makes him the most likely candidate for our leader. We all still vote every six months, but for the last two years, the vote has unanimously been for Sam. Well, except for his own vote of course." She jokingly punches his shoulder. "He hates having so much authority, but in my opinion, that's the best kind of leader."

"That's why you sound so familiar. I heard you on Mel's ear thingie last night. She called you 'Boss.'"

Sam nods. "Mel did good getting to you so quickly."

"Yeah," I agree with him. "She saved my life."

"So," Ember reminds me, "what should we tell your mom for now? Who are we, how do you know us?"

I rack my brain for anything that might be believable. I really hate the thought of lying to Mom, even though right now it's for her own good. Maybe I can find some middle ground.

"Okay, how does this sound? I'm not really comfortable lying to my mom, so let's make the cover story true."

Ember nods her head enthusiastically. "Sounds good to me! Tell me what to do."

I tell them my plan and we use Ember's smartphone to put it into action.

I'm excited at the thought of having friends over for dinner. Real friends. I haven't had a real friend in who knows how long. When we get to my house, Mom is in the kitchen getting plates out of the cupboard and Jana is slicing cucumbers for a salad.

"Mom, Jana, these are some friends of mine. This is Ember and Sam." I motion to each in turn. "Guys, this is my mom, Margaret Shepherd, and my sister, Jana." Everyone shakes hands and exchanges the standard pleasantries. I can't help but notice that Jana saves her warmest welcome for Sam. She flashes him her best smile and holds on to his handshake a second or two longer than necessary. I fight the urge to roll my eyes.

"I hope you're all hungry," Mom says eagerly.

Sam asks if he can wash up before eating, so I point him down the hall to the restroom. Ember and I help set the table.

"So, you have to tell me, Ember," Mom starts out, "where did our Addy meet such good-looking kids?"

Ember doesn't even miss a beat. "Oh, it's funny really. We hadn't even met her before today. Not in person anyway. We're all members of the same fan club. Have you heard of the band Souls on Board?"

Jana lights up. "Oh yeah, they're really good. I didn't know you were a fan club member, Addy."

"Yep," I say. "I joined online." *Ten minutes ago from Ember's phone.*

Ember continues, "Well, Sam and I came out here from our hometowns. We bought tickets to their show in Phoenix for tomorrow night. When we got here, we thought we'd come meet Addy." I take note of how she words her response. She's good. Everything she said is the absolute truth. She bought the tickets from her smartphone right before coming in.

"Oh, that's wonderful. I'm so glad you did." Mom smiles at her.

We're almost finished setting the table and Sam hasn't returned yet. Mom asks me to go check that he's not lost as she puts some rolls into a basket.

I head through the living room, intending to go to the back of the house where the restroom is, but I stop when I see him in the entryway. He's standing and looking at a painting hanging on the wall to the right of the front door. It's hung over a side table where we drop our keys when we come in. I go and stand next to him and look up at the painting.

It's a portrait of my father in his uniform. We both stand there and look at it for a little while.

"Did you do this?" he asks quietly. I look at him, but his pensive expression makes it hard to tell if he likes it or not.

"Yeah. It's not that great. I was only thirteen at the time. I know it's pretty basic, but it was done at a time when I still had a clear image of him." I study the picture too. I pass it every day, but it's been a while since I actually looked at it.

"It's really good. You're talented." He indicates one of the items on the table directly below the picture. "Did he die in the line of duty?"

I pick up Dad's old police badge and run my thumb over the front of the shield. "No. Nothing like that." I shake my head, a familiar frustration bubbling inside my gut. "He goes to work every day, puts himself in grave danger, risks his life, and he dies on the side of the road, in the middle of a rain storm."

He's quiet for a moment. Then he asks, "What was he doing?"

I sigh and look up at him. "He was driving me home from a party one night during a storm. He saw a neighbor of ours stranded on the side of the road, so he stops, gets out to help her, and some inexperienced teenage driver in a sports car comes barreling down the road and hydroplanes right into him." It's been four years, but it's still painful to remember.

"Adelaide, you should know something." He takes his eyes off the painting and faces me. He looks at me with conviction in his eyes. "Your father is a hero. He did die in the line of duty."

I look back at him, puzzled.

"Your father took an oath as a police officer. He vowed to serve and protect—not just in uniform, but always. It's not only a career; it's a way of life. And that's exactly what he was doing that night. He saw someone in distress and he knew it was his duty to aid them. Your father's a hero." I'm speechless, and I fight back tears of shame. All I can do is stare back at him. Why did it take a stranger explaining this for me to understand? Of course my father died a hero. I feel the need to apologize for not realizing sooner. Gosh, I wasted so much time being angry.

I was angry because I thought he had died doing some mundane task. I was angry because I knew he was worth a more heroic ending. I was so angry that I couldn't see what was right in front of me the whole time.

I open my mouth to say I'm sorry to Sam, but I realize he's not who I need to apologize to. It's the memory of my dad that I've wronged. I say a silent vow to never forget that he died trying to fulfill his oath. He died a hero's death.

"Thank you," is all I can say to him. He nods almost imperceptibly and heads back in the direction of the kitchen. I follow him with my eyes. Does he know he's helped heal the biggest hurt inside me? I think he must know. I don't know how he can be so perceptive, but I'm overwhelmingly grateful to him.

This must be what it takes to be a great leader. You heal your peoples' wounds, and they will not only follow you but throw down their lives for you. I have no doubt that any and all of the Realmwakers would follow Sam into hell and back. And I think maybe I would too.

CHAPTER 8

WHEN WE RETURN, Mom insists we sit and let her serve us. She's probably thrilled to finally meet some friends of mine who aren't stuck up like Tori.

"Mrs. Shepherd, your pot roast is the best I've ever had," Sam says, making Mom's day.

She beams and waves her hand in a dismissive gesture. "Well, eat as much as you like then."

Jana has been watching Sam surreptitiously. I wonder if she's as obvious to anyone else as she is to me, but I doubt Sam and Ember ever miss anything.

Jana asks Sam, "So where are you two staying tonight?"

Sam glances at Ember before he answers, and I know that in that quick look an unspoken question has been asked and answered. I can't wait to know these people well enough to be able to have entire conversations with only a glance.

"We'll find a hotel nearby. Any recommendations?" he asks.

Mom answers quickly, "Yes, I know the best place. It's

called the Casa de la Shepherd! And the best part about it is it's free!"

"No, ma'am," Sam says adamantly. "We didn't come here with intentions of burdening you and your family. I appreciate the offer, but we can stay in a hotel."

"Absolutely not. I simply won't hear of it." I'm surprised and grateful at Mom's insistence.

Sam points out, "Ma'am, you don't know me from Adam-"

"Are you implying I shouldn't trust you?" Mom interrupts. Before Sam can say anything, she continues, "If I can't trust you, a police officer, then whom can I trust?"

What? I whip my head around to look at Sam. Did I miss something?

Ember laughs. "Wow, that's impressive, Mrs. Shepherd!"

"What gave me away?" Sam asks her with a curious grin.

"Well, when you're married to a police officer for twenty-four years, you learn to spot the signs." She seems proud of herself.

"Your haircut, for one, is a fairly standard police cut. You're in great shape. You walk and talk like a cop. Don't worry—it's not arrogance, just confidence," she assures him. "And if all that weren't enough, you give yourself away by presenting your left side when you greet people." Mom smiles triumphantly.

Jana looks confused. "What does that have to do with anything?"

Sam laughs quietly and explains, "In the academy, they teach you to keep your gun side farthest away from individuals you encounter in the field. It makes it harder for them to grab your sidearm. After years in the field, I guess it's been ingrained into my daily habits."

I understand now why Sam seemed passionate about my father and how he died. Knowing Sam has dedicated his life "top-side" to the same cause as Dad, and that he's taken the same oath, makes me feel closer to him.

"Not only is he a police officer," Ember brags, "but he's the Los Angeles Police Department's SWAT commander."

I'm completely impressed but not at all surprised that he leads such an important and dangerous task force.

"Wow!" Jana coos. "That's so cool! That's pretty impressive for someone your age, right?"

Sam shrugs. "No, it's not really like that. I'm not THE commander. I'm a member of the command team. I still have people over me that I answer to."

Jana insists on not letting this go. I'm suspicious she's really trying to get Sam's age out of him. "Still, that's amazing! How long have you been a police officer?"

He takes a big bite of food to avoid answering, so Ember answers for him. "It's been, three years, right?"

Sam nods. I try not to laugh. I can practically see Jana doing the math in her head.

"So you're what, twenty-four? You have to be at least twenty-one to join the force, right?" she persists.

Again, Sam nods his head.

"Wow. Twenty-four and leading SWAT. I'd definitely call that an accomplishment." I'm sure Jana thinks she's endearing herself to him by singing his praises, but I have the feeling she's only making him uncomfortable. I try to change the subject for his sake.

"I've got a grandmother in Glendale. I go there every summer to visit. We go to L.A. nearly every day that I'm there. It's my favorite city—away from here that is."

Sam gives me a quick look of appreciation before saying, "Yeah, it's a great city. I've lived there a while now."

We continue the small talk and learn a little more about Ember. She lives in Omaha, Nebraska. She's seventeen and graduates from high school next Friday. Her passion is animals and she wants to study animal behavior at UCLA. Her dream would be to tame and train exotic animals. I have every reason to believe that she can do anything she sets out to.

As Jana and I are clearing the table, Mom asserts one last time that Sam and Ember are to be our guests and that she won't accept "no" for an answer. They both agree to stay and thank her for her kindness. Jana's thrilled that they (mostly Sam) will be staying. She asks if anyone's interested in playing a board game and Ember picks Pictionary.

Sam immediately points at me. "I get the artist."

"Hey, that's no fair! I didn't know Addy was an artist!" Ember pouts. She isn't the only one put out about it either.

Jana tries to hide her disappointment at not being on Sam's team. "It's all right, Ember. We'll kick their butts."

The rest of the evening is spent playing Pictionary and other fun guessing games like Charades and Taboo. Ember proves to be hilarious and keeps us all in stitches. Even the ever-serious Sam seems to be having a good time. I get the feeling that seeing him this way is a rare treat. I'm glad to see that even though these two live dangerous lives in Chaos, they seem like normal, unaffected people. I try to memorize every detail about tonight to add it to the collection of precious memories I keep in my heart.

It's beginning to get late and I'm hoping for a chance to speak with Ember and Sam again before we fall asleep. Mom's already turned in for the night, but before she did, she checked that the guest room was ready for Sam and she put some extra pillows in my room for Ember.

Ember yawns and I realize something. "Hey," I ask her, "isn't it a lot later where you're from?"

She checks her watch. "Yeah. It's the middle of the night there." She laughs it off but this is the out I've been looking for.

"You poor thing! You must be so tired. Sorry I didn't realize it sooner. We'll let you get some sleep. I've had a crazy day today and frankly, I'm ready for bed now too."

She gets the hint. "Okay, sounds great. Thanks Jana for being an awesome partner. The games were a good idea."

"You're welcome! Tonight was so much fun. You guys need to make it out this way more often."

Sam gets up. "I should get some shut-eye myself. Ember, I'll bring your stuff in from the truck."

When he returns, Jana says goodnight to everyone, and I take the two of them to the back of the house.

"Here's the guest room, Sam. Ember, my room's right here."

After we get ourselves ready for bed, I open my door

and check that Jana isn't in the hall. When I see she's not around, I motion for Sam to join Ember and me in my room. Ember sits down on the bed. I close the door and sit down next to her. Sam sits backwards on my desk chair so he's facing us and rests his arms on the back and his chin on his arms. I'm secretly thankful I cleaned my room a few days before.

"Thanks for staying, guys. My mom loves having visitors. You probably made her year."

"She's so sweet, Addy," Ember says fervently. "You don't know how lucky you are. I wish my mom was half as nice as yours is."

The way she says it makes me wonder about Ember's mom and their relationship. Maybe I'll ask her about it when I know her better. Right now I have questions I want answered before returning to Chaos.

I look at Sam. "Are you two at Major Calm?"

"We are. As soon as we get back there, I'll put together a team and we'll come and get you and bring you back to Major Calm."

This raises a ton of fears and questions. "You mean we'll have to go back out into Chaos?"

He senses my fear. "You don't have to be afraid," he assures me. "We spend a lot of time out in Chaos fighting Shades. We're very experienced."

"Yeah, plus, I'm sure we'll get a ton of volunteers to come with us. Meeting a new Realmwalker is seriously exciting. You'll be surrounded by seasoned warriors, all bent on getting you to Major Calm safely," Ember says comfortingly.

Sam explains further, "The whole process will only take an hour or two. Then we can spend the rest of the night showing you around Major Calm and explaining life in Chaos to you."

I try to think what the other Realmwalkers will be like. "How many of us are there?" I can't believe I haven't thought of asking before now.

"You make thirteen. Lucky number thirteen!" Ember laughs.

"It's a good thing I'm not superstitious." I cross my fingers jokingly. "Gosh, I'm so anxious, I'm not even sure if I *can* fall asleep tonight."

"No worries," Ember says. "Sam can help with that. He's got some telepathic abilities."

I'm surprised. "You can read minds?" I ask him, suddenly feeling insecure.

"No, nothing like that. I can suggest things to your mind. That's all," he tells me.

"Like how?"

"Well, for example, let's say I'm chasing down a suspect on foot. I can suggest fatigue to his mind, and even though he's in top physical shape, he suddenly finds he's exhausted to runs much slower."

I am astounded at this information. What an amazing ability. It reminds me of another question I have. "How is it that you can all do these insane things? Mel can stretch herself to be super tall. Ember can somehow make fire? And now this?" I gesture at Sam. "How is it that you're all superheroes? I can't do anything even remotely fantastic."

"Don't worry about that," Sam says. "We all start out that way. You'll learn how to do some really neat stuff once you're in Chaos. It's a bit complicated to explain and would take too long to get into right now. Be patient, Adelaide. We won't leave you out to dry. We have a really good system in place to help new Walkers adjust."

All I can do is take his word for it. I can't think of anything else that's really pressing. I guess I've delayed the inevitable long enough.

"Is there anything else I should know right now? Before going back?" I ask them.

"Nope!" says Ember cheerfully. "Gosh, I can't wait for you to get to Major Calm!"

"Well, I guess I'm ready then." My stomach is a tangle of knots.

Ember climbs over to her half of the bed. "Don't worry, Mel and Crank will take good care of you until we get there. Hey, you wanna see something cool?"

"Sure," I say, wondering what else she can do while simultaneously hoping she doesn't do something to set my house on fire. Instead, she gets under the covers.

"Good night!" she chirps and falls back onto the pillow. She's perfectly quiet except for her soft breathing.

"She's not asleep, is she? Seriously? Just like that?" I ask.

Sam smiles a little. "Yeah, that's one of the first things you'll learn. It's a very important ability to be able to get to Chaos on a moment's notice."

"Wow." I look down at my hands. How will I ever measure up to these people? It's intimidating to think they expect me to learn these things. What if I'm a dud? What if I get there and find that I can't do anything special?

"Don't worry, Adelaide," Sam says. I look up to find him watching me intently.

"You must have lied earlier, about not being able to read minds," I say to him.

His expression softens and I can tell he's trying not to smile. "I can't read your mind. But anyone can tell what you're thinking just by watching your face. You're not so great about hiding your feelings."

Embarrassed, I cover my face. Shaking my head back and forth, I say into my hands, "Sheesh, what you all must think of me."

"It's not a bad thing," he insists. "It tells me you're a passionate person. That's a good thing in our line of work."

He stands up and I remember he's supposed to help me fall asleep.

"Oh, right," I say nervously. "So, I just lay down? Like normal?"

"Yeah." He waits for me as I climb between my sheets. When I'm lying down with my head on my pillow, he walks to the edge of the bed. There's a light fluttering in my stomach, and I'm finding it hard to look at him.

"I know you're nervous," he says quietly as he sits on the edge of my bed.

Am I that obvious? I think.

"But this won't be like last time. You'll fall asleep and wake up safe in Minor Calm."

Oh.

With relief I realize he thinks I'm nervous about what I'll find when I fall asleep. I'm glad he doesn't know I'm nervous because he's really attractive and really close to me-on my bed even-and we are basically alone.

"Okay, you need to look at me," he says. His voice is so gentle it contradicts the tough image I have of him. I turn my head and look at him. His eyes are such a clear blue; it's hard not to get distracted looking into them. He places his hands on the sides of my face and looks into my eyes.

"Peace." Almost as soon as the word escapes his mouth, my anxiety melts away. I'm comfortable. Everything feels wonderful: the soft pillow under my head, the warm blankets covering me, Sam's rough hands on my face. It's euphoric. I can't stop myself from smiling blissfully.

"Courage," he whispers fiercely. I feel like I can do anything. Send me to Chaos. I want to go. I want a chance to prove myself. *I'll make you proud*, I think as I'm looking into Sam's eyes. *I'll make you all proud*. Sam smiles knowingly.

"See you on the other side, Addy," he whispers.

"Sleep."

CHAPTER 9

I KNOW I'M awake and in Minor Calm, but I keep my eyes closed. I'm not ready to lose the feeling and image I just left behind. Before I know it, however, I hear voices whispering nearby. I open one eye and peek out. I'm in a bed. Two figures sit at the end, talking in hushed voices. I open both my eyes and look around. I'm in a comfy-looking bedroom with lavender walls. As I look around, I draw the attention of the two people at the foot of the bed.

Mel and Crank both turn around and shout simultaneously, "WE TOLD YOU SO!" And then we're all laughing. "You didn't think we'd forget that part, did you?" asks Mel.

"I have to admit, as crazy weird as all of this is, it's good to see you guys." I look down at myself and see I'm still wearing yesterday's tattered and bloodstained pajamas. "Please tell me we can do something about this." I indicate my clothes.

"Oh, absolutely, mate. Come with us." I follow Mel and Crank out of the room. We go down some halls and through a series of rooms before we reach two large blonde oak double doors. Mel pulls one open while Crank gets the other. Crank fumbles for a switch on the wall and flips the lights on. Rows of large florescent lights along the high ceiling flicker on in sequence, the ones closest to us first, then down the length of a very large, very long room.

"This is the Minor Calm warehouse. You can find about anything you need here. And what you can't find here, you can find in Major Calm's warehouse, which is nearly twice this big," Crank explains.

Mel motions for me to follow her. As we walk down the center aisle, we pass all different kinds of furniture and appliances. There are bed frames and mattresses of all sizes to my left. Dressers and vanities to my right. Farther down we pass some sofas and an assortment of electronics. I'm amazed at the variety and quality of everything here. We arrive at a section that looks like the inside of an apparel store you see at a mall. There are clothes racks here and there and tables with folded stacks of clothing. Toward the back wall are rows and rows of shoes.

"Wow," I say insufficiently. I'm at a total loss for words.

"Go ahead and help yourself. There's basically every size here, so I'm sure you'll find something," Mel says. "This side is for sheilas. That should help ya out."

"Thanks, guys, but, um… how does this work? Do I need to pay?"

Mel and Crank both laugh at me.

Crank shakes his head. "Oh, hermana, you've got a lot to learn."

I delve through all the clothes on the racks and tables

until I find some things that look comfortable. I grab some extra stuff too in case not everything fits. I find a pair of shoes that fit and the three of us head back to the room I woke up in.

"This place is so nice. It's huge! How many rooms are in here?" I ask them.

"There are twelve bedrooms here and about five comfortable lounging areas," Mel says.

"And this is only the 'way-station'?" I'm amazed at the size of everything. I can't even imagine how they pay for everything inside it, let alone get it all here.

"Yeah, the Realmwalkers who made the Calms wanted to make sure it was big enough to comfortably house all of us in case of an emergency," Crank informs me.

"You'll learn all about it soon." Mel smiles encouragingly. "Essentially, your whole first week is spent learning the basic history of Chaos, as far as we know it. That includes learning how the Calms were made and how we keep them stocked and updated with the latest technology. It's pretty interesting stuff. Well, we'll leave you be so you can get cleaned up. The lav is in there." She points to a door at the back of the room.

They close the door on their way out. I assume that when Mel says "lav" she means the bathroom. Sure enough, behind the door she pointed to is a fully functioning bathroom. I find all the necessary toiletries in drawers and cupboards. After showering, I dress myself and examine the finished product in a full-length mirror by the bed.

I chose a comfortably snug black cotton T-shirt and

some olive green cargo pants with a matching woven fabric belt. I decide I've fallen in love with the pair of shoes I chose—black boots with thick soles, not the gross clunky kind that are easy to trip over. These manage to look military and feminine at the same time. I pull my hair back into a high ponytail using a hair band I found in a bathroom drawer.

I toss my old, bloody clothes into a wastebasket by the dresser and make the bed before heading out to look for Crank and Mel. I find them in the living room I remember from last night. As I join them, I catch the tail end of a conversation Mel is having on her ear device.

"Sounds like perfect conditions. What's your ETA?"

Sam's voice is a little muffled, but I can make out what he says, "Twenty minutes."

"All right, Boss. We'll be ready. Mel out."

I start to get nervous again as I think about actually having to go out into Chaos. I sit next to Crank on one of the sofas. "Can you tell me what to expect? What's it like out there?"

"Boss was just telling Mel there's little to no activity right now. Looks like Fate is smiling down on us today. The trip to Major Calm should be pretty uneventful," Crank explains.

"So there aren't many Shades out?" I ask for clarification.

"That's right. Which is lucky. We normally come across at least a dozen Lesser Shades mulling about between Major Calm and here."

"Holy crap! A dozen of those things?" I blurt out. "The

one I saw last night was enough to last me quite a while, thank you very much."

Mel waves her hand back and forth. "Things aren't normally that way. You see, Lesser Shades are a lot like cattle—big stupid cows that roam around searching for a tear to pass through. It's pretty rare to come across one like we did the other night. If you're out in the open and alone, the way you were last night, and a Lesser Shade is close by, they'll seize the opportunity and try to kill you. But most of the time, if we're in large numbers, they tend to stay clear of us."

"But wait, I thought all you guys did was fight Shades. If they aren't aggressive all the time, when is it that we're supposed to fight them? Do we attack them as soon as we see them?" I'm getting confused again.

"Okay, it's like this," Mel goes over to the large flat-screen monitor on the wall that Crank used last night. She touches the screen, pulls up some files, and scrolls through them until she finds one titled "Known Shades."

"Crank, can you get the lights?" Once the lights are off, she selects the folder. From two small units on the floor, one located on each side of the screen, come projection lights. Where the two lights meet, in the air above the coffee table in front of me, they form a 3-D holographic image of a dark, beastlike creature, similar, but not identical to the Lesser Shade that nearly killed me.

"There's a hierarchy among the Shades. Both types, the Lesser and the Greater have their roles and purposes. This is a Lesser Shade, like the one last night." The image of the Shade is slowly rotating so I'm able to see it from all angles. This one reminds me of a large dog, only instead of four legs, it has six, three on each side. Each leg ends in three bulgy finger-like appendages that look able to grab things. It's disgusting.

"There are all different types of Lesser Shades." Each time Mel touches the screen, a new type of beast appears. Some look insectile, some amphibious. To my horror, I see a few of them have large spanning wings. Mel continues, "The Lesser Shades' main goal is to find a tear in the fabric of Chaos and get through it. That's when we need to watch out for them most. Try to stop them and they get spewin'!"

"So other than that, we basically leave them alone?" I ask her.

"Not exactly. When we aren't busy hunting Greater Shades and sealing tears, we do a bit of what we call 'population control.' If we don't kill 'em off when we can, before we know it, there are too many to deal with. We also try to discourage Lesser Shades from herding. They're more dangerous when they gather up in groups, so we break them up, thin out their ranks."

"You really shouldn't worry too much about Lesser Shades," says Crank. "Honestly, they're stupid creatures. They may seem terrifying at first, but they act purely on instinct. They're simple to outsmart and they always fall for the same old tricks."

"Oscar's right. It's the Greater Shades you need to watch out for." She touches the screen again and the image in front of me changes to what I can only assume is a Greater Shade. "Now, don't let their appearance fool you. These blokes are as cunning as a dunny rat."

So this is a Greater Shade? In terms of "scary," it doesn't look like much—not compared to a Lesser Shade anyway. The creature stands erect like a man. It has arms and legs similar to a human's, only slightly off. Disproportionate. It's as if the monster tried to emulate a man, but this twisted, mutated form is as close as it can come. It seems to be made up of the same blackness as the Lesser Shades. It's hard to get a real idea of its size as I've nothing to compare it to.

"How large are these things?" My voice comes out quieter than I intended. She turns to the screen and types something in. I watch in awe as the hologram steadily expands. When it's finished growing, it's about eight, maybe nine feet tall. Seeing it this large makes it easier to see details.

Even though I know it's only an image and not the real thing, the hairs on my arms stand up and a sudden coldness runs along the length of my spine. Up close like this, the creature looks as though its flesh is made of a thick, oily, black sludge. I wonder how it's able to hold its shape. Under the swirling shadows surrounding the beast, I can see that where its eyes and mouth should be are only gaping, black, empty holes.

"These hooligans," Mel continues, "are the rippers.

They are the only ones who are able to tear holes into Chaos. They're also considerably more intelligent than the Lesser Shades. Still nothing compared to us, but underestimating them can be dangerous. Every once in a while one will do something surprisingly clever."

She then goes into another folder and pulls up a different hologram. In this display, I'm looking at a frenzied image of Lesser Shades. They appear to be stampeding, climbing over each other, the flying ones dive-bombing. All of the Lesser Shades are converging on one point. Looking closer, I see they are all trying to get to a single Greater Shade.

"Here is a typical tear site. This is where we see the most action. That Greater Shade there," Mel indicates the one humanoid creature, "is seconds away from creating a tear. It's our job to destroy him before he does. This is when the Lesser Shades become *really* pesky. When we attack the Greater Shade, the Lesser Shades attack us in an attempt to stall us long enough for the ripper to do his job. See, they want to get to Earth Realm as badly as he does. In this way, the two Shades have a symbiotic relationship. Neither can get to Earth Realm without the help of the other."

I try to imagine being attacked by all those Lesser Shades at once. It's a marvel there are any living Realm-walkers at all! Crank reads my expression and chuckles.

"You won't worry so much once you see us in action. Don't count us out yet!"

I try to let their nonchalance reassure me. It can't really be as bad as I imagine if they are so lighthearted about it.

"ETA five minutes," Sam's voice echoes from both Mel and Crank's earpieces.

Mel shuts off the display as Crank turns on the lights. My palms are sweating as my anxiety grows.

"Well, we best head down to the garage. Boss will expect us to be ready to move as soon as they get here," Mel says as she motions for me to follow her.

Once in the garage, Mel and Crank approach a large

locker unit toward the back. From out of their individual lockers labeled with their names, they remove what look like motorcycle helmets. Crank's is blue with crashing waves on it, and Mel's is a pretty purple with white swirling tendrils.

I look around and see that one of the strange motorcycle-like vehicles matches Mel's helmet and I figure it's hers. Crank grabs a plain black helmet out of an unlabeled locker, I'm guessing for me. I hope they don't expect me to drive one of these things.

I'm not sure what to expect when everyone gets here. I try to remember how it was when Mel first carried me in through the garage door, but everything happened so fast and I was hiding my face for most of it. Just then, I hear a distant buzzing sound, almost like a swarm of bees. As it gets louder, I recognize the sound as the roar of exhaust pipes. It's difficult to tell how many bikes there are, but the sound is impossibly loud.

"You might want to stand to the side!" Crank shouts over the noise. I back up as close to the wall as I can get and watch the inside of the garage door, waiting for it to open. I'm astonished at what I see next.

The large motorcycles come straight through the garage door as if it weren't even there! First one, then two. Each bike is brightly decorated, and they all appear to have different gadgets and apparatuses protruding from them. One after another, they come through the door until the noise echoing off the garage walls is deafening. I'm covering my ears and it's still incredibly loud.

When they all seem to be through, they start turning

off their engines. Finally, I can hear again, though my ears are buzzing from the abuse. I quickly count the vehicles; there are six in all. Everyone's wearing helmets, but I immediately see one bedecked in flames and know that it must be Ember.

The vehicle in the lead is painted jet black and has a sleek design. It looks built for speed. I have a suspicion it's Sam's and am proven right when he removes his helmet and the others follow suit.

"Everyone," Sam says and indicates me, "meet your newest Realmwalker. Adelaide Shepherd."

CHAPTER 10

I STAND THERE feeling insecure while they inspect me.

"Hi," I say nervously and wave at them. I make eye contact with Ember and I'm no longer so anxious. She is grinning and waving ecstatically at me. Her excitement at seeing me warms my heart. She hops off her motorcycle and runs to hug me.

"Well don't just sit there!" She hollers at the others. "Sheesh, you'd think they've never met a new Realmwalker before."

The others get off their bikes and make their way over. Sam walks over to Mel and Crank and speaks with them quietly. I look over the group of Realmwalkers in front of me and the diversity among them is surprising. Other than Ember and Mel, there's only one other girl here. She looks Asian, maybe Japanese. There're three guys among the mix. One is really tall with carrot-orange hair. The other two are shorter than he is but still fairly tall.

"Guys, this is Addy. She's way cool," Ember says matter-of-factly.

The other girl steps forward and smiles at me, her cheeks dimpling. She looks maybe a year or two older than I am. She's very pretty with glossy black hair that falls, stick straight, to her waist. It's like the kind you see in shampoo commercials, and it looks so soft that for a second I'm tempted to reach out and touch it. She has long black eyelashes and is wearing purple eye shadow. I can see the definition in her biceps as she waves at me—she's obviously in great shape. Strapped to her back is a long, slightly curved sword in a case. I'm pretty sure it's called a katana.

"Hi Addy. I'm Kira. Nice to meet you. I'm so glad we got another girl. We can always use some extra girl power around these parts." She flexes her arms for show.

"Nice to meet you too." I smile back.

"I'm Timothy. It's a pleasure," the tall orange-haired guy says in a very heavy Scottish accent. I instantly remember Mel and Crank's story and try not to picture him riding naked behind Sam. Timothy looks like he's in his late twenties, but there's a sort of easy youthfulness about him. Strapped to nearly every available space on his body are guns and ammo of all shapes and sizes.

"Hi Timothy." I smile, wishing I had something witty or charming to say.

"Adelaide." My attention is drawn to a stunningly handsome Asian guy about twenty or so. His chestnut brown hair is styled long and falls in his face in just the right way. He is trim but very fit. I can't see any obvious weapons on him.

"Lang-hao," he says, his voice like silk as he gently takes my hand and kisses the top of it. My cheeks grow warm and

I know I'm blushing. He smiles as though this is the reaction he expected. Timothy rolls his eyes dramatically behind Lang-hao.

"Oh, ni-nice to meet you," I stammer stupidly. Feeling totally embarrassed and awkward, I'm grateful when Ember rescues me.

"And this is Mikhail," she indicates a guy I hadn't noticed before. He's standing off to the side, away from everyone, hands crammed in his pockets, his eyes cast down. He also looks to be in his early twenties. On his back I can see the handles of two long, curved blades. I have no idea what they're called, but they look too long to be knives and too short to be swords. He's got a short buzz cut and light gray eyes. With a strong jaw covered in scruff and a heavy brow. He's built similarly to Sam, though slightly broader in the chest and shoulders.

Is everyone here beautiful? I wonder.

Mikhail says nothing but nods his head in greeting. I smile and wave.

Looking at everyone, I'm bewildered by the overwhelming fondness I have for them. I know Mel and Crank already explained it to me, but it's unbelievable that I can feel so attached to perfect strangers. I can't wait to get to know them all.

"I'm happy to meet everyone. Thanks for coming. Seeing all of you makes me feel much better about having to go out there again."

"Yeah, Mel told us about your first night here. You must have been pretty freaked out, huh?" says Kira. "How are you holding up?" She reaches out and squeezes my shoulder affectionately.

I laugh a little. "Well, I was pretty scared at first, then I calmed down because I thought it was only a dream. Then I found out it wasn't a dream, and I was terrified again." They all laugh and tell me they've been there, all except Mikhail who has wandered back to his bike.

Sam comes over and holds out an ear device to me. "This is yours. Put it on. Make sure it fits." I do as I'm told and once it's in, Sam examines it to make sure I did it right. I take the chance to look him over. Since the first second he entered Minor Calm, Sam has been all business. I was hoping for a warmer greeting from him, considering how laid back he was last night at my house. I remember him relaxed and happy as we played games around my family room. The image in my memory seems foreign now as I watch him move with military precision.

He looks like a warrior with a row of grenades strapped diagonally across his chest and a wicked-looking gun attached to each side. An assortment of weapons hangs from a belt around his waist, many of which I've no name for. The only one I recognize is a lethal-looking dagger at least eight inches long.

"You'll be able to hear all of us through your ear-com device. When you want to be heard," he takes my hand and runs my fingers over the button on the outside, and even this simple gesture makes my heart stutter, "hold this button down and speak. You won't need it while wearing your helmet. It has its own com-link built in."

Crank hands me my helmet as Sam gives the orders. "The scene outside is the center of a major city. We'll stick to the streets to avoid the skyscrapers. Stay in a tight "V" formation. I'll take center point. I want Ember on my right. Timothy, you stay to the right of Ember. On my left I want Mikhail, then Lang. Adelaide, you'll ride with Mel directly behind me in the center. Kira and Crank, you two take up the rear. This should be a quiet trip. Even so, report any activity as soon as it's detected. Any questions?"

"No, sir," most of the Walkers respond. It's plain to see they respect Sam and trust him completely.

Mel motions for my attention. "Come on, Addy. I'll introduce you to my Big-Bike." I follow her to the purple bike and she helps me put on my helmet. Once it's on, I'm able to see that the visor has some sort of digital readout running along the bottom. I have no idea what it means, but I assume I won't need to know since I'm not driving. Everyone mounts up and Mel reaches out and helps me get on behind her. The Big-Bike is huge under me and I feel like I'm straddling a Clydesdale.

"You're gonna want to hold on tight. We usually travel pretty fast," Mel's voice comes through the speaker in my helmet. Everyone revs up and I'm thankful the helmet helps dampen the roar. I look around at everyone. They are all in business mode and ready to go. This is it. I glance at Ember and she gives me a very enthusiastic thumbs up.

Sam's voice comes through the speaker. "All right, let's move out."

Just like that, we're off. Mel's Big-Bike jerks forward,

and I squeeze her tightly so I don't fall off the back. I close my eyes, not wanting to see us phase through the garage door. I know exactly when we pass into Chaos—the warmth of the Calm is suddenly gone, replaced by and empty hollow ache.

Kira's in my ear, "Looks all clear. Sorry we won't be able to give you much of a show today, Addy."

"Don't get complacent. Stay on your guard," Sam warns.

I finally open my eyes and take in our surroundings. As we race down the street, I'm surprised to find the suburban neighborhood from last night is nowhere to be seen. Instead, we're surrounded on all sides by huge towering buildings and parking garages and convention centers—all bleached and faded out. I'm reminded of the time Dad took me to a big stadium in Phoenix to watch a ball game. A few cars line the streets parked in front of parking meters. I can't understand how we came out of Minor Calm into a completely different part of Chaos.

I tap Mel to get her attention. "What happened? Where's the neighborhood?"

Mel nods knowingly. "Chaos is constantly shifting outside of the Calms. We think it's trying to emulate Earth Realm. It's pretty good at it, only it can't populate its towns and cities, so it comes off a little eerie."

I wonder if that means none of this is real. I look around. Everything is so detailed and clear. I can see our reflections in the sides of the glass buildings. I can even see that some of the parking meters have expired. Being an artist, I'm able to appreciate that whatever is orchestrating these scenes has a great eye for detail. Everything *seems* real. That neighborhood street I slammed into last night certainly *felt* real.

As I'm looking around at the city rushing past, I happen to glance into the wide opening of a parking garage and see a patch of total blackness in the shadows of the garage slink around a corner and out of sight. I would've chalked it up as my imagination, but something in my helmet's visor recognizes it and highlights it in white, just before it's gone.

"I'm not sure if it matters much," I say, unsure of myself, "but I'm pretty sure we just passed a Lesser Shade hiding in a parking garage back there." I wait for a response, hoping my voice transmitted.

A voice that I recognize as Crank's says, "Yeah, he better be hiding from us! Dumb beast probably saw us coming and is terrified!"

"I don't know, Crank," Kira says uncertainly. "I'm getting some pretty strange readings."

There's silence for a little while, but I notice everyone looking around more attentively than before.

Sam says suddenly, "Something's off. Something doesn't feel right."

"I'm getting the same vibes, Sam," Ember chimes in.

"Let's pick up the pace, everyone," Sam instructs.

We increase our speed, which makes it harder for me to look for Shades. Then I remember the holographic image Mel and Crank showed me of the Shade with wings. I look up and scan the skies for flying Shades, but I don't see any.

My relief, however, is short-lived. There on a skyscraper to the left, hanging over the top and looking down on us, is a huge black beast resembling something like a giant bat with a muzzle full of large jagged teeth. My visor highlights it in white. I nudge Mel's arm and point out the Lesser Shade.

"Flying Shade, on top of that building there, ten o'clock," Mel says. Then, to my horror, as we approach, more flying Shades begin to peek out from around the tops and sides of other skyscrapers. Some are clinging to the sides of the buildings with impossibly strong, clawed feet. One without wings looks to be crawling lizard-like down the side of a building.

"Whoa. We could be in real trouble here, Boss," I hear a Scottish voice say. As if on cue, dozens of Lesser Shades come rushing out from side streets, from around corners, and out of parking garages.

"AMBUSH!" Kira yells. And like that, the scene erupts into total madness. Most of the Realmwalkers draw their weapons. Horrible snarls and screeches and growls and roars fill the air—loud enough to be heard through our helmets. Shades are charging everywhere. Under the bike, the earth shakes from their pounding gallops. Flying shades are swooping down. Mel skids her Big-Bike to a stop right in the center of a circle created by the other Realmwalkers.

"Mel, your job is to protect Adelaide. If this gets too hairy and you see an opening, take it. Get her safely to Major Calm," Sam says over the com as Realmwalkers fight all around us. I see Timothy with a gun in each hand, expertly picking off the smaller Shades with only one shot. His precision amazes me as his bullets rip through vital parts of the beasts, splattering black sludge through the air.

Kira has ditched her Big-Bike and is moving like a blur through the nearby mass of converging Shades, slicing them apart with her katana. My mind can't make sense of the scene as she flips and spins here and there, leaving oozing and twitching black pieces of Shades behind in her wake. I scan the frenzied scene, looking for Sam and Ember.

Ember is the easiest to find, off on a side street to our right, behind a giant, swirling vortex of fire. Reaching twenty feet high, it ignites the surrounding Shades. Their agonized shrieks and wails fill the air as they burn. Waving her hands and arms around expertly, she controls the direction and speed of the fire tornado, grinning through the bright red hair that whips around her face.

Just then, a buffalo-like Shade zooms through the air above us and crashes into the side of an office building, shattering windows and sending debris sailing. I hear a shout of victory over the noise of the battle and turn to see Lang-hao punch the air upward. As he does, a feline-like Shade in front of him flies up off the ground and hovers in the air. Lang holds his hands above him and starts twirling an unseen object. Simultaneously the giant cat-like Shade starts to spin rapidly and is then thrown down the street as Lang thrust his hands forward.

I'm impressed by my comrades' abilities but it's beginning to look like it won't be enough. There are too many Shades. Just then, I see a Shade charging down the street toward us. It's the same rhinoceros-looking beast from last night and it's headed right for us.

Mel says, "This guy again? I think he's got a crush

on you, Addy!" Crank spins around in time to see him approaching. He's nearly to Crank when he's bowled out of the way and into a building by a giant surge of... water? Water is shooting out of the hydrant at the side of the road, pushing with such force that it's shoved the Shade inside the building and is continually pounding it.

"Good on ya, Crank!" Mel says through the intercom. I glance at Crank and see he's concentrating on the water shooting out of the hydrant. He must be controlling it somehow.

"We need to fall back! There are too many," Sam's voice sounds strained, but I finally see him. He's taking on two Shades at once, fighting with his bare hands. He strikes a charging Shade and sends it sailing as though it weighs nothing. He jumps unbelievably high and grabs a huge, grizzly bear-like Shade on his right in a headlock. Somehow, he manages to get his arms around its neck and with one violent jerk the monster's head twists grotesquely around. Its body goes limp and Sam falls with it, landing on top of it.

Before he can get up, the other Shade pounces on him but Sam's legs meet it and kick it up and back. It soars back and over the head of another Shade, smashing into some cars parked on the street. It doesn't get back up.

"Fall back now! Get to the bikes. Double up if we have to," Sam orders.

All around Mel and me, Realmwalkers are trying to make it back to their bikes while fighting off the attacking Lesser Shades. It seems an eternity before everyone is back within range. The fear in my chest overwhelms me as a tight wall of ravenous, hate-filled beasts encircle us. I have no idea how we are going to get out of this. If the Realm-walkers turn their backs to mount up, they'll be vulnerable.

"I got this guys!" Ember shouts as she starts to swirl her arms around her. Fire grows out from her palms and stretches out like a rope, snaking itself around us, encircling us in a lasso of flames. Following some unseen command from Ember, the thread of fire grows until it is a huge, raging wall.

Heat licks my exposed skin as I witness of Ember's awesome ability. A Shade attempts to breach the barrier but shrieks in pain and quickly retreats. Everyone climbs onto their bikes, which are in surprisingly good shape. I'm still wondering how we'll escape. We're still completely surrounded outside the wall of fire.

Just then, Mel's bike gives a small jerk, as if it's shifting gears. She revs it up and instead of jumping forward, the bike begins to rise. The engine feels different, not as rumbly. The sound is a lot higher in pitch and smoother than the before. I grab onto Mel and hold tight. One by one the others begin to rise. When we're about three feet in the air, Sam raises a hand.

"On my go." He says as he counts down with his fingers. When he gets to one, he points up. Together as one, the Big-Bikes push forward at an alarming rate. We arc upward and climb up the inner wall of fire until we shoot out the opening at the top. We continue to gain altitude at an insane vertical angle.

Right as I feel like we're out of danger, I hear a loud

screech to my right and turn in time to see a wicked-looking Lesser Shade flying like a rocket right for Mel and me. The pterodactyl-like Shade crashes into the back of Mel's bike before zooming away in a blur.

My hold on Mel slips as we spin out of control. I slide down the back of the bike. I think I'm going to fall off completely, but I'm able to grab hold of the rear-wheel fender. I'm dangling out in the open air from the back of the bike.

"We've been hit! We need help!" Mel shouts through the com system as she struggles to regain control of her bike. Everything around me is a blur. I'm only hanging for seconds when I'm grabbed around the middle and ripped from the back of the bike.

I can see the ground above me as I'm dangling upside down. I look to see what has me and am horrified—I'm in the grip of huge, black, oily-looking claws of the flying Shade that crashed into us. Everywhere the talons touch me, my skin burns ice cold.

The flying beast is getting closer to the ground. As it prepares to land, it slings me into a concrete wall. Every bone in my body rattles as I hit the wall and slide down. The visor of my helmet cracks when I hit the ground, making it impossible to see. I want to lie there, rolling in pain, but I don't have time. The flying thing could be on me any second. I wrench my helmet off in one swift move.

Sure enough, the creature is slowly approaching, walking on wings and claws toward me. It climbs over a car and crouches down to shriek at me. The sound is deafening and blows my hair back out of my face with the sheer force of it.

I get to my feet and back up against the concrete wall. It's the side of a business. To my left is a faded green door labeled "Employees Only." A small awning above the door throws it into thick shadows.

I dive for the handle, pulling at it desperately, but it doesn't budge. I turn to face the oncoming beast. It's nearly reached me. I scan around me for any Realmwalkers, but I can't see anyone. Do they even know I'm missing?

As the Shade reaches the sidewalk in front of me, it snaps its head to the right. Whatever has caught its attention is beyond my sight, hidden by the next business over. Behind the Shade, I see other Shades running in the opposite direction, apparently away from something. The flying Shade that brought me down is suddenly lifted off the ground and thrown backwards in the air. It tumbles awkwardly, unable to get its wings out before it crashes down into a streetlight on the other side of the road.

My hopes soar as I wait for the Realmwalkers to ride into view from the direction the Shades were running from. My hopes are dashed when I see what it is that has frightened the Shades. Stepping into view, nearly fifteen feet away from me, is a Greater Shade.

Through the swirling shadows that cling to it, I'm able to see that the demon is easily ten feet tall and is darker than all the other shades I've seen. Its deformed arms and legs drip a clumpy black sludge. I retch involuntarily when I see that its flesh is bubbling and churning, as though hundreds of creepy, crawly things are just under its skin trying to get out. Its searching gaze stops on me.

It turns in my direction and steps closer. I look around me, trying to decide on the best direction to run. It reads my intentions and suddenly holds up a crooked, mangled arm. It points at me and I'm unable to move, held in place by some power. I look at the Greater Shade, at where its face should be under the ever moving cloud of darkened mist that surrounds it. Terror shoots through me like electricity. I've seen this shade before.

Everything in me knows with absolute certainty that the evil being in front of me is the very same demon from my dream. The demon masquerading as Tori. The one trying to keep me from going through the door that brought me to Chaos. As this realization dawns on me, I feel an unmistakable pulse of pleasure emanate from the Shade. I don't know how, but it knows I recognize it.

I hear a revolting, wet, choking sound coming from the area of its mouth and I realize it's laughing. I'm terrified as it inches closer. I try as hard as I can to move but I'm frozen where I stand. I can't even release the scream that's built up in my throat. It turns its outstretched hand sideways and curls its fingers into a claw. As it does this, I feel cold, invisible fingers wrap around my neck. I'm lifted off the ground by the force tightening around my throat. I can't breathe! I'm still frozen, so I'm unable to even reach up or kick my legs.

While I fight for breath, all I can do is plead with my eyes for the Shade to release me. As I'm searching the shadows over its face, I feel a strange sensation in my mind. I feel vulnerable, as though my every thought is exposed.

I see you. You are weak. You are nothing.

A searing pain shoots through my brain as the deep, demonic voice echoes around in my head. Everything in me screams! The edges of my vision are beginning to grow dark. I'm dizzy and lightheaded, on the verge of losing consciousness. I won't survive my second night in Chaos. I'll never get the chance to prove myself. The worst thing about dying now is that the last image I'll ever see is this evil, hateful creature.

The Greater Shade is in my mind. He hears these desperate, dying thoughts and his response is loud, wet laughter. For the second time in two days, I accept that death is inevitable.

CHAPTER 11

As I'm dangling, seconds away from death, I hear the greatest sound I've ever heard. Big-Bikes. Through my failing vision, I'm able to make out first two, then a third Big-Bike land directly behind the Greater Shade.

"LET HER GO!" shouts Sam as he throws something shiny, disc-like, and wickedly sharp-looking at the Greater Shade. I fall to the ground as the Shade releases its grip on me and whips around. While I gasp for breath, the Shade deflects the spinning weapon with ease. It hunches defensively in front of me, making its intentions clear. I belong to it and it isn't going to give me up without a fight.

I struggle to sit up, hoping maybe I can make a run for it, but I'm too weak. I watch as Sam, Lang-hao, and Timothy unleash everything they have at the Greater Shade. Lang's arms are extended and his face is crumpled in concentration. Sam and Timothy are both firing their automatic weapons at the demon but shockingly, to no avail. The Shade seems to be stopping all of the bullets before they can reach it. It's even somehow preventing Lang's ability from having any effect.

I manage to stand up, using the wall for support. I scream out as the Shade uses its power to thrust Timothy back into a parked car. *Get up. Get up Timothy*, I plead silently. Before I can see if he's okay, something happens.

Arms reach out of the shadows under the awning next to me. They wrap around my chest and fiercely pull me backwards and into the shadows with them. The moment we're completely under the awning, I see nothing but darkness. I sense I'm falling, spinning and flipping end over end, all the while being held tightly by strong arms.

As suddenly as it began, it ends. The person holding me steps out into a light-filled street. The street looks much like the one we just left, only with different buildings and cars. Directly in front of me is a silver Big-Bike.

What just happened? How did we get here? The arms release me and I spin around to see Mikhail. I look around frantically for other Realmwalkers but see none.

"Where is everyone? Where are we?" I croak, voice raspy from the damage the Elder Shade's grip caused my throat.

His only answer is to scoop me up and place me gently on his bike. As he gets on behind me, I hear an explosion in the distance.

"What was that? Do you think that's them?" I'm asking him but he isn't answering me. He revs up his bike and we're speeding down an empty street. There are no Shades anywhere to be seen.

We're coming up to an overpass above a freeway. Right when we crest the top, Mikhail's bike gives a small jerk as he changes gears and we lift off the road. We continue to gain altitude and speed. I scan the city below for signs of my friends. It's only when I've craned all the way around that I see a giant column of smoke rising from that part of the city and random flashes of light from either fire or explosions, I can't tell.

"Mikhail! Look! There they are!" I try to point around him at where the fight must be going on. He doesn't even turn to look. His eyes are focused straight ahead and he remains silent. All the while, we get farther away from the Realmwalkers.

It's then that I realize he has no intention of going back. He's taking me to Major Calm without the others. I think of what they must be going through back there. I think of the Greater Shade and how powerful he is. I think of Ember and Sam. Is Mel all right? The last time I saw her was on the back of her Big-Bike spinning out of control. Did she steady it? Did she fall to her death? And Timothy. Did he get back up after being slammed into that car?

No! This isn't right. That's my new family back there. I belong with them. I can't leave them to die!

"Mikhail, please. They need us. They need you! Please?" I beg, crying now as I pound his chest. Still he remains silent.

I stop pleading. I know he won't take me back there. He's following orders. I watch the smoke cloud get smaller in the distance as we get farther away. Everything is silent but the air whipping past us and the sound of my crying. I say a silent prayer that my friends are alive and try to control my emotions. Tears won't help anyone. I manage to calm myself enough to turn and look Mikhail in the eyes. He's still staring straight ahead.

I watch him for a moment. His jaw is clenched tight, and I feel through his chest and arms that he's trembling.

"Will they make it?" I whisper up at him. It takes a moment, but he shifts his gaze downward to look me in the eyes.

"Let us hope," he says in a quiet voice. I can hear his concern through a thick Russian accent. I nod my head and sigh as I face forward. Though my anxiety is strong, all I can do now is hope and wait.

Through our silence, I look at the endless city below as we soar over the tops of the skyscrapers. I scan ahead, trying to find any change in scenery but everything is the same. Buildings, streets, freeways, repeated endlessly as far as the eye can see. Then something interesting begins to happen.

In my chest, a familiar warmth begins to grow. Without ever having been there, I know we are approaching Major Calm. In fact, given the controls of Mikhail's bike, I'm sure I could take us the rest of the way there. It's almost as if I can hear it calling. However comforting the feeling may be, it's not enough to dispel the fear I have for my friends.

As Mikhail begins a descent to street level, I scan the area for signs of any Shades. I don't see any but I continue to search anyway. We land on an empty street and head in the direction of a building with a slanted top. The architecture is modern and a little out of place with its surroundings. I instinctively know that the front of the building is the doorway to Major Calm.

I try to control the rushing flood of emotions that come when I think of how I'll soon be safe while my friends could be dead. I have never felt so helpless, so useless in my entire life.

I don't even flinch as we drive straight through the front display window of the artsy building and into a huge garage, easily twice as large as the one we left in Minor Calm. As Mikhail slows his bike to a stop, I notice a tall, curvy brunette marching toward us angrily.

Though everyone I've met in Chaos so far has been beautiful, this woman is easily one of the most gorgeous beings I've ever seen. She is thin and has long, flowing chocolate hair. Her big blue eyes would be breathtaking if they weren't narrowed into angry slits. Behind her, I barely have time to notice a tall man in a white lab coat before the woman starts shouting.

"What's happening out there! The coms have been cutting in and out. All we can hear are intermittent sounds of distress. Where is everyone?" this woman demands with an absolute air of authority. Mikhail says nothing but shuts down his bike and gets off. As he reaches to help me down, she says in a snarky tone, "I'm not at all surprised to see you here ahead of everyone. It's just like you to sneak off and disappear whenever you're needed!"

I'm completely taken back by this hateful woman's accusations. Suddenly my grief and anxiety turn into rage as I snap at her.

"You don't know what you're talking about! Mikhail was brave. He saved my life!" I fume at this snotty stranger.

The woman looks at me and raises an eyebrow. She looks me up and down as she says, "Oh, and you know Mikhail much better than the rest of us, don't you?"

Before she can say anything else, I march closer to her, livid at her insensitivity. "He only came back because he had to. He was following orders!" I shout.

Her snippy reply is cut off by the sound of a Big-Bike revving to life. I snap my head around to see that while we've been arguing, Mikhail has gotten back on his bike and is now riding back out through the door to Chaos.

I run after him, intending to yell at him to be careful, but he's gone before I can get the words out. I stop right in front of the garage door and fall to my knees. I can't hold back the fresh wave of despair as another friend is added to the list of possible deaths.

I try hard to keep from crying as my mind's eye imagines the worst. I can't stop seeing the image of Ember lying lifeless in the street. I see Sam's bloody and broken body crumpled at the foot of the triumphant Greater Shade.

I rock back and forth hugging myself. I feel a warm hand on my shoulder and I don't even look up. It can only be the man in the lab coat as offering comfort doesn't seem to be in the angry woman's nature. I realize now in hindsight that perhaps I overreacted when I yelled at her. Even though my emotions were running high, I shouldn't have let them get the best of me.

I decide to put the bratty woman out of my mind and focus on only positive thoughts. I picture the other Realmwalkers riding into the garage, smiling victoriously. Everyone is safe and sound and we all celebrate together, laughing as they tell how they defeated the Greater Shade. The hand on my shoulder squeezes me gently, and

I hear a man's voice say with a British accent, "We best move aside. I can hear the Big-Bikes approaching."

Excited and anxious I jump up and run to the side of the garage. I can hear the sounds of the bikes now too. I start to bounce in place, unable to contain my anticipation. First to come through the door is Lang-hao, followed shortly by Kira, then Crank. They stop their Big-Bikes and get off in a hurry.

"Get Doc! Now!" Lang shouts at the tall man in the lab coat. He immediately turns and runs swiftly to a staircase that I assume leads up to the main levels of the Calm.

I examine the three recently returned Realmwalkers and notice only a few small injuries. Lang limps slightly as he hurries to a supply cabinet near the back left corner of the garage. Kira's elbows are grisly to look at and Crank's forehead is dripping blood. The two of them are setting up what looks to be a portable hospital gurney. I run over to them.

"What can I do to help?" I ask, knowing they don't have time to answer any of the other questions that are running through my mind.

Kira points to a large unit of cabinets along one of the walls. "Get some pillows from out of there," she orders.

I run over and throw back the doors. As I'm bringing two pillows back, the remaining Realmwalkers return. I look up at the sound of the Big-Bikes and see Mikhail ride in with Timothy in front of him on his bike. Timothy is conscious but looks to be in a lot of pain. Behind them come two more bikes.

It's Ember, who looks unharmed, and Sam who is

cradling Mel in front of him on his bike. I can see Ember's worried expression as she jumps off her bike and runs toward Sam. Together they get Mel off the bike and carefully carry her to the bed that Crank and Kira have readied. She's unconscious. I pray she is only unconscious.

"Mel!" I turn as the man in the lab coat re-enters the room and runs to Mel as she is laid on the gurney. He gently brushes her hair back out of her face as his expression fills with dread.

Everyone gathers around the bed except Mikhail who is helping Timothy into a chair. I hug Ember fiercely.

"I'm so glad you're safe," I whisper in her ear. She hugs me tighter.

"Move aside," says an older woman's voice.

I look up to see the Realmwalkers make room for a woman in her forties. Her face and arms are covered with gruesome-looking scars. She looks down at Mel. "What happened here?" she asks solemnly as her hands hover inches above Mel's body. She, like the tall man in the lab coat, sounds British.

"We were ambushed. Mel fell from her bike," Sam tells the woman. "It was about a thirty-foot fall onto the pavement."

"Can you help her, Faye?" the lab-coat guy asks.

"I don't know. I need silence. Everyone leave. Except you, Ben. You stay. Mel needs you here."

Everyone but the two Brits move back from Mel's bed. Sam motions everyone to join him around where Timothy and Mikhail are sitting. Everyone huddles closely together in a circle.

"What the hell-"

"What happened out there-"

"Boss, has that ever-"

Everyone's talking at once, and even though they're all speaking softly, the ruckus soon becomes a loud buzz of anxious and urgent voices. Sam puts a hand up, silencing everyone.

"There are a lot of questions, I know. We need to meet in the briefing room and discuss everything in an orderly way. Lang, you go and wake Harmony. This is a priority-one meeting and I want everyone there. Crank, stay here with Timothy and make sure he's all right." Crank nods.

"As soon as Mel is healed up, have Doc take a look at him. Send the others along ahead of you and when Timothy's healed, you and Doc join us too. Doc can tend to the smaller injuries after the briefing. We'll wait until everyone is present to begin. Understood?" Sam looks around and makes eye contact with everyone as they nod and say, "Yes, sir".

Until now, I'd assumed that what happened out in Chaos, while dangerous, was par for the course. From everyone's reaction, however, I'm beginning to think that maybe the Lesser Shades' ambush was something of an anomaly. The circle breaks and everyone starts to head off toward the stairway leading out of the garage. Ember takes my hand.

"Come on, Addy. I'll show you to the briefing room," she says as she leads me toward the stairs. I can't help but steal one last look at Mel as she lies motionless on the bed. The woman who is "Doc" continues to hold her hands above

Mel though nothing miraculous appears to be happening. Mel's eyes are closed and her face is peaceful. Mel was the first Realmwalker I met here. She saved me. She made me feel welcome. I pray this isn't the last time I see her alive.

CHAPTER 12

"CAN THE DOCTOR save Mel?" I ask Ember quietly as she guides me up the stairs.

"Faye is the best healer Chaos has ever had. Mel will be fine." Though Ember's words are confident, her voice sounds troubled.

I'm feeling completely drained from all the overwhelming emotions. My fatigue, however, is probably nothing compared to how the others must be feeling. I examine my friend next to me as we walk through a large living area. She's covered in soot. Her clothes are singed in places and she has an abrasion on her left cheek. Her hair is messy and windblown and her emerald eyes are indeed weary. She catches me watching her and smiles encouragingly.

"This isn't typically how we greet a new Walker. You'll have to be patient with us until we can figure out exactly what's happening in Chaos."

"That's fine," I assure her. "I'm as eager as everyone to understand. I only wish I could be of more help. I feel like all I've managed to do is get in the way. I hate that I'm a burden during something like this."

Ember throws her arm across my shoulders. "You can't help what's going on out there. We all understand that. You're a noob and we only want to make sure you're safe. Don't worry, Addy. Soon you'll be trained and you'll be able to contribute." She winks at me and gives me a squeeze. My fear of being a dud resurfaces. I can't imagine ever having a cool super-ability like these people around me. I'm just *me*.

"Unless she can't do anything useful at all," I hear someone mutter under their breath behind us. Ember and I both turn around and see the tall brunette smirking. She nudges her way past us.

"Like you can talk Simone," Ember says to her. The brunette flashes her a venom filled look but keeps walking.

"Who is that? And what's her deal? She started tearing into Mikhail the second we entered Major Calm." I'm still bewildered that there can be a Realmwalker who treats the others with this level of contempt.

"That's Simone, aka 'Frenchie.' She's got issues. We really don't have time to go over them all now. Stay clear of her and pay her no attention," Ember explains.

I ponder this as we walk through a labyrinth of halls and rooms until we reach a heavy-looking door with a glass window on the upper half.

"I'm sorry we don't have time for a tour," Ember says as she looks at her wristwatch. "It's almost four in the morning in your hometown. We really only have time for this briefing tonight. Hopefully things will be settled down enough by tomorrow night to give you a proper tour." She pushes open the door and leads the way in.

The room is large with white walls and bright, clean lighting. There are two rows of four rectangular tables with two chairs behind each one. Along the entire front wall of the room runs a whiteboard much like the ones in my high school classrooms.

In front of them and a little off to one side I notice a simple speaking podium. Above the whiteboards are some rolled-up pull-down displays, and a projection machine hangs from the center of the ceiling. Ember and I take a table toward the back of the room.

A few Realmwalkers are already here. They're gathered around the room talking with each other in hushed, anxious voices. Simone has Sam cornered at the front of the room and looks to be drilling him with questions. He seems calm and not at all bothered by her persistence. Mikhail is sitting alone at the table behind us.

The most surprising thing I see is Kira and Lang sitting together at a table and talking animatedly to a young girl who looks to be about eight or nine. She is sitting cross-legged on the table in front of them.

"Am I seeing things?" I ask Ember. "Is that really a child?"

"Oh yeah, that's Harmony. She's the youngest Realm-walker. Ever," Ember tells me.

"She can't be more than nine!" I exclaim quietly.

"She's nine now. When she first came to Chaos, she was only five. She's been here longer than me."

"That's cruel. How could anyone think this place is safe for a child? For a five-year-old girl!" I can't help but feel sorry for the kid. She looks so fragile, so vulnerable. "Tell me she doesn't fight," I plead.

Ember laughs quietly. "You don't need to worry about Harmony. She's one tough cookie."

I study the girl sitting on the table listening wide-eyed to Lang-hao. She has platinum hair that curls into loose ringlets at the ends. Her deep blueberry eyes stand in stark contrast to her flawless porcelain skin. I'm in awe of her precious perfection. If I were to pull up an image of an angel in my mind, this is what I would see.

"She's an angel." I'm not even aware I spoke my thoughts aloud until Ember laughs.

"Yeah, that's what we call her. Hey Angel! Come meet our new family member!"

The little girl looks up and when our eyes meet, I feel a feather-soft touch on my mind. Angel grins a dimpled grin at me and my heart melts. She gets down off the table and practically skips to us.

"Angel dear, this is Adelaide Shepherd. She prefers Addy. Addy, meet Harmony," Ember introduces me.

"I'm so happy to meet you. And I'm relieved that you made the journey here safely." Her voice is angelic as well. Her countenance is surprisingly mature for a girl her age. I realize that being surrounded by so many other adults may have had something to do with that.

"I'm pleased to meet you too, Harmony. I'm only here and in one piece because of the Realmwalkers. They were amazing out there. So brave. And Mikhail saved my life and got me out of danger." I turn to smile at Mikhail. When our eyes meet, he looks down shyly though I'm pretty sure he heard my praise. "That's twice now that I was sure I would die. Both times, I was rescued. I only hope I can return the favor someday."

Ember nods her head and grins. "Oh, I'm sure you'll get the chance. We've all saved each other countless times now. No one keeps track anymore."

I look up as Sam approaches with Simone trailing behind.

"I see you've met Harmony," he says as he pulls over a chair from another table and sits on it backwards. I'm thrilled to have him so near. He's felt distant this entire night. Maybe now that he isn't in combat mode, he'll loosen up a bit. Simone seems unsure whether to join the circle or not. She decides on making a sour face and stalking off to sit alone.

"Normally, Harmony would be evaluating you right now. I'm sorry, Adelaide. Things probably won't be back to normal for a little while," Sam says.

"Everyone keeps apologizing. You don't need to. Sometimes bad things happen. Let's take care of one thing at a time. I can be patient." I know everyone is worried about what happened out in Chaos. The last thing they need is to be worried about me. Besides, the longer I can put off having them find out I'm useless, the better.

"That's the spirit," Sam says approvingly. I'm pleased with even this small praise.

"What do you mean by Harmony evaluating me?" I ask for clarification.

Sam puts a hand on Harmony's shoulder. When she smiles at him, the adoration in her eyes is obvious. "Harmony is really special. She has an incredibly strong mind. With your permission, she'll search your mind. She'll be able to recognize areas in your brain that are the strongest. With this information, she can point you in the right direction to discovering and developing your ability."

"Whoa!" I look at Harmony through new eyes. "What an amazing gift."

Harmony smiles bashfully at me and turns a little pink. All this girl is missing is a pair of large, white, downy-soft wings.

Sam pats her shoulder and says, "That's not even the tip of the iceberg when it comes to our Harmony. Because she can see into people's minds, she can also see exactly what goes on in their brain when they perform their abilities. Once she knows how we do our tricks, she can do them too. She's our little Mimic."

"So wait," I try to comprehend what this means. "Are you saying that Harmony can do everything? That she has all of your abilities?" I can't believe this sweet little girl contains so much power.

"That's exactly right," Ember confirms this fact. It's obvious how proud they are of her. I hope she can help me. I really hope she can find something in my mind that I can use to help the others. Again, I feel that feather-soft touch across my mind as I stare into Harmony's eyes. Quietly and softly I hear her sweet voice in my head.

Don't doubt yourself, Addy. Everyone called to Chaos has their purpose. You will find yours.

A small gasp escapes me. Before I have time to consider what just happened, I hear a commotion at the door. We all turn to look and I see one of the happiest sights ever. First Crank, then Ben comes through the door, grinning, followed by a perfectly healthy-looking Mel. Everyone jumps to their feet and gathers around her, giving hugs and high fives.

When I get to her, I hug her tightly. Tears of joy spring to my eyes as I tell her how happy I am to see her safe and sound.

"Addy, I'm so sorry I lost you. I'm so sorry. I should've seen that Shade coming at us. It's my fault we got hit," Mel says in my ear as we hug.

"Don't you dare think that. I don't blame you at all! What happened was no one's fault, Mel. All I care about is that you're okay."

We're interrupted again by more noise at the door behind us. I turn to look and in walk Timothy and Doc. Everyone greets each other enthusiastically, with the exception of Simone and Mikhail. Simone hasn't left her place at her table, but Mikhail is at least making an attempt and hovering awkwardly around the group. After a few more moments of happy reuniting, Sam calls everyone to attention.

"All right, Walkers, we've got a lot to discuss. Please find a seat," Sam says as he takes his place behind the podium at the front of the room. As Ember and I sit back down at our table, I take note of everyone here. I count heads once we're all sitting and find there are twelve others, plus me, making lucky number thirteen.

So this is everyone.

I take note of the ones I have just met and try to remember names. There's Harmony, sitting beside Doc, who I believe is named Faye. Mel is sitting in front of me and Ember, and she's holding hands with the tall British man named Ben. They make an odd-looking pair, but it's obvious they care a great deal for each other. Simone is sitting cross-armed at the front of the room.

"Okay, first things first, I want to recognize Adelaide Shepherd as our newest Realmwalker. Adelaide, could you stand please?" Sam asks. Everyone's eyes are on me as I stand up.

"Adelaide is seventeen years old. She's an American from central Arizona. Tonight is her second night here in Chaos. Let's all try and make her feel welcome."

From around the room come various whoops and hollers and applause. My heart warms at the sight of the smiling faces around me. I really feel like I belong here with these people.

"I'm sorry we don't have time for a better welcoming. For those of you who haven't yet met Adelaide, please take time later to introduce yourself and get to know her." I sit back down and soon all of our attention is back on Sam.

"For the benefit of the Walkers who were not out in

Chaos with us, we'll start back at the beginning. I'll do my best to recount all of the details, but seeing as how I've only one person's point of view, I'm sure to miss some things here and there. Please feel free to comment or add anything I've missed that you feel may be important information." Sam pauses a moment to make sure everyone understands.

"At oh-one hundred hours, L.A. time, I gathered a team together to travel to Minor Calm and retrieve Adelaide, Mel, and Oscar. The team was myself, Ember, Lang-hao, Kira, Timothy, and Mikhail. The first abnormal occurrence that we encountered was that no one spotted any Shade activity during the entire trip to Minor Calm."

A few heads nod in agreement around the room. Sam is so professional. Everything about him is confident and authoritative. He really is a natural leader. I imagine he runs the Los Angeles SWAT much the same way.

"Once at Minor Calm, Adelaide was assigned to Mel and a defensive formation was decided. Upon leaving Minor Calm, there was still a notable absence of Shades, both Lesser and Greater. After a few minutes, however, there were a couple reports of Lesser Shade activity."

Ember raises her hand and Sam nods for her to contribute. "I feel like I should make a point here. Before anyone spotted any activity, I was feeling really on edge. Something felt wrong but I didn't speak up. I apologize. In hindsight, I probably should have said something sooner."

Sam adds, "There was definitely something wrong about the situation. I think we all felt it to a degree." Again many Walkers nod in agreement.

Sam continues. "Quite out of nowhere, we're ambushed by dozens of Lesser Shades. We were under attack, outnumbered and overwhelmed. We fought back as best we could until it was obvious we would not gain ground. I ordered a retreat and we eventually made it back to our bikes and prepared to withdraw."

Here, Kira raises her hand. Sam indicates her and gives her the floor. "You all need to understand this wasn't a crazy free-for-all by the Lesser Shades. This was like nothing we've ever seen. It almost seemed…" she pauses to find the right word.

"Organized," Lang supplies.

"Planned," agrees Crank.

Kira nods her head. "Exactly. The whole thing felt orchestrated."

"That's not possible," interjects Simone. "Lessers are too stupid to do anything like that. They've never worked together. Even when they are in a herd, it's always been every Shade for itself. There has to be some other explanation."

"Right," Sam says. "And I think there is."

The room is silent as everyone waits for Sam to continue.

"As we were leaving, a flying Shade grabbed Adelaide from the back of Mel's bike. I'm not sure exactly what happened immediately afterward, but when we found Adelaide, she was in the grip of a very powerful Greater Shade." Still, the room is silent. A few eyes turn toward me. "Adelaide, could you fill us in on the parts we missed?" Sam prompts gently.

"Sure," I say. I'm surprised to find my memories of the

event are so clear. I can see every precise detail in my mind. I wonder briefly if this is the eidetic memory that Crank mentioned we all experience here. "After that flying Shade grabbed me, it dropped me down by a building. Pretty soon a Greater Shade came and chased off the Lesser Shade."

"Wait a minute," Harmony speaks up. "I'm sorry to interrupt you, Addy. I want to make sure you don't leave anything out. Can you be really specific? Even if you think you're being overly specific, any tiny detail could actually mean something very important."

"She's right," Sam says. "Please start over and don't leave anything out."

"Okay. Well, after the flying Shade dropped me, I did notice something. Behind the Shade I could see other Lesser Shades. They all seemed to be running away from something. I guess I thought it was you guys coming to the rescue. I really started to hope when an invisible force picked up the flying Shade and flew it backwards across the street." I look at Lang-hao. "I remember seeing you have that kind of ability and I thought it was you." Lang nods in understanding.

"But then the Greater Shade came around the side of the building, and I realized that's who'd done it."

"That's interesting," Mel says. "We know that the two types of Shades co-exist, but have we ever really seen them interact on this level?" The Walkers all shake their heads, some say "no" and "never."

"Please continue," Sam says to me.

"Well," I take a deep breath and continue, "when the

Greater Shade saw me, it immediately came toward me. It lifted me off the ground without touching me." I cringe, remembering its icy, invisible fingers around my throat and the sound of its disgusting laughter.

"What are you thinking about now? It could be important," Harmony insists.

I continue uncomfortably, "I could feel its hand on my throat, squeezing. But it still wasn't physically touching me." I reflexively touch my throat and feel tender, bruised flesh under my hand. "And it was making a noise, like it was choking almost. But I knew it was laughing."

"What?" The word comes from more than a few startled Walkers.

"Did you say it made a sound?" Sam asks.

"Yes." I nod. "It was definitely laughing at me."

The room erupts into chatter. Some voices sound anxious, some doubtful. Sam holds up a hand and everyone quiets down.

"Angel, what do you think?" Sam asks Harmony. "Is it possible?"

"For a Greater Shade to vocalize? I'm not sure. I suppose so. Addy says it happened and I believe her, so it must be possible."

"But how? We've never heard one before." Timothy says. "And the records don't say anything about the Shades communicating vocally."

"Angel?" Ben asks. "Could the Shades be evolving?" The room is dead silent at the thought of this. I'm a little surprised by how many of the Walkers are asking Angel the hard questions. Even Sam seems to defer to her on issues concerning Shades.

"I can't tell you 'no' for certain. This is Chaos after all, and here we learn to expect the unexpected. I certainly hope that evolution is *not* the explanation."

"Great," Says Simone bitterly. "Before you know it, they'll be speaking to us!"

This immediately reminds me of the demonic voice of the Greater Shade as it spoke in my mind. I tentatively raise my hand.

"Yes, Adelaide, you want to share something?" Sam asks me.

I nod in affirmation. I'm reluctant to share, however. What happened between the Shade and me feels strangely personal. Ember senses my anxiety and puts an encouraging hand on mine.

"Something happened while the Greater Shade had me," I say hesitantly. Everyone stares at me and waits me for me to finish. I take a deep breath. "The Shade actually did speak to me."

Stunned silence.

"In my head, I mean. Um, I mean I heard it in my head. Its voice. It spoke to me, in my mind," I stammer, hoping everyone believes me.

"That Greater Shade… are you saying it communicated with you telepathically?" Kira asks me.

"I guess. I mean," I look at Harmony, "it was similar in a way to what you did earlier. Only, your voice in my head was soft. Its voice was harsh and actually physically painful. It gave me a screaming migraine."

More silence. Everyone looks to be processing this information. "This has never happened before?" I ask the room.

"No," Sam says. "Greater Shades have never made any effort to communicate with us."

"What did it say to you?" Doc asks.

Again, everyone is quiet as they wait anxiously for my response, and again I feel reluctant to share.

"Nothing earth-shattering really. It just said, 'I see you. You are weak.'" The next phrase seems to stick in my throat. "'You are nothing,'" I murmur quietly, feeling as though somehow uttering those words makes them true.

Ember looks at Sam. "What is this, Boss?"

Sam seems deep in thought for a moment. "I think it means that we have a very dangerous Greater Shade loose in Chaos. We've gotten a little sidetracked with this, and I need to finish my report in order to better inform those who weren't there." Everyone turns forward again and gives Sam their full attention.

"After the flying Shade took Adelaide, our attention was on Mel, who had fallen from her bike. Timothy, Lang, and I went in search of Adelaide as the others tended to Mel. When the three of us found Adelaide, she was indeed in the grip of the Greater Shade. When we began to attack, it released its hold on her. It then, at least to my perception, took a possessive stance in front of Adelaide."

"I agree," says Timothy.

Lang adds, "I definitely got the feeling that it had targeted her and didn't want to give her up."

Some of the Walkers turn and look at me as if trying to discern why it chose me.

"The most interesting part came next, though, didn't it, Boss?" Timothy points out.

"Yes, I'd say so. As the three of us attacked, the Greater Shade managed to deflect all of our bullets AND neutralize Lang's telekinesis at the same time. He was untouchable."

"This is bad," Ben says quietly.

"Very," Ember agrees.

Sam goes on, "It gets worse. Mikhail came and retrieved Adelaide through shadow travel. The instant she was gone, the Greater Shade went berserk. It took everything we had to escape with our lives. In all of my experience here in Chaos, I have never come up against a more difficult opponent. Even the junior nukes had no effect." When he says this, I immediately picture the grenade-like weapons strapped across his chest. That must have been the source of the explosions I had heard, and the cause of the column of smoke.

"So let me get this straight," says Crank, holding up his hands. "We are dealing with an incredibly powerful Greater Shade, unlike anything we've experienced before, who has a strong enough mind to communicate telepathically, has an unholy fixation on our own dear Addy, *and* he is completely indestructible. Did I cover everything?"

"Unfortunately not. I think tonight's events speak of another troubling aspect of this Shade," Harmony says.

"I think you're right, Angel. Go ahead and explain it if you like," Sam encourages her.

"Well, the strange behavior of the Lesser Shades and how they ambushed you seems to suggest that it was all orchestrated by this Greater Shade," she explains.

"So he's controlling them? With the power of his mind?" asks Kira.

"I can't be sure how he's doing it. We are all agreed that the Lesser Shades are too ignorant to organize something of this complexity on their own. So that only leaves the influence of the Greater Shade. Whether he gets them to do it by mind control or simple fear of him, I can't know. But either way, it speaks volumes about the strength of his abilities."

The room is quiet again as everyone considers the implications. I shiver involuntarily as I think of an army of Lesser Shades and, at the helm, the Greater Shade who seems bent on my destruction.

"Why her?" I turn to see Simone sneering at me. "I mean, she doesn't even have her ability yet."

The faces of my friends turn contemplative as they look me over. Again, I feel insecure as I'm examined. What was it about me? I'm the least special person here.

Angel gets up and walks to me. "Addy, when the Greater Shade touched your mind, it's possible he left an imprint behind. Do you mind if I delve into the shallows of your consciousness? It's not very invasive. I'll only access your thoughts concerning the Shade. Anything he left behind may help me better understand him."

"Sure, Angel, whatever I can do to help." I only just met her, but I trust her entirely.

"I need you to think of the Greater Shade while I do this. It will help me in my search." She walks closer to me and places her little hands on the sides of my head, right over my temples, the way Sam did the night before.

I'm looking into her eyes, thinking how beautiful she is when she giggles and says, "Not me silly! Think of the Shade. It may be difficult, but try to imagine it. Think of how it made you feel when he confronted you, when he touched your mind."

I close my eyes to better picture it. I feel that familiar tickle on my mind that I now recognize as Angel's ability. Once I pull up an image of the Shade, it's as if Angel is scrolling through my thoughts at will. My consciousness travels through each of my senses and how they reacted to the Shade.

I feel fear so intense I begin to shake, then that fades and I can hear its strangled laughter. It's as if it's right in the room with me. As the sound fades, I can see the Shade so clearly my stomach turns again at the sight of its bubbling, sludge-like flesh. Then my attention is on its dark face. As I study the shifting shadows, I'm able to catch glimpses at the horror underneath. Again, I'm reminded of the demon in my dream from the night before. The Tori-Shade.

Angel inhales sharply and removes her hands from my head. When I open my eyes, I see that many of the Walkers have gathered around the two of us. I wonder how much time has passed. I look at Angel and she is wearing a look of complete surprise.

"Angel? Did you learn anything?" Sam inquires.

Angel looks bothered and impatient. "Yes and no," she says with her little hands on her waist. "I learned that the Greater Shade has definitely targeted Addy here." She turns to face the others. "And that he is as strong as we suspected, and more. His mind is so strong, in fact, he was able to project his consciousness outside of Chaos and into Earth Realm."

"No way!" Kira shouts. "That's crazy!"

"It's true," Mel says. "I've been suspecting it for the last ten minutes or so, but now I'm sure."

Ben turns to her. "Mel?"

She looks up and finds Crank. "Do you remember, Crank? Addy's first night here, in Minor Calm. She mentioned a demon in her dream." They both look at me.

"Oh yeah, that's right!" Says Crank excitedly. "You said you dreamed of a demon with a shadow face before the fall—which means you hadn't entered Chaos yet!" He starts bouncing in place as he puts the pieces together.

"And most importantly," says Angel, "the demon in her dream was trying to stop Addy from answering the call to Chaos." She looks at me. "That Greater Shade was bent on stopping you from coming here at all. The frustrating thing about it is that I don't have the time right now to properly evaluate you for your potential ability. I have a feeling that when we find out what it is you can do, we may have a better idea of why this Shade is targeting you."

Oh great, no pressure or anything.

"Well then," Ember says, smiling at me, "our course of action is to make sure Addy gets evaluated and trained ASAP, right? I mean, if this super-strong Shade is afraid of her, then it makes sense that it's because she'll be able to take it down."

I groan inwardly. I know Ember means well, but she's only making me feel worse. Now suddenly, it's up to *me* to stop the Greater Shade? I'm paralyzed with fear in its presence, but I'm supposed to vanquish it somehow? I'm starting to feel lightheaded and queasy. I wonder briefly, if I throw up here, will I wake up 'top-side' covered in sick?

Sam must be able to read the fear on my face. "Whatever happens, Adelaide, you won't have to do anything alone. We don't work that way here."

"That's right, mate!" Mel grins at me and rubs her hands together eagerly. "I've got a score to settle with that brute, and if he thinks he's getting a one-on-one fight, he's got another thing comin'!"

"That's for sure!" Timothy shouts. "I had to abandon my bike because of him! That can't go unanswered!"

We all laugh and it's relieving to feel the mood lighten a little.

Once again, Sam is the voice of reason as he brings us all back to the pressing issue. "What we need to discuss now is how do we continue to protect Earth Realm with the threat of an ambush every time we go out into Chaos?"

Everyone is silent as they search for possible solutions.

"I don't really think there is anything we *can* do," says Simone resolutely. "It's simply too dangerous."

"Not so."

I turn, along with the rest of the room, at the sound of the Russian behind me. This is the first time Mikhail has spoken throughout the whole meeting.

"Oh really?" Simone snaps. "And what-"

Sam cuts her off with an upraised hand. "Go ahead, Mikhail. What are your thoughts?"

Mikhail's arms are crossed over his chest defensively. He looks around at everyone. When his eyes land on mine, I smile encouragingly at him. When he finally does talk, he keeps his eyes on me, as if talking to me is easier for him than addressing the whole room.

"We are Realmwalkers. This is what we do. We fight." I nod my head in agreement. I like his attitude—and his voice, quiet but assertive. "When it gets hard, we don't give up. We are warriors. They may have the numbers but we are smart, right? They lose element of surprise now. They can't catch us that way again." When he finishes, he lowers his eyes down to the table.

Everyone slowly turns back to Sam. I see a lot of raised eyebrows, a few sheepish looks, and a giant eye roll from Simone.

"What Mikhail said may be difficult to hear, but I agree with him. This IS what we are for. We weren't summoned to Chaos to stay hidden away in the Calms. I can't force any of you to do your duty, but I'm telling you now, I won't give up." Sam looks around the room, making eye contact with everyone.

After a short silence, Timothy stands up. "I'm with you, Boss." Sam acknowledges him with a small nod.

Harmony jumps up. "Me too, Boss!" She smiles encouragingly around the room, and it's like the sun melting away the layer of ice around our hearts. The rest of the Realmwalkers stand nearly as one to show Sam their support.

He smiles proudly back at us. "This will be hard. I'm sure of it. But we'll get through it together, like we always do."

"That's right, Boss!" Ember shouts next to me. Everyone follows suit and expresses their support with cheers.

"All right, everyone, that's enough for now. Unless there is anything pressing left to discuss, I think we should let Doc make her rounds. This is one beat up, ragtag bunch of Walkers, and frankly, I'm tired of looking at your sorry faces," Sam jokes.

We all laugh as Doc gets up. "Sorry Boss, I can heal any injury, but I can't do a thing about their faces." This earns another laugh as she starts her examination on the nearest injured Walker. Everyone begins to mingle and talk in small groups.

Ember looks at her watch again. "We don't have much time left. Let's see if we can get Doc to fix you up so we can get you in a bed before you wake up top-side."

We get up and make our way to where Doc is healing a very red and swollen ankle on Lang's right leg. Ember and I watch as the swelling reduces gradually until it is gone completely and his skin is its natural bronze color.

"That really is incredible," I say to Doc. She waves the praise away with a hand and motions for me to take Lang's now-vacated chair in front of her.

"Now, let's have a look at you," Doc says, very professionally. I watch her in awe as she slowly moves her hands around my body, finding injuries and miraculously healing them. When she heals my torn-up knees from the previous night, I see there aren't any scars there. Only smooth, pink, new skin. This makes me wonder why she, of all people, is covered in scars. Can she not heal herself?

"Scars or no scars?" she asks. At first, I'm embarrassed and think she means the scars on her face and arms that I've been staring at. Then I realize she's holding my hands and indicating my ruined palms. I remember the day before, feeling Sam's scars on his hands. I remember him and Ember telling me that the scars are a rite of passage and something that all the Walkers have in common. I want to be a part of that.

"Scars please," I say decisively. Doc smiles in approval. I'm given the most relief after she heals my throat. I hadn't realized how bad it felt until all my other hurts were healed and it was the only one left to focus on. I couldn't even swallow without wanting to cry out in pain. As soon as Doc is finished with me, I jump up and throw my arms around her.

"You're wonderful! Thank you so much!"

She pats my shoulder affectionately. "You're very welcome, little dove."

Doc gets up and moves along as I see Sam approaching from the front of the room. When he gets to Ember and me, he gently takes my chin and moves my head to the left and right, examining my neck.

"Much better." He smiles. "You were looking pretty gruesome to be honest. I'm glad you're healed now."

"She's a tough one, isn't she? I didn't hear her complain once!" Ember says proudly.

"Me neither, and to be honest, I've seen grown men cry for less," Sam states. He seems proud of me too, which makes all the injuries worth bearing.

"I'm not tough or anything," I explain. "I'm just so easily distracted it was simple to forget I was even hurt." Ember laughs as she puts her arm across my shoulder, and I notice Mikhail slip quietly out of the room. I feel sad for him.

"Hey," I lower my voice and move a little closer to Ember and Sam. They both lean in conspiratorially. "Is Mikhail really shy? How come he's so quiet?"

Sam and Ember look at each other. Again, it's like a silent conversation passes between them. Sam addresses me. "Ember and I will fill you in on a lot once we are top-side. We'll tell you all about the other Walkers, where they're from, what they're personalities are like. Stuff like that."

I take this as the only answer I'm going to get right now. "And speaking of going top-side, we should probably get you settled in a room. The sun will be up soon, and you're still untrained when it comes to waking up on command."

I'm surprised to hear how late it is already. I'm usually up early on the weekends.

"I'll find her a place, Boss. Why don't you get

things wound up here and we'll meet you up top when you're finished."

"Sounds good. See you two soon."

I follow Ember out of the conference room, saying good-bye to Walkers as I go. Some give me high fives, others hugs. Outside the conference room, we walk through an area that looks to be a huge game room. I see two pool tables and an air hockey table. Arcade games line the walls, except where a huge TV hangs from a wall. Under it, I see every type of major game console. Stacks and stacks of games and movies fill the entertainment center under the TV and everywhere are soft and plush-looking sofas and chairs.

We pass another room that's filled with every type of musical instrument you can think of. The walls are floor-to-ceiling mirrors, and right in the middle of the room is a dark cherry grand piano. I see electric guitars, acoustic guitars, even an electric-acoustic guitar. There are amps and microphones and a drum set. I see cases along the wall that are in the shapes of a various stringed instruments. There's a beautiful pearl-colored full-sized harp. I laugh when I see there is even a didgeridoo and wonder if Mel had anything to do with that.

We stop when we reach an area that branches off into three different hallways. There's one directly ahead and one off to my left and one to my right. Ember points to the right hallway.

"My room is down this way. There aren't any vacant rooms down here now, but if you like, Angel can build you one later."

"Whoa. What?" I ask not sure I heard her correctly.

"Well, not physically. We don't run on child labor here," she snorts. "Manipulating and expanding the space here in the Calms is a mental ability. Angel's the only one of us who can do that right now." My head spins as I try to understand. "It's all right. You'll get it later. Anyway, we have spare rooms down either of the other halls. Take your pick."

"Uh," I hesitate. I point to the middle hall at random. "This works."

The first empty room is the second on the left. Inside, the walls are a crisp, fresh yellow. "This is perfect! Matches your aura!"

Ember motions to the dresser in the room. "There are some pretty standard clothes in here to hold you over for now. Girls' clothes are on the right. Pajamas should be in the top drawer. Once you're changed and cleaned up, go ahead and lay down. I won't wake you up top-side for another twenty minutes to make sure you've had enough time. Everything sound okay?"

"Yeah, sounds good."

"You did really great tonight, Addy. I'm proud of you. See you in a few." Ember heads out and I close my door behind her. I find the pajamas where she said I would. The layout of this room is nearly identical to the one I stayed in last night at Minor Calm. The only differences are the colors on the walls and the bedspread.

As I wash dried blood off me in the bathroom, I realize how surprised and grateful I am to still be alive. I ease myself into clean comfortable pajamas and climb into bed. I figure it's been nearly twenty minutes, so I take deep breaths and try to relax. My eyelids droop suddenly, and I find I can't possibly keep them open another second.

CHAPTER 13

I OPEN MY eyes to see Ember smiling down at me. There's something exhilarating about waking up and realizing I have this incredible secret! And better yet, I get to share this experience with my best friends. The sun is shining through my bedroom window and birds are chirping in my front yard. It's a startlingly cheery atmosphere compared to the terrifying ordeal I went through last night. I turn and look at my alarm clock. Seven thirty-two a.m.

I sit up and take inventory of my body parts, double checking they are all present and in working order. Everything feels great. My palms are completely healed and covered with my "initiation" scars, which might be difficult to explain to my mom and sister. I'll have to keep my bandages on for the next week or so.

I'm feeling surprisingly well after the events of last night. Shouldn't I be exhausted? I haven't actually slept for the last forty-eight hours or so, and the amount of physical and emotional energy I've exerted should have left me a mess.

"How does my body rest?" I ask. "I don't feel tired at all!"

Ember smirks knowingly. "Pretty crazy, huh?"

"Definitely crazy."

"If you think about it, it makes sense. Your body's in two planes of existence. When you're in Earth Realm, your Chaos Realm body is resting, and vice versa. Your body actually is getting the sleep it needs. It's your conscious mind that can't rest," she explains.

"So… that can't be good right? Even our minds need sleep, don't they?"

"Normal minds, yes. The rules of reality in Chaos are different from the ones here. Chaos does something to us physically. It changes our minds, expands them, so we can adapt to the demanding lifestyle. It's pretty cool. Without it, we'd probably all go mad." She says this so casually I can't help but laugh.

"Maybe you are all mad!" I tease. "So, is that also how you can make fire? Because of the different rules in Chaos?"

"That's exactly how. Think of it like this: Imagine the fabric of reality. In Earth Realm, it's solid, immovable, and impenetrable. It has strict rules that must be followed. For some reason, the fabric in Chaos is different. It's like putty. We can shape it, manipulate it, and control it. There are fewer rules. Once we learn how it's done in Chaos, we can do the same thing here, in Earth Realm. But since the fabric here is still tough, it's a little more difficult to manipulate, even though we know how. The result is our abilities are never quite as strong here as they are there," she explains.

"But you can definitely still use them. I've seen it."

"Right!" Ember seems glad she was able to get her meaning across. I'm still marveling over the fact that I'm not even tired. Actually, I'm feeling invigorated, even giddy! And...*famished*. My stomach growls intensely as if to accentuate the point. Ember's rubbing her own stomach too.

"Well, what are we doing in here? Let's go eat!" I say as I throw back the covers. As we leave my room, I also realize how badly I need to tend to other bodily functions, and I make a detour to the restroom. As I'm washing my hands, I wonder if the Walkers ever use the bathrooms in the Calms or if that would only create embarrassing problems for your body back in Earth Realm.

As I'm waiting for Ember to take her turn in the bathroom, I glance down the hall at the guest room's closed door. My stomach gets a funny, tight knot in it.

I wonder if Sam is up yet, and if not, I try to imagine what he's doing in Chaos. As I think of seeing him again this morning, I'm surprised at how much I'm looking forward to it. I mean, I only left him about thirty minutes ago. I guess there's just something about having him here, in my own house.

Ember startles me out of my musings when she opens the bathroom door. "I've got an idea!" she says as we head toward the kitchen. "Let's make breakfast for everyone." Jana's still asleep and I can hear Mom's shower running.

"Sounds like we're the only ones up anyway, so we might as well." I look around for something quick and easy. I feel like I haven't eaten in days. We decide on biscuits from a can and sausage and gravy. We split up the process and soon the kitchen is filled with mouth-watering aromas. The smell works like a charm because first, out comes Mom, soon followed by a sleepy-eyed Jana. Like moths to a flame.

Ember insists they take a seat at the table while the two of us serve. As we're setting the table, I hear the guest room door open, then the bathroom door close. My pulse picks up a little. What's my problem? It's just Sam.

I'm not the only one looking forward to seeing him I notice as Jana gets up and moves to the other side of the table, leaving an open chair next to her. I roll my eyes at her and she sticks her tongue out at me. When Ember and I walk back to get the orange juice and milk from the fridge, we both giggle at Jana's maneuvering.

Ember takes the pitchers to the table, and as I get the glasses, a thought crosses my mind. Jana's gorgeous. Sam wouldn't be completely out of his mind if he fell for her. They aren't too far apart in age—at least not enough to deter Jana.

I can hear him out there greeting everyone. My stomach twists around a little. Ugh! What's wrong with me? I decide the best way to get past this bizarre reaction is to face it head on. I scoop up the cups and march, head held high, out of the kitchen, around the corner, and WHAM, collide right into Sam.

We both fumble quickly to try and catch all of the tumbling glasses. Thanks to his incredible reflexes, we manage to save them all. We're standing awkwardly close, holding the glasses in place between us. I feel like a fool when I look up into his face because my cheeks are burning and I know I'm blushing. So much for facing my fears.

He smiles down at me like an old friend.

"Morning," he says simply.

"Good morning! And good save!" I pray he doesn't pick up on my nervousness. We juggle the glasses around between us so that I'm carrying two and he has three. We set one down in front of each place setting and settle in to eat.

Everyone thanks the master chefs and the rest of breakfast is spent with lighthearted chatter. Jana tells Mom that her friend Katie is coming over to hang out today. I have my own suspicions why, but I don't say anything.

"So what do you guys plan on doing the rest of the day?" Mom asks us.

We all look around at each other. We hadn't really planned anything. I'm not even sure how long they're able to stay. Sam has a pretty demanding job. I'm sure he's expected back soon. Other than the concert tonight, I have no idea what they had in mind.

Ember speaks up. "We didn't really have any specific plans. We were just thinking of hanging out, getting to know each other better." She looks at me. "Maybe you can show us where kids around here go to hang when it's a hundred and eighty degrees outside."

"Oh yeah, I've got the perfect place!" I smile, grateful for the suggestion. This will get us out of the house and somewhere we can talk about Chaos without my family thinking we're insane.

Sam clears his throat. "Mrs. Shepherd?"

"Oh please, Sam, call me Maggie!" Mom insists.

"Thank you, ma'am. Well, Ember and I wanted to know if we could take Addy with us to the concert tonight." I turn to Sam, completely surprised. I look at Ember and she grins and winks at me. "We went ahead and got an extra ticket and were planning on asking her, but it's in Phoenix, and I wanted to make sure you were comfortable with that."

I turn to Mom and give her my best "desperate pleading" face as I bounce in my seat. She looks at me with one eyebrow raised and tries hard to suppress a smile. I take this as a positive sign.

"Mom?" I say as sweetly as I can. I'm smiling because I can already tell she's going to give. "Mommy? Mommy dearest? Mother whom I love above all others?"

At this she starts laughing. "Oh I guess." She draws it out dramatically.

"YES!" I turn and high five Ember. "Thanks guys." Then feeling sheepish, I remember Mom. "Thanks Mom, you're the best." I'm so thrilled at the prospect of seeing a really good band in concert with two awesome people that even Jana's surly, jealous expression can't dampen the mood.

After breakfast, Mom refuses to let us help clean up. We take time to get ready for the day. Ember lets me use my room first and when I'm finished, I find Sam cornered in the front room by two very overly social girls.

Ember's observing the scene from the living room, trying to hide a smile at the sight of Sam stuck on the couch between Jana and her friend Katie. I'm not as amused as Ember is. I decide the sooner we leave the better.

"Hi Katie. You've met Sam then?" She nods her head without even turning to look at me, keeping all of her attention on Sam. I've never disliked Katie but for some reason, this really irks me.

"This is Ember. Ember this is my sister's friend Katie." At least she has the decency to turn and wave at Ember before turning back to Sam and giggling at something he's saying to Jana. Ember wiggles her eyebrows at me and goes to the back to get changed.

I actually look at Sam now. I don't know what I was expecting. I thought I was beginning to understand him and his demeanor over the last few days. While he had shown kindness, he had been mostly assertive, serious, and reserved. I thought he would look bothered, stuck between these two silly girls chatting and flirting with him. If not bothered, then at least a little uncomfortable.

The reality is, he's sitting there, grinning and talking very animatedly with them. He's engaging them more openly than he had the Walkers. For some reason this, plus the fact that Katie and Jana were totally being rude to me, makes me even angrier.

I choke down the snippy, sarcastic comments threatening to slip out of my mouth as Jana plays with a strand of her hair. They all start laughing at something, and Katie puts her hand on Sam's arm as she leans toward him. And it's too much. I'm dizzy and a little nauseous, so I march out the front door without saying a word to anyone.

I walk out to the big tree in the center of my front yard. The morning air is warm and fresh, and I take deep breaths as I lean against the trunk of the elm. I close my eyes and rest my head back against the bark. I'm not being silly. I have a right to be upset, don't I? Sam is supposed to be "family," but he's never been that open with me.

"Addy?"

I turn and see Sam standing a little ways off. He hardly ever calls me that. He looks worried and confused. It's hard for me to look at him right now, so I close my eyes again and rest my head back. I concentrate on taking slow, deep breaths. I hear some leaves rustle nearby on the ground, and I feel goose bumps on my arm as I sense he's moved closer.

"Are you upset?" he asks softly. He sounds sincerely worried and that makes me feel guilty. Here I was upset at some silly girls, and right now, I'm being the silly girl. I exhale deeply.

"No." I shake my head slightly. I open my eyes a little. "I needed some air I guess."

Sam's quiet for a while. He turns and leans against the side of the trunk next to me. Our arms are just touching, and I can feel the warmth of his skin through our shirts. I'm suddenly very aware of the fact that his hand is hanging mere inches from mine. He takes a breath like he's going to say something but then stops. We stand in silence for a while, enjoying the moment.

Sam always seems to have a relaxing effect on me. I wonder briefly if this is natural or if he's using his "mind persuasion" on me. That, however, seems manipulative, and

I don't think Sam would ever do that to me without my permission. Now that I've had a minute to calm down, I feel guilty for getting upset with him.

"You should get back in there." I motion toward the door. "They're probably waiting with bated breath for your return."

He lets out a short bark of laughter. I turn my head and look up at him. He's looking down at me with an amused look. "That's what this is about?"

I make a face at him and turn away so that he can't see my embarrassment. Maybe I shouldn't have said anything.

"Hey," he says plaintively and nudges my arm with his. I lean away slightly.

"Oh come on. I'm only keeping the peace here. If I get along with your family, then they don't question the fact that they've let a perfect stranger into their home."

"That's what was happening? You were 'getting along'?" I say lamely. I know I'm being a brat but I can't stop myself. I'm hurt that he can respond so warmly to them while he mostly gives me his serious side.

"Come on, Addy." He leans closer and lowers his voice. "That wasn't really me in there. I'm acting. Your sister is nice and all, but she's a bit…" He searches for a word.

"Silly?" I supply.

He laughs. "Very."

"And desperate?" I add.

"Maybe a little," he jokes.

"I could go on," I offer.

Just then, the front door closes loudly and we both jump

guiltily. We relax when we see it's only Ember. She walks up to us grinning.

"Hey Romeo, you sure you don't want to stay and visit with the fam longer?" she asks sarcastically.

"Don't even start," Sam says as we walk to his truck. "Let's get out of here before those girls think of an excuse to come with us."

Ember holds the passenger door open and waits for me to get in first, placing me in between the two of them. I swear I see her smirking as I climb in, but once we're all buckled up, she's schooled her expression.

"So where to?" Sam asks.

CHAPTER 14

I GIVE SAM directions to a local ice-skating rink that opens early on Saturdays. They have a bunch of comfortable booths around the rink and a huge snack bar where we can grab some lunch. I figure it's a cool place for us to sit and talk and escape the heat.

"So are we really going to the concert tonight?" I ask. I wasn't sure if that was just some cover story.

"Oh, hell yes!" Ember says enthusiastically.

"Thanks guys! I've never been to a concert before."

"Are you serious?" Ember looks scandalized.

"Well, not unless you count piano recitals when I was younger," I say, feeling a little embarrassed.

"Um. No," Ember says lamely. "I don't count piano recitals." She laughs. "Man we're going to have so much fun. We're lucky such a good band happened to be in town this weekend."

"So how long can you guys stay?" I ask. "Sam, you've got to work eventually, right? And you still have school for another week, don't you?" I ask Ember.

"I have to be back at work Monday by ten A.M." Sam says.

"Yeah, I'll have to fly home tomorrow," Ember says with a scowl. "One more week. Just one more week," she chants.

We pull into the parking lot of the ice rink and get out of the truck. Before we head inside, Sam digs around behind his seat for a small black messenger bag.

The rink's only been open a half an hour, so there're aren't many people around. We sit in one of the empty booths, and Sam carefully tips the contents of his bag onto the tabletop. Out comes an array of small electronic devices. Among these, I recognize a couple of the latest smartphones and five watches, each a unique style. Sam slides me one of the phones.

"Here's your new phone, courtesy of the Walker account. Everyone's preprogrammed in. Make sure you have this phone on you at all times. Here." He pushes the watches closer to me. "Choose one of these."

I look at all the watches. Two are obviously men's watches, and one looks sporty and could be worn by either a girl or a guy. From the two remaining girls' watches, I choose the one with the brown leather band. It's stylish and looks more like a cool bracelet than a watch.

"I'll take this one. So is it like a cool spy gadget? Is there a micro-camera in here or knock-out mist?" I tease. Sam reaches across the table and puts the watch on my left wrist.

"It's cool, but not *that* cool," Ember laughs. "It works as a pager. It's a way for us to alert you if we can't get you on your phone. Green alert means your presence in Chaos is requested but not necessary, in case you can't get away at the moment. Yellow, you need to come to Chaos as soon as you can. Red alert, drop whatever you're doing and get your ass to Chaos pronto!"

"It also displays three time zones: one for our L.A. base, one for where you live, and one for our London base," says Sam.

"What do you mean 'base'?" I ask, thrilled that I'm finally getting answers.

Sam explains it to me. "We have two bases Earth-side. Each Realmwalker has the option to live wherever they please or to move to one of the bases. Having a base on each half of the world helps us make sure there are Walkers inside Chaos at all times. When it's night in England, it's day in California. Get it?"

"Yeah, that makes total sense. Does everyone live at a base?"

Sam answers, "No, not everyone. Ben, Mel, and Timothy live at the London base right now. Lang-hao sort of bounces back and forth between the two, depending on where his job takes him. Crank and I are the only ones at the L.A. house right now."

Ember pipes up, "Not for long though! As soon as I graduate, I am so there. I've already been accepted to UCLA and everything!"

"That's awesome, Ember! It must be fun living with friends like that," I say dreamily. "I'm surprised Crank is in L.A. He's really young, right?" I ask Sam.

"Yeah, he's fifteen. As soon as he came to Chaos and

learned about the L.A. base, he moved his mother and him up from Paraguay," he tells me.

"It was so sweet!" Ember croons. "It was always her dream to come to America. He bought her a beachside bungalow and a scarlet macaw named Big Red."

"Whoa! How did he manage that?" Having a grandmother in Glendale, I know how expensive real estate can be out there. Especially oceanfront.

"Here's a really cool part about being a Realmwalker," Ember says, rubbing her hands together a little maniacally. "All of the cool things we learn in Chaos usually help us here in our daily lives. For example, we call Ben 'The Wizard' because he's been able to really expand his knowledge. He is really, really smart. Like Einstein smart! He uses his smarts Earth-side and has all of his earnings from his inventions deposited right into the Walker account."

"Wow, that's really generous of him. So everyone lives off his money?" Somehow this doesn't seem fair to me.

"No, it's not like that at all," Ember says, shaking her head. "See, imagine decades, centuries even, of Realmwalkers using their talents to earn huge sums of money. Some invested and some left the majority of their fortune to the Walker account in their wills. After a while, it really adds up. And don't feel bad about using the money. We all end up paying it back eventually. Before The Wizard made any money, he borrowed hundreds of thousands of dollars to fund his research."

"Hundreds of thousands?" I exclaim, perhaps a little too loudly. Embarrassed, I look around to make sure no one's looking at us weird. "How much money is in this Walker account?" I ask in awe.

"More than you could spend in your lifetime," she says casually.

I stare into space. I'm aware my slack-jawed expression must look stupid, but I can't wrap my mind around it. All that money? And I have access to it?

"Which brings us," Sam says as he pulls his wallet out of his back pocket, "to this." He takes out a plastic card and hands it to me. I turn it around in my hand. It looks like a debit card. There's no name on it, just a series of numbers.

"This is only a temporary card. It has a three-thousand-dollar limit per day, so try not to go over that. This will have to hold you over until one with your name on it comes in the mail. There are no limits on that one. The PIN is thirteen forty-eight."

I stare at the card in my hand. It feels like it weighs a hundred pounds. I can vaguely hear Ember in the background telling me about the significance of the PIN and how it's the year of the earliest record they have of a Realmwalker.

I'm thinking about what this money could mean. Dad's pension is all we've had for a source of income for the last four years. When the money started to run out and things were getting tight, Mom took a part-time job at the post office. Now Jana's in college and Mom is under-qualified for any decent-paying job. We've been living with the fear of poverty looming over us. And now this? Unlimited funds, in the palm of my hand.

"Hey, Addy. Are you with us?" Ember snaps me out of my trance. I blink and a couple tears escape my eyes. I still can't seem to look away from the card I'm holding.

"Ember, let's give her a minute. Besides, I'm hungry again. Let's see what they have here." Sam gets up and motions for Ember to follow. I'm grateful for the minute alone, but all I can think of is I don't deserve this money. I haven't done anything to earn it. These people, these Realmwalkers risk their lives every night. They deserve it, not me.

But to be able to relieve Mom's stress? That's so tempting. I wonder if this means I'll have to tell her. Maybe I can come up with some way to get her the money she needs without her finding out where it came from.

I glance around the rink and watch people skating. A father's teaching his son to skate by pushing an upside down bucket around. A couple holds hands as they skate, and it makes me think of Mel and Ben holding hands last night. I smile at the memory. I wonder if any of the other Walkers are in a relationship. All of a sudden, an enormous tray of nachos is plopped down in front of me.

"Hope you're hungry!" Ember says. My stomach growls as I stare at the food.

"How can I be starving already? We had a huge breakfast and it isn't even lunch time yet," I ask, a little embarrassed by my appetite.

"Get used to it," Sam says. "We need to keep our bodies fueled. We burn a lot of calories in Chaos. Dig in."

After a minute or two of munching on nachos, I try to

continue our previous conversation as politely as I can while still eating.

"So, about this Walker account. Would I someday be able to help my mom and sister out?" I ask the two of them.

"Someday?" Ember says and looks at me like I have three heads. "Why wait?"

I set the card down and slide it away from me. "I haven't done anything to earn this yet. Maybe someday, when I've contributed enough or risked my neck enough to deserve it."

Sam slides it back in front of me. "Trust us. You'll definitely earn it, so stop worrying. Honestly, Adelaide, you could spend a million dollars and no one would even blink."

I choke on a nacho and have to cough a few times before I manage to speak. "That's an obscene amount of money. I can't imagine ever needing to spend that much," I say adamantly.

"Of course you don't *need* to. No one *needs* to spend a million dollars," Ember tells me. "Relax, Addy. Have some fun! You've got to remember something. The Realmwalkers' unofficial motto," she pauses dramatically, "we work hard, we play hard!" I shake my head in disbelief.

"Come on, spoil yourself. The first thing I did when my card came in? I went and bought myself my own car."

"How did you explain that to your parents?" I ask her.

"Oh, I told my mom about Chaos. It's not a big deal. She doesn't care about anything," she says off-handedly. No matter how nonchalant she says it, I can still feel pain in her words. I move the conversation along to get her mind off it.

"So, how would I be able to help her? I mean, it's not

like I can drop a huge amount of money on her lap. She'll probably think I robbed a bank."

Sam nods. "That's why we have 'The Walker Foundation.' It's for the Walkers who choose not to tell their families about their double lives. We set up this foundation that makes donations for whatever reason we can think up. For you, it will be easy—a donation to the surviving family members of a fallen officer."

"Oooo, we should get on that," Ember says around a mouth full of nachos.

"I bet there are a lot of people out there who think this Walker guy is pretty wealthy," I say as an afterthought. Ember and Sam chuckle a little.

"*Forbes Magazine* has been trying to hunt down the allusive Mr. Walker for ages," Ember tells me.

"Thanks guys. I can't tell you what a relief it will be to have my mom taken care of. She's done a lot for me and Jana." I can imagine her face when she gets the donation. I can't wait for that moment.

We finish the nachos and Sam goes to get us some drinks.

"So let's see. What else should you know?" Ember taps her fingers on the tabletop while she thinks.

"I was hoping to learn a little more about the other Walkers, if that's okay," I suggest.

"Oh yeah, that's right! Okay, where should we start?" she asks me as Sam gets back with the drinks. I grab a water bottle and think about the Walkers.

"Why not start with the last person to enter Chaos, besides me, and then work backwards?"

"Good idea," Sam says.

"So that would be... Timothy! Oh! This is great!" Ember laughs.

Sam shakes his head and looks annoyed. I decide to rescue him. "It's all right. I've already heard this story. Mel and Crank told me all about how Timothy used to sleep in the nude." As I say it, I find it harder to keep a straight face than I thought it would be. Ember's still laughing though she's struggling to get control of herself. "So he's from Scotland?"

"Yes," says Sam. "Timothy Fairweather is twenty-nine years old. He answered the call about ten months ago. Timothy's an expert marksman. While he prefers guns, his precision applies to any type of projectile. He's good with a bow and arrow, a crossbow, and throwing knives as well. He's also our weapons specialist. He can build and upgrade any piece of weaponry you can imagine, literally. If you can think it up, he can build it."

"Oh, so that explains why he was strapped with all those guns last night." I picture the tall, orange-haired man with a friendly smile. "Yeah, I didn't recognize any of those weapons."

Ember's calmed down enough to contribute. "He's also working on making us some armor. It's still in the works, but I've seen his prototypes and they're amazing."

"Right now, Earth-side, he has a few contracts with

some weapons manufacturers. He helps upgrade models of weapons that soldiers use in the field."

Ember looks serious now. "He could be making millions outfitting the world's armies with new and advanced weapons if he chose. Once I asked him why he doesn't, and he quoted Robert Openheimer after he invented the atomic bomb. 'I am become Death, the destroyer of worlds.' He says he doesn't want to give them too much destructive power and then be responsible for the misuse of it."

"Wow," I say, letting that sink in. I guess Realmwalkers can have a bigger influence on the world than I'd ever imagined. It's a good thing that most of the Walkers seem to be really good people.

"Next is Oscar Torres," Ember says, "or, as we tenderly call him, Crank."

"Why do you call him that?"

"Oscar," Sam says, "is our resident mechanic. He builds and maintains our vehicles. He collaborates with Timothy on the weapons and defense systems on each vehicle."

"So he built all of those Big-Bikes? He knows how to make them fly?" I ask in awe.

"Yep. And he's not only a mechanical genius," Ember brags. "He can also control and manipulate water."

"Oh, that's right! I saw him do that last night." I picture him pulling water from the fire hydrant.

"Before Crank, came Kira Sato," Sam goes on. "Kira's nineteen and from Japan." I think of the sweet girl with dimples and long, perfect hair. "Kira uses a katana when she fights, but she doesn't really need to. She's a mixed martial arts world champion."

"I thought she looked like she was in really good shape," I say. I remember her fighting in Chaos. She moved so fast I could hardly follow her movements with my eyes. "What's her ability?" I ask Sam.

"She has two. First, she can manipulate the flow of time."

"Whoa," I interrupt. "She can time travel?"

"No, it doesn't work like that. She can only slow time down around her in little increments. Or speed it up. So for example, if a Shade's charging her, she can slow its progress down while speeding herself up."

"And they don't stand a chance," Ember says, holding her head high. "She's all about girl power! We're lucky to have her."

"Kira's also a Sealer," Sam says. "That's a really important ability in Chaos. She puts the protective wardings on our Calms to keep the Shades out. She also seals the tears that the Greater Shades make in the fabric of Chaos."

"That does sound important." I think how we Walkers would be pretty useless without a sealer.

"Who came before Kira?" Ember asks rubbing her temples.

"Lang-hao Su," says Sam. "He came to Chaos two and a half years ago."

"How could I forget?" Ember says as she plays with her smartphone. "Here ya go, Addy. Meet Lang-hao Su." She passes me her phone. I'm watching the screen when a video starts. Music begins to play and people in flashy costumes start dancing. It's a music video. I've never heard the song but it sounds like something I might like. Then the video shows the singer dancing and singing in what sounds like Mandarin.

"That's Lang!" I shout. I watch amused as he effortlessly performs incredible dance moves. "Whoa, he's really good!" Already the catchy song is in my head even though he's singing in another language.

"Most of China thinks so too," Ember says. "He's huge over there. I mean HUGE!" She spreads her arms out wide. "You should Google his name and see all the cheesy merchandise they have with his face on it. I told him I was going to buy a bed set with him all over it so I could lay my head on his face every night." We both laugh at that. He's a really good-looking guy. No wonder he acted so suave when we met the other night. He's probably used to girls throwing themselves at him all the time. I blush at the memory of him kissing my hand.

"He can move stuff with his mind, right?" I ask, remembering him spinning that cat-like Shade around in the air last night.

Sam nods his head. "He's telekinetic. Comes in real handy."

Everyone has such amazing gifts. Each new ability I learn about, though, puts more fear and doubt in my heart. Again I hope I'm able to do something useful like the rest of them. Maybe I could be a Sealer, like Kira. It wouldn't hurt to have two of them.

I'm a little startled as a group of pre-teen girls sit at the booth behind us. I look around the rink and see it's starting to fill up with families. The noise level has risen enough that I'm not concerned about anyone overhearing us.

"Before Lang there was Mel. You know her already," Sam says.

"Yeah, the Aussie, and our age, right Ember?" She nods. "I saw what she can do. She stretches."

"She can take any shape, large or small," Sam says.

Ember adds, "She's a sealer too, like Kira."

There goes my idea of being a Sealer.

"Who was before Mel?" I ask the two of them.

"Frenchie," Ember says with a sour face.

"Her name's Simone Renard," Sam corrects Ember. Ember rolls her eyes and crosses her arms.

"Oh yeah, her," I say flatly as I remember the snooty brunette.

"Simone's from France and is twenty-six," Sam says. He doesn't comment on her attitude or rude behavior. I guess he's trying to remain neutral because he has to lead everyone.

Ember though, has no such reservations. "She's famous too, like Lang."

"She's a singer?" I ask her.

"No, she's an actress. And a model," Ember says resentfully.

"Hmm, I wonder if she's in anything I've seen before," I think aloud.

"I'm sure she is, just not the version of her that you've seen." At my confused look, she explains further.

"Frenchie—I mean Simone," she emphasizes as she glances at Sam, "is a shape-shifter."

"Like Mel?" I ask.

Sam clarifies, "No, Mel can stretch or shrink her own form. Simone can actually change her form into another's. She can become another person."

"That's why you don't recognize her. When she acts, she's Silvia Redding," Ember says.

My jaw drops. "No way!" Silvia Redding is hugely famous. I'm talking "A list." In fact, Mom and I watched her latest movie in the theaters two weekends ago. I actually like her!

"Silvia's a blonde. She looks nothing like Simone!" I say still in shock.

"She looks nothing like the version of Simone you saw last night," Ember corrects me. "And she also looks nothing like Shay Rendle." When she says the name, I immediately think of the famous redheaded model from Italy.

"What does she have to do with anything?" I ask.

"That's also Simone," Ember says matter-of-factly.

"What? She's both Silvia Redding *and* Shay Rendle?" I ask. Ember nods her head. I look at Sam for confirmation.

"It's true."

"You know the magazine that puts out the list of the world's top one hundred beautiful people?" Ember asks me.

"Yeah, my mom just got that issue in the mail a couple months ago. I think it might still be lying around somewhere," I say.

"Well, she'll be the first to tell you that she stole both the number one *and* the number two rankings this year."

"No way," is all I can say. I think of what it would be like to have that ability. I could make myself look like anyone. I could be taller. I've always wanted to be taller. And have blue eyes like my mom and sister. Or green like Dad. The possibilities are endless.

Ember brings me out of my fantasy. "Simone's always changing. Even in Chaos. She's a different woman every week it seems. Only those of us who were here when she first arrived know what she actually looks like."

"Why change so much though? Is she not happy with any of her looks?" I ask.

Ember laughs. "She's thrilled with her looks. She knows she's beautiful. As to why she's always changing, well, I have a theory." She grins at Sam and wiggles her eyebrows at him. He looks away and ignores her.

"What am I missing?" I ask the two of them.

"Well, when Simone first got here, it was Sam that came to her rescue. He swooped in like a knight in shining armor. She's been crazy for him ever since." I look at Sam to see his reaction. He watches the people ice-skating as if we aren't talking about him.

If this was true and Simone was in love with Sam, I couldn't really blame her. He's a strong, good-looking guy. He isn't trying to deny any of this, so it must be true. Wow. So Sam can have his choice of any version of Simone? That could be pretty tempting for a guy.

"Only problem is," Ember says, watching Sam, "Boss

isn't interested." I turn and watch Sam again. He seems to be watching one of the families out on the ice. "She keeps changing her appearance, hoping one of them will strike his fancy. It's kind of sad, really, and pathetic. She can change her outside all she likes, but she can't ever change the ugliness inside of her."

"All right, Ember, that's enough," Sam admonishes.

"Sorry, Boss," Ember says, not looking sorry at all.

"Um," I begin but hesitate, not wanting to upset Sam.

He indicates for me to go ahead. "Can I ask, why does she seem so…"

"Mean?" Ember asks.

"Yeah. I mean I don't even know her, but I'm pretty sure she hates me."

Ember looks at Sam expectantly.

Sam sighs and says, "We don't really understand where the attitude comes from. Although some of us think Simone lashes out at others because of her insecurity."

Did I hear him right? What could someone like Simone have to be insecure about?

"I know what you're thinking," Sam says. "But you don't know the whole story. Simone's been working really hard with Angel, but so far her shape-shifting ability seems to be the only one she has. There isn't a whole lot she can do with that to fend off Shades."

"Oh," I say as it dawns on me. I understand now. She feels useless. I can definitely relate to that. I try to imagine what it must be like for her, surrounded by Walkers with incredible abilities and all she can do is change her appearance.

Ember shrugs. "That still doesn't give her the right to be a total bi-"

"Ember." Sam snaps, giving her a look of disappointment.

Ember sighs submissively. "All right, all right. Anyway, I came to Chaos right before Simone. It's been almost four years now for me," She beams proudly.

"What's your last name?" I ask her, feeling dumb for not asking earlier.

"Ember McGinnis, at your service." She salutes me. "Well, I used to be Amber McGinnis, but I took the privilege of slightly altering my first name once I discovered my abilities."

"Wow, like, legally?"

She winks at me. "It's official."

"Well, I think it suits you." I smile. "And you can control fire. And isn't there something else you can do? Something about auras or mojo or something?"

She laughs. "Mojo! That's funny." Even Sam cracks a smile. "Yes, I can see people's auras when I want to. It isn't a super-useful skill, really, but it can help in knowing a person's personality or countenance." She puts an arm around me and pulls me into a side hug. "That's how I knew you and I were going to be best friends. Your aura says a lot about you."

Ember had said my aura was a sunny yellow. "So, what do the colors tell you?" I ask, still a little confused.

"Well, it's not so much the colors as it is the brightness," she explains. "The colors only tell me a little about the personality of the person. That's not nearly as important as the countenance. For example, you're a bright yellow. So bright, in fact, it's almost distracting. It's like stepping out into the sun after being indoors all day. It's so bright it takes a moment for your eyes to adjust."

"And that's good?" I ask self-consciously.

"That's very good. Where someone's hue tends to go with their personality, their brightness directly correlates with the quality of their character. I guess you could call it their morality scale."

"So if I was dark, we probably wouldn't be friends?"

"If you were dark, you would not be a Walker. That's for sure." I'm starting to really wish I had this ability. How cool would it be to know if someone you just met is trustworthy or not. "How about the rest of the Walkers? Are they all bright too?"

"Yep. You're right up there with the brightest. In fact, I've only seen one person brighter, and that's Angel."

This intrigues me. "I'm no Mother Theresa," I say, making her laugh more.

"I've never seen her in person, so I wouldn't really know! Actually, you and Sam are both the same brightness." Sam and I look at each other. I strain my eyes trying to see even an inkling of what Ember's talking about.

"What color is he?" I ask, not taking my eyes off his.

"Guess," she says. Oh great. This is some kind of test and if I fail, does it mean I really don't know Sam at all? I look into his eyes and I'm drowning in ice-blue waters.

My first instinct is to say the color of his eyes, but before I open my mouth to guess, I hesitate. While the color is mind-numbingly beautiful, it's a cold color.

I close my eyes and imagine Sam—how I feel when I'm around him. I remember this morning under the tree in my yard. I can still feel the warmth of his arm on mine. Sam's not an icy cold blue. He's warm. Everything about him says warmth and comfort. I open my eyes.

"Red."

Sam's eyebrows shoot up. Ember coughs as she chokes on her soda. After clearing her throat and catching her breath, she turns to me.

"How did you know that?" She seems really impressed. "Can you see it? His aura?"

"No, I can't see it," I say embarrassed. "It was only a guess."

She shakes her head, bewildered. "And a lucky one. I never thought you'd get it."

Sam's still staring hard at me, contemplatively. My cheeks warm under his scrutiny, and I search for a way to change the subject.

"So, who came before you, Ember?" I ask her.

"The Wizard," she says.

"You said that's what everyone calls Ben, right?"

"Yes. Ben Miller. He's a twenty-six-year-old Londoner. He's incredibly intelligent. He understands everything there is to know about everything. He's also our resident IT guy—as in information technology," Ember explains.

"Is he the one who got you guys, I mean us, access to the satellites?" I ask them.

Sam nods his head. "He's a technical genius."

"And he and Mel are together?" I ask.

Ember smiles warmly. "Yes. He fell head over heels for her the second she came to Chaos. It didn't take much convincing on her part either. It's funny—they don't look like they fit together, but they're two peas in a pod." The thought of Mel happy and in love makes me smile.

"Addy?" I hear my name a short distance away. Startled, I turn to see who called me. My brain stops functioning as I see Kevin Ludlow standing ten feet away from our table.

CHAPTER 15

KEVIN IS LOOKING at me and smiling uncertainly. I
think he's trying to decide whether to come over or not.
He's holding the hand of a four-year-old girl who's tugging
wildly at his arm. I know I should be smiling and greeting him but I'm completely at a loss for words. I'm sure
he's heard everything we've said about Chaos, and now he
thinks I'm a huge freak and is going to tell everyone.

"Come on Kevin! I want some cotton candy!" The four
year old screams as she tugs on his arm. She has dimples
just like him.

"Stop, Millie, or I won't buy you anything," he scolds
her as he walks to our table. I realize my fear of being overheard is paranoid thinking. Still I'm worried about how to
introduce Sam and Ember and am still searching for words
when he gets to us.

"Hey Addy," Kevin says to me. "How are you?" He
briefly looks at Ember and Sam. I'm really wishing I didn't
blush so easily as I'm reminded of how cute he is.

I finally find my voice. "Hi Kevin." I smile back. "I'm

really good! Thanks." Ember gently nudges my elbow with hers. "Oh! These are my friends Ember and Sam." I indicate each in turn. Kevin nods at them and says hi. "Is this your little sister?" I ask, smiling at the cute little girl holding his hand. She sticks her tongue out at me and turns her back on us with a "hmph."

"Millie!" Kevin chastises. "Yeah, sorry. She's having one of those days," he apologizes.

Ember and I laugh. "It's all right," I say. "I'd be grumpy too if I had to wait for cotton candy." This earns me a sideways look of curiosity from the girl.

"Yeah, she's pretty used to getting what she wants," he says. "Anyway, it was good seeing you, Addy." His smile and casual use of my name makes me a little dizzy. Ember has to nudge me again to clear my head enough to respond.

Smiling, I say, "You too, Kevin. I'll see you at school Monday." He waves bye to Ember and Sam and flashes me one last heart-stopping smile as he heads to the snack counter.

"Well played," Ember says sarcastically.

I roll my eyes. "Yeah, I'm not so good with stuff like that," I say quietly. Embarrassed, I look from Ember to Sam. Sam is still staring at the back of Kevin's head from across the room.

"He's super-cute, Addy! He seems really nice too," Ember says. "Are you guys friends?"

"I don't really know him that well. He's in my fifth hour but we've only talked a couple times."

"Hmm," Ember muses. "We'll have to fix that." She smiles conspiratorially.

"So," Sam interrupts, "before Ben, there was Harmony Tanner." It takes my mind a minute to pick up where we left off before.

"Angel," I say. "She must have been so young." I'm still unable to accept it.

"She was five. I found her sitting cross-legged right outside the door to Major Calm. She had found the place on her own." Sam grins at the memory.

"She was just sitting there, waiting for someone to greet her. When I first saw her, she looked up at me and smiled. She said 'Hi Sam, it's a pleasure to meet you.'"

I try to imagine what it would be like to hear that coming from a five year old. All I can think of is the petulant Millie we'd met a few moments ago.

"Angel must be really special."

"She really is," Ember agrees.

"So I'm pretty sure I understand her ability. What else is there to know about Angel?"

"Not a whole lot, really," Sam says. "We hardly know anything about her. We don't even know where she lives though we're pretty sure it's somewhere in America."

"Really? How come?"

"She's just a kid. I can imagine she wants to live her life top-side as free from Chaos as she can," Ember says.

I think about it and it makes sense to me. I can't imagine what it must be like for her being so young. I don't blame her for wanting to enjoy her childhood. Besides, I doubt her parents would be thrilled to find out their nine-year-old daughter is secretly fighting demon Shades every night.

"Mikhail came before Angel," Sam says. As I think of the quiet Russian, a dozen questions come to mind.

"That's right," Ember says. "He's been in Chaos almost as long as you, Sam." Sam nods.

It's quiet for a while as I wait for them to continue. The mood feels different, and they both seem reluctant to go on.

"Actually," Ember continues, "Angel, Mikhail, and Faye all came within a month of each other."

"Wow. Is that unusual?" I ask.

"Yes, very," Ember says somberly. Sam is staring hard at a scratch in the tabletop. He seems to be far away in thought, maybe remembering something. "About seven years ago, there was a terrible accident in Chaos," she looks at Sam with sorrow in her eyes. The silence is deadening as I wait for her to go on.

"One of the sealers made a mistake on the wardings that guard Major Calm. Lesser Shades found the weak spot, and thinking it was a way into Earth Realm, swarmed through." She's speaking so quietly now I have to strain to hear her. "The Walkers were caught completely off guard. Almost everyone was awake top-side, leaving their bodies in Chaos completely defenseless. It was a massacre."

I stare in horror at Ember. I can't even imagine how awful that must have been. I think of how terrified I was at the thought of losing Mel the other day. To lose multiple Walkers? It was unthinkable.

"Six Walkers died that day. In the month that followed

there was a surge of new Walkers. I guess the 'powers-that-be' recognized the need and issued more calls."

I watch Sam's face as he stares off into space, reliving whatever horror that day held. There's sadness there. I wish I could comfort him. Underneath the pain in his eyes, I can see strength—and a righteous anger that must come from having lived through such an event. I fight tears back for the loss of those Walkers. I never knew them but I know that we are all connected in a way. We sit in silence for a while. I can't think of any words to say that wouldn't sound too small and inadequate.

After a short time Sam clears his throat. "Mikhail Kozlow is Russian. He's twenty-two." Though he still seems subdued, the moment of sadness has mostly passed.

Eager to move the conversation along, I ask, "What's his story?" Ember and Sam do that thing again where they exchange a silent conversation with a single look. They still seem reluctant to talk about Mikhail. Confused, I ask, "What is it?"

"Um," Ember starts awkwardly, "Mikhail is just... different."

"Yeah, he seems kind of shy," I say. They both avoid eye contact with me. "What? Is it more than that?"

"It's difficult to explain Mikhail," Sam says quietly. "He keeps to himself, so no one really knows him."

This doesn't make sense. He's a Realmwalker like the rest of us. Doesn't that make him family? "Has anyone tried to get to know him?"

"Of course," Ember explains. "But it's like talking to a brick wall. He shuts down… or disappears."

"Maybe he doesn't have any people skills," I try.

"I don't know." Ember shakes her head. "He doesn't even try. Plus, he puts out a really strange vibe."

"What do you mean? He didn't seem strange to me," I say in his defense. "Besides, he can't be that bad if he's a Walker, right?"

"Well," Sam says grudgingly, "there have been Walkers in the past who've gone sour. Being a Walker doesn't imply sainthood. We've the agency to choose right from wrong like everyone else."

"I actually think it's harder for us to be good, given all of our capabilities," Ember muses. The thought of a Walker gone rogue is a frightening thought indeed. I picture Mikhail in my mind, appearing out of the shadows with his deadly arched blades flashing lightning quick.

"No," I say, unable to accept that image. "I just don't see it. I mean, he saved my life."

Sam concedes my point. "He is a great warrior."

"When he doesn't go MIA on us," Ember mutters under her breath.

"What?" Unsure I heard her clearly.

Sam sighs heavily. "He's been known to go AWOL in the middle of battle before. When asked about it, he clams up. That doesn't exactly inspire faith in him for the rest of us."

I'm a little surprised at Sam's willingness to express doubt in a fellow Walker. He refuses to speak ill of Frenchie, who is an obvious tyrant and pain in the ass, but he shares his uncertainty about Mikhail openly. This makes me want to defend him even more.

"But he hasn't done anything outright bad, though, has he? I mean…" I try to think of a way to defend him. "What about his aura, Ember? Can't you tell if he's good or bad?"

"That's just it!" Ember slaps the table. "When I try to see his aura, there's nothing there! It's like he doesn't have one." She says this as if it confirms her point that he can't be trusted.

"Have you asked him about it?"

She shakes her head. "Nah. Honestly, I try to avoid him. He gives me the heebie-jeebies." She shivers. "Even his powers are creepy."

"What are they?"

"We aren't exactly sure," Sam says with a furrowed brow. He looks frustrated. "We know he can travel through shadows."

I remember him pulling me into the shadows and holding me tightly against him as we fell through darkness. It was a startling few moments but nothing about it felt evil. It actually seems like a really cool ability.

"Angel senses he can do more than that," Ember says, "but he's never let her fully assess him. That's another reason we don't really trust him. Being secretive like that, it's not right. Makes you wonder what he's hiding."

Sam sighs. "We really should let you form your own opinion of him."

"I will," I say adamantly. I'm surprised at the defiance in

my voice. I don't like that every Walker seems to have made up their mind about Mikhail. It doesn't seem right to gang up on one of our own. I make a promise to myself to do everything I can to reach out to Mikhail. I won't give up on him. He's one of us. He was called to Chaos for a purpose, and he belongs there as much as everyone else.

Sam and Ember can tell that I'm upset. We sit in an uncomfortable silence for a moment. Sam clears his throat and continues.

"So, shortly before Mikhail came Faye Devon."

I think of the kind healer covered in scars. "She's much older than everyone else, isn't she?"

Sam nods. "She's forty-seven."

"Is that strange? For someone of her age to be a Walker?" I ask delicately.

"A little," he says. "It's not unheard of though. Whenever an important skill is needed, the best person to fill that role is called to Chaos. Even though Faye is older than most Walkers, she was the best person for the job."

"And she really is," Ember says enthusiastically. "It's amazing, the things she can do. Each time one of us gets hurt so badly I'm sure there's no coming back from it, she fixes them, good as new."

Sam nods in agreement. "She's the best healer I've ever seen in Chaos. I don't think there's anything she can't do." This reminds me of a question I had.

"If she can heal anything," I start, but I hesitate as I can't find a polite way to word it.

Ember thankfully understands what I'm getting at. "Her scars?" she asks.

"Yeah. I mean, how did she get them in the first place?"

"Car accident," Sam says, looking as though he's got a bad taste in his mouth.

"She didn't heal herself?" I ask, not understanding.

"It happened three months before she came to Chaos. She didn't have her ability then."

Ember elaborates for me. "She could heal them now if she wanted, but she chooses not to. You see," her green eyes are red rimmed, "she lost her husband of twenty-two years in that crash. Then, when she found out a few short months later that she has the ability to heal practically any wound, it was too much for her. I think she feels so guilty for not being able to save him. Keeping her scars is her way of punishing herself."

"But that's not fair! It wasn't her fault! The call just came too late." They both nod in agreement with me.

"Sometimes Fate's a bitch," Sam says angrily. "She's a doctor now, top-side I mean. She works in London's busiest emergency room. She's there every spare second she gets, forever trying to make up for losing her husband."

This makes me angry too—that someone like Faye would have to suffer like this. To be given the power to save lives, just months too late to save the one most dear to her. It was like a cruel joke. And poor Faye is reminded of it every time she looks in the mirror.

Thinking of Faye's loss makes me think of my father and the day a car stole his life. I wonder at the similarities.

A question comes to mind, but it may prove too personal to ask anyone else. My instincts push me forward, however.

"Can I ask you guys something personal?" I ask quietly.

"Course, Addy," Ember says encouragingly.

"Well," I think of how to voice my question, "I lost my Dad four years ago, and Faye lost her husband."

"Yeah," Sam says before I can go on, "we've all lost someone close to us."

With my suspicion confirmed, all I can do is shake my head slowly and ask, "Why?"

"We don't know for sure," he says.

I look at Ember. "My older brother," she says simply. Sam doesn't offer to share who he lost and I don't ask. I can understand his not wanting to talk about it.

I take a deep breath and try to dispel some of the gloom I've been feeling. Our conversation has taken a heavy turn these last few minutes, and I'm anxious to get on to a happier topic. I mentally go over all the Walkers we've covered so far.

"So," I say a bit more cheerily, "it looks like you're the only one left Sam..." I let it hang in the air, waiting for his last name.

"Dixon," he provides with a crooked smile and mock bow. Seeing him act silly makes me giggle and I appreciate his efforts to lighten the mood.

"Sam Dixon," I say, liking the sound of it. I frown thoughtfully. "Let's see how much I know about you so far." I rub my hands together eagerly, the way I've seen Ember do. It earns a laugh from her. "You are Mr. Boss Man

Extraordinaire. Longest in Chaos, current leader of the Walkers, and SWAT commander." I tick things off my fingers as I go on. "Bad-A warrior man wiiiiiith…," I remember him tossing those shades around with ease, "super strength?" I ask, crossing my fingers and hoping I guessed it right.

They both laugh as Ember says, "Pretty much nailed that one."

"It's not exactly like that though. I mean, I'm not Superman or anything," he says bashfully. It's about time someone else did the blushing for once and I'm finding I very much like the way it looks on him. I can't help but grin at how adorable he is right now.

"Oh please!" I say, planning to milk this for all it's worth. "I saw you snap that huge bear Shade's neck like it was a twig!"

Ember joins in. "It's not only strength, he's agile too. Like a cat!" she teases.

He fidgets uncomfortably under the praise and it makes Ember and I laugh even harder. He shakes his head in exasperation.

"Okay, okay. We'll be good." I give him some relief.

"It's really not all that special. It's not like magic or anything."

"Explain it to me," I encourage.

"It's like this. Let's say Average Joe is lifting weights."

He puts his arm on the table and mimics an arm curl. I'm completely distracted by the sight of his drool-worthy bicep flexing. I nod absently, trying to show that I'm following along.

"His brain is sending a message to his muscle to contract. But the problem is that only a fraction of the muscle fibers is doing any work."

"Seriously?" I ask.

"Yeah. Most of us will go through life never using our muscles to their full potential. But when my brain sends messages, all of my muscle fibers respond."

"Even still," I say, not completely convinced, "I mean, you're a strong-looking guy and all…" He raises his eyebrows and waits. "Those Shades you fought, they were huge."

"It's like when you hear a story about someone doing something impossible when hit with an adrenaline rush." And when he says this, I get it.

"Like a dad who lifts a two-and-a-half-ton van off his child. I've heard those stories."

"Sam can harness that kind of strength anytime," Ember says proudly.

"Wow, Sam. All teasing aside, that's really impressive." He shrugs like it's no big deal.

"I'm also pretty convinced his ability to lead others isn't just a talent," Ember says. "I think it's another power of his. The way he can make and execute a tactical plan with absolute precision is superhuman. Angel seems to agree with me."

"Anyway, that's everyone," he says abruptly, in an obvious attempt to change the subject. He looks around the ice rink as he says, "I don't know about you guys, but I'm hungry again."

CHAPTER 16

ON OUR WAY out of the ice rink, Ember insists we stop at the mall. "I only had a moment's notice when Sam called me to fly out here. I didn't have much time to pack, and I had no idea I would be going to a show this weekend. I need to shop!" she says, fist clenched with fierce conviction.

"That's fine," Sam says. "I've got some calls I have to make for work. I'll drop you two off and you can call me when you're done."

Ember fist pumps the air. "Yes! Girl time!"

Once at the mall, I discover Ember's ulterior motive behind her need to shop. "I really don't need to get anything. I just wanted to get you here so I could buy you a new outfit for tonight."

"Wait a second-" I begin, but she doesn't let me finish.

"No 'ifs,' 'ands,' or 'buts'!" She says firmly. "You've never been to a concert before. I want tonight to be memorable and fun. You're getting spoiled today whether you like it or not." She grabs my hand and pulls me into the nearest clothing store.

Two hours and over three hundred dollars later, Sam pulls up to the east entrance of the mall to pick us up. I feel defeated and look undoubtedly shamefaced about the number of bags hanging off my arms, but Ember radiates a victory glow. Sam jumps out and helps us load our loot into the back of the truck.

"Hope you can find room for all of this in your luggage, Ember," Sam says. Ember smiles and winks at me.

"I'm sure I'll manage," she says slyly.

Once back at home, Mom makes us some sandwiches for a light dinner. Afterwards, Ember helps me piece together an outfit from the new wardrobe. All in all, I'm pleased and a little surprised with the outcome. I end up in a pair of jean shorts and a black Led Zeppelin shirt. I leave my hair down but at Ember's suggestion, I cram a hair band into my pocket for later.

"Trust me, it's going to get sweaty and gross in the crowd, and you are going to want to put your hair up," she informs me as she laces her high-top Chucks.

"Are there going to be mosh-pits?" I ask worriedly.

"No. Not for the band we're seeing. That kind of stuff usually only happens at hard rock or metal shows. Besides, Sam will be there so no one would dream of messing with us."

She looks me over. "You look great! Here, wear these." She hands me some thin black bracelets. On our way out, I hug Mom and thank her again for letting me go.

"Now, Sam," she says seriously, "I'm counting on you to look out for these girls. Have fun, but bring them back safe."

"Yes, Ma'am." Sam nods respectfully.

Ember has me sit in between her and Sam again on the drive to Phoenix. I don't complain. I can smell a faint trace of cologne coming off of Sam. It's a warm, woodsy smell. I realize now that my palms are sweating and I'm having a hard time keeping still. I try to relax. I want to absorb everything about tonight. I know it'll be over soon, and we'll be back in Chaos facing the same troubles we left behind last night. Tomorrow morning will come and Sam and Ember will have to leave. Who knows when I'll be able to see them again top-side.

No. I'm not even going to think about any of that until I absolutely have to. Ember asks if we can stop at a convenience store so she can grab an energy drink.

"I need some caffeine so I can stay amped up! You guys want anything?" she asks as we pull into the parking lot.

"I'm good," Sam says.

"Do you want me to come with you?" I ask.

"No, no. I'll only be a second." She hops out of the truck and inadvertently leaves me in a very awkward position.

Do I stay where I am, squished up next to Sam while there is an open seat next to me, or do I scoot over until Ember gets back and then scoot back again? All of a sudden, it's too quiet in the truck. What do I do? I'm panicking and trying to make up my mind when I realize it's probably too late now. The moment of indecision has passed and if I moved now it would only be more awkward. Now I'm stuck trying to think of something, anything to say when Sam breaks the tension.

"This was a good idea," he says quietly.

I let out a relieved sigh. "The concert?" I ask.

"Yeah. I haven't seen Ember this happy in a long time." I follow his gaze through the store's windows. I can see the top of her bright red head over the aisles. "It's easy to forget that Realmwalkers are normal people too. They need stuff like this every now and then to help them cope."

"So you're saying, being a Realmwalker isn't all glitz and glam?" I scoff. He chuckles under his breath. "What's it like in L.A.? Do you and Crank ever do anything fun? Or is it just SWAT and Chaos? Do you have friends outside of all that?"

He reaches up and scratches at the stubble on his jaw as he answers. "It's mostly just work and Chaos. Sometimes I volunteer to teach a class or two on self-defense at the women's shelter. Sometimes I'll catch a meal with a co-worker."

"Any family?" From the look on his face, I instantly regret asking. His brow furrows and the skin around his eyes tighten.

"Hmm, no." He shakes his head. "It's just me."

Our earlier conversation at the ice rink comes to mind. Ember had said that all of the Walkers had lost someone close to them. I silently kick myself for ruining the light-hearted atmosphere. I search for a way to salvage the moment.

"So Ember's headed out there soon, right? That should liven things up," I say with a smile. Then I realize something. "Hey! I'm actually going out there this summer to visit my Gram. I should stop by the base and check it out!"

Ember comes jogging back out to the truck. "What'd I miss?" she asks when she climbs in next to me.

"Adelaide was telling me she plans on visiting base this summer."

"Just visiting? Heck, Addy, why not move there?" she asks excitedly.

"Move?"

"Yeah, why not? I mean, you're planning to go to college somewhere right? Why not UCLA? With me? Oh my gosh!" She grabs my shoulders and shakes me. "We would have so much fun!"

"Oh. I hadn't even thought about that," I say as I run through the possibilities in my head. I'd be close to Gram. UCLA does have a great art program. Normally there would be no way I could afford it, but now, with the "donation" money coming, tuition shouldn't be a problem.

"Really, Addy, think about it. Maybe mention it to your mom, see what she thinks," she pleads. Her expression makes me laugh.

"Okay I will! It actually sounds like a great idea. Only, let me think about it a bit."

The rest of our night proves to be one of the most memorable and happy nights I've ever had. At the concert, the three of us manage to get a spot in the crowd fairly close to the stage. The place is so crowded Ember, Sam, and I are crammed into a tight circle. When the band comes out, everyone squeezes up to get in even closer.

The energy of the place, of the band and the fans singing together, is electrifying. Everyone's jumping and dancing to the familiar songs. I can feel the bass from the speakers pump through my chest. I can even feel it in the bodies of the people pressed up against me on all sides. Everyone's happy and having such a good time. The three of us smile and laugh the entire drive home as we tell our favorite moments of the night.

Once we get home, I tiptoe into Mom's room and kiss her goodnight.

"Did you have a good time?" she asks sleepily.

"The best ever. Thanks so much for letting me go mom," I whisper.

"Mmm-hmm," she murmurs as she pulls her sheets up to her chin.

Even though it's late, the three of us take turns showering. While Ember had warned me about getting sweaty, she failed to mention how I would come home covered in other people's sweat as well. Yuck.

With my ears still ringing from the loud concert, I climb into bed next to Ember. She squeezes my hand.

"All right, girly. Tonight's the night!" I smile nervously back at her as she collapses into her pillow, already asleep. Sam comes in and sits on the edge of the bed, facing me.

"When we get back to Major Calm, Ember will take you to Angel. I've got to organize a test run with some of the Walkers, but I'll come by and check on you before we head out."

"You're going back out into Chaos tonight?" I ask surprised. "Already? Isn't that dangerous?"

"It won't be that bad. It'll be a scouting mission. We

need to know what we're up against and whether we're going to face an ambush every time we leave a Calm or not."

I nod, understanding but still worried.

"With this mission and your evaluation, it's going to be a big night. Are you ready?" His steady gaze is confident, and I take strength from it.

"I guess I've gotta have faith that whatever or whoever brought me to Chaos knew what they were doing."

"You'll do fine, Addy," Sam says reassuringly.

I want to reach out and touch him. I want to hug him and steal comfort from his arms. Instead, I lie back on my pillow and close my eyes. He places his hands on my face.

"I'm ready," I say, focusing on the warmth of his hands.

"Sleep now, Addy." I listen as his voice fades away to a soft and lingering whisper.

CHAPTER 17

WHEN I AWAKEN in my temporary room, the familiar warmth and comfort that comes with being in a Calm wash over me. It helps ease my apprehension about my evaluation. I figure the best thing I can do now is relax and accept the inevitable.

I throw on some of the generic clothes I find in the guest dresser and glance at my reflection in the mirror hanging on the back of the door. My hair is a tangled mess and my eyes are puffy. I'm combing my fingers through my hair when there's a quiet knock on my door. I open it to find a radiant and perfectly groomed Ember.

"How did you do that?" I ask perplexed.

She laughs as she hands me a small, decorative bag. "I figured you would need some basic essentials."

I unzip the bag and find a hairbrush, hairspray, deodorant, and even some makeup (which I doubt I'll use).

"You are my HERO!" I motion her in as I head to the bathroom to tidy up.

"So what are you doing next weekend?" she calls from the bedroom as I'm attempting to tame my bed-head.

"Next weekend? Friday night is graduation rehearsal, and Saturday I have my art show at the school."

"Oh, okay." She sounds a little disappointed.

My hair is as good as it's going to get without a shower and hair dryer. I find Ember waiting on the edge of the bed.

"What's next weekend?" I ask.

"Graduation," she says nonchalantly. "Some of the other Walkers were going to come and I thought it would be cool to have you there too."

"Oh bummer! I would love to be there." I try to come up with some way I can make it.

"Don't worry about it. You've got a lot going on. And you can't miss your art show. That's a big deal." She's smiling but I can tell she's a little bummed.

"Sorry Ember." I frown at her. I remember Ember's an only child and that she doesn't seem to have a close relationship with her mom. It would probably mean a lot for me to be there. "I'll make it up to you—I promise," I say with conviction.

"No biggie. Really," she insists. "How about this? On my way to California, I'll swing by your place. That way I can be there for your graduation!"

"That's perfect!" I feel a little better now. "Come as soon as you like! You can stay all week if you want."

She gets a mischievous look in her sparkly green eyes. "Maybe, if I'm lucky, you can leave for California with me! A few well-placed hints and suggestions to your mom could go a long way," she says enticingly with raised eyebrows. I laugh at her persistence. It feels good to have someone really want me around, not out of a sense of guilt like Tori but because they genuinely like me.

"I'm sold." I decide right then. "I'll convince my mom."

"Seriously?" Ember jumps up from the bed and grabs my shoulders.

"Seriously." I smile. Ember's the sweetest, coolest person I've ever met. This is the kind of friendship I should surround myself with. "I'll do whatever it takes. Even if I have to fight dirty. One way or another, I'm going to California with you." I hope secretly that I have the kind of persuasive power I'm boasting of. The look of triumph on her face is priceless and I know I'll never forget it for as long as I live.

After a few minutes of "Oh my gosh!" and "I can't wait!" and "We're going to have SO MUCH FUN!" we remember I'm supposed to be meeting with Angel right now.

I follow Ember through the hallways of Major Calm. As we pass Walkers here and there along our way, I'm greeted with various wishes of good luck. Lang-hao winks and flashes me a heartbreakingly beautiful smile while Ben offers me a firm handshake and a nod. I'm not too disappointed when we pass Simone lounging in a bean bag and she ignores us completely.

"Are there normally this many Walkers here?" I ask once I notice how most of the Walkers I'm seeing are living on the opposite side of the world. It must be the middle of the day for them.

"Nope. Not normally. Everyone's been on high alert

though since the ambush last night. I think everyone's hanging around in case anything new develops. Plus, not to make you nervous or anything, but everyone's probably curious about what your ability will be."

I try not to think about that as I follow her through Major Calm to a hall I haven't been down before. We reach darkly stained oak double doors that open into a large octagonal room.

Everything's richly lit by a crystal chandelier hanging from the high ceiling, throwing the corners of the room into shadows. The room is beautiful and cozy. All around are formal but comfortable-looking sitting chairs, sofas, and loveseats. The most remarkable thing about the room, however, is that the walls are actually bookshelves—thick, glossy, mahogany bookshelves. And they're filled with books. There's even a ladder attached to a bar that runs along the top of the walls. It's on wheels and I can see how it can roll around the entire circumference of the library. The room looks like something out of a fairy tale.

"Pretty cool, huh?" Ember says quietly as I'm gaping at my surroundings. I nod my head, not wanting to speak and break the almost reverent spell in the atmosphere. "I'll go get Angel if you want to wait here and unwind. I'm sure you're pretty anxious right now. I remember I was back when it was my turn."

After she turns and leaves, I make my way into the room. I'm trying to read some of the titles of the books lining the shelf nearest me when I'm nearly startled out of my skin by someone clearing their throat. I turn around in a circle, checking everywhere until I find the source.

There, sitting in one of the corners, hunched over a book propped on his knee, is Mikhail. No wonder Ember and I didn't see him; he's buried in shadows. I wonder how he can manage to read at all. Maybe one of his abilities is night vision.

"Hi Mikhail." I smile at him and head in his direction. He nods politely at me but then returns his attention to his book. It's an obvious attempt to avoid socializing, but I'm determined to get to know him. After what Ember and Sam said about him yesterday, I have to decide for myself if Mikhail is a good person. I refuse to rely on borrowed opinions.

A high-backed chair sits close to him, but I decide to scoot it closer. As I go to lift it I'm surprised at its weight. I'm barely able to budge it. Things get awkward when Mikhail doesn't offer to help. In fact, he doesn't even look up and acknowledge my efforts. I'm almost tempted to give up. I manage however, to at least scoot it an inch in his direction and angle it so that I can face him. I sit down.

"What are you reading?" I ask.

After a few silent seconds, he looks up from his book. He doesn't look directly at me but instead gazes somewhere in the vicinity of my hands resting on my lap. He lifts his book up a little and shows me the front. It's difficult to see through the shadows, but on the cover I'm able to make out an image of a big ship on a storm-tossed ocean. I can see the title and author but it's in another language.

"That's Russian, right? What's it called?"

After a brief hesitation, he says in heavily accented English, "Star of the Black Sea."

It's obvious he isn't comfortable speaking to me, but I get the feeling it's more out of shyness than from blatant snobbery. He's here in the library reading a book, so I decide to exploit that angle. Maybe talking to him about something he enjoys will help him open up more easily.

"What's it about? Is it fiction?" I ask.

He nods his head. He's quiet for so long I start to think that's all I'm going to get from him. Then he surprises me.

"There is an old story in Russia of a ship that was found out at sea by the Navy. The nine crew members were not found onboard, though the life boats were all accounted for and nothing was missing or stolen from the ship. It is a well-known mystery. This book is a fictional account of what happened written from the first mate's perspective, like a journal, which is said to have been found among his things in his cabin."

"Wow. That sounds really good! How is it so far?" I'm encouraged when he finally looks me in the eyes.

"I've read it before. It's good." Once he says this, I can see that the cover and pages of the book are aged and well worn from repeated readings. I smile at the sight of it.

"I have a few books like that. There's one I must have read at least a dozen times."

"You read much then?" He's asking me questions now? This is a good sign.

"I'm always reading!" I say, jumping on the opportunity.

"Call me a nerd but books are my best friends. I love disappearing into a good story. Being able to leave everything behind and become part of something else," I say dreamily, "it's magic."

He looks at me for a few seconds as though he's contemplating his next comment. I'm disappointed though, when he looks back down at the book in his lap and starts reading again. Angel and Ember aren't here yet, so I'm not willing to lose this chance to get to know him better.

"Do you know if there's a version in English? I'm almost finished with the book I'm reading now, so I'll need something new soon." He starts to look back up at me but just then I hear Ember's laughter coming from the hall outside. Knowing my time with Mikhail is up, I turn to thank him for talking to me. And there's nothing in front of me but an empty chair.

Shocked, I gasp audibly.

"What's wrong?" Ember says from the doorway, looking concerned. I turn back to make sure I'm not completely losing it. Sure enough, Mikhail is nowhere in sight. I sit there for a minute, looking wide-eyed and pointing stupidly at the empty chair in front of me.

"Mikhail…" I manage to say. That's when I notice Angel standing next to Ember. She's looking especially cherubic tonight in a white sundress with matching ballet flats.

"Oooh," they say in unison, nodding their heads in understanding.

"He does that sometimes," Angel smiles and says in

her sweet, little-girl voice. Sam appears behind them in the door frame.

"Angel, Adelaide, are you two ready?" he asks us. Angel looks questioningly at me. And just like that my mind is off the disappearing Mikhail and back to the business at hand. I take a deep breath and try to steady my nerves.

"Well, I'm as ready as I'll ever be," I say weakly through a thin smile. Angel comes over and takes my hand.

"You don't have to be worried, Addy. Everyone has a place and a purpose here in Chaos." She leads me to a soft brown leather chair near the center of the room. I sit down and she stands in front of me the way she did the other night in the conference room.

I'm suddenly very aware of Sam and Ember hovering over us. I can read the appraisal in their intense stares and I begin to feel uncomfortable. To fail is one thing, but to fail in front of these two would be miserable.

"All right, you two," Angel says. "You know the rules."

Ember's shoulders slump in defeat and Sam nods in acceptance.

"Ugh, fine. We're leaving," Ember says begrudgingly. She pats my head on her way past. "Good luck, sweetie. Make us proud." I cringe inwardly even though I know she means well.

Sam stops next to me and looks unsure of himself for a second. It's strange and unnerving to see a crack in his normal, unwavering confidence. He swings his arms nervously back and forth a few times and finally decides that an offered fist bump is the best option for well-wishing. After I bump my fist to his, he quickly leaves the library.

Angel giggles quietly. "He's nervous for you. Everyone's anxious and excited tonight. I know this is overwhelming but you really don't need to worry. You'll see, Addy." She places her tiny hands on my head, directly over my temples. "Are you ready?" she asks through a grin. Looking into her blueberry eyes has a calming, almost hypnotic effect on me. I nod and she begins her instructions.

"You don't need to do much for this. Just try to clear your mind as best you can. This won't be like the other night in the conference room. I'm going to go much deeper into your mind tonight. You won't be aware of me or what I'm doing. It will almost be as if you are asleep. Okay?"

"Okay," I answer. I try to think of nothing, which is impossible. Instead, I'm thinking about how I'm failing at thinking about nothing. I'm starting to get worried that maybe this isn't going to work at all when my eyesight goes fuzzy. I can't seem to focus on anything. Everything seems to be going dark. All of a sudden, there is a ringing in my ears. It's not a loud ringing, just that sound you hear when there is no other sound at all. It's as if your ears invent a noise to fill the emptiness.

Then the sound stops and my vision begins to clear. The first thing I see is blue. I'm staring into Angel's eyes again as they seem to rise up out of a murky haze. Or maybe I'm the one rising up, toward her. I can hear her voice now but it's muffled.

As the rest of her face comes into focus, I can see that

instead of her typically porcelain skin, her face is flushed red. Her eyes are red rimmed and her cheeks are wet with tears. I'm trying to make words match the movements her mouth is making when she takes her hands from the side of my head and throws her arms around me.

"Finally," I think I hear her say. I can feel her little body shaking with quiet sobs.

"Angel, what's wrong? Did I fail?" I ask.

She explodes into giddy laughter as she pulls back, and shaking her head, she says, "Oh, no, Addy! You did not fail." She's grins as more tears escape her eyes. "I've been waiting for someone like you for so long! And you're finally here." She sighs contently. An almost visible weight seems to lift right off her shoulders.

"You mean I have an ability?" I ask. I hold my breath and wait for her response.

"Yes, Addy, you have an ability." She lets out another peal of silvery laughter. "Addy, you're a Mimic!" I try to remember where I've heard that familiar term before. Then Angel explains, "You're just like me!"

CHAPTER 18

"WHAT?" I ASK numbly. I'm lost in a hundred thoughts at once. Did I hear her right? Did she say I'm a Mimic? Could she be wrong? What does that mean for me? I can do what everyone else does? How is this right? I don't feel like I can do anything, let alone *everything*.

"Adelaide." Angel waves her hand in front of my eyes. "Woo hoo!" she calls. "Snap out of it." My eyes refocus and I can see her smiling. "You. Are. A. Mimic," she says slowly and clearly.

"But how?" I wonder aloud. "Are you sure?"

She nods her head adamantly. "I'm very sure. To be a Mimic, you must have two abilities. One, you must be able to project your consciousness. And two, your mind must be very adaptable. You have both of these abilities, Addy," she says excitedly. She puts her hands on her hips and looks contemplative.

"You know, there's something else about you. I can't quite put my finger on it." She taps her foot as she thinks. "It's something that you have that I don't. An understanding of things, or of the nature of things?" she muses aloud. She waves a hand dismissively. "Oh, it'll come to me."

She walks over to the door and opens it. Ember peeks in.

"So?" she asks with clasped hands and raised eyebrows. "Can we come in?"

"She's all yours!" Angel says. As Ember and Sam clear the doorway, other familiar faces appear from the hall. Mel and Ben walk into the library hand in hand, followed by Kira and a very exuberant Crank.

Crank bounds to my side. "Hey Addy! How are you? So how did it go? What can you do? No, wait! Let me guess... oh, I have no idea—tell me already!" I laugh with the others at his intensity.

"Give her a moment, Crank," Sam says calmingly. Then he glances at Angel. "What's the matter, Harmony?" He sounds concerned. "Have you been crying?"

"Oh." Angel's little hands go to her cheeks. She laughs and assures him, "It's nothing really. I guess I'm just so relieved to finally have another Mimic in Chaos besides myself."

The small group erupts into shocked exclamations.

"Whoa! No way!" shouts Crank.

Kira slaps me on the back with a "That a girl!"

Mel hugs me warmly. "I knew you'd be a strong one, right from the start. I said it, didn't I, love?" She nudges Ben with her elbow.

"She did. Congratulations, Adelaide," Ben says with a smile and a handshake.

"Thanks guys." I'm blushing from all the praise and

attention. It feels weird being congratulated for having an ability I don't even know how to use.

I look to Ember who's shaking her head back and forth and grinning smugly. "And you were so nervous. I told you there was nothing to be worried about!" She pulls me into a side hug. "This is so great, Addy. You're going to be such a kick-ass Walker!"

Sam's staring at me, his thoughts a mystery behind his steady gaze. He nods his head in approval and any lingering fear and uneasiness I have melts away completely.

I look around at everyone and sigh. "So what now?" I ask them.

"Now," Sam says, "you train. Angel, do you mind getting Adelaide started on her basic training?"

"Sure thing, Boss!" she beams.

"I want her self-waking by the end of the night. The rest of you, don your 'coms.'" Sam taps his ear as he makes eye contact with the small group of Walkers around me. "Timothy, Lang-hao, and myself will be leaving shortly to perform a scouting maneuver and we need you listening in. I want you all ready to provide back-up on a moment's notice. Understood?"

"Yes sir."

"Copy."

"Wil-co."

Various replies are heard from the Walkers.

As everyone says their good-byes and heads off to prepare for the coming mission, I grab Sam by the arm. He turns and looks at me questioningly. For a moment, I struggle with what I want to say.

"Are you sure you want to take just the three of you?" I shudder as I remember the horror of last night's events.

Sam is in "boss mode" and looks every bit the commanding officer. "This will actually be safer than taking a large group. This is only a reconnaissance mission. The fewer Walkers the better. We can move faster and have a smaller chance of being spotted."

I understand what he's saying makes sense tactically, but it still means he's going out into Chaos at a very dangerous time. It does little to ease my fears.

He exhales and I can see some of the rigid formality drain from his bearing. He steps a little closer and softens his tone. "Don't be worried, Addy. We'll be okay."

I try to take comfort from his words. This is what he does for a living, after all.

"Yeah, of course," I say, nodding my head, more to convince myself than anyone else. He squeezes my arm reassuringly before he leaves.

Angel and I are the only ones left in the library. "Do we have a com we can keep handy while we work, just in case?" I ask her.

"I've got one right up here!" she says, pointing to her head.

She sees my confused expression.

"I can sense if any of the Walkers are in trouble."

"Whoa." This blows me away. "Wouldn't you have to be reading everyone's mind all the same time to know if they were in trouble?" I'm not sure how I'm going to be able to do these things that Angel can do. I've never been one for multi-tasking.

"No, it's not like that at all. I don't have to be actively reading someone's mind to pick up on their distress." She motions for me to sit next to her on one of the plushy sofas.

"Think of it like this. People are like radios. We broadcast ourselves—our personalities, our moods, our states of being. Our volume depends on what we broadcast. Most of the time, we're humming along, barely audible. But when someone's in a state of distress, that kind of excitement gets broadcast *very* loudly. I can't help but pick up on it."

I consider this. "Even from far away?"

"It depends on how familiar I am with the individual. But yes, I know all of the Realmwalkers'…" she makes quotes in the air, "'frequencies' by heart. I can access their moods at all times from anywhere on Earth or Chaos."

"Wow. That's actually really comforting," I say, feeling much better about the scouting mission tonight.

"You'll learn to do it too!" Angel says happily. "But first things first. Adelaide Shepherd, are you ready to begin your basic training as a fully-fledged Realmwalker?"

CHAPTER 19

"THERE ARE SOME standard essential abilities that everyone must learn to do right away," Angel instructs. "The first necessary ability is to be able to put yourself to sleep and wake yourself up in an instant. Okay?"

"Okay," I say, rubbing my hands together. I'm both nervous and excited to be learning my very first trick. "What do I do?" I ask eagerly.

"You might want to lie back on the couch. Get as comfortable as you can." She jumps up and sits in a chair across from me. I lie back on the sofa. The ceiling of the library is the same rich wood as the shelves lining the walls. My eyes go to the chandelier and again the peaceful beauty of this room amazes me. I take deep, relaxing breaths and once I'm comfortable, I close my eyes.

"Perfect," Angel says quietly. "Now I'm going to walk you through this a few times before I actually let you do it. I want to be sure you completely understand how it's done beforehand. That way you can bring yourself back to Chaos on your own."

"That makes sense."

I start to feel a soft, familiar presence in my mind. "Is that you?" I ask.

Yes.

"Wow," I whisper. I can feel Angel's amusement at my awe.

You don't need to speak anymore. Try thinking a direct thought at me.

"At your body? Or at the 'you' that's in my head?" I ask.

At my presence in your mind.

"Um, okay," I say uneasily. "Here goes." I try to direct my thoughts toward Angel's gentle voice.

HELLO?

Not so loud!

"Oh! Sorry!"

I open my eyes and see Angel wincing with her head between her hands.

"Try to be... softer. More subtle," she says through gritted teeth.

"I'm really sorry. Oh, I'm going to be bad at this aren't I?"

"No, Addy. You're actually very good. Too good—that's the problem. It took the others much longer to even grasp the concept of this, but you found me right away. The others had to put an immense amount of effort into it. For you, however, it comes so naturally that you need to concentrate on restraining yourself."

I try to see this as good news. I can do it. I can actually find Angel and talk to her with my mind. I only need to pull back a little.

"How can I be gentler when I don't even know how I'm doing it exactly?" I ask her.

"You have a strong imagination. Use it." She closes her eyes and I expect that's the only help I'm going to get from her.

Now let's try again, I hear her think to me.

I try to think of how to push my thoughts at her without screaming. She said to use my imagination. Okay… think, think.

Then I realize I already have the answer! Before, I thought about "pushing" my thoughts, and that's what I'd done. I'd shoved my thoughts toward her, and in doing so I overcompensated. But what if I slowed it down?

Angel? I think at her very slowly.

Ah. That's much better, Addy. It's a bit slow but once you get the hang of it, you should be able to gauge the proper speed and volume. Congratulations! I can feel the pride radiating off her mental presence.

Where are you now? I mean, in my mind? Can you hear what I'm thinking?

I'm at a level of your consciousness where I can hear only the thoughts you directly send to me. You'll eventually learn the different levels of the mind and how to access each of them. There's a proper etiquette to all of this. You can't go swimming around in people's deepest darkest secrets.

Oh! I wouldn't dream of it! I impulsively think at her, horrified at the thought of knowing someone's every thought.

Quietly, remember?

Sorry. This time I concentrate hard on restraining myself. *I'll do better. So, what now?*

Well, normally, and with any other Walker, I would show you how to sleep and wake by actually putting you to sleep and waking you up repeatedly until you learned how to do it yourself.

Normally?

Yes. But, since you're a Mimic, I would like to have you learn how to do this in the way that Mimics learn all of their abilities. By observation. She pauses a moment while I consider this.

So, I think slowly to her, **instead of doing it for me, I watch you do it and then try to copy you?**

Yes. Only, don't watch with your eyes. Watch with your mind.

Watch what with my mind? Your mind? How can I watch your mind when you're in my head?

You must project your consciousness out of yourself, the way I'm doing. You must push yourself into my mind.

Trying not to get too worked up, I think, **But I'm not ready for that. Even if I can figure out how it's done, I wouldn't know how deep and how shallow to stay. I could inadvertently read your most private thoughts! I don't want to do that!**

Trust me, Adelaide. My mind is very strong, and I've learned ways of building walls around things I wish to keep to myself. You couldn't break those walls even if you wanted to.

Are… are you sure it will be okay? I think at her hesitantly.

I'm certain. Now, to move your consciousness to mine is easier than it seems. Simply feel where I am in your mind. Try to get a sense of me. When you feel me start to move, follow me. I'll guide you into my own mind.

Whoa. This was all so incredible, so surreal. *Will it be difficult? Leaving my own mind?*

It shouldn't be too difficult for you. If you feel any resistance, give your thoughts a push. We both know your "pushes" are very strong, she teases.

Okay. I'm ready to try.

Follow me.

Slowly, I feel her shift in my mind. The light, feathery sensation I've begun to associate with her travels upward, lifting higher and higher. I concentrate all of my thoughts on following her. I follow her until I feel as though she's going to leave me completely. And then she's gone.

I hesitate, unsure of my next move.

I feel the barrier at the edge of my own mind, and beyond it, a great emptiness. I imagine myself standing on the very edge of a cliff. The chasm below is vast and unknown. I still feel a little of Angel's presence, in the air above me, just out of reach.

I feel as vulnerable as a baby bird, its mother beckoning it to leap from the comfort of its nest. What will happen out there? Once I push my consciousness out into the open, will I lose control? What if I can't find my way back? Will I literally lose my mind? I hear Angel's comforting voice from the chair next to me.

"Don't be afraid, Addy. I know you can do this." I nod in determination. I feel around the barrier in my mind. I find the place where I can sense Angel the strongest, just on the other side. And I push.

CHAPTER 20

I CAN SEE everything. I mean... *everything*. Everywhere, almost at once. I see myself lying on the sofa. Angel's resting with her eyes closed on the chair next to me. I can see every detail of the library. Given the time, I could count all of the books on the shelves. Across the room, a pretty book bound in deep blue catches my eye, and then it's as if I'm in front of it, able to read its title, *The American Civil War*.

I feel like a helium balloon bouncing around the room, instantly drawn to anything that piques my interest. The reason I don't completely panic is that I still feel an attachment to my mind, like I'm tethered to it by a thin thread.

I'm so distracted by this new freedom that it takes me a moment to remember what it is I'm supposed to be doing. I worry as I remember I'm supposed to be following Angel. I force myself to be calm. I remember how Angel's energy feels to me. I put out imaginary feelers and search for that soft, feathery presence. I'm shocked when this actually works and I find her!

I focus only on the feeling of her presence, blocking out

all of the conflicting visual input from the library. By doing this, I'm able to sense her start to move again. I put all of my trust in this ability as I begin to follow her blindly.

I follow. I feel another slight boundary but this time I don't even hesitate. I push straight through.

Once through, I'm contained again, and the comfort of it is a relief. Even though I realize I'm not in my own mind, my instincts tell me I'm in a safe place. The feeling of Angel's mind is much like her personality: happy, bright, warm, and loving. It's a comfortable place to be, like the feeling I get when I'm visiting Gram's house.

You did great, Addy!

I sense her voice and realize she's a bit higher than I am. I must be deeper down into her consciousness than she would prefer. Briefly, before rising up to find her, I can't stop myself from wondering about her wall that she mentioned. And with that thought—that tiny little thought about her wall—I slam into it. Like before with that blue book in the library. I need to learn to control my impulses better.

Being here, against this wall in her mind, curiosity gets the better of me. I reach out tentatively and can definitely feel I'm being blocked from going any further. I feel the strength and enormity of the wall. I'm aware of every aspect of it. In fact, just being here, "viewing" it, I'm pretty sure I know how it was made and put up. I know that if I ever needed to, I could do the same thing in my own mind.

In fact, I could do it better. I could make it stronger because I can see the weaknesses in this one. I'm also certain that, despite what Angel believes, I could get through this wall if I pushed hard enough. Not that I ever would of course. I respect Angel too much to violate her privacy that way. Still... I wonder what kind of secret such a sweet young girl would feel she has to hide.

Never mind. It doesn't matter. It's none of my business. As quickly as I can, I rush up toward where I know Angel is.

There you are. See! You're a natural. I feel a little guilty

as I realize she thinks I got lost on my way to her. Out of embarrassment and shame, I decide not to tell her about my detour, and I'm grateful she can't read my thoughts unless I let her.

Thanks, Angel. You're a great teacher.

Now, she thinks at me, *I'm going to put myself to sleep and then wake myself back up again. Try to be aware of what my mind is doing during this process. If you can see how it's done, you can make your own mind do the same thing.*

Okay. I'll watch as you do it. I try to expand my consciousness to cover her entire mind. I don't delve deeply; rather I float atop the surface looking down. I keep my feelers out, ready to sense any changes from her current state of mind.

Briefly, I wonder in amazement how I already know what to do. It's like being handed the keys to a car for the first time ever, and somehow, without ever being taught, I already know how to drive.

I begin to notice activity in Angel's mind, and I focus on it. I see exactly what she's doing and how she's doing it. She's creating in her mind all the feelings that come with sleep: exhaustion, warmth, comfort, rest. Only, instead of letting it occur naturally, she's manually triggering it. Like flipping a mental switch. The effect is instantaneous. Her mind goes quiet and I can tell her body is asleep now.

Before she awakens, I have a moment to consider whether I'll be able to do this with my own mind, and I know that I can. This sense of self-assuredness is new to me. Never have I felt so confident in myself or my abilities. It's refreshing and exciting.

I begin to sense more activity. This time it's muffled, almost like a conversation you hear through a door. I realize I'm sensing what she's doing to her mind over on Earthside. The process is identical. She's putting her mind to sleep over there. As she does this, she immediately wakes up here in Chaos.

Were you able to understand what I did just now?

I answer her excitedly, but manage to do so without shouting. ***Yes! This is so amazing. I know what you did and I'm sure I can do it too. I never thought this would be so easy!***

It isn't easy for others. You have your ability to thank for that. Even so, I'm surprised at your rate of learning. I knew you'd be a fast learner but not THIS fast. At this rate, you could finish your training in a week. Way to go! Are you sure you don't need me to repeat the process a few more times? I don't mind.

Sure. Once more would probably help. This time, I try to anticipate the steps she'll go through. I run through it all seconds before she does and find that I'm spot-on the whole way through. In fact, I play with the idea of whether or not I could induce sleep in not only myself but in others.

After she awakens the second time, I'm eager to return

and try it myself. I find the return journey is the simplest part of all. It feels as easy as retracting an outstretched arm.

Once I'm back, I open my eyes and sit up. "Is it okay for me to try now?" I ask the perfect little girl sitting across from me.

Her face brightens and she smiles at my enthusiasm. "If you feel like you're ready, then go ahead! If you succeed in waking up top-side but find you can't get back, I'll help you."

As I lie back down, I feel her in my mind again. This time I can tell she's hovering at the highest levels of my mind so that she can observe. I close my eyes and, keen to prove myself, I immediately find the areas in my mind I need to activate. Without hesitation, I repeat the process of inducing sleep I witnessed in Angel's mind. I fleetingly notice how my body begins to feel heavy as I slip into a deep sleep.

A sleep I don't get to enjoy as I instantly open my eyes to my darkened bedroom. I did it! I actually did something with my mind. Something that normal people can't do. While I realize it's nothing spectacular, it's at least a start. I glance over and see Ember sleeping soundly. I notice her eyes are moving back and forth underneath her eyelids, and I wonder what she is seeing right now.

I decide to put myself back to sleep before Angel can start to worry that I'm stuck here. I find the second time through to be even easier, and when I awaken, Angel's clapping ecstatically and bouncing in her seat.

"Bravo, Addy. Bravo! What a perfect Mimic you make."

Again, I notice how her eyes get a little misty at the mention of my ability.

"Thanks Angel." I say, genuinely grateful for her help and encouragement. "You made that so easy. I guess it's helpful to learn these things from someone who thinks like me."

"I'll teach you everything I can that the others can't teach you. And if you don't mind, I'd really like to make it a crash course. Things are going to be so hectic these next few weeks, and the faster we get you out into Chaos the better."

"Wow. Okay, sure. Whatever you think is best."

Angel looks pensive as she explains, "But you need to know, Addy, no one's expecting you to take on this Greater Shade all on your own. I really hope you don't carry the weight of that around with you. We're a family and a team here and we all work together, okay?" She looks at me with concern.

"Okay. Thanks, Harmony," I say with relief.

"Anyway, to be honest with you," she sighs in a way that I've only seen adults do, "the Greater Shade is not behind my reasoning for wanting you to learn quickly." A strange thing happens as I look at her. Suddenly she doesn't look nine years old to me. It's as if all the weariness, worry, and fatigue you would expect to see on an elderly war veteran is etched into her tender young face.

"What is it, Angel?" Her eyes tear up and I realize she's done a lot of crying tonight. "Why are you so upset?"

Her hands flutter to her eyes to wipe away tears before they can fall. She laughs and says, "Oh, I'm not upset at all! I'm sorry I'm so emotional. It's just…" she looks me in the eyes, "you can't realize what a relief this is for me! I've been so worried for so long now. I kept thinking, what if something happens to me? What if I get killed out there one night, or if Chaos decides it's done with me and releases me? What will happen to the Walkers? Who will do the things that only I know how to do? It's a lot of pressure and it's been a constant sense of trepidation for me."

"But Angel, nothing's going to happen to you. I'm sure you'll be around for a long time. Ember says you're one tough cookie and I believe her."

Angel smiles and nods her head. "I know. Trust me—I don't plan on being Shade food. But all the same, you know, accidents happen." She says this as she fidgets with some frill on her dress. "I'm very comforted to have you here, Addy. I'm eager to train you as quickly as I can to permanently relieve my worry. Can you understand that?"

"Of course I can. I'll do everything possible to learn quickly." This seems to cheer her up. She bounds off her chair and grabs my hand and pulls me after her out of the library.

"Wonderful! Let's get started with an official tour!"

CHAPTER 21

"OUR FIRST STOP should be Logistics. There's a map on the wall there that will help you with memorizing the place." I follow Angel through the halls of Major Calm. As we go, we pass rooms and halls, some I'm familiar with already and others that are new to me. We stop once we reach a room located in between the briefing room we met in last night and the hallway that leads to the garage.

Inside, the room appears to be a large office-like space filled with computers, desks, and planning boards and charts along the walls. An image of the world map, along with corresponding digital clocks atop each time zone, takes up an entire wall. About a dozen little flag pins protrude from the map at different locations. On the North American continent there are five flags: two in California, one in Nebraska, one in New York, and one in Arizona.

"That's me then?" I ask Angel as I point to the one in central Arizona.

"It is. At least until you move. Do you plan on moving to a base?" she asks me.

"I hope to move with Ember to the L.A. base, but it all depends on whether I can convince my mom or not," I say, crossing my fingers.

"I'm sure you'd have a good time there, Addy. Well," she says, indicating the room, "this room has a few purposes. Sam can usually be found in here assessing data, reviewing past missions, and planning new ones. Over here," she points toward a wall with an expansive floor plan, "is Major Calm. I'll give you a few minutes to really study this map. You'll come to find that here in Chaos our minds have a remarkable knack for memory. You should be able to recall this map perfectly after we leave here."

Excited to really put this to the test, I go over the map extensively. Each room is labeled, so it's easy to get an idea of what Major Calm is really like. I notice that most of the rooms are grouped off into separate wings. The wing on the west side of the map is labeled "Training Wing." That's where we are now, and north of this room is the briefing room from the night before. The other rooms in this area are massive and have various titles like, "Gym," "Pool," "Target Practice," "Obstacle Course A," "Obstacle Course B," and "Practice Rooms A, B, and C."

The north wing is the Living Quarters area, complete with sixteen bedrooms, the library, and the music room.

The east wing is labeled "Laboratories." Here I see rooms called "Weapons Lab," "Infirmary," and "Science and Tech." The largest room of all is located in the southeast corner of the map and it's titled "Storage." Attached to this room is a smaller room labeled "Armory." In the southwest corner are the garage and a side room attached to it labeled "Garage Shop." Connecting all the rooms are hallways that lead to a large central area simply labeled "Living Rooms."

Once I'm pretty certain I've got it all down in my head, I turn to Angel. "Okay, I think I've got it."

"Let's go see the real thing," she says as she leads the way out the door. As I follow her around Major Calm, she plays tour guide and describes what we're seeing and what each room is used for. We find Kira in a practice room beating a padded target into submission. I watch her in awe as she flips and darts around the target with skill and ease.

In the Science and Tech Lab, Ben is stooped over an expensive-looking microscope. He looks up and waves at us as we enter. His safety goggles hang around his neck, but they've left deep impressions around his eyes and his raccoon-like appearance makes me laugh.

When we get to the living quarters, Angel stops a moment to talk. "One of the first things you should learn is how to create and manipulate the space here in the Calms. In a day or two when things have settled down, I'll create a bedroom for you more attuned to you and your tastes. You can watch my mind as I do this so that later you can do it yourself."

"Okay," I say doubtfully. "But is it really hard? It seems like it would be."

"It's not too difficult. You're a fast learner so I'm confident you'll do fine." Angel's confidence in me is reassuring. Knowing she will be here for me, to walk me through everything, is comforting. I can't screw up too bad with her helping me, right?

As we're walking, I notice an odd-looking door. It's the only door I've seen that appears to be made of metal. There's a large latch on the outside and big heavy bolts around the edges.

"What's that room?" I ask.

"Oh, I always forget about that room. Thankfully, we never use it." We walk over to it, and she lifts the latch and heaves open the heavy door. Inside is a small, square room. The walls are cement and there's a metal bed attached to one of them. There's also a metal desk and chair in one corner; both are bolted to the floor and immovable.

"Wow. This kinda looks like a jail cell," I say jokingly.

"It should. It is," Angel replies lightheartedly.

I look at her, stunned. "Seriously? A jail cell?"

"This is Inner Silence. A place even the strongest Walker couldn't break out of. The walls, ceiling, floor, and door are all sealed with special wardings that can be removed only with three Walkers simultaneously working together."

"Why would we need a jail for Walkers?"

"Well, hopefully we never will. This room's been here for as long anyone can remember. Thankfully, it hasn't been used in nearly a hundred years. In the Walker Chronicles—a detailed account of our history you can find in the library—there's a log for Inner Silence. The last Walker to be logged in was back in the nineteen twenties. A man named Wesley Fischer."

"Whoa. What did he do?" I ask.

"The log doesn't say. Only that he was held in Inner Silence for a period of two weeks then released."

"Crazy." I can't imagine one of us turning on our own. The thought seems weird and unnatural.

Angel closes the door and leads me down the hallway to finish our tour. I'm completely blown away at the enormity of Major Calm's storage room. It makes Minor Calm's storage look like a tool shed.

"I can't wrap my head around how you manage to have all of this stuff! I mean, you didn't make it all here in Chaos, did you?"

"It seems mind-boggling at first, but it's actually very easily explained. Because we're safe from Shades here in the Calms, we create our *own* tears to Earth realm here within the warehouse. Top-side, we protect the tear sites with wards, the same way we do down here, so no Shades can pass through. Then we ship whatever we need here in the Calms to the protected tear sites top-side and send them through."

"Whoa," I say as I contemplate the idea.

"And before you wonder about it, no, we cannot physically pass through the tear ourselves. Nor can we send through any living thing. For some reason, the laws of Chaos won't allow us to breach the tear," she explains.

"So Shades can pass through tears, but we can't?" I ask to clarify.

"As far as we know. Must be something in the way that we're different," she muses thoughtfully.

When we finish our tour, we head back to the central

living area. We sit on a pair of beanbags facing each other in a quiet alcove. She looks lost in thought for a moment. I watch her and wonder if she's checking up on Sam and the others out in Chaos. I hope they're all right. And then I wonder, *Do I know Sam well enough to sense if he's in danger?* I'd like to think so, but I've really only known him a few days.

"Addy," Angel brings me out of my musings. She hesitates, wearing a worried expression as she tugs a strand of hair. "I need to ask you to do something for me, and I'm afraid you aren't going to like it at all."

CHAPTER 22

OF COURSE I want to help Angel. Her reluctance to ask me to do what she needs, however, makes me pause.

"What do you need, Angel? I'll help you however I can," I assure her.

"Well, it's Simone," she says quietly. And now I understand why she seemed so hesitant. Already a knot of dread is building in the pit of my stomach.

"Okay, what can I do?"

"Well, I've been working with her for quite some time now. I've been trying to find some other ability she may have—one that could help us fight the Shades."

Even though Simone is a stuck-up brat, I feel sorry for her that her only ability is something completely useless here. It's got to be hard being surrounded by Walkers with amazing abilities. Maybe if I were in her place, I'd be bitter too.

"Okay, so what do you need *me* to do?" I ask wondering what I could possibly do that Angel couldn't.

"I need you to take over for me."

"What?!" I ask startled.

"I've done everything I can to help her, but to no avail. I don't have the heart to tell her I've exhausted my efforts. This means so much to her. I know she may seem harsh," she says apologetically, "but she really is a Walker at heart. All she wants to do is help, but I simply have hit a brick wall with her. Maybe bringing some fresh eyes to the situation will help."

It takes me a minute to process what she's asking me to do. "So, you want me to... what? Evaluate her? The way you do all the Walkers?"

She nods. "Yes. You really *should* start with a full assessment. And after that, if you haven't found anything promising, keep working with her. Follow your gut. Try to get to know her and how her mind works."

I think knowing how her minds works is one of the *last* things I want.

"I don't know, Angel. She really doesn't seem to like me, and that's putting it lightly. I doubt she'll even agree to let me try."

"Oh, she'll agree," Angel says very sternly. The command in her little voice is hard to ignore. "I've put in a lot of hours with her and she owes me. Plus, she trusts my judgment, and when I tell her this is her best chance, she'll listen."

I resist a sigh of defeat. It looks as if I'm going to be spending a lot of time with my least favorite person.

"Will you teach me how to evaluate? I haven't the foggiest idea how to begin."

She smiles gratefully at me. "I knew I could count on you! Of course I'll explain."

"There you are!" Ember runs up to us. She's wearing an earpiece and she looks relieved to have found us. "The guys are back! They want us all together for the debriefing."

Ember grabs my hand and pulls me up, and the three of us head to the briefing room. I know Sam, Lang, and Timothy must all be safe, but I'm still anxious to see them with my own eyes to be sure.

When we get to the briefing room, everyone's standing around talking in hushed, excited voices. I scan the group, ignoring all other faces until I find the one I'm looking for. When I see Sam, our eyes meet. Relief washes over me. He holds my gaze for a moment then clears his throat.

"All right, everyone's here. Have a seat please, guys, and we'll get started." We all shuffle to nearby chairs, anxious to find out what's going on out in Chaos.

Ember and I sit at the table closest to the front of the room where Sam's standing, leaning back against the podium. I look at him closely for any signs of injuries. He seems to be unscathed.

"Well, I know you're all on pins and needles," Sam says in his quiet way, "waiting to hear about our exciting trip, but I'm afraid I'm going to have to disappoint you." I hear a few confused murmurs around the room.

"Timothy, Lang, and I had a fairly routine trip out into Chaos. No ambush, no Greater Shades, nothing out of the ordinary at all." He reaches up and rubs the back of his neck. "We even did a little hunting while we were out."

I look at Ember, confused, only to find her giving me the same expression.

Kira speaks up from the back of the room. "What's that about?"

"I'm not sure. I have a couple of ideas but none of them could be right. The truth is we don't know enough about this Greater Shade, how he thinks or what he wants."

"He probably wants what they all want," says Doc. "To get top-side."

Sam nods in agreement. "I'm sure that's his ultimate goal. But I think there's more to it. Why get creative with it? Why change up the usual methods? Why does it seem like he's targeting Adelaide?"

"Too many questions, not enough answers," Crank says glumly. "So what do we do about it, Boss?"

"Keep doing our job, Crank," he answers. "Try and be as prepared as we can. Always leave here expecting the worst. Keep finding tears and sealing them. That's the most important thing we can do. Find weak spots in the fabric of Chaos and strengthen them. We must, at all costs, prevent this Greater Shade from getting to Earth Realm. That's all we can do for now."

The room is silent for a few moments.

"We could approach this scientifically." Ember and I turn toward where Ben is sitting with Mel.

"How so, Ben?" Angel asks.

"Well, in science, when there are a number of unknown variables, you perform certain tests or experiments to get you closer to the truth."

"Okay," Sam says. "What do you suggest?"

"Well, for starters, we know that the ambush occurred once Adelaide entered Chaos. Today you went into Chaos without Adelaide and there was no ambush. This seems to suggest to me that Adelaide might very well be the catalyst. To find this out, we simply take Adelaide back out into Chaos and gauge the reaction of the Shades."

"Absolutely not," Sam says abruptly before I even get a chance to consider what was said.

"Well now, wait a minute," Lang-hao puts up a hand to hold off Sam's objections. "Ben has a point, Sam."

"I'm not going to allow that," Sam says adamantly. "She just got here. She's in no way prepared to go back into Chaos." His expression alone should be enough to kill the topic then and there, but this is me they're talking about. Don't I get an opinion?

"I want to do it," I say. Despite the death look I'm getting from Sam, I continue. "I'm not saying I want to go out there right *now*. I know I'm not ready yet. Going out there now, I'd only be more of a problem than any kind of help," I explain. "But soon."

"You will finish all of your training before you go back out there. Complete training is required from every Walker before they are allowed to fight, and I won't make any exceptions," Sam replies.

I open my mouth to argue some more when I hear Angel in my mind.

Let it go, Addy. I agree with you, but let it go for now, and I'll speak with Sam later.

Unaware of Angel's thoughts in my head, Sam takes my slight hesitation as acceptance and continues.

"All right, everyone, I think we're done here. Let's resume our normal schedule of hunting and sealing." Sam makes eye contact with each of us as he speaks. "I don't want any teams with fewer than three Walkers at a time. Remember to be extra careful out there and keep your guard up always."

Walkers nod their heads in acknowledgement. A few "Yes sirs" are heard here and there.

"Happy hunting." This must be some cue that the meeting's over because everyone is either getting up to leave or turning to talk with others around them. I try to see if Sam still looks upset, but I catch only a glimpse of his back as he leaves the room.

"Well, that was interesting," Ember says with raised eyebrows.

Before I can reply, Angel's standing next to our table with an annoyed-looking Simone behind her.

"Addy, do you have minute?" Angel asks politely.

Ember takes the hint. "I'll see you top-side, Addy," she says as she gets up to leave.

"Bye." I watch her leaving, silently longing to be leaving with her.

Angel pulls herself up onto the table and sits cross-legged, the way she was the first time I saw her. She motions for Simone to take Ember's empty seat next to me. Instead, Simone folds her arms and stares at the front wall.

"Please sit, Simone." I notice a slight edge in Angel's

voice. Surprisingly, Simone sighs dramatically and plops down on the seat next to me.

"Addy, I've briefly spoken with Simone about you working with her. I've explained to her the importance of her cooperation, and she has agreed to give you *full* access to her mind in hopes of discovering her additional skills and abilities."

I glance at Simone, who's still staring straight forward, refusing to acknowledge me. This is the nearest we've been to each other, and it's annoying to find that despite her haughty expression, she's still the most beautiful woman I've ever seen.

Angel continues, "I suggest the two of you set aside one hour each night to work together, starting tomorrow. Find a time that works best for both of you. And please," she leans forward and places a tiny hand on each of us, quietly adding, "be patient with one another." She stares meaningfully into our eyes to emphasize her words. "Be kind. Understand that each of you only wants what's best for Chaos."

Simone's hardness seems to melt away at Angel's earnest sincerity. Her shoulders slump in defeat. This earns a big grin from Angel.

"Thank you," she says to both of us. As this responsibility passes from her to me, I can see more weight lift off her shoulders. "I'm due to wake up top-side very soon, so I'll say good-bye. Addy, you have a busy day tomorrow. Come prepared to learn." She smiles and winks before she slides down off the table and practically skips out of the room.

Next to me, Simone sighs again—though less

dramatically than before—and looks at me expectantly. The dread creeps back into my stomach.

"So," I start hesitantly, "I guess we should pick a time."

"I'm usually awake by seven in the morning, but to be safe, let's meet for one hour at five a.m. You'll come to my room," she says quickly. Before I can comment, she adds, "Now that's New York time, so you'll have to do the math." With that, she stands up and marches out, leaving me alone in the room.

"Fantastic," I say to the deserted room.

CHAPTER 23

WHEN I WAKE up in my bed, Ember's already dressed for the day.

"Good morning!" she says in a sing-song voice as she shoves clothes into her suitcase. I sit up and rub my eyes. I can't help but make a sour face as I watch her pack. Seeing me, she laughs.

"Don't worry, Addy! I'll be back in a week, remember?"

"I know," I grumble. "It's just, I have a feeling this next week in Chaos is going to be insane. I'm gonna miss having someone *here* who understands what I'll be going through."

Ember sits down next to me. "You can call me anytime you need to, okay?" She squeezes my hand.

"Thanks."

I get ready for the day while Ember finishes packing. Once we're done, Ember grabs her suitcase and heads out. I intend to follow her, but before I can leave, something catches my eye. I turn and look at my bedside table. Something seems different about it, and then I see it—next to my suspense novel is another book. I pick it up and examine it closely.

Star of the Black Sea. Goosebumps rise on my arms. On the cover is the same picture of a ship at sea that was on the book Mikhail was reading in the library last night. I sit on my bed as I examine the book. It looks brand new, and as I thumb through the pages, I see it's printed in English.

"How did YOU get here?" I murmur. I snap my head up and quickly glance around my room, half-expecting to find Mikhail himself, but it's just me. Still, there's only one way for this book to have gotten here.

I'm lost between being touched by Mikhail's thoughtfulness and feeling uneasy at the implications of what it means to find this book in my room.

He had been here. In my room. Sometime last night. He must have found my address in the logs in the Major Calm computers and got here somehow—most likely by Shadow Travel. How long did he stay here last night while I was busy in Chaos? I try and push the troubled feelings down and focus on the kindness of the act. It's the thought that counts, right? And I did promise myself to give him the benefit of the doubt.

"Is everything all right?" Ember startles me so badly I nearly drop the book. Her expression turns from concern to amusement at my reaction.

"Gosh, Ember!" I laugh with relief. "Don't sneak up on me like that!"

"I didn't. You were so enveloped." She glances at the

book in my hands. "Really, are you okay? I thought you were right behind me."

I set the book back down on my nightstand. "Yeah, it's nothing. Sorry." I get up and follow her out. I decide not to mention Mikhail to Ember. She'd probably make a big deal about it and turn Mikhail's intentions into something nefarious.

I'm surprised to find Sam already awake and in the kitchen. I'd been a little apprehensive about seeing him this morning after the tension in the briefing room last night. I was worried that arguing with him about me going out into Chaos again might have upset him.

Instead of finding the surly, distant Sam I was dreading, I find him wearing a very floral apron and stirring a big bowl of what I assume to be pancake batter. The sight of him in the feminine frock makes me giggle.

Looking up at me, he shows off the apron and says, "You like?"

"Very fetching," I assure him.

Mom is tending to bacon and sausage on the griddle, and Jana's sitting on a bar stool admiring Sam.

"What can I do to help?" Ember asks politely.

"Nothing, sweetie. It's our turn today," Mom says. "But Sam was telling us about last night! Did you really crowd surf?"

We laugh as we relate our concert experience from the night before. Breakfast is over too soon and before I know it, we're loading luggage into Sam's truck bed.

Sam plans to drop Ember off at the airport in Phoenix

for her noon flight on his way out to California. We all gather on the front lawn when it comes time to say good-bye. Mom hugs the two of them and kisses them on their cheeks.

"Please come back any time. You both are so welcome here," she tells them. Jana gives hugs and says her good-byes. I'm grateful to Mom when she meaningfully tugs on Jana's sleeve and motions her back in the house, leaving the three of us alone.

Ember immediately throws herself at me and hugs me with a fierceness that threatens to re-crack some of my newly healed ribs.

I hug her back and tell her, "Have a happy gradu-ation, Ember! And I'll cross my fingers that next week comes quickly."

She leans back and gives me a serious look. "Your mis-sion this week? Convince your mother to let me steal you away to California. I can't be the only girl at L.A. base," she says dramatically.

"Wil-co," I say as I salute her. She gives me an approv-ing slap on the shoulder and bounces over to hop into the passenger seat of the truck.

I realize it's only Sam and I, and suddenly I'm nervous. Unsure what to say, I kick at the grass and wait for him to speak.

He clears his throat awkwardly. "Well, I probably won't see much of you in the coming weeks, what with you train-ing and all. I'm sure Angel will keep you busy as much as she can, and I'll be running missions non-stop." I look up at him. His hands are crammed in his pockets and his stance is rigid.

Seeing him look so uncomfortable right now is comical to me. Could he be as nervous as me? I chuckle to myself and he must understand the humor because he grins too. It breaks the spell of tension long enough for me to get up the nerve to hug him.

He wraps his arms around my shoulders and pulls me in close. Closer than I'd been expecting. For a brief moment I'm frozen, taken aback with sensory overload. He smells so good, it's overwhelming. He feels softer than his physique hints at. I'm so comfortable here in his arms that I melt into him even more. I can even feel his heart beating in his chest. I don't ever want this to end.

"I'm proud of you, Addy. The way you've handled yourself. You're very strong, and you have a good heart," he says quietly in my ear. "Your father would be proud of you."

My throat tightens up at the mention of Dad. "Thank you, Sam." I want to say more, but I'm not sure what or how. My heart drops as he pulls away. I find I'm a bit dizzy from the encounter. Embarrassed, I steady myself and try not to let my face show how sad I am that he's leaving.

"Well, drive safe, all right?" I say to him.

He nods. "Sure. Thanks. I'll see you later, Addy."

I stare one last time into his eyes, trying to memorize the way they look. "Bye, Sam." I force a smile and wave.

He waves and gets in the driver side. Ember's grinning at me like a fool. I'm pretty sure she's wiggling her eyebrows at me, but I can't be sure from this distance. I shake my head at her and laugh.

They wave once more as they drive past the house and down the street. I'm not sure how long I stand there after they're out of sight. Eventually though, the sound of the front door opening brings me back to the present.

Mom leans out of the house. "Come on you. Wishing won't bring them back." She gives me a knowing smile.

I sigh dramatically and walk slowly back into the house.

CHAPTER 24

I SPEND THE rest of my Sunday trying to relax. Jana and I catch up on the rented chick flicks we never watched from Friday night. On the way to return the movies we have a good, long-overdue sister-to-sister talk, and when we get home, we're both happy to find dinner waiting for us.

All through dinner I wrestle with ways to mention UCLA to Mom. I struggle to find a way to tell her I want to move to California and go to the same college as someone I just met without sounding too impulsive. This will be tricky, but by the end of our meal, I think I've got my best arguments sorted out.

"So, Mom," I say as nonchalantly as I can.

"Mm-hm?"

"I was talking with Ember and I found out that she leaves for UCLA next Saturday."

"Wow, that's really soon. Does she have housing already?" she asks with motherly interest.

"Yeah, she does actually. Anyway, she's driving by herself

all the way from Omaha, and I was wondering if we could invite her to stop here along her way and visit for a bit."

Mom claps her hands together happily. "You know I love her. She can stay here for as long as she wants."

"Great, Mom. Thanks." I smile, tallying an imaginary mark for me on my mental chalkboard.

"I'll probably ask her to stay for my graduation then if that's all right."

"Sure, sounds fun, Addy."

"Okay, I'll call her and ask her after I clean up dinner." I figure doing the cleanup and dishes will help keep me in her good graces.

Instead of calling Ember (since I already know what her answer will be), I lie on my bed and rest for a moment. As I lie there, I'm curious about something. Ember had said that the abilities we use in Chaos we can use here, but it was more difficult. I wonder how difficult it would be to do what I learned last night.

Tentatively, I send my consciousness up to the barrier around my mind. Less afraid than last night, I push through. I expect this to be much more difficult here in Earth Realm, so I'm surprised when I'm met with virtually no resistance. I'm outside myself now, looking down on my resting body. I travel with ease around my room, bewildered with how natural it feels.

Now that I don't have an immediate goal, like following Angel into her own mind, I take the time to hone my ability. I try very hard to subdue my impulses. Instead of zipping around my room on the slightest whim, I try to focus all of my thoughts on making precise and deliberate observations.

At first I find it very difficult. I try to focus on the book Mikhail left me, and my conscience is thrown at it. I try to return to the ceiling where I was before, and I'm there again in a flash. This quick traveling is dizzying and I hate it. I try harder. I slow my thought process down. Concentrating hard, I move slowly through the air back to where the book lies on my nightstand.

It's a grueling task—like exercising a muscle you never knew you had before. I accomplish the feat, and though I'm thrilled I managed it, I'm left mentally exhausted. I retreat back into my own mind to rest but make a promise to myself to practice more later.

I figure it's been long enough for me to have made a phone call to Ember, so I head out of my room. I find my mom reading a book in bed.

"Hey! What did Ember think?"

I climb into bed next to her. "She's way excited! In fact, as we were talking, we both kind of had an idea. A great idea actually, but I told her I had to ask you first."

"Okay," she puts her book down and gives me her full attention. "What is this great idea?"

"Well, you know how I go to Glendale every summer to see Gram?"

"Sure."

"Well, what if I moved my visit up a bit?"

She furrows her brow in thought. "To when?"

"Well, why not after graduation? I can drive over with Ember. That way she isn't alone for the rest of her trip."

"Hmmm," is all she says. I can see her running through the risks and benefits in her head.

"That way, I can help Ember get settled into her new place. And also, I can bring her by to meet Gram."

"Well, I have to call Gram and make sure it's all right with her."

"So that's a yes?" I ask trying not to sound too excited.

"Sure, honey. Sounds like a fun trip. You can call it your senior trip if you like."

"Thank you!" I squeal as I hug her. I know this isn't the same as getting permission to move to California and go to college there, but I have a feeling that the key to winning that discussion is going to be patience. *One battle at a time,* I think as I mentally tally another point for me.

Tired and anxious to get to Chaos for more training, I say good night to Mom and head to bed. As I climb under the covers, my attention again falls to the new book on my nightstand. I feel somewhat guilty for having questioned Mikhail's actions. This book is a gift, given out of kindness. I'm filled with gratitude as I picture the shy and awkward young man and think what a big step out of his comfort zone it must have been for him to reach out to another.

With this happy thought on my mind, I lie back, take a deep breath, and fall asleep.

CHAPTER 25

THE FIRST PART of my night in Chaos flies by. I find Angel in the living area and she quickly drags me to the library.

"Okay, Addy. Normally, we would spend an entire week on Chaos history alone." She indicates a very large leather-bound book displayed on the main desk in the center of the library. It appears ancient and fragile.

"This is the *Realmwalker Chronicles*. It gives an account of our history as far back as the year thirteen forty-eight. It's an interesting read but very time-consuming, and there is little to be learned that can actually be used to save your life out there in Chaos."

She motions me toward a sofa as she says, "So for you, we are going to skip it all together."

"Wow. Okay," I say a little shocked.

"You can always come back to it after everything else. It's something that you can do on your own time. And our priorities have changed since you've gotten here."

"All right," I say, sitting on the sofa we used the night before. "So where do we begin?"

"It comes down to what's most important right now." She lowers her eyebrows in a frustrated expression. "I'm torn between whether I should focus on teaching you all the responsibilities that come with being the only other Walker who can perform my duties and getting you physically prepared to defend yourself out in Chaos."

"What's more important?" I ask, trying to help.

"I believe they're equally important. So perhaps we'll split your time each night. Half of the time, you train with me. The other half you'll dedicate to learning first your basic self-defense, then you'll make rotations. You'll spend time with each Realmwalker, studying them and learning their abilities."

I interrupt her. "Wait—I have a question about that."

"Go ahead," she says patiently.

"I'm not really sure I'm comfortable with taking others' abilities from them."

"Taking?" She looks perplexed. "You won't be stealing them, Addy. You'll be learning them in order to make yourself into a better warrior."

"I know, but..." I try to put my hesitancy into words, "everyone here is so unique. In a way, their abilities are their identities. It feels strange to take that away from them."

"I understand what you mean, Addy." She nods. "But you have to think about it this way: What if, heaven forbid, Faye and I are both killed on a mission?"

I cringe at the thought.

"In the same mission, another Walker is critically wounded, and the injuries are too severe for Mel's limited healing abilities." She lets her words hang in the air as I contemplate their meaning.

"Then that Realmwalker would die," I say morosely. "And we would be left without a healer."

"Do you see the importance of learning others' abilities now?" she asks gently.

"Yes," I say. "I get it. But I still feel off about it. It seems like such an invasion of privacy."

"I promise you, Addy, no Walker would ever choose to withhold their ability out of pride or selfishness. They all understand the necessity of sharing their talents. The protection of Earth Realm comes before everything else. You'll see," she promises.

I nod to show her I'll comply, but I decide then and there to never take anything from someone without their complete willingness.

With a game plan decided, we move on to training. The first thing Angel teaches me is how she evaluates others for potential abilities. We start with this because I'll be needing it during my session with Simone today.

We work together, going through the process again and again, practicing on each other. It's not a difficult concept. It involves hovering at the top of someone's mind and spreading out to encompass it entirely. Then you extend "feelers" down into every part of the individual's mind, searching around for the overdeveloped areas which signify their strengths. She teaches me how to recognize these areas and how to interpret them into practical uses to be developed into abilities.

It's all incredibly fascinating and I'm enjoying myself so much that before I know it, an angry Simone stomps into the library where she stands, glaring at me accusingly.

"Oh shoot," I say as I look down at my wrist. "I'm sorry, Simone. I got carried away."

She opens her mouth to say something but Angel cuts her off.

"I'm sure Simone understands, Addy. It's your first day of training after all. Have a good session, you two."

I'm grateful to Angel for intervening. Simone spins around and heads out of the library. I guess that's my cue to follow.

"Bye Angel. Thanks." I shout as I rush out to follow Simone before I lose her. I hear Angel giggle as I run out of the library. At least someone is amused about this.

I catch up to Simone and follow her through Major Calm to the living quarters. She takes the farthest left hall of the three, and I make a mental note to avoid this hall in the future.

She stops at a large black door I can only assume is her room and turns to face me before going in.

"This is my room," she says in a matter-of-fact tone. "No one else has ever been in here except Sam. You should consider yourself lucky."

Uhhhh, am I supposed to be impressed? I almost say aloud. Instead, I bite the bullet and take her crap. Arguing with Simone would only cause tension among our ranks, and that won't help anyone at this stressful time. I'm determined to remain civil. *For the greater good*, I tell myself.

The inside of her room is not at all what I expected. I'm completely floored at the enormity of the living space. Her "room" is more like an entire apartment. The floor plan is open and spread out and includes a large sitting area, a sleeping area, and an entertainment nook complete with a television, stereo, and computer. I also see a door that leads to what looks like a large walk-in closet.

Everything is ultra-modern and posh. The décor is mostly black and white with a few accents of color here and there. All the furniture is high-end and has the tell-tale, clean, sharp edges of modern design. I'm sure it's considered to be luxurious to some, but the place feels like a museum to me. Or maybe a morgue. I can't ever imagine being comfortable here.

Simone sits on her bed and folds her arms. She looks as if she's already made up her mind about me and my ability to help her.

I'm not about to sit on the same bed as her so I look around for something to sit on. There's an odd-looking metal thing that is either a very questionable work of art or a chair. I decide to give it a try.

"Close the door," Simone orders before I can even move. I clench my jaw and do as I'm told. I move the bizarre metal object closer to her bed and sit on it so that I'm facing her. She doesn't object, so I figure I haven't offended her by placing my rear end on a priceless art piece.

I watch her as she stares at the wall across from her bed.

I still can't believe this woman is the famous Sylvia Redding *and* Shay Rendle. I'm curious if she's this much of a diva in her everyday life. I'm pretty certain I know the answer to that.

"So how do you want to do this?" I ask, not wanting to put off the inevitable any longer.

"Do what?" She finally looks at me, and I wish she was still staring at the wall.

"This." I point a finger back and forth between us. "Do you want to talk first? Get to know each other? Or just jump in there and get it done."

She rolls her eyes, a gesture I'm beginning to view as synonymous with her. "Oh please. You sound like a nervous little virgin about to get laid for the first time."

Her snark doesn't surprise me, but her reluctance to be of any help is really beginning to get on my nerves.

For the greater good, I remind myself.

"I'm only trying to help you Simone," I say with forced civility.

"Ha! Like I need help from you!" she sneers. "Look, I'm only doing this for Angel. You can sit there and tell me all about your pathetic little life, but there is no way in hell I'm letting you into my head."

My mouth falls open.

"But—"

"But nothing, sweetheart. It's not going to happen."

"Then why bother pretending? Why even bring me here?" I ask, angry now.

"So Angel would think I'm letting you meddle in my

business. She deals with enough. She doesn't need any added stress right now," she says quietly.

"Wow," I say sarcastically. "You mean you actually care about someone other than yourself?" I regret it instantly. I told myself I wasn't going to stoop to her level. Damn her and her vileness.

She gives me a withering look and I sigh in defeat. "Fine, Simone. I won't force you. If you refuse to even make an effort to become a useful member of this team then fine. That's on you. But if you think for a second that I'm going to sit here and waste an hour of my life every night on you, then you're very mistaken." I get up and head toward the door.

"Refuse to make an effort?" Simone shrieks from behind me. "You don't know anything about me!" As my hand reaches for the door knob, a small throw pillow slams into the wall next to me, narrowly missing my head. "So don't pretend you do!" I shut the door behind me, gladly leaving the fuming *prima donna* behind.

CHAPTER 26

MAJOR CALM SEEMS eerily empty as I walk the halls. I figure Sam, Ember, and probably Crank must be out on a mission and everyone else is most likely top-side.

I have a few questions for Ben, so I decide to head to the Science and Tech Lab. I'm not surprised when I find the place empty, so I find a note pad and a pen and start writing.

In the note, I ask him if he knows of a way to pull some strings with UCLA to get them to accept an application from me for the fall semester. I explain how I'm sure I missed the deadline and my chances of getting in on my own are next to nothing. I thank him for his help and tape the note to the middle of his very neat desk where I'm sure he'll find it.

On my way back to the living room, I hear what sounds like someone playing a drum set, so I head to the music room. Sure enough, I find Lang-hao pounding out a drum solo. He looks up and smiles. I wave back at him and lean against the door frame and watch him finish. He really is talented and looks every inch a pop star.

When he finishes, he comes over and gives me a hug. "Hey beautiful," he says. Even though I'm beginning to get used to Lang's flirty personality, I still can't help blushing at his words.

"Hey! I'm surprised to see you here. Shouldn't you be top-side?" I ask him.

"I'm actually thirty thousand feet in the air right now." He smirks at my confused expression. "I'm on a plane to L.A. I've got some recording to do at a studio there."

"Oh, I see. Long flight then?"

"Very. And why be cooped up in a plane for ten hours when I could be here having me a jam session."

Every time I speak with Lang, his American accent impresses me.

"For sure," I say. "Hey, I wonder if you could help me."

"Anything for you, Love."

I laugh. "Well, I'm supposed to be getting my self-defense training, but I never really got the details about it."

"I can definitely help you. It's Kira or Boss who does the self-defense training. My guess is that Boss is going to be too swamped this week to teach you, so you'll need to find Kira."

"Hmm, this is going to be difficult. Isn't she at London base?"

"She is, but you're in luck. Kira's a work-out-aholic. She's almost always in the training center here working out."

"Oh great!" I say with relief. "I knew Angel really wanted me to start today. I was worried about disappointing her."

"Well, if you get to the Training Wing and Kira's not there, come get me and I'll train you for tonight."

"Thanks so much, Lang." I hug him again before I head out.

Sure enough, as I enter the main hall leading to the separate practice rooms, I hear Kira's familiar grunts and shouts. When I find her, she's decked out in boxing gear and is severely abusing a punching bag. When she sees me, she stops and takes off her gear.

"Hey girl," she says to me, only slightly out of breath.

"Hi Kira! Do you feel up to doing some training?"

The rest of my night is spent there in the Training Wing. First, Kira takes me to the supply room where I find some comfortable workout clothes. Then she shows me where the showers and locker rooms are so I can get changed.

Once I'm dressed, we head to a practice room with a padded floor, and I learn basic defense maneuvers for the better part of an hour. Once I've got all the positions memorized, Kira stops pretending to attack me and actually does.

While I realize that she must be going easy on me, she's still managing to kick my butt. Time and time again I end up on my back staring at the ceiling. She's very patient and tells me it's okay to get knocked down as long as I keep getting up. So I do. I get up every time, and gradually, things begin to get easier. Kira's too tough an instructor to take pity on me and ease up, so this can only mean that I'm improving.

By the time my watch says six a.m., sweat falls in streams from my clothing. My limbs feel a hundred pounds heavier, and my pulse pounds in my face. I shake my head when I see Kira isn't even breathing heavy.

"Same time tomorrow?" she asks me cheerfully. I'm too exhausted to speak, so I give her a halfhearted smile and a thumbs up. I pat her on the shoulder as a way of saying thanks before I head back to the showers to rinse off.

I manage to make it back to my temporary room minutes before my alarm is set to go off. As I collapse on my bed, I concede to myself that I had a pretty great night tonight. I accomplished a lot, apart from the spat with Simone, and I'm proud of myself.

Now that I have a pretty good idea of what this next week is going to be like for me, I have fewer worries about my own inadequacy. I'm actually looking forward to tomorrow night as I fall asleep with a comforting sense of satisfaction.

CHAPTER 27

MONDAY MORNING IS agonizing. A long hot shower before school does little to relieve my aching muscles. The only highlight of my morning is the heaping piles of waffles I consume at breakfast.

"Whoa." The sound of my sister's voice breaks me out of my hunger-induced binge mid-bite. She's sitting across the table looking perplexed and more than a little disgusted.

"Hungry much?" she asks.

I think back to last night's exertions and the calories I must have burned. *Is it always going to be like this?* I shrug at her and make an effort not to inhale my food quite as fast as before.

After breakfast I say good-bye to Jana. She's heading back to Flagstaff today and I won't see her again for a while. I hug her and tell her to please try to drive carefully (something nearly impossible for her). I say a silent prayer that she survives the three-hour trip back.

Before I leave for school, I make sure I've grabbed both of my cell phones. I'm going to have to get used to keeping my Walker phone on me at all times. As an afterthought, I also snatch up my new book from Mikhail on my way out.

School's the worst part of my day. I try to be patient and pleasant to Tori before the first bell, but I'm finding it abnormally difficult this morning. Her comments and attitude are shallow and obnoxious as she gossips about people she partied with over the weekend.

I'm having a hard time concentrating on playing the attentive, listening friend as my mind constantly wanders. If I'm not going over everything I learned from Angel yesterday, I'm playing back all my defense training, making sure I still remember it all. And then I'm wondering how the others are. How were the missions last night? Is everyone safe? Have they learned anything new?

It's fortunate Tori doesn't require much input from me in our "conversations," or maybe she'd would've realize how distant I am, or how unimpressed I am by her list of scandals that occurred last weekend.

As bad as it is being around Tori, my classes are even worse. Since finals are over, there's little to hold my attention. I can't stop thinking about Chaos. I wish I were back there training. This is pointless being here when I could be learning how to protect myself and help my friends.

I glance at my watch again only to find just a few minutes have passed since the last time I checked. My leg bounces impatiently, and I'm so frustrated I feel as though I could burst from my skin.

I try to pass the time by practicing some mental abilities. I send my consciousness out and explore the classroom.

I watch from above as students visit and exchange yearbooks with each other for signing. I play with the idea of going into some of their minds for practice, but I can't get past the feeling I'd be trespassing.

By third hour I've become brave enough to push my consciousness out of the classroom and into the hall. I do this slowly and carefully, trying to spread my awareness out rather than send it completely to one area. I can't risk leaving my body inattentive in case the teacher calls on me. Even though it's good practice, it doesn't do much to ease my frustrations at not being in Chaos.

By lunchtime I'm starving. Tori finds me in some shade under a tree on the edge of the central courtyard. She looks pointedly at the three slices of pizza I bought from a vendor on campus.

"I missed breakfast," I lie.

She gives me an exasperated look as she pulls a yogurt and bagel from her bag. I roll my eyes, not caring if she sees.

She frowns at me and starts to say something, but a buzzing sound coming from my bag cuts her off. I reach for my phone and stare at it in confusion when I see it isn't ringing. Then I realize my other phone is buzzing.

"Oh no." I panic as I dig through my bag, thinking a hundred horrible things at once. I find my phone and answer before I can even read the name on the screen.

"Hello?" I ask anxiously, gripping the phone tightly.

Ignoring the confused look on Tori's face, I get up and walk a few paces away for privacy.

"Adelaide?" a man's voice says. I recognize the English accent.

"Yes? Ben? Is everything okay?"

"Everything's fine," he reassures me. Relief washes over me. "I'm calling about your note."

"Oh right!" I slap my forehead. "Of course. Wow, I didn't expect to hear from you so soon."

"Well, it was a simple matter, so it's no problem," he explains. "I did not get UCLA to agree to accept a late application from you."

My heart sinks. "Oh." I think of how disappointed Ember will be and of all the fun I'll miss out on next year.

"You see," he says, "there's no need for an application. I simply placed you on the roster as a full-time student with a full-ride scholarship. Your acceptance packet is in the mail."

"You what?" Did I hear him right? "Wait, you can do that?"

"Adelaide," he says patiently, "I can access any and all of the world's satellites. Did you think I could not get you into a university?"

"Wow," I say a little embarrassed. "I feel stupid."

He laughs. It's a warm, infectious sound that spreads a grin across my face.

"Well, we can't have that. You're a university student now. Mel suggested I enroll you in the art program there. I hope that was all right."

"That's perfect!" I can't believe how easy this was. "Thank you, Ben. Thank you so much!"

"Of course, Addy. If there's anything else you need from

me, let me know." I can hear what sounds like Mel in the background shouting 'hi' at me.

"Tell Mel I said 'hi' back and give her a hug for me."

"With pleasure," Ben says, and I can hear the smile in his voice.

"Thank you again."

I field Tori's questions about who called me and when did I get a new phone as best I can. I tell her it was a graduation gift and that it was just a friend calling. She looks at me expectantly, waiting for me to elaborate, but I shove pizza in my mouth instead. Before she can grill me further, I pull out my new book and start reading.

She makes a huffing sound. "Well, I'm not going to sit here and watch you read. Have a good lunch." She gathers her things and leaves. She's angry, but for the first time, I really don't care.

This last weekend I learned what real friendship is, and I'm acutely aware that it is not what Tori and I share. I'll try and be civil toward her. I'll always be grateful for her being there for me when Dad died. But I'm done making myself miserable over her.

I really do read as I eat, and I find the novel intriguing. I get so enveloped in the story and characters that I nearly miss the bell signaling lunch is over. As I cram the book into my bag and get up to rush to fourth hour, something strange happens.

I feel like I'm being watched.

I look around, searching for a familiar face gazing my way. Students are all around me, talking and heading in different directions—on their way to class, horsing around, laughing and flirting with each other. No one's looking at me. No one's watching me.

And as abruptly as the feeling came, it's gone.

I shake my head and blame it on stress. This is my school. This is the most normal aspect of my life right now. Surrounded by students and teachers, with things as mundane as calculus and gym class, I'm certain this is one place the mysteries and dangers of my new life can't reach.

My theory proves right when nothing life-threatening happens on my way to my next class. In fact, while abhorrently slow, the rest of the school day passes without incident.

At home, I rush through the evening as quickly as I can. I do chores. I do homework. I help with dinner. As soon as Mom and I finish eating and the dishes are cleared, I feign exhaustion and say goodnight, anxious and excited for what the night holds.

CHAPTER 28

BEFORE MAKING MY way to the library to train with Angel, I knock on Ember's door. No answer. I drop my head against her door. I was hoping to check in on her, see how things were out in Chaos. I look down to the end of the hall toward Sam's room. I know I won't find him in there either. My frustration is renewed as I think of the two of them hunting every night while I remain unable to help them.

Train, Addy. The only solution is to train as quickly as possible. I turn and jog down the hall, determined not to waste another second.

Running through the halls of Major Calm, I encounter no one until I round the corner entering the main living area. I'm running too fast to stop the full-body collision. Completely startled, I bounce back off a dark figure hard enough to land me on my butt.

Before I can see who I crashed into, strong hands wrap around my upper arms and lift me with ease. Once on my feet, I look up into a pair of light gray eyes.

"Oh," I say inadequately.

Mikhail lets go of my arms once I steady myself. "Are you hurt?" he asks quietly, concern on his face.

"No, I'm okay," I say embarrassed. "I'm so sorry, I wasn't paying attention, I—"

"It is nothing," he says as he steps around me to leave.

"Wait!" I say impulsively. He hesitates before turning to face me. I can't let myself pass up any chance to get to know Mikhail. I know the others haven't had any luck, but he came to my home and left me a book. That must mean something.

"I wanted to thank you," I start uncomfortably. He isn't looking me in the eyes, so it's difficult to gauge his reaction.

"For the book I mean." Still, his gaze only flicks in my direction before shifting to the walls or the floor. This is awkward. I wonder briefly if he's intentionally making this difficult or if he just has a complete lack of social skills.

Not willing to give up yet, I continue. "It's really good! I started it at lunch yesterday and couldn't put it down." He nods slightly in acknowledgement.

"Well," I say, shifting my weight from one foot to the other, "it was really nice. Of you. I mean," *am I stuttering? What is wrong with me?!* "you didn't have to go out of your way. But you did." Gosh. Is his social ineptness contagious?

I feel as though I'm de-evolving right here in front of him.

Again he nods, still withholding conversation. I sigh inwardly. On an impulsive whim and as my last attempt to salvage this, I reach up and place my arms around his shoulders in a hug.

Mistake.

Instantly, he's stiff and unmoving, like the way a deer freezes when caught in the beam of headlights from a car. I'm pretty sure he isn't even breathing. Things have just escalated from awkward to miserably humiliating.

What must he think of me, if he won't even accept a friendly embrace? The other Walkers hug me with nearly every encounter.

Leaving me the book was a kind and thoughtful gesture. I knew Mikhail was shy but I never expected this extreme reaction. I force back feelings of hurt and confusion at his mixed signals.

I step away, eager to leave. "Well, it was good seeing you," I say quickly, not looking up into his face. I wave briefly, and head down, walk swiftly in the direction of the library. The whole way there, I try to convince myself not to let the meeting with Mikhail discourage me. This might be the point at which another person would give up, maybe say, "Oh well, I tried." But I couldn't do that.

An image of Mikhail flashes in my mind. He's standing alone, hovering awkwardly by his Big Bike in the garage of Minor Calm as the other Realmwalkers are greeting me for the first time.

What's it like for him? It's hard enough to have to face the evils and dangers of Chaos, but to do it all alone? No. I won't give up yet.

A smiling Angel greets me in the library. "Are you ready for tonight?"

I grin back at her. "Let's do this." I clap my hands together, ready to begin.

"First, we start with manipulating and shaping the space here in Major Calm."

"Whoa, already? Isn't that one of the more difficult abilities?" I say surprised.

"It's one of the more important abilities," she stresses, "which is why we'll tackle it tonight. Don't worry, I'm confident you're capable."

I follow her out of the library, nervous and hoping I'm ready for this. There's no sign of Mikhail or anyone else as we make our way toward the residential wing. Angel stops once we get to the area where the three halls of rooms branch out.

"I believe you're down this hall?" I nod as she points down the middle hall.

"Would you like to stay there, or do you have a preference elsewhere?" I briefly note how easy it is to forget I'm speaking to a child. What nine-year-old says "elsewhere"?

"Well, I'm particularly fond of Ember," I say through a grin as I think of the spunky redhead, "but there aren't any empty rooms down her hall."

Angel smiles meaningfully. "Just because there are no available rooms doesn't mean there's no space to build one."

This hadn't even occurred to me.

"It just so happens there is space available. Plenty, actually."

The next few hours are spent creating a living space for me directly across the hall from Ember's room. I observe

Angel's mind as she examines the fabric of Major Calm. She walks me through the steps she'll take so I know what to expect when she acts.

I watch, amazed, as she pushes and pulls at the substance of space, creating a pocket. With her help and guidance I'm able to stretch the pocket. I spread out the space, in a way that's similar to the way I had spread my consciousness out the day before in school, only now I give this space a defined shape, structure.

Together we form a room, large enough to fit all the necessities and furnishings I would need to live comfortably. At Angel's insistence, I create an additional wing to be an art studio.

"It's important for us to have hobbies here. We need the option to busy ourselves with tasks that make us happy. Without some creative outlet, we'd probably all be really grumpy."

"Sounds like a good idea. I could always use the time to try to improve."

"You know, you may come to find that the gifts you possessed before coming to Chaos have dramatically improved." She smiles mischievously.

"How's that?"

"You already know that Chaos has physically changed you in order to help you cope with the demands of this lifestyle. Your mind has been expanded, strengthened."

"So having a quicker mind will help my art?"

"It's not just quicker." She waves her tiny hand dismissively. "Oh, you'll have to see for yourself. You'll be busy for a while training but do try and grab a few minutes to your-self sometime soon. Give your artwork a try here— you'll see what I mean."

With my room complete, we make a trip to the ware-house, and I select furnishings as Angel records them on a list. She says she'll leave it for the next shift of Walkers, and they'll move everything over for me. I feel bad that the others will be doing all the work and heavy lifting, but Angel insists it's nothing out of the ordinary.

"Besides," she assures me, "the boys enjoy throwing their muscles around whenever they can."

When we return to the library, we're surprised to find a distraught Lang-hao hovering over a squirming form laid across one of the sofas.

"There you are," Lang-hao says urgently and darts toward us. I'm able to see now that the person on the couch is Crank. He's grimacing and writhing in obvious pain.

"Crank!" I gasp as I see his leg is twisted and bent in an unnatural way. One of the bones that runs from his knee to his ankle is broken. The sight of it pushing sideways against the skin of his leg is enough to make me retch.

"Angel, Faye is busy top-side and we need a healer," Lang says in a rush.

Angel hurries to Crank's side. "Hang in there, Oscar. I'll try to be quick." He nods his head as he breathes heavily through clenched teeth.

"What happened?" I ask Lang quietly. Angel speaks up before he can respond.

"Addy, come here please."

"What?" I ask surprised.

"Please come here. You need to learn to heal and there's no time like the present," she says calmly.

I'm shaking and dizzy as I approach the sofa.

Don't pass out. Don't pass out.

"Watch me very closely, Addy. I don't want to drag this out too long, for Oscar's sake."

I nod quickly. I try and push my thoughts out toward Angel, but all I can think about is the leg that's twisted grotesquely in front of me. Like a car wreck, it's horrifying to see, but I can't tear my eyes away from it. I try again to push my thoughts out but it's a weak attempt. Oh gosh. I can't do this.

I can't do it. And Crank is suffering because I'm failing. This thought forces me to look into Crank's face. The pain I see there rocks me and snaps me out of my panic. My friend is hurting. I can do this. I have to.

I take a deep, slow breath and force my hands to stop trembling. With renewed purpose, I send my mind out to join with Angel's. Her process is clinical and emotion-free. She's not uncaring in her manner; she's merely saving herself from being overcome by the clutching grip of panic.

I watch as she extends her awareness deep into Crank's body, into his actual leg around the area of the break. She mentally examines the injury.

She narrates as I observe. *If the injury is not life-threatening, the first thing we do is block the pain signal to the mind.* I watch in fascination as she travels to his mind and stops the flow of information entering the area that interprets pain.

A huge sigh of relief escapes Crank. "Gracias," he says wearily, lapsing into his native tongue.

"You might not want to watch this Oscar," Angel warns him gently.

He throws an arm over his eyes and nods. "Go ahead." For a moment I'm nearly overwhelmed with concern and sympathy for Crank. Lang is too apparently. He steps closer and kneeling by the sofa, grips the boy's free hand. I force myself to focus on my task.

Angel places her small hands on Crank's leg and with surprising strength for her size, she sets the bone, all the while observing with her mind to make sure she accurately aligns the two pieces of bone.

What happens next is peculiar. I can sense Angel sending out information. She's sending it to the bones, muscles, and tissue of Crank's leg. It's almost like a foreign language. While I can't understand the words, I instinctively understand the meaning and purpose. It's as if she's entreating the body to heal itself. Encouraging it.

Incredibly, it listens. The cells already have the blueprints and instructions. Angel's just giving them a shove to get them going. Torn muscles begin to repair themselves. Inflammation reduces. Bone builds more bone as the broken pieces stretch out like a bridge to join and fuse with each other.

All this happens at an alarming rate. All the while Angel nudges and shoves the process along, not letting it slack.

This is unbelievable. I think to Angel.

She stops sending her message out and the body stops healing.

Now you finish. She thinks at me.

But I can't. I don't know how. I don't know where all the pieces go.

You don't need to, she insists. *The body will do the work. You must understand—the body WANTS to heal itself. All you do is press fast-forward.*

Without knowing exactly what I'm doing, I push my thoughts out to Crank's leg. I think of Angel's message and try my best to mimic it, sending it out tentatively. Very slowly, hesitantly, the broken pieces begin to mend again.

Very good. Now, be more firm. It must not be a question, not a request for the body to heal itself. It must be a command given with authority.

Certain now that the message I'm sending is correct, I send it out more forcefully and am filled with wonder as Crank's body responds to my command.

The moment turns surreal as I realize what I'm doing. I'm healing a broken leg with the power of my mind. I'm actually doing it and I'm suddenly giddy. I'm suppressing excited laughter as Crank's leg finishes healing. I'm staring at a perfectly structured and intact leg.

"You're a true Mimic, Addy. A natural," Angel praises. "Well done!"

I release a pent-up breath as relief and pride wash over me. Oscar jumps up and begins testing his leg out by stretching and bouncing.

"Good as new, Addy! Maybe even better. Way to go,

thank you!" He hugs me tightly. At this close proximity, I'm overwhelmed by a horrid stench coming off Crank's entire being. It's horrible yet indescribable. I've never smelled anything even remotely comparable to this putrid scent.

"Ugh." I hold Crank at arm's length to look him over. "What *is* that?" I notice thick black sludge splashed all over his body and clothing. Clumps of it hang from his dark hair and black grease smears his right cheek.

"Oh yeah," Crank says sheepishly. "I kind of forgot about that. Sorry."

Lang-liao laughs out loud. "Addy fixes you up and you thank her by sliming her with Shade guts. Very thoughtful, Crank!" he teases. The brown skin of Crank's face turns a shade of red.

"It's all right, Crank," I say, trying to make him feel better. "I don't mind. I guess having Shade guts on me makes me feel more like a Walker," I laugh.

He smiles now, visibly pacified. "No outfit is complete without it!" he says.

We're all laughing when a very tired and disheveled-looking Ember comes into the library. I look behind her expectantly but no one else follows her in. She too is covered in Shade guts, only hers are intermingled with singes and black smoke residue.

"Hey!" I say happily, wanting to hug her but not badly enough to endure that awful stench again.

"Hi girly. How goes training?" she asks as she drops herself down into a high-backed chair.

"It's going great. But what about you guys?" I ask the three sludge-covered Walkers. "How's Chaos been?"

"Busy," Lang says.

"Busy?"

"Very busy," Ember agrees. "There's been a massive increase in the number of Lesser Shades the last few nights. It seems all we've been doing is fighting Lesser Shades."

"Is that unusual?" I ask.

"A little." Crank answers. "But it happens sometimes, I guess. The population of Shades is always fluctuating."

The others nod in agreement. "Crank, are you ready to go back out?" Ember asks with some reluctance. "Boss is restocking the bikes, but I know he's eager to leave as soon as you're well enough."

"I'm good as new thanks to these two here," he says as he pulls Angel and I into simultaneous side hugs. We both laugh and squirm to try and get away from his horrible odor.

"Go on, get out of here!" With a crinkled-up nose, Angel pushes Crank toward the door.

Once the others leave, Angel turns to me. "We got a lot done today, Addy. You should be proud."

"Thanks, Angel. I kind of am," I say cheerfully. The good mood doesn't last long, however.

"Well, Simone's probably waiting for you. We went a little over again today on time. You'll have to give her my apologies."

"Oh, right," I say evasively. "I'll head that way now. Thanks again!" I leave as quickly as I can, hoping to avoid questions about how last night's session with Frenchie—no,

Simone—went. I can't let Angel down. I can't bear to disappoint her. It's her trust in me that drives me through the halls until I'm standing in front of Simone's closed bedroom door.

I knock quietly, half hoping that if she's inside, she won't hear me.

"What?"

She heard me.

"Simone, it's me," I say.

No answer.

How do I get her to let me help? I can't force her.

"Simone," I call again.

Silence.

Then, "WHAT?"

I drop my forehead against her door. *For the greater good. For the greater good.*

"Come on, Simone," I call plaintively. "You know this is what Angel wants. Let's just get through it. For her."

Silence.

I almost think she's done talking and am about to leave when I'm startled by the door opening.

"What the—" I nearly shout with surprise. I'm looking at a total stranger.

"Who—" Is all I manage to say as I stare with confusion into the face of a shockingly beautiful, though unrecognizable, face.

The five-foot-three, dark-skinned, exotic-looking young woman sneers back at me. What did I ever do to her? And when did we get a new Realmwalker? I thought that kind of thing was a big deal. I'm starting to think that there's something disturbingly familiar about that smirk when it dawns on me.

This *is* Simone.

The cocoa-haired beauty from last night is gone, replaced by this different, though equally breathtaking persona.

"You're not that bright, are you?" she says, looking up at me with mock sympathy.

I sigh and find I'm gritting my teeth again—a bad habit I seem to exhibit often in her presence. I'll soon grind all my teeth away if I can't manage to control the frustration this woman causes me.

"Are you going to let me evaluate you?" I ask her bluntly, choosing to ignore her previous insult.

She stares at me for a long time, viscously, hungrily, like a wolf about to devour its prey.

I force myself to maintain eye contact, not wishing to give her the satisfaction of thinking she can frighten me.

Finally she responds. With an overly dramatic sigh she says, "I guess we could work together."

"Wonderfu—"

"IF!" she interrupts loudly. Holding a bossy finger in the air, she continues, "And *only* if you apologize first."

"Excuse me?"

"You heard me."

"Apologize? For what?" I search my memory trying to find some instance that would warrant an apology from me.

"For your behavior last night," she says matter-of-factly.

I can't believe I'm hearing this.

"*My* behavior?!" I nearly shout, trying hard to rein in my anger. I slowly turn my head from side to side.

"Unbelievable," I say to no one in particular. I turn around and walk back down the hall.

"Fine!" she raises her voice. "Have fun explaining to Angel why you're blowing off our sessions."

I'm so upset at this moment that even the threat of letting down Angel isn't enough to entice me to waste any of my time in that hag's company. Whatever the consequences.

CHAPTER 29

I AWAKE TUESDAY morning as tired and achy as I did the day before. I get out of bed stiffly and spend the next ten minutes stretching, hoping I'll even be able to walk today.

After my failed attempt to help Simone last night, my rigorous training session with Kira was cathartic. I'd like to say that it wasn't Simone's face I pictured on the head of the practice dummies I pummeled for the rest of the night, but I'm not that altruistic.

My fighting skills continued to improve as Kira taught me how to spot and exploit weaknesses in my enemy. My confidence grew with each properly placed strike. While I realize my level of lethality is nowhere near Kira's, I feel as though I'm shaping up to be a fairly competent combatant.

School's monotonous and crawls by at a painfully slow pace. Again my thoughts continuously drift back to Chaos and my training. I begin to realize that while I exist in this realm, I'm becoming a creature of Chaos.

I belong to it. It consumes my mind so entirely that there's no escaping it, which makes me sad in a way. Realizing how completely different I am from the students around me makes me feel alone here. Alienated.

I look around the halls as I walk from class to class. I search the faces of people I know, friends and acquaintances. Can they sense it too? Can they feel how I've changed, down to my very core? I suddenly long to be in California at L.A. base, surrounded by my people. *My* people. I hold on to that comforting thought, and it helps get me through the rest of the day.

When I arrive home, I intend to shower off the day's worth of sweat I've collected from the hot Arizona sun. On my way to the back on the house, however, I'm stopped by a truly upsetting sight.

Mom's sitting at the kitchen table. Her face is in her hands, and her body's shaking, racked with uncontrollable sobs.

"Mom!" I drop my bag and run to her side. Dread overwhelms me. This is how I remember her after Dad died. *Jana's dead.* I'm certain of it. Or Gram. Gram or Jana is dead.

"Mom, what happened?" I ask desperately, not wanting to hear her answer.

"Oh Addy," she chokes out and looks up from tear-soaked hands. I'm surprised and confused to see her smiling. No, grinning. And now laughing.

She picks up a stack of papers from the table in front of her and hands it to me. Under a speckling of tear drops, I read the following::

To Mrs. Margaret Shepherd,

On behalf of the Gregory Walker Foundation, I present you with this donation in honor of your late husband, Officer Henry Shepherd. Subsequent to a thorough review of Officer Shepherd's career and achievements contributing to the good of his community, the Walker Foundation is granting you and your family a contribution in the amount of $3 million. We thank you for your sacrifice and sincerely wish you the very best.

Regards,

Gregory Walker IV

I look up at my mother and stare at her in stunned silence. Three million dollars? I read the letter again. *Three million dollars.* I read the letter a third time. I did not misread it.

"Look," she says as she takes the papers from me and shuffles them until she finds the one she's looking for. In front of me now is what appears to be a printed record of a transaction. It's a copy of a bank deposit for three million dollars, posted with yesterday's date.

"It's real, Addy." She sniffs as she wipes more tears from her face. "I've been on the phone with the bank for the last hour. It's real."

Tears spring from my eyes as I'm overwhelmed with gratitude. I knew money was coming. I never expected it would be so much.

"Good, Mom," I manage to say, emotions making my

words thick. "You deserve it." She stands and we hug tightly for a long time.

She spends the next hour on the phone with Jana. As I try to concentrate on finishing my homework, I overhear bits of the conversation.

"No. I've researched it. There's a website for the foundation but there's so little information about it. All it really says is that it's an organization that awards donations and grants." She pauses as Jana says something.

"I can't find one. There isn't a phone number or address or e-mail address. I can't even find a picture of the man who signed the letter."

I hide a smile while thinking of the elusive "Mr. Walker".

Later that evening while clearing off the table for dinner, I find a stack of letters and bills. It's the rest of the day's mail. Absently going through it, I spot a business envelope with my name on it. Inside is a shiny plastic credit card bearing my name and a single, hand-written note. On it are four numbers and one word.

"1348

Enjoy"

In the excitement of the donation, this envelope must have been overlooked or forgotten. I'm grateful for the distraction since I would have been at a loss as to how to explain the card.

For the rest of the night, my mother sits at the kitchen table with a stack of bills and a checkbook, paying off debts one by one. Occasionally, she starts crying again only to end up laughing out loud like before. Watching her from the living room, a deep peace settles over me. She'll never have to scrimp and scrape for money again. No more holding her breath, praying we make it through to the next paycheck.

Now I'll be more comfortable moving away from home. I can live in California and go to school there without worrying about how she's getting by. Knowing she's taken care of is the best gift anyone could have given me, and I'm all the more eager to prove my worth to the Walkers. Determined to train extra hard tonight, I kiss my happy mother good night and go to bed.

The next two nights make the previous two look like a carefree stroll in the park. I push myself harder than I ever have before, mentally and physically. With Angel's guidance, I'm able to master a dozen new vital mental abilities. I learn to detect weak spots in the fabric of Chaos and mend them before they can attract the attention of the Greater Shades. In a practice room, Angel repeatedly tears gaping holes in the essence of Chaos. I repair them, each time improving upon previous mistakes until Angel is satisfied with my work.

I learn how to make my own tears. I learn how to protect and guard them with wards. I'm continually surprised by each new ability I learn, and how the shroud of mystery and magic is removed from my perception of them. Each ability has a logical, almost scientific process behind it.

Before, the ability to sense my fellow Walkers' level of well-being, even down to their moods, seemed like voodoo. Now I understand that everyone transmits a subliminal signal, unique to them, at all times. I only have to broaden my sensitivity to the signals. The more I spread out my own awareness, the easier it is to pick up their "frequencies."

In relation to this skill, I learn how to recognize when a new or unfamiliar frequency is approaching. This is how Angel knew that I would soon come to Chaos. She felt me each night, getting closer to the barrier surrounding this realm. This capability is essential. Angel tells me she suspects that some of the Greater Shades may have this ability as well, which makes it all the more important to be prepared to reach new and defenseless Walkers the minute they cross over from Earth Realm.

An interesting and unexpected aspect of learning these mental abilities in Chaos is that instead of my mind becoming fatigued and used up, I seem to get stronger with each new accomplishment. It's as though my mind is a well, but it doesn't fill up and threaten to overflow. It gets deeper and wider, allowing for an even greater capacity.

One of the most personally benefiting abilities I learn over the next few nights is how to manipulate my own body. Each morning when I awaken with sore and aching muscles, I heal them. I encourage them along their process of growing, thickening, and becoming stronger.

Kira still continues to push me to my extreme physical limits, but I continue to push back. During workouts and combat training, I'm able to use my mind simultaneously with my body, maximizing my accuracy, strength, and endurance. It's refreshing and encouraging to find that each night I'm a little less tired, a little less sweat-drenched, and a little more prepared to defend myself and cause some Shades some serious damage.

My "sessions" with Simone, however, are much less progressive. Each night I show up at her door at our designated time. Each time I knock, she answers. Each time she demands an apology, and I always walk away, unable to comply.

I realize I'm being prideful and stubborn. I know if I just submit and apologize (even pretend to!), this stalemate could end and I could help her. But every time I open my mouth, intending to say the words "I'm sorry," I envision myself as a helpless creature on my back exposing my belly to a many-fanged beast hovering over me.

The image is always enough to make me walk away. I refuse to lose any of my dignity or self-respect to Simone. I won't cower and placate her infantile behavior. I simply cannot.

Instead, I spend the hour in between training sessions in my new art room. After finding a wealth of high-quality supplies in a craft section of the warehouse, I waste no time stocking up on all my favorite products.

I quickly come to understand what Angel was trying to explain to me about other talents improving because of Chaos. As I sketch, charcoal, and paint various scenes and subjects, I find myself delighted by the improved quality of the work I'm creating. It's uncanny. It's as if by altering my mind, Chaos has also altered my perception of color and composition and enhanced my ability to recreate it.

On the few occasions I run into other Realmwalkers, it's always the same experience. We exchange a brief greeting as they rush from one task to another, anxious to get back out into Chaos to continue hunting the increasing numbers of Lesser Shades. They always look tired and overworked and are always covered in the oily black blood of Shades. My concern for them is a constant incentive to put everything I have into my training.

School continues to be a necessary evil—an obstacle in my Chaos-consumed life. During classes, time drags on with cruel indifference to my desperation. Tori and I grow further apart as I spend all of my free time with my nose in my novel. The book Mikhail gave me has become my only way to escape the torturous minutes of spare time, and I'm dreading the end of it.

On Thursday as I walk to my truck after school, the feeling that I'm being watched returns. I stop mid-step and quickly glance around me. I search the parking lot, in between parked cars, in the shadows of the few trees dotting the pavement.

I turn a complete circle, unable to find the source of my unease, yet the feeling persists. While unnerved, I don't really feel threatened. I'm more curious than afraid, which may be due to my growing sense of confidence in myself and that, thanks to my training, I no longer feel completely helpless.

I try to shake off my apprehension as I climb into my truck. The feeling fades as I travel, and by the time I pull into my driveway, I'm almost convinced the whole thing was my imagination. The entire ordeal, however, is completely forgotten the second I walk through my door. In front of me, standing stiffly, arms crossed, is one very angry mother.

CHAPTER 30

I'M FROZEN IN place as my mother skewers me with a frightening look.

"Um," I swallow nervously. "Hi?" I try tentatively.

"We need to talk. Now," she says in a dangerously quiet voice. She turns and marches out of the front room. Heartbeat quickening, I follow her, filled with a sense of dread that only a mother can inspire. I try anxiously to think of what could have upset her. Receiving the donation has made the last few days the happiest, most cheerful we've shared in a long time. What could possibly have upset her enough to chase that joy away? As we sit down at the kitchen table facing each other, a sickening thought hits me.

She knows.

I search her eyes. Could she possibly have found out about Chaos? Does she know about my new life? I wouldn't blame her for feeling angry, even betrayed.

"Explain this," she says through tightly pursed lips. She slides a large white envelope across the table. I look down at it, fearing at first that she has found my Walker account credit card. Instead, this envelope is new. It's been opened. I pull out the papers and briefly skim over the words on the first page.

"Oh," I say as I realize what it is. I look up at her meekly. Her expression doesn't change.

"UCLA?" she says with deceptive calmness. "Next fall?"

"Uh," I say, tapping my fingers on the table while searching for some way to explain. In the hustle and bustle of the last few days, I'd forgotten I was supposed to be easing my mom into this. My oh-so-clever plan had been eclipsed with my new training priorities.

"When were you going to tell me?" Her voice rises as she begins to lose control of her temper.

"I'm sorry, Mom. I guess I forgot," I apologize. She gives me an incredulous look.

"Forgot? To tell me you were planning on leaving home? Moving out of state for school?"

"I applied forever ago! When I didn't hear back right away, I figured that meant I was rejected. I never even thought I would get in." I try this excuse out, mentally crossing my fingers.

She puffs air out and hangs her head down, rubbing her forehead with her fingers.

"Well, you got in," she says shortly.

"Oh."

We sit in silence for a few moments as she massages her skull.

Quietly, in a softer voice she asks, "Why there? Why UCLA?"

"Mrs. McCowen suggested it." I pull the idea out of the blue. "She gave me the application, said their art program was great."

"Your art teacher?" she asks, looking back up at me.

I nod. "And well, Gram lives there. I thought, on the off-chance that I even got in, it might not be such a bad idea."

I could see the wheels turning behind her eyes as she reluctantly considers this.

"I meant to tell you, Mom, really. But then I thought, why stress you out about tuition for an out-of-state university when my chances of getting in weren't great anyway?"

Her expression finally begins to soften. "And why wouldn't you get in? Your grades are above average, your art has won awards. Of course they were going to accept you."

I shrug, hoping to play up on the youthful ignorance angle.

She looks at me steadily. "I don't like secrets, Addy."

"I'm sorry."

"When I saw this, I thought..." she trails off.

"What?" I prompt gently.

In a self-deprecating manner she says, "I guess I thought, I don't know, that you were trying to get away from me."

"What? No!" I insist. "How could you think that?"

"Well, you never mentioned UCLA before," she says defensively. She seems to be questioning herself now. Shaking her head, she says, "I always worry. Constantly. I can't help fearing that I'm not doing enough. Since Dad, well..." tears brim on her lower lids. "Sometimes I feel like I'm failing. I thought, 'Addy's sneaking around, applying to colleges out of state so she can get far away from me.'"

"Mom. That's crazy." I lay my hand over hers. "You're not failing. You're the greatest! I won't go, okay? I won't go to UCLA."

"No, that's not what I want." She laughs at herself through her tears. "I'm sorry, Addy. I guess my hurt turned to anger. I haven't really thought about this."

"It's okay," I say, eager to pacify her and stop her tears.

"No, it's not. You got a full ride, Addy. A *full ride*," she emphasizes. "I should be telling you how proud of you I am. And I am. I'm so proud of you. Had I known you applied, I would have expected no less." She's smiling now, draining the tension out of the atmosphere. She scoffs, "Can we chalk this one up to pre-empty nest syndrome?"

Laughing with her, I say, "Sure, Mom. Only, don't ever think those things again," I say more seriously.

She nods, too choked with emotion to say anything.

Over dinner we discuss UCLA more. She even remembers, without any prompting from me, that Ember's moving there this summer. I can't believe my luck when she suggests we get an apartment or dorm together. Victory! While it isn't the way I envisioned achieving this goal, it's a victory nonetheless.

As I'm getting ready to sleep, I hear an electronic chirp come from where my phones are charging by my bed. Looking at my Chaos phone, I see I have a text waiting for me. It's from Sam.

Adelaide, please join Harmony and Kira in Logistics

first thing tonight to give a progress report of your training. Thank you. –Sam

Will Sam be there too? Suddenly I'm filled with hopeful anticipation. It's only been days since I last saw him but it feels like weeks. Nervousness spreads through me as I think of reporting my progress from the last week to him. I hope I've done enough so far, but there's only one way to find out. I crawl under my covers and pass through the gateway of sleep.

CHAPTER 31

BEFORE HEADING TO Logistics, I take some extra time to make myself presentable. I shower and fix my hair so that it's slightly curlier than normal. I put on my favorite outfit—navy cargo pants and a snug, dark grey T-shirt. As I'm getting ready, I notice how my physique has changed. My frame is more slender, not as soft as it used to be. There are defined lines of muscle along my arms. The change is good. It's evidence of my hard work.

Satisfied with my appearance, I head to Logistics and find Angel, Kira, Sam, and—surprisingly—Timothy waiting for me. They're gathered around Sam's desk, talking, with Angel sitting cross-legged on top. I'm willing to wager she's the only Walker who can get away with sitting on top of the boss's desk.

"Hi guys," I say from the doorway, nervous again. This is a performance review after all. It would be impossible for me to *not* be a little edgy.

"Adelaide, come in. Have a seat." Sam indicates an open

chair next to Kira. I examine him as nonchalantly as I can, looking for any signs that he is injured or unwell.

He looks good. Aside from a few days' worth of stubble on his chin and a vague kind of tiredness around his eyes, he's the picture of health.

One of the first things I notice as I sit down is the way I'm increasingly aware of each individual and their "frequencies." Each person's output has a different feel to it, as unique as their personalities. If I'd entered the room with my eyes closed, I would've been able to tell you exactly who was present.

Angel smiles warmly in greeting. "Kira and I were just telling Sam how far you've come this last week."

Sam nods, approval in those crystal blue eyes. "They both tell me you've been working hard. They say they've taught you nearly all they can. Very impressive for a short week," he says.

"Really?" I look from Angel to Kira in surprise.

"It's true," Kira says. "Your physical basic training is complete. Now is when we'd typically start your field training."

Field training. Finally. I'm filled with an odd mixture of apprehension and excitement at the thought of actually testing out my skills on real live Shades.

"Let's not get ahead of ourselves," Sam cautions. "Your case is anything but typical."

"I can't field train?" I protest.

Sam holds his hands up defensively. "Now hold on. I didn't say that," he explains. "I just think we should be more cautious about this. None of the other Walkers have had to field train with a Greater Shade keen on their demise."

As disappointed as I am, I have to concede he may have a point. Reluctantly, I remind myself that he is Boss and try to trust his judgment.

Timothy interjects, "He's right, Addy. Something strange is happening out there, and we really should have a better understanding of the situation before we send you out."

"Do you mean the increase in Lesser Shades?" I ask, looking from face to face.

"It's not really anything to worry about," Kira explains. "The Lessers are easy to defeat. It's just the sudden influx has kept us running near-constant hunting missions just to keep the numbers under control."

"An exceptionally clever and dangerous Greater Shade shows up in Chaos," I say, "and all of a sudden there's swelling numbers of Lesser Shades? It can't be a coincidence."

Sam runs his hand wearily down the side of his face. "That occurred to us too."

"So, what does it mean?" I wonder aloud.

"We aren't certain," Timothy says, "but we have an idea."

"Of course," I say as it dawns on me. "It's a distraction. We're being kept busy on purpose," I offer, looking to the others for confirmation.

"That's what we think," Angel says.

"What's that Greater Shade up to?" I muse.

"A very good question," Sam adds. "One we need more time to answer."

Angel jumps down from her place on the desk. "And in the meantime, Addy, as a Mimic you should begin learning as many of the other Walkers' abilities as you can."

"Starting with mine." Timothy claps me on the back. "Feel up to some target practice?"

The others take this to mean the meeting's over. As I follow Timothy out of the room, I glance back regretfully at Sam. I wish we had more time to visit. I've missed him and the comforting effect his presence has on me. When our eyes meet, one corner of his mouth lifts in a half smile. That simple gesture, that smile just for me is enough to make my heart skip a beat. I smile back and wave good-bye, unsure when I'll see him again.

Timothy leads me to an area of the training wing that I haven't used before. The large room runs the length of my high school's gymnasium. Along the far wall are a number of targets. Most of them are shaped as various Shades, both Lesser and Greater, which makes sense. Some however, are shaped like men—with the target rings focused on the head and chest—and others are simple, traditionally shaped circles. In an attached room there's an array of weapons, most of which I'm seeing for the first time tonight.

Timothy has a way of making everything he does look effortless. As I stretch my mind out to observe his process, I'm intrigued and startled to find that it's mathematical in nature.

Each time he takes aim, equations run through his mind telling him where to point, the exact angle to throw, the force required behind it, and the precise moment to release.

This information is sent at lightning speed to the rest of his body, coordinating perfectly with his muscles, and takes just a fraction of a second to transpire. The best part is he isn't even aware of how he's doing it. It comes naturally to him.

He's patient with me. We move from one projectile to the next as I mimic him and master each one in turn.

"You see, it's conceptually the same for any type of projectile," the Scotsman says matter-of-factly. "Once you know how it's done, you only need to become familiar with the different types of weapons."

We manage to get through most of the arsenal, save for the larger weapons (like the grenades and "Junior Nukes") that aren't safe to practice with inside Major Calm.

Throughout the night I come to know Timothy and his personality well. The towering carrot top is kind and humorous. I grow quite fond of him through our training and am grateful for this one-on-one time.

As the hours pass away, the holes I create on my targets slowly migrate closer to the center ring. By the end of the night, I'm hitting bull's-eyes with perfect consistency.

"Well done, Grasshopper," Timothy teases.

I thank him profusely before saying good-bye. I'm excited about my newly acquired talent, and buzzing with adrenaline, I nearly skip all the way back to my room. Before I put myself to sleep, I remember that I have my art exhibit tomorrow evening. After such a good night here, it will take all my effort to stay present and pretend to still be a part of that world.

CHAPTER 32

THE MOMENT I awake Friday morning, I can tell something's wrong. The air in my dark bedroom feels different. It's too thick. It feels full, pregnant. Eerily still. I'm sure I'm not alone. My hand darts to my lamp, bathing my room in light, while at the same time I throw back my covers and spring out of bed. Crouching in a ready stance, I quickly look around me.

Nothing.

I drop to the floor and look under my bed.

Nothing.

I throw my closet door open.

Nothing.

A bird sings outside my window at the same time I hear Mom's bedroom door open. The moment's passed.

What's wrong with me? This is starting to happen too often to be my imagination. Or maybe I'm cracking. Maybe having an active mind around the clock, with no chance for rest, is taking its toll. I'll become famous for being the first Realmwalker to go insane. Shaking my head in annoyance,

I resolve to speak to someone about it. I'm sure Ember can help me. Besides, she graduates tonight and I need to call and congratulate her.

At school I'm excused from most of my classes so I can spend my time in the library putting the finishing touches on my section of the exhibit. Once I'm happy with the arrangement of the display, I offer my help to the other students there. At times I'm again overcome with the sense of being observed, but I can never find any cause for my suspicion.

I call Ember the minute I get home and congratulate her for surviving high school, and she wishes me good luck at my show. We both commiserate about how unfortunate it is that they're happening on the same night. And then, before I can change my mind, I tell her about the odd instances over the past week when I've felt watched.

"I'm crazy, right?" I ask her, hoping she'll have an easy explanation for me.

"Hmm, I don't know," she says uneasily. "You're a Mimic, Addy. You've got some mad mental skills. If anything, your perception is better than most. If your gut's telling you someone's stalking you, I'm inclined to believe it."

"Well," I say, trying not to panic, "I wouldn't say *stalking*. I mean, it's annoying, I guess, but it doesn't feel like there's any malice behind it."

"Well, there's your answer then!" she says cheerfully. "You've probably got a secret admirer and you're sensing him gawking at you. Maybe it's that boy from the ice rink!"

I laugh. "If only. That would definitely make me feel better."

"Well, be extra careful just in case, okay? I'm headed your way early tomorrow morning, but I'm driving so I probably won't get there until sometime Sunday. Once I'm there, I'll make sure no one messes with you."

I feel better after talking about it. I love that I can rely on Ember. We visit a while longer and discuss our plans for the summer. She sounds excited to meet Grandma. We talk about spending long days on the beaches and maybe even hitting some of the big theme parks out there. It's a happy conversation, full of the promise of great things to come.

With my mood considerably lightened, I change into some of my nicest clothes. I decide on a snug-fitting royal blue dress that's cinched along one side and ends right above my knees. Mom does my hair for me and loans me a pair of cream-colored peep-toe heels so I'll be "extra lady-like" as she puts it.

"Look for me around seven-thirty, okay?" she says as she kisses me on the cheek. "Knock 'em dead!"

The parking lot is already starting to fill up by the time I get back to school. Once in the library, I notice an easel in front of my display that wasn't there before. On it is a poster with the large golden words "Tomorrow's Star Award." There's a big blue ribbon attached along with a list of awards and acknowledgements I've received for my art-work over the last few years.

"Addy dear," I turn at the sound of my name through the crowd. Mrs. McCowen rushes over. Her eyes dart across me and my art display then bounce back to the growing crowd of people. "You look lovely Dear try to stay close to your display in case anyone has questions for you about your work and remember to be polite and that you're representing our student body oh but you're always so nice...." I miss the end of what she says as she rushes off to greet the next student.

As the evening progresses, the library fills up with patrons. The crowd seems to be made up mostly of families and friends who have come to support students whose work is on display. Appraising comments can be heard here and there over a background of soft classical music.

I greet people I know and tell them about my projects and pieces, even answering the occasional question from curious strangers. While I'm mostly occupied, I still find myself periodically glancing at my watch, wishing the night was over. Just before eight o'clock, I catch sight of Mom through the mingling crowd. She rushes over to me.

"I'm so sorry!" She hugs me hastily. "I hadn't realized my dress would need ironing. How's it been?"

"Fine so far. People seem to be enjoying themselves. It should be over soon." A sudden draft of freezing air hits me, forcing goose bumps to rise on my flesh. As I'm thinking that the air conditioning must have kicked on, or that I must have absently moved underneath an air vent, I feel a tap on my shoulder.

"Excuse me, miss?" Shivering visibly I turn toward the voice. "Is this your artwork?"

I'm startled at how close the man is standing to me. I take a reflexive step back as I stare into his face. Before I can form much of an opinion of him, my eyes are drawn to the area immediately behind his right shoulder.

There, no more than two paces from me, towering eight feet tall with hollow eyes gaping directly into my face, is a Greater Shade.

CHAPTER 33

TIME STOPS. A myriad of thoughts rush through my mind. First is denial. This isn't happening. This is my school. My school's library! There's no way evil of this magnitude can be here in such a mundane, safe place.

My next thoughts turn to my mother. My sweet, vulnerable mother is standing inches away from pure malevolence and she doesn't even know she's in mortal danger. No one here does. There are easily a few hundred patrons here tonight, and none of them know they share their company with a man so wicked he has attracted the patronage of a Greater Shade.

The Shade stares back at me openly, blatantly. Does it recognize me? Does it know I'm a Realmwalker? Can it sense that I see him? While all these questions hasten through my mind, one thing is certain: This is not the Greater Shade from my nightmare. I have never seen this Shade before.

What do I do? I search my mind for answers. With horror, I realize all my training, all my preparation for a time such as this has fled. My mind is a complete, stunned blank. Panic has taken hold of me. I grasp for something, anything, and come up empty.

With great effort, I pull my eyes away from the monster. I mustn't draw its curiosity on the chance it doesn't know who I am. Instead, I give my full attention to the man who addressed me. He gazes at me expectantly, eyebrows raised, waiting for an answer. In an instant, I take in every detail about him.

He's handsome—shockingly so. He's wearing dark jeans and a navy plaid button-up shirt. I'd wager he's somewhere in his mid-forties. He's a few inches taller than me and has an average build with rich brown hair and dark eyes. Everything about him is appealing—except that from him radiates such an overwhelming sense of abomination that I am physically sickened.

I must say something, but my throat's gone dry. I swallow a few times, trying to find my voice.

"Yes. This is my display," I manage to croak. I force a smile.

His head tilts to the side slightly as he returns an equally fake smile. I must have messed up. Perhaps I hesitated a fraction of a second too long in responding because something passes behind his eyes. For the briefest of moments, his façade cracks, and the beast within the man stares back at me. In that second, I can see in his eyes that *he knows*.

He knows, even if only instinctually, that *I* know. He knows I see the evil inside him. And just as quickly, the beast is gone.

The man extends a hand. "Matthew Crowe," he says through a grin.

I can't hesitate again. I have to try to convince him he's wrong—that I don't suspect him of anything other than admiring my art. I reach out and shake his hand enthusiastically.

"It's nice to meet you Mr. Crowe," I say warmly, inwardly choking down my revulsion at the touch of his skin.

"You're a very talented young lady." He releases his grip on my hand.

"Thank you, that's very kind." As he turns to face my display, I scramble for a way to get my mother as far away from this man as possible.

"Mom," I turn to her and speak quietly. "Heather Eldridge's work is over there." As I point across the library toward my friend's display, I notice Mr. Crowe watching us from the corner of his eye as he pretends to examine a charcoal piece. The Greater Shade, while no longer gazing in my direction, still hovers close behind him, standing out like a cancerous smear on reality for only me to see.

"You should go say hi," I say shakily. "I know she'd love to see you."

"I haven't seen Heather in ages!" She glances in that direction, trying to see over the heads of passersby.

"In fact, why don't you take a trip around the library and check out everyone else's work too."

"That's a good idea, Addy." She kisses me on the cheek before she leaves.

I look back at Mr. Crowe, who's made it to the other end of my display wall, and wonder what kind of man must he be to attract a Greater Shade? What kind of evil? Is he smart? Calculating? Or is he an animal fed by blind rage and desire? Are there bodies in his basement? Unmarked graves in his backyard?

Aware of my scrutiny, he looks toward me. Again I catch a brief glimpse of the monster behind his eyes. How can no one else see what I see? Even without the proof of the Greater Shade, surely these people can sense how wrong this man is. Weeks ago, before I myself knew of the existence of Shades, would I have been able to sense it?

Mr. Matthew Crowe approaches and again stops too close to me. "I find your work very pleasing," he says quietly. His voice is heavy silk, rich and warm, and I'm convinced he uses it as a weapon, perhaps to lull his victims into trusting him.

"Would you consider a commissioned piece? I have more than a few blank walls in my home that are aching for this level of workmanship." He fishes in his back pocket before drawing out a business card and pen.

I hold my breath as he leans even closer and says conspiratorially, "Perhaps I could get a number or address from you, some way I could get a hold of you to work out the details."

I force a laugh. "Oh, I would love to, of course. It's just, you see I'm leaving town soon… to go to school…" I stutter, "so, I'm afraid I wouldn't have the time."

"Hmmm," he *tsks* and shakes his head. "That's too bad." He steps back and makes a show of fully looking me over. "I guess it's my loss."

"I'm very sorry," I say as he offers his hand again.

His eyes are a little too knowing and his grip on my hand a little too firm as he says, "I understand. You have a nice night, miss." He turns and walks toward the exit, not bothering to stop at any other exhibits on his way. And like that he's gone, out of the library and into the night, with the towering demon trailing in his wake.

CHAPTER 34

I NEED HELP. I can't handle this on my own. I reach for my Walker phone and realize with dread that I left it sitting on the passenger seat of my truck. How could I be so careless? I consider running out to the parking lot to get it, but I'm afraid of leaving my mother unprotected.

I find her and stay by her side the rest of the evening, never allowing her to stray more than a couple feet. As the night winds down and fewer people remain, I grow more anxious about leaving and what's waiting for me once I do.

"I'll walk you to your car, Mom," I say when it's time to go. I put her arm through mine and hold her close as we head out into the darkened parking lot. Only a couple dozen cars remain, sprinkled in small groups here and there. As we walk, she chats about what great talent our community has, and I try my best to act like I'm listening as my eyes dart around us.

Fear has pushed my imagination into overdrive. Every noise is a monster approaching. Every shadow holds a pair of gleaming eyes. I wait for Mr. Crowe to rush at us from behind a bush or from around a parked vehicle. As we approach Mom's car, I purposely drop my keys. As I quickly swoop down to pick them up, I glance under her car to make sure no one waits there.

Please let me get Mom out of here. Please. As she unlocks her car, I glance at her back seat. It's empty.

"I'll see you at home," she says cheerfully as she climbs in and starts her car.

As she backs up and pulls away, I'm filled with relief. It's short lived, however, as I realize my truck is at the other end of the parking lot and I'm now completely alone. I look around me, desperately searching for a group of parents or students. There's no one.

An image of my phone resting on the seat of my truck flashes through my mind. If I can only make it to that phone. If I can just get to my truck, I can lock the doors and call for help.

I scoop down and jerk my heels off my feet as fast as I can.

And I run.

I keep my head up, constantly looking around me in all directions. I avoid shadows and clusters of cars where one could easily hide in ambush. I can see my truck now and swear silently because I didn't park underneath a light. Worse yet, a large, dark SUV is parked next to my driver's side. When I'm fifteen yards away, I stop, unsure what to do.

Should I wait for people to show up? Should I make a dash for the truck? I peer intently into the shadows around the two vehicles. Could Matthew Crowe be there, crouched in hiding? Try as I may, I can't make out any shapes through the thick blackness.

I hold as still as I can and listen. Holding my breath, I strain to hear any sound that might give someone away. A creak of metal from a car. The soft thud of a shoe on the pavement. I hear nothing.

If attacked, I'll have to defend myself, so I try to remember what I've been taught. I've been trained to kill Shades. Demons. I've expected it, even anticipated it. But a person? Could I do that? Could I bring myself to actually kill another human being?

The longer I stand indecisive and exposed, the more the dread grows. The longer I wait the more certain I am that I'm in danger.

I can't stand still any longer. Panic forces me to move. Pulse pounding, palms sweating, I take a step toward my truck. And then another. Once close enough, I peer through the windows of the SUV, expecting to see a shadowed silhouette sitting inside, waiting. It looks empty. When I'm five feet away from the bed of my truck, I bend and look under the vehicles. I can't see much, but I don't think anyone's there.

I grip my keys tightly, regretting now that I drive such an old vehicle, one without automatic locks. Getting the right key ready, I make up my mind to move. I look around one last time for any help, and, finding no one, I rush forward.

I make it to my door. I try desperately to find the key hole in the enveloping shadows. In my blind panic my senses have dulled. This is taking too long. All I can hear is my breath and my heart pounding and the frantic jingling of keys.

Come on. Where are you?!

Finally I find it. I slide my key in and turn. The old, heavy door creaks loudly as I pull it open. I can see the phone on the passenger seat. I climb inside and, reaching for the phone, pull the door closed behind me.

Made it!

Only the door doesn't close. At the last second, it stops. I pull harder, choking down a sob of terror, not wanting to turn around and see what's stopped it.

No. I'm so close!

The phone's in my hand. I push the home screen button and it lights up as the door is yanked open and out of my grasp.

And then I hear it—a distinctly metallic *click-click*. A sound I easily recognize.

"Give me the phone," the silk voice says.

When I turn around, I'm looking into the barrel of a large, black handgun.

Chapter 35

Cold dark eyes stare back at me from behind the raised gun.

"I said," he repeats in a quiet but deadly voice, "give me the phone."

Numbly, I pass the phone to him. He slips it into his pocket.

"Get out." He reaches behind him and opens the back passenger door of the SUV.

I know my reflexes are fast. I try and gauge the distance to the gun and whether or not I can reach it before he squeezes the trigger.

"Don't try it." I look into his eyes. "I will shoot you. I will shoot you right…" he presses the gun hard into the center of my forehead, "here." He licks his lips eagerly as a dreamy smile spreads across his face. "I have no qualms with that."

He means it. I have no choice for now but to do what he says. I slide down off the seat, which puts me very close to him. I can smell his acrid breath.

Now that I'm out of my truck, I see the Greater Shade

hovering in its usual place behind Crowe. It seems to be pulsating with eager anticipation for the horrors undoubtedly planned for me. Grabbing my left arm above my elbow, Crowe guides me into the SUV. He's surprisingly gentle. This isn't comforting; rather, it leads me to imagine he's done this many times before and is sure of himself and his methods.

"Atta girl," he whispers.

My father's voice echoes in my mind—advice he gave me years before. *If someone ever tries to harm you, Addy, tries to take you, never leave with them. Even if threatened, you fight back. The chances of someone surviving an attack dramatically decrease after they're taken to a second location.*

I hear the truth in my father's words. If I leave this parking lot tonight, with this man, I will be killed, so I decide that if I'm going to die, I might as well die here, fighting. As Crowe leans across me to buckle me into my chair, he takes his eyes off me for a fraction of a second.

NOW.

Before I can move, however, something flashes and catches my eye. Behind Crowe, in the shadows surrounding the Greater Shade, a glint, a gleam of silver appears and disappears. I stare into the darkness trying to identify what I just saw. I look at the Shade. Its face is frozen, its maw opened in a noiseless scream as its head slowly slides from its shoulders and thumps to the ground.

Crowe, though unaware of even the existence of his nefarious partner, must sense the beast's demise in some instinctual way because he whips his head around to look behind him—and I strike.

Sweeping my left forearm out, I knock the gun from Crowe's hand while simultaneously shifting my body to the right. I put all my strength behind the kick I deliver to the center of his chest. The force of it sends him back into the side of my truck bed, striking hard enough to leave a dent.

Eyes wide in disbelief, Crowe slides down the side of my truck and lands in a puddle of thick, oily Shade blood that has seeped from the headless corpse next to him. Wheezing, he rolls onto his side and attempts to get back up.

Two curved, silver blades reach from the darkness and strike with viper-like speed. Again and again they work their deadly craft on Crowe. I witness the bloody scene in a state of shock, watching but not really seeing. When the deed is done, the Shade and the mad man lie in a messy heap on the ground.

Mikhail stands and wipes his blades on his pant legs. Sheathing his weapons into place on his back, he turns to me and speaks quickly.

"Adelaide, we must go." He reaches out a hand.

I stare at the blood on his extended arm—dark red mixed with black oil.

"Quickly!" he snaps urgently.

I grab his hand and he yanks me from the SUV, wraps his arms around me tightly, and together we fall backwards and into darkness.

CHAPTER 36

WHEN THE WORLD stops spinning, I'm lying flat on my back under Mikhail's full weight. We're lying on something soft though it's too dark to see exactly what it is. I feel the Russian's weight shift and a light clicks on. I recognize my own room around me.

"Stay here," Mikhail says as he rolls off me and darts to my closet. He opens the door and, still stunned, I barely manage to sit up in time to see him disappear into the blackness within.

I don't know how long I sit there on my bed staring at the closet. At least ten minutes pass before the roar of a familiar engine snaps me out of my stupor. I get up and look out my window to see my truck parked in the driveway. It's already turned off and the cab is empty. A jingling draws my attention back to the closet. Mikhail steps from the darkness and places my keys and a blood-smeared phone on my desk.

"Did he hurt you?" he asks, his steel-colored eyes anxious.

Even though I shake my head "no," he still takes a minute to examine me.

"How—" I begin, but he interrupts me.

"You should keep your phone on you," he chastises. "You were completely unprepared."

"I know. I'm sorry," I say lamely.

As if on cue, my phone buzzes on my wooden desktop.

I loathe to touch the blood-covered phone, so I use a towel from my laundry basket to wipe it clean as best I can. It buzzes again in my hands and the screen lights up.

Nine missed calls. Six voicemails. Twelve text messages.

I read the first few texts.

From Ember: "Addy are you okay?! Angel says you're in trouble."

From Sam: "Adelaide. Call me now."

From Mel: "Addy! Why aren't you picking up? Are you hurt?!"

From Oscar: "I am worried about you chica. Please call and tell us you are okay."

Another from Ember: "What's going on?! PLEASE CALL ME!"

Another from Sam: "Dammit Addy. Stop whatever you are doing and call now."

I look up at Mikhail. "Is this how you knew I needed help?" I ask, holding up the phone, my hand visibly shaking. "Did they call you? Did Angel tell you?"

Mikhail avoids my eyes. "You should call them. Let them know you are safe."

I ignore this. "You saved me. *Again*."

His gaze drifts toward the closet and his only exit.

"Please don't go," I say, desperate now. "If my life is worth being saved, twice, aren't I worth a few words?"

He sighs and his shoulders droop. Finally he meets my gaze.

"Thank you, Mikhail. I can't believe you got to me so quickly, but I'm grateful. Thank you."

He stares at me for a moment as if deciding what to say. Then, hesitantly, "I-I check on you."

He spoke quietly, and his accent is so thick I'm not sure I heard him right. He reads my confused expression and explains further.

"Sometimes, when there's nothing else," he gestures vaguely with his hands, "I check on you. You are new and... vulnerable."

"Wait," I say as I begin to understand, "you've been checking on me? For how long?"

He shrugs his shoulders. "Since you came." He rubs the back of his neck awkwardly.

I think of all those times I felt watched. All those times when I knew there was someone observing me. I could never find a source. And now I know. It had always been Mikhail, watching from the shadows. No wonder I never felt any malice behind it. He sees the realization on my face and seems embarrassed.

"And you were checking on me tonight? That's how you knew I was in trouble?"

He nods shortly.

How did I not recognize it was him all those times?

Each Walker has a distinct frequency. I should've known it was him. As I try to remember the unique feel of Mikhail's output, I realize I've never actually sensed it. Even now, as I reach out my feelers toward him, I get nothing. Empty space surrounds him. How is that possible? I remember now what Ember told me about him not having a visible aura. I study him curiously, lost in thought.

My phone buzzing in my hands brings me back to the present. I look down to see Sam's name shining on the screen. My wish to keep talking with Mikhail is strong, but my desire to hear Sam's voice is stronger.

"I should answer," I tell Mikhail.

"Goodnight then." For a second I think he's going to embrace me then he looks down at his blood-covered clothes and instead walks toward my dark closet.

"I owe you, Mikhail," I say abruptly. He turns before disappearing. "I know that sounds lame and incredibly inadequate but I mean it. I'll pay you back for this…" I nod insistently, "somehow."

He smiles shyly at me then turns and, stepping forward, fades from view.

CHAPTER 37

"I'M ALL RIGHT," I say into the phone as I sink onto my bed.

"Where in the hell have you been?" Sam demands.

Surprised at his anger, it takes me a second to find my voice. "I—"

"I've been calling you nonstop. Why didn't you answer?"

"I left my phone in my truck. There was a Greater Shade. I couldn't get to it," I spit out as fast as I can.

"A Greater Shade? There?"

"Yes. At my art show."

"Is it still there?" Sam's voice sounds urgent but controlled.

"No. It's dead. Mikhail killed it."

A pause, then, "Are you in any immediate danger right now?"

"No, I'm at my hou—"

"Then get to Major Calm as quickly as you can," Sam orders and hangs up before I can say another word.

What's going on? Why does he sound so mad? So

much has happened in the last half hour that I can barely process anything. I stare absently at some faint blood smears Mikhail left on my comforter. I look down at my dress. Blood splatter has forever ruined it.

Blood.

Blood from Matthew Crowe. That disgusting man's tainted blood is on me. On my bed!

In a rush I kick off my shoes. I pull the dress up and off my body and take off everything I have on underneath. I even rip the pins from my hair. Everything from this night must go—even the Walker phone and the towel I used to clean it.

I throw all of it onto my bed and frantically ball up the comforter around them. I yank my sheets off and even my pillows. I take everything and shove it into the farthest corner of my closet and slam the door closed. Panting and sweating, I lean back against the door.

I wish my closet was a furnace. I wish everything inside would go up in flames. At the very least, I wish this door had a lock.

A flash in my mind—Crowe, licking his lips eagerly.

The thought of the blood and Shade ichor behind the door is enough to make my skin itch and crawl. I won't be able to sleep in this room tonight.

Sam wants me in Major Calm right now. He sounded angry and though I don't want to upset him even more, there are things I have to take care of. I wrap an old towel around me and walk to the bathroom. In the shower I make the water as hot as I can stand it and scrub myself from head to toe.

A flash—blood sprays across the front of me as Mikhail slashes a deadly arc through Crowe's darkened form.

I scrub harder, rinse, and start again.

There's a knock on the bathroom door.

"Addy?"

I have to struggle to speak. "Yeah Mom?"

"I didn't hear you come in. Are you all right, honey?"

I turn the water off and step out.

"Mostly. Just a little queasy. I must have eaten something bad."

Crowe's body in bloody, unrecognizable pieces. Lumps on the pavement.

"Okay, well, maybe you should go to bed," she says through the closed door. "Let your body rest."

"I will."

I don't go back into my own room. I go straight to Jana's and pull some of her clothes from her dresser. I stare at the ceiling from under the covers of her bed. I try with difficulty to push violent images from my mind, and for the first time in a while, I think of how grateful I am that I can no longer dream.

CHAPTER 38

BEFORE I CAN even open my eyes I feel hands in mine. I awake to find Ember sitting on my right and Mel on my left. Both have one of my hands in a tight grip and both carry expressions of relief and curiosity.

I sit up and throw myself into their arms.

"I knew you'd make it through!" Mel says happily.

"Was it bad?" Ember asks.

I nod, too choked with emotion to speak.

Leaning back, I watch two pairs of eyes quickly scan for obvious injuries.

"I'm not hurt. Just freaked out a bit," I say, smoothing my hair back out of my face.

Ember nods knowingly. "For good reason too."

"Boss wants you in the conference room," Mel says apologetically. "He's already got Mikhail in there. We have an idea of what happened, but he still wants a full debriefing."

"He's angry," I say, worried about facing him.

They both shake their heads.

"No, he isn't, Addy," Ember says reassuringly. "He's worried, like the rest of us."

I look into her emerald eyes and notice they're red rimmed. "I'm sorry I worried you."

She smiles. "We're Realmwalkers. That sort of thing tends to happen now and then."

"Will you come with me?" I ask them.

"Of course." says Mel.

Buoyed by their encouragement, I get up and make sure I'm not a complete mess. I pull my hair back in a quick ponytail and straighten my rumpled clothes.

In the conference room, Mikhail's sitting behind one of the tables, and Sam's in his usual place by the podium at the front, his face a storm cloud. Angel's also here, along with Crank and Ben. Mel joins Ben while Ember and I take a seat at one of the empty tables.

"I've heard from Mikhail," Sam starts as he shuffles through some papers on the podium. "Now it's your turn. This is an incident report. It's standard procedure after any Shade encounter top-side."

"Okay," I nod. Even from where I'm sitting, I can feel an unhappy energy emanating from him in waves.

"Start at the beginning," he prompts.

I recant in detail the events of the night. I tell Sam about first seeing the Greater Shade and Crowe during my art show. Reluctantly, I admit I left my phone behind. I tell how Crowe found me in the parking lot, cornered me in my truck, and then forced me into his vehicle. I look at Mikhail as I tell how he showed up and killed the Greater Shade and then Crowe. I push the images of gore back down when they threaten to rise up and overtake me.

Through the whole retelling, Sam glares down at the papers on his podium. Occasionally he'll jot down a note here, a detail there. When I'm done, I sit quietly and wait for him to finish scribbling.

After a minute he asks, without looking up, "Is that all?"

"Yes," I say, taken back by his coldness and apparent disinterest.

"Okay. Good work, Mikhail." Mikhail inclines his head in acknowledgement.

"Adelaide," Sam says, finally looking at me. "Mikhail says you fought back, kicked the man?"

"Once, yes."

"Good. Though next time, don't leave your phone behind. That was negligent and I expect more from you."

My cheeks get hot as the blood rises in my face. I stare at the table and nod, too embarrassed to even apologize.

Ember covers my hand with hers in a comforting gesture.

"All right, everyone," Sam finishes, "happy hunting."

The briefing now over, the others begin chatting and making their way to me. Mikhail promptly gets up and leaves. I'm saddened to see that no one notices. He's the hero here and no one has any kind words for him.

As Crank, then Angel and Ben hug me and try to squeeze any remaining details out of me, I sense Sam leave the conference room. I try to ignore the hurt I feel at his lack of concern for me.

"Does this happen a lot?" I ask the others.

Mel answers. "Not often. But it does happen."

Ben nods. "I'm sure it was frightening, Adelaide, but it's actually a very good thing. This means one less Greater Shade walking the Earth."

"Do you think it had anything to do with the Shade that's here? The one that's so powerful?" I ask.

Angel frowns thoughtfully. "It's not likely. We haven't had any breaches here in a while, so the Shade you ran into tonight has probably been top-side for quite some time."

"But what are the odds of him being there at my art show? And of its human targeting me?" I wonder aloud.

"It's not really that strange," Ember says.

Crank bounces on his toes. "Oh that's right. One came after you once too!"

I look at Ember, surprised. "Really?"

"Yeah. A few of us have had encounters with them top-side. It's rare, but it happens. They're probably drawn to us. Maybe they sense who we are." She shrugs. "There's so much we don't know about Greater Shades, even after centuries of fighting them."

After a few more minutes visiting with the others, I'm weary and eager for the whole ordeal to be over. After asking Ben if he could ship me a new Walker phone in the mail, I excuse myself to go get ready for the night of training ahead of me.

Mel has agreed to work with me and help me learn her ability to alter her shape. I agree to meet her in the training wing in a half hour.

As I head back to my room alone, I mull over the numerous emotions running through me. I'm frustrated. I should've fought back more. I hate that after everything I've learned I could still be so helpless. I have to learn to master my fear. My abilities are useless if I can't get past the paralyzing panic.

I'm mortified and ashamed that I could slip up so badly as to forget my phone. I knew it was important to keep on me at all times. That seemingly simple mistake could have cost me my life. It could have cost the lives of others tonight too, including Mom's.

When I think of Sam, I'm surprised to find I'm angry. After the terrifying encounter with Crowe, I was looking forward to seeing him, to hearing his voice, to the comfort I feel from being around him. I clench my jaw as I remember the anger on his face and the cold way he spoke to me in the conference room.

I'd be lying to myself if I didn't admit that my wounded pride had a lot to do with it. I hate the way he called me out in front of the others. It doesn't matter that he was right. It doesn't matter that I was wrong and stupid. It hurts that, at a time when the other Walkers are so obviously worried about me, he could seem so uncaring. So distant.

Once back in my room, I begin rummaging through my dresser to find some comfortable workout clothes. Before I can find anything to wear, there's a knock at my door.

I sigh.

What now?

My sour mood's made me bitter. I don't want to talk to anyone. I only want to lose myself in training.

I've barely turned the knob when Sam pushes through the doorway and into my room. Startled, I stumble back a few paces. He grabs both of my arms and pulls me toward him. His hands slide along my back as he wraps his arms around me, molding us tightly together.

For the moment, I'm stunned. Last night I had choked down fearful tears, determined not to show weakness. Earlier tonight, I managed to stave off tears of anger, shame, and frustration. But now I'm finally broken. Water falls from my eyes as I bury my face in Sam's neck. This is all I wanted. After everything I've been through in the last couple of hours, this is more than I could have hoped for.

"I'm sorry," I say, my voice muffled through my tears. "I'm so sorry. Please don't be angry anymore. I can't take it." He holds me tightly, almost desperately.

"I'm not angry," he assures me quietly. "Not really. I just... I felt so helpless. I hate feeling that way."

I scoff quietly. "Now you know how I feel every time you go out into Chaos."

I absorb as much comfort from him as I can. I need this. The way he makes me feel—it's like medicine. His steady confidence calms me, brings me back down, centers me. His unwavering strength feeds me and makes me stronger.

"I was so worried, Addy," he whispers into my hair. "I've never been so afraid."

I'm surprised—though deliriously happy—to hear

this. Sam, who's not frightened of anything, was afraid of losing me?

As he holds me, I begin to grow more aware of him and how he feels in my arms. The soft rise and fall of his chest against mine. His familiar smell, thick and rich. His strong arms along my back and shoulders. The places where his hands lay begin to burn under his touch.

Too soon though, he pulls away. I can feel my cheeks warm as our eyes meet. He clears his throat and steps back.

"You've had some pretty rotten luck the last couple of weeks," he commiserates.

"No I haven't," I disagree.

He smiles crookedly at me and my heart melts. "You don't think so? Do I need to remind you about all the close calls you've had since coming here?"

"I don't see it that way." I lift my chin stubbornly. "At least... I don't want to."

"Then how do you see it?" He indulges me, blue eyes sparkling.

"Chaos is the best thing that ever happened to me."

"Oh really?" He raises his eyebrows.

"Yes, really." I insist. "I've done things I've never thought I'd be able to do. I'm stronger than I've ever been."

"Go on," he goads.

"My mom's a millionaire now. She's set for life!"

He laughs out loud at this. "And?"

"And most importantly, this is where I belong. I have friends here. Actual friends. Family really. I'm surrounded by people who care about me, people who fight for me."

His smile becomes genuine, all trace of teasing gone, and a deep warmth spreads throughout my chest.

"These have been the best two weeks of my life. I've never been more fortunate." Saying the words aloud I realize how much I mean them.

"I'm really glad Mikhail got to you in time." His eyes narrow thoughtfully. "Addy?"

"Hmm?" I thrill at the sound of him using my nickname.

"Did Mikhail say how he knew you needed help?"

"He didn't tell you?" I ask, somewhat guarded.

Sam shakes his head. "He doesn't carry a phone, even though I've asked him to repeatedly. So he couldn't have heard from any of us." He studies me carefully.

"Didn't you ask him about it?"

"I did. He refused to tell me." Exasperated, he runs a hand through his short hair. "Mikhail's weird about some things. He seemed uncomfortable when I asked, and I was so grateful he saved you that I didn't press him."

He senses my hesitation.

"What is it?"

I'm reluctant to share what Mikhail obviously didn't want to tell, but looking into Sam's face I realize I can't keep anything from him.

"He's been…" I remember the way Mikhail put it, "checking on me."

Sam's eyebrows lower and come together. "What do you mean? Like, visiting you?"

I lift a shoulder in a shrug. "Sort of…"

"Addy," he says, crossing his arms.

"I didn't know about it until now. I mean, I kind of did. I knew someone had been watching me, but I didn't know it was him until tonight."

"So he's been spying on you."

"No!" I say defensively. "It's not like that. He just said he was worried and was checking to make sure I was okay."

I don't like the suspicion on Sam's face.

"Why does everyone always assume the worst from him?"

"You don't think that's weird, Addy? That he's been watching you? Why not come out and say he's there? Why creep around in the shadows?"

"I don't know." I search for a way to defend him. "He's shy?" This doesn't seem to pacify him. "Come on, Sam. If he hadn't been checking on me, I'd probably be dead right now."

"I know," he says gravely. Without taking his eyes from mine, he reaches out and takes my hand. Slowly, he threads his fingers through mine. "And for that I'm thankful to him."

Of all the unbelievable things to happen to me recently, this is one of the most surreal. Since first laying eyes on Sam I've been trying to ignore the undeniable attraction I've felt for him. Sometimes I'd daydream that he felt it too, but every time my heart would whisper hope to me, my mind would squash it down with thoughts of reason and logic. *I'm only a kid to him*, or *He could never see me that way*.

Feeling his rough hand in mind, I forget to breathe. He's so close. His gaze travels down my face and rests on my mouth. Instinctively I move closer. His free hand lightly traces a path up my arm, over my shoulder. He touches my cheek, his face barely inches from mine.

Something in the open doorway behind him draws my eye. Standing in the hallway, glaring back at us, is Mikhail. Surprised, I gasp and step back. Sam looks at me puzzled then turns quickly to follow my gaze. No one's there.

"What is it?" he asks, worried and confused. "Mikhail," I say, staring at the now-empty hallway.

"What?" Sam moves to the doorway and steps out into the hall, looking both ways. "There's no one here. Are you sure?"

"Yes."

"That's it. I've had enough of this." I'm surprised at his anger. "I'm going to find him."

"He was probably just walking by, that's all," I say, trying to defuse the situation. The trouble is I don't believe my own words. The look on Mikhail's face...

"His room isn't even in this hallway. There's no reason for him to be down here. If he comes back, if he bothers you in any way—"

"That's nonsense," I cut him off. "Mikhail's a good guy. He's a good walker, Sam."

"I'm still going to talk to him."

I think of the expression in Mikhail's eyes. There was something there, something I've never seen in him before. It wasn't anger—it was beyond anger. Hatred even. I nod finally.

"Just... be careful," I say quietly.

"I will. You should go train. Mel's probably waiting for you."

As he leaves, I wonder how I'll manage to focus at all tonight. I change quickly and leave for the training wing. The whole way there I can't stop replaying what just happened—how close I was to kissing Sam. The cold fury in Mikhail's eyes. Will Sam even be able to find him? If Mikhail doesn't want to be found, I doubt anyone will.

CHAPTER 39

"OKAY, GOOD. ONE more time now—only faster," Mel instructs patiently. "Remember, don't completely let go of your original structure. Don't let it change. *Mold* it."

"Okay." I shake my arms and legs out in preparation. "Here goes."

I repeat the process I've watched Mel do in her mind and body. I watch my reflection in the mirrored wall of the practice room as I shrink down to the floor and stretch myself out into a long snake-like form. I giggle at my appearance. I can't get past how ridiculous I look.

"You laugh now, mate, but wait until you're in a real jam and changing your form is the only way to survive," she says defensively, sounding a little miffed.

"I'm sorry, Mel. I'm not laughing at the ability. It's a perfectly legitimate one and extremely useful." I release the form I'm in and watch in amusement as I expand upward and out, back into my original shape.

"It's surprisingly fun." She can't understand how grateful I am for this distraction from the stress and drama.

"Besides, without you and this ability, I'd be road kill right now." I remember fondly the elongated rollerblading girl who saved me from being trampled to death.

She smiles at the memory. "You were so confused that night."

"Can you blame me?" I stretch up while pulling my sides in until I am a nearly identical replica of how she had looked then—minus the rollerblades and helmet.

"Much better, Addy!" Mel claps encouragement.

Mel's ability is so unique and fascinating it's been surprisingly easy to get lost in training. Her command over her own body is incredible. It's also the reason behind her limited healing abilities.

While I've managed to suppress my worry about Sam and Mikhail for most of the night, once we're finished training, my uneasiness returns.

"Mel? Can I ask you something personal?" I ask when we get to the locker room.

"Sure," she says through a grin.

"What's it like with you and Ben?" I hesitate. "I mean, is it difficult? Both of you being Walkers?"

Her expression serious now, she takes a minute to answer. Different emotions dance across her face: Joy. Love. Then fear. And finally a deep sadness. "It's the most wonderful and terrible thing." I picture Sam's face in my mind and feel those same emotions run through me.

I don't press her further. Instead, we both clean up and change in a companionable silence. I hug her before leaving and thank her for sharing her ability with me.

On my way back to my room, I pass Simone in the hallway leading out of the training wing. She's still the dark-skinned vision she was the last time I saw her. Fully dressed in workout clothes, she looks like she's just finished a photo shoot for a Nike ad.

"Heard there's been some drama," she says conversationally.

I stop and face her, suspicious of her neutral tone. "Looks like you survived." She smiles at me.

Eyeing her warily, I answer, "Thanks to Mikhail."

Her smile grows and stretches into a toothy sneer. "Yes, that's right. You can't seem to get anything right on your own, can you? Even after all this training you've done." She shakes her head. "I thought Mimics were supposed to be useful."

Shattered by her words, I can't manage to find any of my own in reply. Looking pleased with herself, she turns on her heel and walks away down the hall, a happy bounce in her step.

How does she do it? How does she manage to get right to the heart of the matter *every time*? It's like when I was afraid of being assessed by Angel. She knew I was terrified of finding out I had no abilities. She knew, and she rubbed it in my face.

Devastated, I realize the worst part is that she's right. I have no defense against her accusations. I'm perfectly capable of getting myself out of trouble. I've been given the tools. I just haven't used them like I should. I'm a liability, not an asset, and everyone knows it.

But no more.

By the time I'm lying in bed, I've made up my mind. Tomorrow night I'm going out into Chaos. I'll never learn to fight unless I'm tested in actual combat. The only way to overcome this fear is to face it.

Head on.

CHAPTER 40

"BUT THAT'S NOT fair!" I know I sound like a petulant brat, but my anger's making me inarticulate.

"I don't have time for this, Adelaide. I've given you an answer." Sam stands solid as a totem pole, crossed arms, stern face, and all.

"I've done everything you've asked." I try hard to control my frustration. "Not only have I finished my basic training, I've learned every Walkers' ability, except for Simone and Mikhail. I've worked my butt off this weekend. I'm getting tired of asking."

"And I'm getting tired of telling you. The answer is no."

It takes all my effort not to stamp my foot in rage.

When I woke up Saturday morning, I told Mom I was still feeling sick from the night before. She suggested I stay in bed and try to sleep it off. I spent nearly the entire weekend in Major Calm finishing my training. The other Walkers were eager to help.

First, Ember taught me how to create fire from nothing, then how to control it. Later that night Crank taught me how similar his ability to manipulate water was to Ember's ability to use fire. Once I mastered one element, I could more or less figure out the others.

I worked around the clock, only waking Earth-side to take care of certain necessities and to consume astonishingly large amounts of food. When fatigue threatened to slow my progress, I would practice my healing abilities, strengthening and revitalizing my own body and mind. With each new ability, my confidence grew. So did my determination.

The moment Sam returned to Major Calm Saturday night, I asked him about field training. I'd barely gotten the words out of my mouth before he shut me down.

"You're not ready yet," he said. "You still haven't acquired everyone's ability." Disappointed, I quickly learned arguing was pointless. Even pleading was out of the question. The only way I was going to get what I wanted was to give him what he wanted. So I set about finishing my training as quickly as I could.

Lang-hao's approach to his ability was surprisingly spiritual.

"Everything is a part of God's creation, from human beings to the smallest particle of matter. There's a natural order to all things and God has given us that order. As humans, and His children, we are given command over all other matter." The red brick he brought into the target range with us zoomed around the room, hitting target after target, as he continued to explain.

"Once you 'see' this brick, all the way down to its

smallest part, you can command it to do anything and it must obey. This is our privilege, our divine birthright."

Sunday morning Ember pulled up outside my house in a cherry red '67 Mustang convertible. She insisted she'd be fine on her own and encouraged me to sleep when I could to continue my training. She seemed as eager to get me out into Chaos as I was. I was thankful for her support.

Ben's ability was the most complicated. I watched his mind as he worked in his lab on a number of different equations and experiments. It was difficult tracking his lightning fast thoughts. There were so many things happening at the same time in different parts of his brain all at once. It was nearly impossible to follow everything going on in his head.

I quickly realized this was an ability that would take a long time to learn. While incredible, I didn't see Ben's ability as essential to my defense and determined to train more with him another time.

I was ready to confront Sam again.

So here I am, standing in the doorway of Logistics, obstinately refusing to move from Sam's only exit. I'd gotten lucky finding him here—between running missions and trying to find Mikhail. I'd caught only brief glimpses of him this entire weekend. I also suspected he'd been purposely avoiding me in order to postpone this conversation.

The missions had been a success. I'd heard from other Walkers that the number of Lesser Shades was starting to thin out though Sam had been unable to locate the Russian. Some Walkers had reported seeing him out in Chaos fighting Shades, but he was never in one place for very long.

"What's your excuse now?" I challenge, raising my voice.

Sam exhales, a frosty look in his eyes, reminding me of a bull forcing steam out his nostrils.

"You're not going out there until we know more about this Greater Shade and what—"

"There's been no sign of him!" I cut him off. "Not one sighting since that night."

"For all we know, he's saving his energy and biding his time until you leave the safety of Major Calm."

"So, what then? You're going to make me stay here forever?"

"If I have to." His determined gaze is unwavering.

"No," I say meekly, my rigid defiance draining from my body. "Sam, please." I place a hand on his chest. "I was brought here for a reason." For the first time he looks away, unwilling to look me in the eyes as I say what he knows is the truth.

"That reason wasn't to sit here and hide. I'm ready. I know I can do this." The muscles in his jaw flex as he clenches and unclenches his jaw.

"Don't you believe in me?" I choke the words out, hating how vulnerable I feel. Hating how much I desperately need his approval.

He places a hand over the one I've laid on his chest. He squeezes it gently but still refuses to look at me.

"Of course I do." He nods. "But I believe in Timothy and Lang-hao as well. And together the three of us couldn't even scratch this bastard. Until I know what he's up to and how to stop him, I'm not letting you anywhere near him."

He reaches out and grabs me by the shoulders. Before I can react, he's lifted me up and out of his way and has disappeared around the corner.

The following week is miserable. Sam manages to avoid me almost entirely. On the rare occasions when I do see him, we both adamantly refuse to acknowledge each other's presence. I'm angry and hurt. He's stubborn and bossy. We're at an impasse, both believing that we're the one who's right.

This is not the way I'd envisioned things. Instead of getting closer to Sam, we're growing farther apart. Instead of fighting Lesser Shades, I'm stuck here in the library memorizing this enormous, ancient, leather-bound book *The Walker Chronicles*. Without the other Walkers' support and sympathy, I'm sure I'd have gone loony by now.

Nearly all of the Walkers at one point or another this week have expressed mild confusion and disbelief at Sam's insistence that I remain within Major Calm.

Angel's been especially helpful in keeping me distracted. On my first night of what I'm calling "lock-down," she tasked me with pushing my "feelers" out as far as I could into Chaos so that I could be aware of everyone's state of mind. Once I managed to do this, she told me to stay that way all night.

"This must become a constant habit for you. You need to be able to recognize danger at any time, all the time."

At first it's difficult to keep my feelers out while performing other tasks, like working out with Kira or studying history in the library, but by the end of the night, it's become automatic. Like breathing.

Each night Angel finds me and charges me with an additional task. Be aware of the space in Major Calm at all times in case a weak spot appears. Be on constant alert for any approaching unfamiliar "frequencies" in case a new Walker is being called to Chaos.

My respect and admiration for this little girl grows each night as I come to realize how much work goes into maintaining safety here. And with each new responsibility I take on, Angel's burden becomes lighter. The effect is obvious.

She seems to grow visibly younger. Nearly every time I see her she's smiling or laughing. I even catch her skipping through the halls. I don't mind the extra work if it means that Angel gets to be a kid for the first time in her young life.

It's Thursday night now and I'm in my usual chair behind the giant oak desk in the library, buried deep in the accounts of the nineteenth century Realmwalkers. I'm trying very hard to focus on the writings, but as I read the entries—stories of adventures and battles and amazing abilities—I find it difficult not to be jealous and feel sorry for myself.

I sense a Walker approaching and immediately recognize it as Angel's bright, sunny spirit. My sense is confirmed when I look up in time to see her jog through the door of the library, grinning widely, her corn silk hair bouncing behind her.

"Hi Addy! It's a lovely night, isn't it?" she says cheerfully, hopping into the chair opposite the desk.

"I can't say I agree," I grumble. Even Angel's exuberance isn't enough to lighten my mood tonight. "More tasks?"

"Nope. Not tonight!" She grins and spreads her arms out dramatically. "You're done! I've taught you everything I can teach you, aside from what you'll learn from experience," she rambles excitedly, "and that you'll have to learn on your own. Once you get out and test yourself, of course. Oh, and you'll be great. I know it!"

I smile. She's a young bird chirping up a storm, excitedly bouncing around on its spindle legs.

"I just wanted to check on you, ya know? I know this has been a long week. How are you doing? How are things with Simone?"

I'm caught completely off guard. My mouth hangs ajar as I try and scramble for some excuse or another.

"Uhhh..."

"Hmmmm, not good then, huh?" She puts her hands on her hips and pushes her mouth over to one side of her face as she considers.

"I'm sorry, Angel. I've tried! I mean, you can lead a horse to water and all..."

"And Simone can be one stubborn horse."

More like jack-ass. I think to myself and then shoot Angel a guilty look, hoping she didn't overhear that thought.

"Please, Addy, don't give up." The pleading in her eyes cuts me deep. "You've helped me so much this last week, taking over my responsibilities. I can't tell you what it means. But Simone is suffering and it weighs on me." The youthfulness leaves her and she's again an adult in a child's body.

Simone's suffering? I reach for Simone's awareness and find her in her room. I lightly skim the surface of her mind.

What I find is anger. Anger and bitterness. I'm not surprised by this. I dig a little farther down, avoiding thoughts and focusing instead on emotions. What I find below the anger surprises me. There's doubt there. Insecurity. And even deeper than this, a tender, raw ache.

I try hard to understand. I think of how a normally passive animal will become nasty when wounded and cornered. Is this who Simone really is? Under the meanness, is she just a scared, wounded creature?

Someone clears their throat and startles me out of my thoughts. Looking up, I'm surprised to find Faye standing behind Angel. She holds her hands folded in front of her, a kind but tired smile on her face. Her gray hair is pulled back into a haphazard bun, and a few stray wisps fall around her scarred face. I haven't had much opportunity to get to know Faye. She's rarely in Chaos, spending nearly every waking minute at work in the E.R., forever trying to make up for her imagined crime.

"I'm sorry. I hope I'm not interrupting," she apologizes.

Angel motions her forward. "Not at all! Have a seat."

"I won't take too much of your time," she says somewhat breathlessly. Faye always seems to give the impression that she's in a great hurry. Even when she's talking directly to you, she still seems to be a bit preoccupied.

"Everything's all right?" I ask, feeling outward to make sure she's in a calm state.

"Of course, of course." She waves away my concern. "I was thinking, Addy, about your predicament." Her English accent, I note, isn't as pronounced as Ben's. "I hate to stir up trouble, but I really don't agree with Sam's decision to keep you from fighting. It's not right, and I wanted to let you know that there *is* a way around this."

"What?" I spit out.

"Boss's word is not law," she says matter-of-factly, eyebrows raised.

I stare wide-eyed at her. "But, what can I do?"

Angel's face lights up. "Faye, you're brilliant!"

"What?" I demand.

Faye explains, "The newest Walkers might not know this, but the Boss's decisions are not the final word. This is a democracy. If there's ever dissent within the ranks, we can put the issue at hand to a vote."

Chapter 41

"Stop squirming! You're making this way harder than it should be." Ember tugs at the corner of my eyelid as she traces my eyes with black liner.

"Do you think he'll come?" I ask her. She's so close to me that I catch a whiff of smoke and ash, a comforting and familiar scent that always seems to surround her.

She screws up her face in annoyance. "If he doesn't then he's an ass. There." She leans back and tilts her head to one side as she appraises me. "Spin around. Let's see."

I make a show of twirling around in the little black dress she and Mom picked out for me. It's snug, sleek, and shimmery. I never would've chosen it for myself, but now that it's on I'm surprised by how much I love this piece of fabric.

Ember "oooos" and "aahhhs" dramatically. It's Friday evening and I'm graduating in a couple hours. I turn and look at my reflection in the mirror hanging on the back of my door. My hair is swept to one side, held in place by unseen pins, and falls in big dark rings over my right shoulder. Ember has somehow managed to make my eyelashes thicker and longer, my eyes brighter, and my lips fuller, without making it seem like I'm wearing makeup at all.

I've never felt more feminine. I know this is probably the last time in a long time that I'll feel this pretty, and I hope more than anything that Sam comes to my graduation so he can see me this way. After the scene last night in the briefing room, however, I won't be surprised if he's a no-show.

Last night, after Faye's revelation, Angel summoned everyone to the briefing room. It took about twenty minutes to assemble everyone, but I was surprised that all the Walkers, save Mikhail, showed. The room buzzed with curiosity, and Sam seemed the most perplexed. There was a nervous wariness about him, as if he knew what might be coming.

Once everyone quieted down, Angel stood at the front of the room and announced why she had called us all there. I'm not sure what I was expecting—maybe for the room to suddenly explode into commotion as Walkers shouted support for either Sam or me. Maybe shock or even outrage at the thought of openly challenging the Boss—anything but the complete blanketed silence that followed.

The atmosphere in the room was so tense it almost overwhelmed me, being plugged into the emotions the Walkers were broadcasting. Everyone's extreme unease filled me up so much that my hands quivered.

Sam, as expected, was furious. As the Walkers tentatively raised their hands in support of me, he skewered them with piercing glares. One by one, every Walker present voted that I be given a proper field-training experience.

Even Simone raised her hand on my behalf. I was so grateful for this, whatever her motives, that I made a silent vow to swallow my pride and recommit to helping her.

As my friends filed out of the briefing room, they avoided looking directly at Sam. I smiled and thanked them somberly as they left. The guilt they felt was evident on their faces, and it was hard to look at them, knowing they just did something very uncomfortable to help me.

This was a victory. It should have felt like a victory. But as Sam walked out of the room without even a glance in my direction, all I felt was hollow.

Now, as I smile for Mom's camera, the sounds of excitement are a muffled, muted backdrop to the worry in my heart. As the light from the flashes temporarily blinds me, all I can think is *Will he be there? Will he forgive me for what I had to do? Will he ever understand why I had to do it?*

I stumble through the next few hours in a fog, and at some point I'm vaguely aware that I'm sitting in a row of students in black graduation gowns. Someone is speaking at a podium on the stage.

Tonight. I return to Chaos tonight. Can I do this without his support?

I'm standing now with the rest of my row. When I reach the edge of the stage, I look up and see my principal staring at me expectantly. They must have called my name because I'm nudged from behind. I force a smile as I accept my diploma.

When I committed to being a Walker that day in the shade

of a tree on my neighbor's property, I didn't do it under the condition that I would be loved and accepted.

I see Dad's smiling face again as he waves good-bye for the last time. I watch him walk away through the rain and out of sight.

Because it isn't about me. It isn't about having amazing friends who love you. It isn't about finding someone you could love for the rest of your life.

My fellow graduates cheer and throw their caps in the air. As they fall back to the earth, they turn into raindrops. Under a dark gray sky I see a graveside funeral, and a rain-slicked black casket is being lowered into the ground. My mother and sister are huddled together under a black umbrella. They're weeping.

It's about doing what's right—simply because it is right. It's about helping those who are unable to help themselves, refusing to let evil prosper, and if it's demanded of you, forfeiting your life—or love—to the cause.

With this new creed etched into my heart, I force the fog from my mind, determined to enjoy the night as best I can. Families flow down from the stadium seating to find their graduates among the gown-clad students on the football field.

As I try to pinpoint my mom, sister, and Ember in the crowd, I feel a familiar presence to my left. Before I can turn to see if it's really him, a rough, warm hand wraps around mine. I look up into icy waters.

"You came," I whisper through a mix of surprise and relief.

Sam stares back at me for a moment before answering. I try to read his expression. He seems calm, resigned.

"I needed to," he says simply. He smiles, though a bit sadly. "You look amazing."

I can feel my face warm at his words. "Thank you, Sam."

And those words are all we need. No apologies. No mentions of the painful events of last night.

"Congratulations, Addy!" I hear a group of people shout. Turning, I find a happy sight. Mel, Timothy, Crank, Kira, Lang, and Ember are rushing forward with grins and flowers and hugs. When Mom and Jana find us, everyone's introduced as "friends I met through Sam and Ember," and they're all invited back to my house for dinner and games.

Before leaving the field, I make it a point to find Tori. When I do, we hug and make small talk for a moment. All the while she curiously eyes the gaggle of interesting-looking people waiting for me. As I hug her good-bye and wish her a fun trip to Paris, a part of me realizes this is probably the end of our friendship. I'm not just saying good-bye to Tori but to the old me and my old life. She must sense it too because her hug is tight and her good-byes and well wishes are genuine.

The evening is full of laughter. There hasn't been so much joy in this house since before my father died. The Walkers fit seamlessly into my family, and at the end of the night, Mom and Jana are begging everyone to stay. Makeshift beds are made on couches and floors, and by one in the morning, everyone's ready to turn in.

Anxiety fills me as I think of the night ahead. On my

way to bed, Sam grabs my hand and pulls me into the guest room where he'll sleep. It's dark, but a sliver of light enters from the hall—just enough to see by. We don't have much privacy. Kira and Mel are chatting right outside. He tugs me close to him.

"You have to know, Addy," he says quietly. "I do believe in you."

For a moment I'm afraid he's going to try one more time to change my mind.

"You were right. The whole time I knew you were right." He shakes his head. "I just didn't care."

I take my hand from his and lean into him, putting my arms around his waist. His arms lift and wrap around my shoulders.

"We'll take it easy, okay? Nothing too crazy," I try to reassure him.

"Try to stay close to me tonight, okay?"

"I will," I say into his chest. He kisses the top of my head. "Good."

I hear Kira call out in a loud whisper. "Addy! Come on, girl! Let's go kick us some nasty Shade butt!"

Sam growls a bit at her eagerness while I try to stifle a chuckle.

"Goodnight, Sam." I squeeze him tight, wishing for more times like this. "See you on the other side."

CHAPTER 42

I'M SUPPOSED TO head directly to the armory to meet up with those who will be joining me on my very first mission. There we'll don protective gear, arm ourselves with our favored weapons, and receive instructions from Sam, our mission leader. Instead, I head to Angel's room.

This last week, between being in the library and working on my fitness, I've had plenty of time to ponder the problem of this Greater Shade, and I stumbled upon an idea. At first it seemed crazy, but as time went on and the more I considered it, the more certain I became that it was our only option. Before pitching it to Sam, I wanted to get Angel's opinion, and hopefully, her support.

Angel's door is wide open, the way it always is. Her room's one of the most surprising—yet coolest—in all of Major Calm. Though Angel is far from your typical nine-year-old girl, her room is a typical nine-year-old girl's dream come true.

The walls are pastel pink with the floor a matching shag. Posters of British boy bands, young actors, and puppies line her walls. An entire half of her room is piled with an enormous variety of stuffed animals. I quickly scan the heap, half-expecting to see her little porcelain face peeking out of the plush collection of spotted, striped, and whiskered creatures.

The room's brightly lit, so the sequined and glittery gowns lying around her dress-up area shine and seem to dance in the reflected light. Tiny high heels peek out from under a mound of fuzzy pink and purple feather boas. A gold conical princess hat, complete with white tulle cascading from the top, hangs from an elaborately carved, gilded coat rack.

Stepping over Hula-Hoops and bottles of nail polish, I make my way to the stairs at the back of the room. The walls and steps of the spiral staircase are papered to resemble the gray stone insides of a castle tower. Halfway up the stairs an arched, stone window is pictured on the wall with a scene overlooking a rose garden and a pond.

The top of the stairs opens up into a large round room, in the center of which sits a giant four-poster bed. The castle tower theme continues here, with more faux windows along the curved wall and wood beams depicted on the convex ceiling. Layers of pink tulle drape over the top of the bed frame and are parted open on the sides.

Angel's on her stomach reading a book, legs kicked up behind her with her ankles crossed. When she sees me, she smiles and sits up.

Patting the bed in front of her, she says, "Big night tonight, huh?"

I drop onto her bed, feeling heavier than I should. "That's what I came to talk to you about."

"Cold feet?" She looks concerned.

"No! Not at all," I insist, even though my heart does a quick double-beat. When I glance down and see the book in her hands has a unicorn on the cover, I forget my uneasiness and a smile breaks over my face. For a second I'm nearly done in with a rush of overwhelming emotion. The love I have for Angel couldn't be stronger if she were my own flesh and blood.

"I've been thinking..." I hesitate. She nods encouragement. No turning back now. "I think I might have a way of taking down this Greater Shade."

"Go on, Addy. Let's hear it." Her gaze is intense and mature, the level of solemnity clashing dramatically with the dreamy-eyed girl I came upon moments ago.

"Well, he seems untouchable, right? I mean, the Walkers really threw everything they had at him that night. It seems like he's too strong for us."

"It does seem that way."

"But it can't be true. There has to be a way to beat him. Because," I try to think of how to put my gut feeling into words, "you see, there's a trend. There's a balance." Angel tilts her head to the side a little.

"Okay, so you know how I've been studying the *Chronicles*, right? Well, I've noticed a pretty clear pattern in our history. Whenever there's an influx of Shades or a loss of Walkers, more seem to show up. It's as if whatever's calling us here is trying to maintain a balance. Like, it's not possible for one side—theirs or ours—to have too much of an advantage over the other."

"And this Greater Shade, it seems, is a huge advantage for their side," Angel adds.

"Yes! So you see? It can't be *impossible* to defeat him. And, well, maybe we're looking at it the wrong way."

Her eyebrows lift thoughtfully.

"Maybe," I continue, "if we can't hurt his body, then maybe we should attack his mind."

Angel's eyes widen.

"He's projected himself into *my* head. Why can't I do the same to him?"

"And then what? Even if you could get into his head, what would you do once you're in there?"

This one's easy. I've thought about it a lot.

"Shut him down."

CHAPTER 43

"CAN IT BE done, Harmony?" Sam asks Angel. "Realistically?"

We all huddle in the armory, shoulder to shoulder in a circle. This is my first tactical briefing and I stand wide-eyed and alert, using my Chaos-improved mind to absorb every minute detail.

"I don't see why not." Angel shrugs. It's strange seeing her in full body armor. Timothy's latest prototype has a sleek design and covers the entire body from ankle to neck. The plating incorporated into the fabric is oddly supple. I'm amazed at how weightless the dark gray suit feels and try to force down my doubts about its actual competency. I trust Timothy, and that will have to be enough.

"I don't know," Sam says in a lowered voice, his internal struggle evident on his face. "It sounds dangerous."

"It won't just be Addy. I'll be there too. We'll both attack him together."

Sam rubs his forehead. After a few seconds he looks at me. "This was your idea?"

"Yes," I say, afraid of a rebuke. Instead, I'm surprised to see pride in his eyes.

Others in the circle indicate their approval as well. Mel grins and winks, Lang-hao fist pumps the air. I look around, into the faces of seasoned warriors, and am met with nods and smiles of acceptance. There are ten Walkers here tonight, eleven including me. Even Faye insists on being a part of this.

I understand why Simone would choose not to be here, but I feel an empty sort of ache at the loss of Mikhail. He should be here. He belongs here. The void he leaves behind is impossible to ignore. Like a nagging itch I'm unable to scratch.

"This is it, Boss." Ember draws our attention. "This is why that Shade was so bent on killing Addy last time."

Crank bounces excitedly in place. "Because she figured out how to stop him, and now she's going to end him. Tonight. Yessss! You're going down desgraciado!" As the others laugh, I embrace the outpour of excitement and adrenaline coming off them. I draw it inside me and imagine it filling me up completely, leaving no room for fear or doubt.

Sam clears his throat and everyone's silent. "All right, this idea of attacking the Greater Shade's mind is a good one, and I think it's worth a try. This is a tricky situation, however. We all know this Shade's particularly clever. He uses the Lesser Shades as distractions. He has telepathic abilities and he's damned near invincible. We have two objectives for this mission. One, find the Greater Shade. Two, protect Angel and

Addy so they can focus on using their mental abilities to take him down. You two—" he indicates Angel and me, "once we find him, don't worry about anything but getting into his head, clear?"

We nod in unison.

"Okay team, let's go get him."

On our way to the garage, Sam tells me I'll be riding behind Timothy and Angel will be riding with Lang. Angel doesn't drive a Big Bike, and Crank's still building mine, but even if I had one and knew how to drive, I'd still be assigned to another Walker. This task will demand my full attention.

"Remember," he says once we get to the garage, "don't leave my sight."

"I won't."

"And if things get bad, say the word and we'll abort."

"Okay."

For a moment he breaks his stoic businesslike persona and hugs me tightly before heading to his Big Bike, helmet in hand.

"I've gotcher back, girl!" Ember cheers at me as she passes.

A familiar, deafening rumble fills my ears as the Walkers start their bikes. I swing my leg over Timothy's powder blue bike and try to find a comfortable position behind the ginger giant. It's difficult because of all the guns and ammo strapped to him. Once situated, he gives me the thumbs up and I put my helmet on, significantly dampening the roar of the engines.

Time slows.

My throat tightens up. I try to swallow, but my mouth is too dry and my tongue sticks to the roof of my mouth. I feel like there's a jackhammer in my chest, smashing against my ribs, trying to break free. The Walkers rev their engines loudly, eagerly. I grip Timothy tighter around his middle and lean into him to compensate for the force of acceleration.

I have to do this. I *have* to succeed. Everyone's counting on me. This is my purpose. I'm the only one who can defeat this monster. I picture the Shade in my mind, its ever-moving flesh glistening wet, its dark empty eyes, its ragged gaping jaw. Suddenly this battle feels personal, like it's only me and him. He may be gunning for me, but I'm gunning right back. He's mine. I *will* destroy him.

Sam gives the signal and together we lurch forward. I force my eyes to stay open as we phase through the door to Chaos. I'm eager and ready for anything. This time I won't flake out. I won't freeze. I refuse to be helpless any longer.

The first thing I notice is green—it's everywhere. Though it's faded in comparison to the richness of colors within Major Calm, it's striking nonetheless. The bikes slow to a stop as everyone takes in our surroundings.

We're in a forest, but this is different from any forest I've ever been in. The trees are gargantuan and surround us in dense clusters. It's a miracle we didn't crash into any leaving the Calm.

The moss-covered trunks are six, maybe seven feet wide with thick roots that expand outward in a tangled, knotted filigree covering the ground. The tops of the trees tower above us, easily reaching heights of over a hundred feet.

Their leafy branches reach out and intertwine with their neighbors, creating a thick canopy that barely lets in the sun. Large, sturdy-looking vines hang from limbs. They're strewn from tree to tree like the lattice work of some giant, prehistoric spider's web.

The thought of spiders draws my attention to the forest floor. Tall, thick vegetation carpets the ground, reaching as high as my shoulders in some places. There are a few narrow paths winding here and there between the trees, but they look difficult to navigate. Our bikes will be useless on this terrain.

The most disturbing thing about this landscape is the near total lack of sound. No birds chirp or caw, no monkeys holler, no insects buzz. It's unnerving.

"Can we hover?" Faye's voice inquires through the coms.

I look to Sam on his bike at the head of the group. He's craned around facing us, and his helmet shakes from side to side.

"The vines would snag us. This is rotten luck, guys. Maybe we should abort."

Five feet behind him, the underbrush moves, quivers. The wind?

"What's the consensus?" Sam asks for our opinions. I haven't taken my eyes off the moving plants behind Sam, so I'm the only one prepared when the thick, anaconda-like Shade launches out of the brush, fanged mouth agape, aimed directly at Sam.

"NO!" I thrust my arm forward, instantly pushing force all along the length of it, from my shoulder to my forearm to my hand and exploding out my fingertips. The Shade, just inches from Sam's neck, is thrown back into the trunk of the nearest tree and chunks of wood splinter and fly in all directions. The snake Shade bursts in half on impact, flinging thick black oil into the raining cloud of wood and pulp.

I'm transfixed as I watch the cloud of debris slowly settle to the ground. I did that. My first kill. And then the ground begins to shake.

"This is it!" Kira hollers.

"Dismount. Spread out!" Sam barks.

A rush of adrenaline thrills through me. As we climb off the bikes, our nervous anticipation thickens the air. I hear strange noises off in the distance but my helmet muffles them. Frustrated and feeling claustrophobic, I remove it. Once off, the sounds are clearer—and more terrible.

It's the trees. They're groaning, creaking, and snapping under the weight of the Lesser Shades as they barrel their way toward us. I hear trees being felled in every direction, and they sound as though they're screaming out in pain. The earth beneath us shakes violently with each thunderous collapse. This once-silent forest overflows with a cacophony as roars, shrieks, and snarls mingle with the sounds of the forest being crushed and broken.

I turn in a quick circle, getting my bearings, and watch the other Walkers remove helmets, draw their weapons, unsheathe swords, and prepare themselves for war.

Sam's at my side in less than a second. He has to shout over the ever-growing noise to be heard. "This isn't a stampede! They're coming from all sides. Addy, I think this is it. Are you ready?"

"Yes!" I shout back. I look to Angel on the other side of me and she gives me a determined nod.

And then they're on us. The forest around us explodes in a black wave as Shades crash down on all sides. The scene is pure madness, and I fleetingly think of how aptly named this realm is. Everyone is spread out among the trees, each fighting their own battles. I can't keep track of anyone anymore—so much is happening. Rapid gunfire to my left, a loud explosion far behind me.

Sam throws himself at a charging Shade with giant, curved ram's horns. They collide mid-air and tumble down in a blur. I run after them, determined to help, and steel myself as I send force out, ready to pull the Shade apart limb from limb. Suddenly I'm struck from the right and bowled end over end as I'm pushed and trampled, all the while feeling the beast's cold flesh against mine.

When I finally stop rolling, I'm lying on my back, pinned to the forest floor by a wolfish devil of tremendous size. One giant front paw digs into my chest, making it impossible to breathe. Black slime drips from its ragged mouth onto my face and neck as it lowers its head for the kill.

"BAD DOG!" I hear Angel's admonishment followed immediately by an ear-piercing keen of pain as the monster throws its head back in anguish. The Shade is frozen in a death howl when it falls sideways to my left, thumping the earth loudly. Strangely, its hindquarters—tail and all—fall to the right of me, spilling its steaming entrails on the forest floor.

Angel stands beside me, offering a hand up. She's entirely covered in clumpy, black Shade blood. Even her beautiful hair's an oily, raven black. The only white I see on her is from a giant toothy grin.

"Did you jump *through* that thing?" I shout.

"It worked, right?" The moment's surreal as I try to reconcile my view of Angel as the sweet innocent child I've come to know with this hardened killing machine that stands in front of me.

An earsplitting trumpeting rips through the air, and we both turn toward the source just in time to see an elephant-like Lesser Shade rear up on its back legs. Its massive front legs slam down onto a tree directly in front of us. The tree snaps like a twig and cuts through the air on its way down to crush us. It's stopped at the last second, inches above my head.

"ADDY! A little help here!" Lang's standing a few feet away, his hands raised, his face contorted with extreme exertion. I quickly lift my hands above my head and together we strain our minds to hold the tree up horizontally in the air. Our burden is lightened considerably when Angel joins in.

"At the Shades, you two!" Lang and I nod our understanding.

Before we act, Angel projects an order out to the Walkers who may be in our path.

EVERYONE DOWN!

On Angel's signal I mentally thrust the mammoth tree out toward the largest group of Shades nearby. Our combined efforts have a devastating effect and Shades are flung everywhere. Like bowling pins, they fall, flatten, and hurl to one side or the other. A crop of trees finally stops our battering ram, but the damage to the other side has been significant.

Lang slaps me on the back. "Great work girls. Again?"

He points to another felled tree and we work together to take out more of the demons. Panting, we look around us through the thinning number of Shades. Where's Sam? We weren't supposed to be separated—he'll be worried.

STUPID GIIIRRRL.

"Aaaggghh!" I scream in agony and fall to my knees, clutching the sides of my head.

CHAPTER 44

MY HEAD. THE pain! Tears squeeze through my clenched eyelids.

Angel's muffled voice rings through my head. *Sam, he's found us!*

I'm on my side on the ground, curling my legs up into my chest and cramming my head between my knees. I can *feel* him. Cold scales slither and writhe under my skull, sending shooting bolts of pain throughout my mind.

"MAKE IT STOP!" I scream as an icy, clawed hand seems to rake across my brain, digging in and shredding everything there. I sense the Walkers around me, and I know they've rallied and are giving all they've got to protect me. The ground beneath me continues to pound and quake as the battle escalates.

Addy! Angel's urgent voice is in my mind. *I can't do it! I'm so sorry, Addy! He's too strong for me. I can't get in. You have to try. Please try!*

YOU ARROGANT CHILD. YOU THOUGHT YOU

COULD KILL ME? YOU THOUGHT YOU WERE THE ONE?

Its wicked laughter is all there is, drowning out everything else. My body is numb. I no longer feel the ground shaking. I can't hear my friends. I can't even feel them anymore. There's only blackness. Blackness and pain.

All I can think is that I have to escape this. I have to escape. With all the strength I have left, I push myself up and out my body—out of my head and away from the dizzying torture. The second I leave the confines of my mind, relief overwhelms me, and in that instant everything comes rushing back at me—the reason I'm out here and what must be done in order to survive.

I can't delay this any longer. Seconds lost could cost me my friends. I scan the frenzied scene around me. My body is directly below. My head rests on Ember's lap as she strokes my hair.

Many Walkers surround me, facing out, fighting more fiercely than I've ever seen them fight. Off to one side I see Faye on her knees on the ground. Her head's bleeding heavily, but she ignores it as she hunches over a motionless body, hands hovering in the air above it. I see Sam fighting back to back with Timothy, holding their ground.

What few dozen Lesser Shades remain are being chopped down one by one. They fall seemingly on their own. I watch closely and catch glimpses of shiny blades darting in and out of shadows all around the unsuspecting monsters. Mikhail!

And then I see it. The Greater Shade. He has Mel in his

arms, and he's pulling her apart as best he can, but she keeps stretching herself out to keep from being destroyed.

Now or never.

I throw myself down toward the demon. Down to where I can feel his mind. A massive amount of sheer force shields him, stopping me abruptly. The Greater Shade throws Mel down and gazes up into the air. His empty eye sockets search the air around me, as if he senses me. A wave of gleeful anticipation pulsates from him.

I push against his mental barrier as hard as I can. There has to be a way in! There has to be a chink in the armor. I just need to find it. I probe and push, straining myself beyond my limits. And then the demon looks directly at me, his mouth open wide in a sinister semblance of a grin. Why is it grinning? Why is it so pleased? What have I missed?

The barrier's suddenly gone. It doesn't shatter. I don't slip through an unseen crack. It's simply lifted. Released. I pass through with ease, as if I've been invited in, and then I realize my mistake. I realize how terribly wrong I've been. But now it's too late.

Screams. Heart-wrenching, blood-curdling screams. I hear women, men, even children, screaming as though they're slowly being tortured to death. Some of the voices are sobbing and pleading. It's more than I can bear. Quick flashes of horrifying images accompany the haunted voices. Death. Decay. People on fire. Mutilated animals. Mass graves. Despair and grief overwhelm me.

Stop! Please Stop!
Laughter.

I recognize the beast's gravely, wet laughter layered over the sounds, the flashes. I try to get away from them but I can't. In every direction I flee I'm met with more ghastly images and sounds. This is the mind of a demon. This was my mistake, thinking I could navigate my way around here as easily as I could a man's mind. How could I not have known that inside this evil being would be a mind so dark and twisted that upon entering I would be driven mad?

It knew.

That's why it welcomed me in so eagerly. And now I don't know if I'll ever find my way out. I've completely abandoned my original purpose of shutting down the Shade's mind. Now I must put all of my focus into merely surviving.

Think. Think, Addy. But I can't think. I can't see past the graphic displays of violence and hatred. I feel like I'm losing myself. The panic has stripped away my control and reduced me to a creature of pure instinct. Fight or flight.

Flight isn't an option. I'll have to fight. But how?

This evil is extreme—I need another extreme to battle it and decide to go in the opposite direction. Love. If anything can neutralize evil, it's love. I dig deep. I force an image to form in the Greater Shade's mind. It's Ember. My head's in her lap and she's stroking my hair. The image is brief but for that short moment the darkness sputters and falters, then returns with renewed strength.

Again.

Concentrating hard and with great effort, I bring up the scene from last night—the laughing Walkers sitting around my living room playing games with my family. I imagine I hear their laughter, warm and hearty, and it begins to drown out the wails and cries of misery.

Again.

Sam. Leaning against his truck in the fast-food restaurant's parking lot. He's smirking at me playfully and his eyes pierce me through the heart, melting away my despair. I hear him saying my name in my ear, his voice thick with emotion.

And again.

Jana and I singing at the top of our lungs on a road trip.

Gram tickling me to the point of tears.

Mom and dad slow dancing in the kitchen.

With each new image my self-belief grows. Faster and faster they come, the happy visions filling my sight as the darkness begins to lift. I'm getting stronger, and for the first time the Greater Shade's confidence wavers. A brief flicker of panic darts across its mind. Now is my chance, while he's flailing. I begin to spread myself out, extending feelers as far and as deep as I can probe.

The layout of this mind is foreign to me. I have no sense of where to even begin to look for the "off" switch. I continue to throw images of joy and love at the Shade's mind while I search.

There.

A wall.

I've come up against a heavily protected area of its mind. If there's anything the Greater Shade would want to protect, it would be its most vulnerable part of itself.

Excited by my discovery, I draw all of my presence to

the wall and spread myself out along it. The wall's strong, but like the one I stumbled across in Angel's mind, not strong enough. I discover flaws in its construction. Imperfections. I find the weakest place and I put pressure on it—as much as I can muster. It takes a few seconds but cracks begin to spread. It gives a little, and I'm pleased when I feel the Greater Shade's alarm.

With one last, hard push the wall caves in and I'm through.

What I find amazes and terrifies me. I absorb as much as I can from this forbidden area, knowledge and secrets I was never meant to see.

OOOUUUTTT! The Greater Shade roars at my presence, and I find myself being hurled from the demon's mind and out into the open air. Disoriented from being so forcefully expelled, I grasp around me, desperate to find the tether back to the safety of my own mind. I find the familiar thread and follow it until I'm home again, back in the confines of my own body.

I open my eyes, expecting to look up from the forest floor and see Ember. Instead, I'm balanced on the front of Sam's bike as he jerkily maneuvers around trees and roots.

"Almost home, Addy. Hang in there," he says through a busted lip.

My head aches so badly. I close my eyes and grit my teeth. I'm alone in my mind. The Greater Shade feels far away now. A warmth starts to spread throughout my chest. We're nearing Major Calm. I feel it the moment we pass through into the garage. Sam lifts me off his bike and carefully rushes me to a nearby cot.

I hear commotion around us, but as I try to sit up and look around, Sam gently pushes me back down.

"You need to rest now. You've been through a lot."

I reach up and touch the side of his face where it's swollen. I lightly run my thumb over his split lip, leaving a trail of rapidly healing flesh behind.

"Stop that," he says softly, pulling my hand away. "No more work for you."

"Sam, I'm okay. Let me help." I try sitting up again. This time when he protests, I push his hands away.

I look around, wide-eyed, at the damage we've received. Bodies fill the cots next to mine. Ben is one of them. Mel's at his side, whispering encouragement as he moans quietly. Oscar's on the other cot. He's completely still.

Frantic to help, I jump up. The movement is too fast for me and the room spins. Sam's arms encircle me, supporting me so I don't topple over.

"If you insist on helping, at least heal yourself first, please. You're no use to anyone this way."

Recognizing the wisdom in his words, I do a quick once-over on myself. I have more injuries than the adrenaline pumping through my veins has allowed me to feel. I ignore the two broken ribs, the torn ligaments in my left shoulder, and the sprain in my left wrist. Those would take too much time to heal. Instead, I clear my concussion and block the pain signals from traveling to my injuries. This will do for now.

"I'm better now." The half-truth is enough to satisfy Sam, and he lets me rush over to Crank's cot to do what I can. I thank the heavens aloud when I see he's only unconscious. His body, however, is broken in so many places, and the broken bones have cut up his insides. He's bleeding internally. I place my hands on him and block out the rest of the world as I begin to heal him.

Nearly five minutes later I remove my hands from a perfectly intact Oscar. My hair's damp with sweat from the effort but I'm pleased with my work. I let him sleep. I swivel around on the edge of Crank's cot so I'm facing Ben and a fretful Mel. Ben's back has been broken in two places. I marvel at his strength as I relieve his pain and heal his spine.

Mel reaches over Ben and hugs me once I finish. "Thank you, love." I nod and stand up, scanning the garage for more victims.

Faye, whose head wound is still bleeding, is healing a gash on Kira's neck and what looks like a broken collarbone. Angel's with Sam, her hands on a swollen knee. Looking around, I see tired but otherwise healthy-looking Walkers, resting on the ground or leaning against walls. When I'm satisfied there are no more life-threatening injuries to tend to, I decide it's okay to heal myself. As I'm returning to my cot, however, something catches my eye.

At the far end of the garage, sticking out from behind a parked Big Bike, I see a pair of boots. Curious, I walk towards them. As I get closer, I see the boots are attached to a pair of legs in dark pants. Concerned now, I run the rest of the way and find a bloodied Mikhail propped up against the wall, barely conscious.

When I kneel down next to him, my hands land in a thick, red pool. Alarmed, I look him over and find the source of the bleeding. Piercing his left side, about six inches under his arm, is a large, jagged chunk of wood.

Idiot, I think angrily. Why would he crawl over here out of sight where no one can help him?

"It's okay, Mikhail. I'm going to fix you." His normally sharp, steel-gray eyes are glazed and out of focus. I don't know if he can even hear me. The first thing I do is turn off his pain. Then, bracing myself, I place one hand around the piece of wood and the other flat against the side of his chest. I pull hard.

As the wood comes free, Mikhail arches his back and inhales sharply. There's a strange, wet, bubbling sound and I realize his lung must be punctured. I place my hands on his ribs and close my eyes. I command the body to expel any splinters or chips of wood and dirt and to repair, regrow, and replace any broken or lost tissue and blood. Once every-thing is back as it should be, I scan for other injuries and find him intact and well.

Withdrawing my mind from Mikhail's body and returning to my own, I feel hands resting over mine. I open my eyes and see Mikhail's holding my hands tightly against his chest. His gaze is so intense I'm finding it difficult to break away from.

"Mikhail," I whisper through a smile, "I'm so glad you're

okay. I'm so happy you're here and that you fought with us. Thank you."

His expression is tender as his eyes travel over my face. His heartbeat quickens under my hands.

"Adelaide," he speaks softly. I lean forward to hear him better.

"There you are." Sam's voice startles me. I turn around to see him standing there with an uneasy look about him. Mikhail's hand drops from mine.

"Is everything all right?" His distrust for Mikhail is written plainly on his face.

"Everything is now." I smile up at him.

"Well, looks like everyone is put back together. We should get to the briefing room and figure out what happened out there."

"Sounds good." I turn back to Mikhail. "Will you come?" I ask quietly, pleading with my eyes. He looks at me for a moment then gives a reluctant nod. Grinning, I stand and offer him a hand up, and after only a moment's hesitation, he takes it.

CHAPTER 45

I'M THE LAST to walk through the doors of the briefing room. On my way here I finished healing the rest of my body. Given the fierceness of the battle, I'm lucky to have fared so well.

An anxious Ember greets me the moment I step inside. "How are you?"

"I'm better." I grab hold of her hand. "Thanks for staying with me." I remember the image of my head on her lap while she hovered protectively over me.

"Always," she says simply.

"All right, everyone." Sam watches from the podium at the front of the room as the last of us find our seats.

"What happened? Did you guys kill him?" Simone's at the table next to Ember and me. Her hair is slightly messy and her eye makeup is smudged. She looks as if she's been crying. I'm surprised—I've never seen her look anything less than perfect.

Sam lowers his head. The room is silent. No one wants to admit defeat.

"Well?" she demands.

"No, Simone." It's Angel who speaks. "He was too strong for us."

She stares in disbelief at Angel. "What about the plan? I thought you and Adelaide were going to get in his head."

"We underestimated him," she says sadly.

The room's quiet again, and the weight of everyone's despair settles down around me like a thick, suffocating blanket.

"I got in."

Everyone turns and looks at me, shock and puzzlement on their faces.

"It was almost easy," I say, staring blankly ahead. "He let me right in."

"What happened, Addy?" Lang-hao speaks up. "One second we were kicking trash and the next you were screaming."

I swallow a few times, trying not to think about the pain the Greater Shade caused me.

Angel saves me. "He found us. He targeted Addy again. He was in her head."

"Did he talk to you?" Kira asks hesitantly.

I nod. "He was mocking me, amused that I thought I could stop him. He said...," I can feel the blood rush to my cheeks as I stare at the floor, "he said I wasn't the *one*."

"I don't understand." Crank sounds confused. "You aren't the one? The one *what?*"

"To stop him," I say miserably. "All this time I was so stupid. I thought that's why I was called here, that I was the one who would be strong enough to destroy him. And I'm not."

"But you have to be," Ember insists. "You got inside his head when Angel couldn't."

I'm shaking my head before she even finishes. "No, no, no, no. I told you guys. I was *let in.*"

Angel inhales sharply. "Oh no. Addy. What did he do to you?"

A powerful wave of nausea hits me as the horrifying sights and sounds resurface. I wretch involuntarily. My hands clutch my head as I try to shake the images away.

"Hey. Hey! It's okay, Addy, I'm right here." Ember's arm is around me, pulling me into her. Sam's stands in front of our table, arms crossed, peering intently at me, worry on his face.

I want to tell them about all of the horrible things I witnessed, how it crippled me, how I never imagined I'd escape. But I can't. I can't let anyone else experience the things I saw. I can't burden them with that.

"What matters is what I was able to find out," I say. "I couldn't kill him from inside his mind. It wasn't possible. I'm sorry." I look around into the faces of my fellow Walkers, searching for signs of disappointment. None, surprisingly not even Simone, show a trace of accusation.

"But I found an area of his mind that was guarded. I managed to get through his defenses there and what I learned changes everything."

"Is it how to kill him?" Timothy asks eagerly. His fists are balled up angrily, and he's leaning forward in his seat.

"No," I say with dread. "I saw his memories. His plans. I know what he intends to do."

"But I thought we already knew that," Simone interjects. When everyone turns her way, she holds up her hands defensively. "I'm sorry. I'm not trying to be a brat. It's just...," she shrugs her shoulders, "he's a Greater Shade. Don't they all want the same thing? To find a weak spot, make a tear, and get to Earth Realm?"

"He isn't just a Greater Shade, and that isn't what he wants."

Ben leans around Mel to better see me. "Not a Greater Shade? Is that what you said?"

"I said he's not *just* a Greater Shade. He's more. When I was in his memories, I saw an awful land." A violent shiver passes through me. "It was a nightmare. The sky glowed a dull red, as if it smoldered. The horizons were littered with jagged mountains, all tapering up and off into sharp, jutting peaks. Everything was black as far out as I could see—the land, the mountains, the cliffs—with bubbling swamps like prehistoric tar pits."

"The Nether Realm." Mel's whisper carries through the whole room.

Nodding my head, I continue. "The blackness was so complete that I almost didn't notice the Shades." A crawling sensation creeps up my arms, and I reflexively try to brush it away as I remember what I saw.

"At first, I thought the ground was a river—a black flowing river of oil. But then I saw that it was the Shades— thousands of Shades, writhing, clambering, and climbing over each other. It was like the ground was bleeding Shades. Lesser and Greater alike."

"Disgusting," Lang-hao spits out.

"At the top of a peak a wide cavern opened up onto a ledge. In the cavern was a large circular slab. Standing around it, as if in deep discussion, were six towering Greater Shades."

I look up at Sam. "But these six, they aren't just Greater Shades, Sam. They're ancient. It felt as though they've always existed, since the beginning of time. I could feel the power ebb from them. It doesn't compare to anything we've ever seen. Not even close."

"What are they?" Sam asks intently.

"They are the Circle of Elders. The Elder Shades." The room feels colder to me than it did moments ago. "Elder Shades?" Angel puzzles.

"Yes. And the Greater Shade that's here in Chaos is one of them. He's the newest of them—the youngest— and he was sent here on a mission. You see, they all have different strengths, like each of us. Not all of the Greater Shades are rippers—very few have that ability. For some reason, the rippers are the only Greater Shades that are called to Chaos. It's as if the two abilities go hand in hand with the call."

Some Walkers nod in understanding, but others still look confused.

"What about the Lesser Shades?" asks Crank. "If there are so many in the Nether Realm, how come only a fraction of them are here in Chaos? You'd think they'd all want to get out of that hell hole."

"Because, Crank, it's the same with us over here. There are billions of people in Earth Realm, but only a dozen or so Realmwalkers in Chaos. Only a few of us receive the call. Same with them. Which brings me to my point. This Elder Shade that's here in Chaos, he isn't trying to create a tear into Earth Realm. He's trying to tear open the barrier between Chaos and the Nether Realm and bring through it, not only the Circle of Elders, but the entire Shade population. Every last one of them."

CHAPTER 46

"No!"

"He can't!"

"That can't be possible!"

Several of the Realmwalkers' shouts are incredulous, others angry.

Sam motions with his hands for the room to settle down, but it takes a minute before it's quiet enough for him to be heard.

"This is serious. What scares me the most is that all of us are in here right now. We need to end this briefing and send out a crew immediately. I'm sorry guys. I know you're all tired, but it's down to the nitty-gritty and we'll need Walkers in Chaos every hour of the day. We simply can't risk the Elder Shade making that tear."

"I'll go. Boss." Timothy stands.

"I'll join you," Kira says gravely, strapping her katana to her back.

"That should be good," Sam says. "Go now."

The two of them rush from the room. "Good work,

everyone. I know this may feel like a defeat, but it isn't. We gained knowledge tonight and knowledge is power. Be prepared to answer a summons at any time. Consider us DEFCON one. Got it?" He waits for each of us to affirm the order. "All right. Happy hunting," he says grimly.

I look around the room at the dazed faces. I wonder at the doubt they must be feeling. We gave everything we had tonight and it wasn't enough. I wish I could give them all hope, but I can't find enough of it for myself.

"Long night, Addy," Ember commiserates. I nod absently. "For all of us."

Simone passes in front of me on her way out and I feel the distress pouring off her. She must have been so frustrated sitting here all alone and unable to help. I feel terrible for her.

When Sam approaches, I stand to meet him and am surprised when he pulls me into a tight embrace. This public display of affection is rare. I take advantage of the moment and melt into him, soaking up as much comfort as I can. He holds me for a long time until nearly all the Walkers have wandered off. Over his shoulder I see Mikhail as he leaves. Our eyes meet briefly, long enough for me to see sadness in his gaze, and then he's gone.

"We need to get top-side. Timothy's asleep on your couch. We should move him to a bedroom so he isn't disturbed while out in Chaos."

I reluctantly pull away from him and check my watch. It's already six a.m. Ember's still here, standing next to us. I look back and forth between the two of them desperately.

"What are we going to do?"

Ember tries to be encouraging. "We'll figure something out."

"I hope so."

"Come on, girly. Let's go."

The three of us walk back to our hall, and Ember gives us a quick wave before disappearing behind her door. Lang's room is a few doors down, and I hear a guitar being played from inside. It's a sad, eerie melody. Sam stops outside my door and lifts my chin until I'm looking in his eyes. I lean into him.

"This isn't so bad, all right?" He traces my cheekbone with his thumb. "We know his game now. That's an advantage we didn't have before."

I close my eyes and open my soul up like a trench and swallow all of the comfort he's sending me. "I wish I could be as strong as you. As confident."

"You are strong, Addy. You were brilliant tonight. Watching you fight out there, it took my breath away." He leans down and kisses my cheek, his mouth warm against my face. "I've got one or two things I need to do here, but I'll be up top-side in a few minutes."

"Okay," I say, backing away slowly, a little dizzy from his presence. "See you in a few."

I close my door and immediately remove the night's clothing and throw it in the waste bin. I shower quickly, washing away Shade blood, dirt, and sweat.

Once I'm in some clean, comfortable pajamas—cotton shorts and a white tank top—I climb into bed, ready for the night to be over. But as I'm pulling the blankets over me, I hear a soft knock on the door. Exhausted, I lie still for a minute, hoping that maybe I was hearing things. Seconds tick by. Then, another soft knock.

I throw the blankets back, walk on quiet feet to the door, and open it. Sam's standing in the hallway.

"Did you forget something?" I smirk at him playfully.

Without saying a word, he pushes through my door and grabs me. He kicks the door shut behind him and pushes me back against the wall of my room. His face is inches from mine and I think my heart stops. He's pressed up flat against me, pinning me to the wall. His breathing is quick, heavy.

"Sam—" I start to say but am cut off when he pulls my face toward his and kisses me. For a second I'm lost in the kiss. My head is spinning, and my once-still heart is now pounding. I lean into his kiss, which makes him even hungrier. He feels urgent, desperate, almost angry. His hands squeeze my waist tightly, fingers digging into my skin. It hurts.

I push back a little. "Wait," I try to say, but he pushes his lips hard into mine. As much as I care about Sam, as often as I've thought about this moment, I'm confused. I never imagined Sam would be so rough with me. I send my mind out tentatively, trying to feel for his mood, searching for some kind of explanation behind this abrupt change in behavior.

Something's wrong.

I can't feel him.

All around Sam, where I can usually feel his strong familiar presence, it's just empty air. A void.

No.

I push back harder this time, managing to free myself enough to get out from between him and the wall.

"Stop," I say, hands out in front of me as I slowly back away. "Please. This isn't like you. This isn't what you want."

He reaches out and grabs my arm. He tries to pull me closer to him but I continue to back away. He jerks me forward roughly, and I use the momentum to twist my arm out of his grasp and pull free. I pull too hard and the force of it sends me tumbling backwards. I trip over my bed and land on top of it. And then he's on me. He's trying to hold my arms down and I'm trying to push him off, but he's stronger than me. He pins my arms to my side and presses his mouth into mine.

Sam! I send out the mental cry as loud and far as I can. *SAM PLEASE!*

My arms are pinned but my legs are free. I'm kicking out at him but I'm not making any difference. Hurt and betrayal pour through me so strongly that I grow weak. I turn my head sideways, breaking his kiss, and sob in desperation and heartache. My cries affect him. He stops fighting me. His weight shifts and with relief I realize he's trying to get up.

Before he can, my door is violently kicked open. Standing in my doorway, silhouetted by the light in the hall, is Sam. MY Sam. His familiar essence is so strong that I wonder how I ever believed this imposter on top of me was him.

He bursts into the room and grabs the phony Sam, lifting him up and throwing him into the nearest wall, his head making an audible crack on impact. He slides down the length of the wall and crumples into a motionless heap on the floor.

"What did he do to you?" Sam demands as he helps me up from the bed.

"He—, he—" I can't get the words out. I'm staring at the unconscious Sam on the ground as he slowly begins to morph into someone else. His hair shortens, and his shoulders broaden. Sam sees it too. He must have lost control over his disguise when he lost consciousness. Sitting limply on the floor is my fellow Walker and—I thought—my friend, Mikhail.

"I'll kill him," Sam says through clenched teeth. He launches himself at Mikhail.

"No!" I scream. I grab his arms at the last second and pull him backwards. "Don't, Sam!"

"What's going on?" Lang, then Ember appear in my doorway.

Sam points to Mikhail. "Help me. We need to get him to Inner Silence quickly." Without hesitating, Lang hurries over and he and Sam lift Mikhail and carry him out of the room. Ember walks over to me, eyes wide as saucers.

"Addy, are you all right? What happened?"

I wrap my arms around myself, trying to fight the

feeling that I'm coming apart. "He came in here, as Sam. He kissed me."

"As Sam? What do you mean?"

"I mean *as Sam*. He looked like him." I feel numb, in shock. And then the look of anger on Sam's face comes to mind. "I have to go. I have to keep Sam from hurting him." I rush out of my room. "Come with me!" I shout over my shoulder as I run.

When I get to Inner Silence, Sam is disappearing behind the heavy metal door. I slip through before it can close all the way. Sam spins around.

"Get out, Addy!" he shouts at me, furious.

Mikhail is laid out on the metal bed, still passed out. I don't see Lang-hao anywhere.

"No."

"GET OUT!"

I stand my ground, refusing to be intimidated. "Not unless you come with me." We stare each other down. "I'm not leaving you alone in here with him. You're too angry. You'll do something stupid, something you'll regret."

Reading the resolve in my eyes, he growls in frustration.

"Come on, Sam," I say softer, reaching out for his hand. "Let's do this the right way." He's still angry, but deep within him he must know I'm right.

He turns to look at Mikhail once more before grabbing my hand and leading me out of Inner Silence.

Seeing Ember, Sam immediately sends her top-side to make sure our sleeping bodies aren't left unguarded.

"Just because he's locked up here, doesn't mean he isn't free to go wherever he wants in Earth Realm," he warns.

Lang returns with Angel and Mel in tow. "The sealers are here," he reports to Sam.

"Good work."

I stand in between Angel and Mel as we put the seals on Inner Silence. It takes all three of us working simultaneously to do it properly. The method is a failsafe to assure that a rogue Walker can't imprison anyone on their own.

Strangely enough, I'm fairly certain I *could* do it by myself if I had to. I only need to perform three different wardings at the same time. It's really only a matter of multitasking, but I keep this information to myself. The wardings are impossible to break from the inside, so there's no reason to worry anyone.

"We'll need to take a vote as soon as we can. Procedure calls for it. I can only hold him in there for twenty-four hours without a majority consensus."

Watching Sam pace, I try to comfort him. "Really, Sam, I don't think he would ever hurt any of us."

He stops pacing. "How can you say that, Addy? He attacked you!"

"But I don't think he was trying to hurt me! He seemed like he was trying to stop. He did stop, right there at the end, before you came in," I insist. "I mean, come on! How many times has he saved my life?"

"Please tell me you aren't defending him," he says incredulous.

"No. I'm not," I say adamantly. "What he did was wrong. I know that. It's just…"

Mel shakes her head. "I'm with Sam on this one, Addy. At this point it's better to be safe than sorry."

I look to Angel for help. "Angel, you know he's not dangerous."

Her blueberry eyes look sad. "I know you believe in him, Addy, but what he did tonight was really bad."

"I know, but—"

"No, I don't think you do," says Sam. "He not only wronged you tonight, he wronged all of us. He's a shifter? What other abilities does he have that we don't know about? He's done nothing but lie to us from the very beginning. We can't ignore that."

The dread begins to sink in. I know Mikhail is secretive, but I've always tried to believe he's had his reasons for that. Has my desire to believe in him been so strong that it's made me blind? Even now, with all the ugly evidence against him, my instincts still won't let me see him as a bad guy.

Angel soothes the tension with her soft voice. "We all need a break from this. We need time to let it settle so we can look at the situation with clear and," she looks at Sam for emphasis, "calm minds."

Sam glares at the door to Inner Silence as though he can see straight through to Mikhail.

"Don't worry." Angel assures him. "He's not going anywhere."

"Fine. Let's get top-side. We need to inform everyone

about what happened. Angel, could you fill in the others who aren't with us at Addy's house?"

"Of course."

"Good. I'll send another pair of Walkers to relieve Timothy and Kira in a few hours."

"Sheesh," Mel says tiredly, "as if we didn't have enough trouble to deal with."

CHAPTER 47

WHEN I OPEN my eyes, I want to cry. *Mikhail. How could you do this?* I know the Walkers are probably all out in the living room where Sam and Ember are filling them in. I'm in no hurry to join them. I don't want to see the looks on their faces as they learn of Mikhail's betrayal. I don't want to hear "I knew it" and "I saw this coming." I lie still, taking my time, as I try to sort through my warring emotions.

Why? How could he think that I wouldn't have known? That I wouldn't have figured it out? Is he really so desperate for affection that he has to lie this way and betray my trust? Why couldn't he talk to me? He knows I care about him. I'm the only one who makes the effort to be kind to him.

And now, of all times, he pulls this. Right when we need him the most. I picture him in battle last night, zipping through the forest nearly unseen, effortlessly hacking down Shades. He's one of our very best fighters. We can't expect to defeat the Elder Shade without his help. I can feel it in my gut. We need him. We'll need every last Walker.

I can hear Kira breathing from her makeshift bed on

the floor. I peer down over the edge of my bed at her. I feel for her presence, searching for her state of mind. She seems peaceful. Chaos must be pretty calm at the moment. It seems Ben was right. It looks as though I'm the catalyst that causes the Elder Shade to attack.

But why? He made it very clear last night that there was nothing I could do to defeat him. I'm no threat to him. So *why*?

The sounds of dishes clanking and cupboards being closed float back to my room. I can't hide back here any longer. I pull myself out of bed and make my way to the kitchen, bumping into Mel in the hall.

"Hey, how is everything?" I ask her warily. "Do they know?"

She nods her head. "Yeah, Ember filled them in. The atmosphere's a little tense right now. It's not easy learning one of our own has done something ugly to another one of us."

"Are they angry?"

"A bit. Also concerned for you. I told them not to worry, that you seem to be handling it better than the rest of us."

I rub the side of my face wearily. "Thanks Mel. I want this to all go away. We don't need this kind of trouble right now."

"I get your concern, Addy, but you have to understand there's a procedural process that we need to go through. We can't forget what he did. There are rules in place that have existed since the beginning of our history, and they're there for a very good reason."

The dread I feel knots and twists inside my stomach.

"Can't we make an exception? Considering everything?"

"I don't know," she says doubtfully. "I wouldn't get your hopes up about that. Boss is pretty upset. I don't think he's going to let it go."

Seeing my dismay, she pulls me tightly to her side. "Buck up, mate. There are still reasons to smile. You graduated last night, remember? And I hear you're off to L.A. base with Ember soon. That's exciting, isn't it?"

Smiling weakly, I say, "Yeah, that's right. Thanks Mel."

In the living room I find a note taped to the television.

Addy,
Jana and I didn't want to bother you
and your friends this morning, so we
snuck out early to run some errands.
Love you!
~Mom

In the kitchen, huddled around the tables and counters, the Walkers eat and talk in hushed voices. A few look up and smile at me, a vague sort of nervousness in their eyes. Others are more obvious, forcing artificial looks of good cheer. They're putting on a good show for me, trying to lighten my spirit. Between failing to kill the Elder Shade last night and then the whole thing with Mikhail, they must know how badly I need it. If only I wasn't so sensitive to their true states of mind, I might actually fall for it.

I love them for trying though, and not wanting to

disappoint them, I smile big and say, "Man, I had the craziest dreams last night."

This earns a hearty chuckle and the tension seems to crack and fall away.

Ember brings me an unholy amount of scrambled eggs, toast, and bacon, and I sit down on a bar stool at the counter to dig in. Sam lets me get through all of my breakfast before getting into the subject of Mikhail.

"I made sure everyone knew the details so they could vote fairly," he says quietly from the stool next to me.

"You already voted?" I ask surprised and feeling wounded.

"Yes, and Angel took votes on her end. It's decided. Mikhail will stay in Inner Silence for three months."

"Three months?"

"And then he'll only be released if he allows Angel to fully assess his abilities. He must give her complete access to his mind or he stays in there indefinitely."

"That's pretty extreme," I say, trying to push down my anger. "No one should be forced to open themselves up like that. It's not right, Sam."

"It's fair. In our line of work we can't afford to have secrets, Addy. It's too dangerous. We have to know we can trust one another."

"Don't I get a vote?"

"Sure. But just so you know, it's unanimous so far, so if you vote against—"

"It won't change a damn thing." I glare at him. "This isn't fair. I'm the one he came after. I should have a say."

"It doesn't work that way."

I fume at my empty plate, too mad to look him in the eyes. "How do you expect to fight without him? You know how badly we need him," I whisper. "Locking him up where he can't fight... I don't know Sam. Something about this is wrong. I can feel it. I can't explain it, but when I think of fighting without him, a sense of dread comes over me. Can't you feel it?"

He's quiet for a while. "His timing is unfortunate," he admits. "I wish things were different. I wish he could fight with us. I wish he never even looked at you." He's whispering now too. "I wish you would've believed me when I told you he was no good. But I can't change any of those things. What happened, happened. We have our laws and we have to follow them."

He places a hand on my lower back. I try hard not to be angry with him. I know he cares for me. I know he's trying to protect me. He's "Boss" and he has a job to do. Even though I know he's wrong, I can't afford to distance myself from him right now. With our gloomy outlook, I really need him.

Sensing me give, or perhaps reading it in my expression, he asks, "Are we good?"

I'm finally able to look up at him. The concern I see in his eyes is heavy, visibly weighing him down. It hurts me to see it.

"Of course we are," I say, wanting to relieve him, happy to know that I'm able to. A softness touches his eyes, and he leans in closer and rests his forehead against mine.

"I'm so glad you knew. That is wasn't me. I'm so glad, Addy."

I lay my hand on his chest over his heart and feel the strong thumping underneath his ribs. For a second I forget all about Mikhail and the Elder Shade. I even forget we're in the kitchen surrounded by friends. For a few short seconds, it's just the two of us.

"I'd know this heart anywhere," I reassure him. He takes my hand and brings it to his mouth, kissing my palm.

"I'll feel much better once you're with me in L.A." My heart skips a beat when I think about living in the same house with him. He'll be so close to me. I'll get to see him all the time.

I lean back to look at him better, my heart warming at the sight of his smile. I love the way he studies my face, as if he's committing every detail to memory. He's playing absently with a strand of my hair when Lang interrupts.

"Okay, you two, hate to break up the love fest, but we've got some details to hammer out." My cheeks warm when I see Lang's smirk.

"I never wish to leave good company, but I've got to be in Bangkok in about twenty hours." He looks around the room at the other Walkers. "I know we all need to get back to our lives, but I'd feel much better knowing we aren't leaving Addy completely alone."

"Hey! What am I? Chopped liver?" Ember says indignantly. "I'm staying right by Addy's side for as long as it's necessary."

"I'll be fine, Lang. I'm heading to L.A. base later today

so I won't be alone. Besides, I'm not completely helpless you know."

He laughs. "Yeah, you were pretty awesome last night. We should go Shade bowling more often."

This starts a bustling conversation as everyone relives last night's adventures. I watch their joy-filled faces as they exchange battle tales, always trying to "one up" each other. I feel so close to these people.

After a little while, Timothy and Kira come stumbling out of the back of the house looking sleepy-eyed and ravenous. Angel, Faye, and Ben have replaced them out in Chaos.

Soon, it's time to say good-bye. Sam sets up a schedule with everyone so that missions in Chaos will run around the clock. I help them all gather up their things and thank them for coming to my graduation.

One by one they wave good-bye as they climb into taxi cabs that will take them to the airport. Sam, Crank, Ember and I will drive back to California later, so when it's just the four of us left, I take some time to pack up a few essentials that I'll need for my new home.

"Don't bring a ton of clothes," Ember insists for the third time. "I'm taking you shopping when we get there. It'll be fun! Plus, you need the distraction." Guilt hits me hard in the chest as I think of shopping with Ember while Mikhail is imprisoned in Chaos. Everything about this is wrong. If I could talk to him, maybe he could explain himself.

I lose my train of thought when I hear Mom shout from the living room, "Addy! We're home. Come here please."

When I find her, Sam's telling her how all of our friends

are sorry they missed her this morning and how they all wanted to thank her for being so gracious.

"Well, they were a pleasure!" she insists.

Jana echoes her sentiments. "Yeah, last night was so much fun. I can't remember the last time I laughed so much."

Sam and I exchange a quick glance. *Our* night wasn't so fun.

"Addy." Mom digs in her purse and pulls out a pretty green box the size of a deck of cards with a bow on it. "Jana and I wanted to get you a little something for a graduation-slash-going-away gift."

"Oh, wow." I say, caught off guard. "Thanks guys." She hands me the box. It jingles a little as something inside slides around. I untie the bow and take the lid off. A pair of keys sit inside. I stare at them blankly.

Ember gasps and disappears, running to the front room. I hear the front door open. I look at my mom and sister, both wearing identical grins.

I try to find words. "Really?" is all I can manage.

"I know you love your dad's truck, sweetie," Mom explains, "but I want you to be safe. Don't worry—I'm keeping the truck here and I promise I'll take good care of it. I don't want to be constantly afraid of you breaking down so far from home."

"Addy! Come look!" Ember shouts from the front yard. My curiosity drives me to her. There, parked in the driveway is a brand-new, dark green SUV. It's one of those sporty cross-over vehicles that are smaller than a full-sized off-roader but bigger than a sedan.

"Whoa!" I shout. Ember's already looking through the front windows.

"Open 'er up already! Come on. Let's take her out." I run back to Mom who's standing in the doorway and hug her fiercely.

"Do you like it?" she asks, laughing.

"I love it, Mom. Thanks! It's perfect."

"Jana picked it out."

I reach over and hug Jana. "Thanks Sis."

"Yeah well, you can pay me back by letting me borrow it when I come visit you in L.A. I'll need something I can fit all my surfer boyfriends into."

Laughing, I say, "Yeah, right."

I motion for Sam and Crank and they follow me out to the car. We take it around the block a few times.

"This will work out great, Addy," Sam says from the passenger seat. "You and I can take your car, and Ember and Crank can take hers. We can take turns. One of us can drive while the other takes a shift in Chaos."

"I can go back out?" I ask, surprised.

"No. I'm sorry, Addy. It's too dangerous."

I didn't really think he would let me, and this time I don't insist. I know there's nothing I can do at this point to contribute. If I go out into Chaos again, it will only provoke the Elder Shade and cause more harm than good.

"There are other things you could do though. Like practice training or studying. Who knows? Maybe there's something in the *Chronicles* that might offer us some kind of clue about beating this guy."

Busy work.

I know as well as he does that there's nothing in the *Chronicles* about Elder Shades. The Walkers have all read it already, and their enhanced memories wouldn't let them forget something like that. I give him a look and his expression turns guilty.

"Just for a while, okay?" he pleads. "Until we figure something else out."

"Yeah, okay," I say, making a point not to look and sound as sour as I feel. Pouting won't help the situation.

Once back home, we eat a hearty lunch and get ready to leave for California.

"Are you sure you don't want to stay another day?" Mom asks, standing in the driveway, starting to look a little panicky.

"Yeah, sorry Mom. I wanna get up there today so Sam can help me move in before he has to go back to work on Monday." Mom doesn't know I'll be sharing a house with Sam and Crank. I've yet to think of a way to tell her that won't keep her up at night worrying about my virtue. I know she trusts me and she adores Sam, but being the perceptive mother that she is, she's picked up on the chemistry between the two of us.

"Well," she wrings her hands absently as Sam throws the last of our bags into the back of my new car. She chokes out a laugh to try and cover up the fact that she's on the verge of tears. "I never thought this day would come so soon."

Jana rolls her eyes behind Mom and I try not to laugh out loud. "I'm not that far away, really. And you can have

Gram come check on me whenever you want." I hug her tightly. "I love you, Mom. Thanks so much for everything. For the car, for taking care of me. I'm gonna miss you."

"Call me at *least* every other day. And you three," she points at my friends sternly, "keep her safe and out of trouble, okay?"

"Yes, ma'am," they say in unison.

I squeeze Jana one last time and get behind the wheel.

"Call me when you get there so I know you made it!" Mom hollers as I wave good-bye. Sam settles back into the passenger side seat.

"I'll see you in a few hours," he winks and smiles at me before closing his eyes.

"Be safe," I say, but he's already gone.

CHAPTER 48

THE DRIVE TO my new home is blissful. After two hours Sam wakes up and we spend the rest of the drive talking. We talk about everything—our favorite music, movies we consider classics, books we've both enjoyed.

We talk about our plans for California. Sam's wanted to get a dog for a long time but was worried about having just him and Crank there to take care of it. With Ember and I there now, he thinks we should get one. "Our L.A. base needs a mascot," he says. We talk about what breeds we like and ultimately decide to get a shelter dog.

We stop to fill the cars with gas, and Crank climbs into the driver's seat of Ember's Mustang.

"Whoa, Crank, are you even old enough to drive?" He and Sam both wear sheepish looks.

"Uhhhh," is all I get from Crank.

Eyebrows arched, I turn to Sam who's replacing the cap on the gas tank.

"What's this, Officer Dixon?" I enunciate his title teasingly.

"Ah," he shrugs. "He might not have a license, but he can drive. I taught him myself."

"Besides," Crank defends himself, "I could take this baby apart and put her back together again in an hour flat! Why shouldn't I be able to drive her?"

"Ha!" I bark. "Good point."

Back behind the wheel again, I take a risk and venture into a topic with Sam that I've been curious about for a long time.

"Hey, can I ask you something personal?"

"Of course you can," he says mildly, but he stares out the window like he knows what's coming.

"Where's your family?" I ask gently. "Did you lose them?" He's quiet for a little while.

He fishes his wallet from his back pocket, gingerly takes out two photographs, and passes them to me. I hold them in front of me and study them over the steering wheel. One picture is of a young woman, maybe my age. She's sitting on a black-and-white carousel horse and smiling at the person behind the lens. She's blonde and has large blue eyes the same shade as Sam's.

"That's Rebecca. My older sister." I glance at him as he says her name. The tenderness in his eyes is heartbreaking.

"She's beautiful."

The second picture is of a young couple, and it's faded and worn from time. The man and woman are sitting on a brownish-orange couch, and their clothes and hairstyles are straight out of the seventies. The photographer caught the woman laughing, her head back and mouth open in a grin.

There's a mischievous twinkle in her eyes. She is breathtakingly beautiful. The dark-haired man was caught admiring her, the look of adoration on his face forever frozen in time. On the woman's lap is a light-haired baby in a pink-and-white jumper.

"Your parents?"

"Yeah."

I pass the pictures back to him and watch as he carefully, almost reverently, puts them back into his wallet.

"We lived in northern California. When I was fifteen, we were in a bad accident. My parents were in the front seats and died right away. Rebecca was next to me in the back. She ended up in a coma for a week before she passed."

My eyes burn and prickle. I slowly shake my head back and forth. I hate how unfair this world can be sometimes.

"I'm so sorry." I know the words are inadequate but nothing I could say would make it any better. We sit in heavy silence for a few miles. I don't look at him because I'm afraid if I see tears in his eyes, I'll lose it and have to pull over.

"I've wanted to tell you," he finally speaks. "I want you to know me. It's just been hard. I mean, it's not something you come right out and say."

"I know. It's okay. Thank you for wanting to tell me. It's rotten what happened and I hate it. But I'm happy to know you better. I think everything we experience, especially the bad stuff—" the sound of screeching tires rings through my memory, "it shapes us. It makes us who we are, for better or worse. I'm glad to know that part of you. It makes me appreciate your strength even more."

He reaches for my hand across the seat and weaves his fingers through mine. "Thanks Addy," he says simply. The genuine gratitude in his voice makes me smile.

Once we get about thirty miles out, we pull over so Sam can drive the rest of the way to the base. I start to get nervous as we cruise into an upscale neighborhood. The homes we pass are huge, surrounded by sprawling green lawns and guarded with heavy security gates.

"Um, is this our neighborhood?"

Sam looks at me sideways and smiles slyly.

We stop outside a large, gilded, two-door gate with a roaring lion's head protruding from the middle of each side. Sam clicks a button on his key ring and the gates swing inward. My suspicions are confirmed when we roll up to the front of the largest red brick mansion I've ever seen.

"Holy crap, Sam! Is this a joke?" I hear the panic in my voice.

Confused, he looks back and forth between the house and me. "You're upset. Don't you like it?"

"How am I supposed to explain this to my mom?" I gesture at the house frantically. "She's supposed to come visit me next month!"

"Oh." He's very unsuccessfully fighting a smile.

"Oh?" I ask, incredulous.

He's laughing–no—he's *giggling*.

"Saaaam," I say plaintively.

"Don't worry, Addy. We'll find an explanation. You're

supposed to be moving in with Ember, right? Who's to say she's not secretly a millionaire?"

"Oh man," I grumble.

Once inside, Crank dashes from room to room as he gives me and Ember the tour, his exuberance making his English hard to understand.

With the high-class neighborhood and the sheer size of the house, I'd been expecting everything on the inside to be opulent and lavish. I'm surprised to find instead the house is completely practical.

The furniture is comfortable and sturdy, the spaces used well. There are rooms for exercise, some for entertainment, some for study. There's even an office that's nearly identical to the logistics room at Major Calm. The kitchen is large with lots of seating areas, an oversized fridge, and a giant walk-in pantry. The place is filled to the brim with food, which is probably a good thing considering how much and how often we eat.

Overall, the house is cozy and welcoming. The only extravagant thing about it is its size. There are eight bed-rooms, each with their own personal bathroom. Ember and I pick rooms across the hall from each other.

I call Mom to let her know I made it safely and then take a few minutes to settle in. It's strange that a brand-new place can already feel so much like home.

Sam and Crank welcome Ember and me to the base by cooking dinner for us. After consuming enough food to feed a small army, we all clean up together.

"I know it's still pretty early," I say once we are finished, "but I think I'm gonna head to Chaos."

Sam eyes me suspiciously. "What do you have planned?" He tries to sound casual.

"Something very unpleasant," I say dramatically.

I smile at their confused expressions. "Well, I can't go on missions so I have to do something useful." My mood sours as I anticipate what I'm about to do. "I'm going to bite the bullet and help Simone."

"Do you think she'll let you?" Ember asks scornfully.

I nod my head. "She will, even if I have to pledge a lifetime of servitude—which is very likely—I'll get her to let me."

I say good night to my friends, Sam last of all.

He seems pleased with my renewed determination to help Simone.

Hugging me good night, he says, "I'm glad you're going to try again with Simone. She may be difficult, but we could sure use the extra help that another ability would give us on the battlefield. Good luck, Addy."

"Thanks Sam. I'll need it."

CHAPTER 49

I STARE HARD at the black door in front of me, hand hovering in the air by my face, knuckles poised inches from the shiny surface. I swallow once, then again, trying to force down the lump of dread that has lodged in my throat. Dread—or is it pride? Isn't that what they say? *Swallow your pride?* I understand that phrase better now.

Here goes.

I rap politely on the door, four short knocks. There's movement inside and after a few seconds the knob turns. I'm beginning to grow used to Simone's ever-changing appearance, so I'm not too startled when a stranger opens the door.

Tonight Simone is a willowy strawberry blonde with light freckles peppering her nose and cheekbones. Her delicate mouth is framed by coral lips, and her large eyes are pale green adorned with long, soft, golden lashes. Again, I'm in awe of her beauty. This one's a kind of natural, dainty loveliness you would expect to see on an elf or a water nymph, if such beings existed. This is the most striking version of Simone I've seen yet.

I'm shocked when her trademark sneer doesn't instantly mar her perfect face. Simone stares back at me with an almost empty expression. The only trace of emotion is deep within her eyes. If I weren't so aware of her mood, I might not catch the misery hiding there.

"I'm sorry," I blurt out.

Her eyebrows rise. We stare at each other for a moment. She keeps her face very still, but I can feel the conflicts within her. So many emotions—fear, anger, longing, frustration.

"Please Simone," I say desperately, "let me in."

Whether she takes me to mean, *Let me into your room, Let me into your mind,* or maybe even *Let me into your heart,* she steps aside and opens the door wide.

After closing the door behind me, I follow her to her bed where she sits cross-legged, propped up against a dozen throw pillows. Without waiting for permission, I climb up and sit across from her. She still hasn't said anything, but I feel the ache coming from her. It hurts me nearly as badly as it does her.

"Don't look at me like that," she says softly, eyebrows furrowed. "Don't pity me."

"It's not pity."

She huffs and looks down at her hands in her lap. "You're my sister, Simone. It doesn't make me happy to see you suffer."

Her eyelashes flutter as she blinks rapidly. Her mood feels heavy and tired. It weighs on me like a cloak of iron.

It must be exhausting for her, keeping her defenses up constantly, always hiding behind a steel exterior, striking out with hateful looks and venomous words.

"I'm not Angel. I'll never be as sweet or as kind as she is. Heck, I'm can be as stubborn as you sometimes." I smile ruefully at her. She sniffs noisily and crosses her arms defensively.

"But the bottom line is," I tell her, "you're family to me just as much as any of the other Walkers. That feeling we all have for each other, the one that connects us, I feel it for you too. And I'll continue to feel it no matter how you treat me. So, I guess what I'm trying to say is I'm not going to give up on you."

She finally looks up from her lap, a hint of a challenge in her eyes.

"I won't ever force you," I assure her. "Ever. But I will bug the hell out of you. I'll beg, I'll plead, I'll grovel at your feet if that's what it takes."

A hint of a smile dances around her mouth. "Grovel, huh?"

"I'd prefer not to. But..." I shrug.

"So, what? We're supposed to be besties now?"

"No. Not besties. Just," I mull a few words over in my mind, "comrades. We're comrades in arms." She searches my eyes for any sign of mockery. Finding nothing but sincerity, she nods shortly.

"Fine."

A grin spreads wide across my face, but she humbles me quickly.

"But I reserve the right to change my mind at any time," she states. "Just because I let you do your mind mumbo-jumbo on me once doesn't give you unlimited access whenever you want."

"Of course," I say, placating her.

"And this does NOT mean we are friends." "If that's how you want it, okay."

"Okay," she throws back at me. She must realize how juvenile she sounds because she makes a visible effort to soften her expression. After a few deep breaths she asks, "What do you need me to do?"

⟡

Simone's mind is much like the other Walkers', clear and quick and strong. I delve deep within her consciousness searching for areas of overdevelopment. I purposely ignore the area of her brain that gives her the ability to morph into whatever she chooses. I'm already aware of that ability. Instead, I search the corners, plunge the depths, and skim the shallows looking for any hint of some other ability.

I find a couple obvious strengths. Her willpower, for one, though others might call it stubbornness, is immense. Her perception of people, or scrutiny as some may say, is unnaturally strong. While these attributes explain some of the more disagreeable aspects of Simone's personality, none of them point to a legitimate ability. At least none that I'm familiar with.

There is, however, a feeling. It's difficult to describe. It's as if I'm right on the verge of discovering something. It's like a secret, like some massive potential is just out of my reach. It's frustrating and disappointing, and I dread telling Simone that I don't have an answer for her. She wants this so badly—to be able to feel like she's one of us.

I withdraw myself from her mind and return to my own. Slightly dazed, she opens her eyes. It takes only a second before she's gripping my arms tightly, a look of desperation on her face.

"Did you find it?" She looks terrified of my answer.

"Yes and no," I tell her, hoping my instincts are right.

She shakes her head in confusion. "What does that mean?"

"It's there… something's there," I try to explain. "I just, I can't tell what it is yet." Her head drops into her hands.

"Simone," I try to comfort her, "this is good news. We need to be patient. I need a little more time with you, to see how your mind works."

"But," she hesitates, "it's there? You're sure?"

"Something's there. I can feel it. I'm sure."

For the first time, I feel a flicker of hope spark within Simone.

"Will you let me work with you? I'll need to be with you often, observing how you think and react to everything. It may be intrusive." I'm afraid she'll say no, throw me out for not being able to help her, and never talk to me again.

"Okay," she says meekly.

"Really?" I ask surprised.

She nods vigorously. "Yes. I… I need…," the words seem almost painful for her to say, "your help."

"Then you've got it," I say matter-of-factly.

At that moment, I feel a strange sensation at the back of my mind, like a nagging, plucking feeling. It's as though my attention is being tugged in a certain direction, and it takes me a moment to realize what it is. Angel had described this to me when she was assigning her duties to me one by one. She told me this is how I'd recognize a weak spot in the fabric of Chaos.

Simone senses my alarm. "What is it?"

"A weak spot. I've got to go." I jump down and rush out of her room and down the hall. As I run, I send out a mental call to all the Walkers within the realm.

There's a weak spot in Chaos.

I immediately feel apprehension from multiple frequencies. I search for Sam and find his familiar presence in Logistics. I run in that direction, finding Ember and Crank along the way.

"Boss is in Logistics," I say as I run past. They follow me with tense, worried faces.

When we arrive, we find Sam pacing in front of his desk. "Where's Angel?" he demands. His intensity startles me.

"What?"

"Angel. Where is she? She's not answering the summons. We need her to show us where the weak spot is since you can't go out there."

"I haven't seen her. Give me a second."

Angel? I call to her mind. I can feel her now, though she's distant. She must be top-side.

Angel, we need you.

"This is strange," Crank says. "Angel's the one who usually tells us if there's a weak spot, and now she's not even here?" There's a hint of accusation in his tone.

"I've been taking over for her," I say defensively. "She's just a kid, Crank. She shouldn't have to do everything all the time."

Crank immediately looks ashamed. "You're right. I'm sorry."

But I barely hear him. I'm concentrating on getting through to Angel. It's never been so difficult before. It feels like I'm trying to talk underwater.

"I may have to go out there, Sam."

As he starts to protest I hold up a hand. "Got her!"

I feel her more clearly now. She's in Chaos though she seems peculiar—muddled, almost groggy.

I'm on my way. I can tell the others received her message too from their obvious relief.

"Go assist her, guys," he tells Ember and Crank. "Lang and Mel are on a mission now. Give them a heads up once you're out there. You may need their help."

"Yes sir." They leave in a hurry.

"Be careful!" I yell after them, feeling useless.

Sam leans back against the edge of his desk, arms crossed, face weary.

"Will you monitor them? So we know if this will be an all-out war?"

"Already am," I tell him. "I think it will be okay though. The weak place hasn't gotten any thinner, so I don't think the other side knows about it yet."

"I'll relax when it's fixed."

I lean back next to him, our shoulders touching. We sit this way, in quiet anxiety, for at least ten minutes. Finally, the tugging sensation at the back of my mind lessens then disappears altogether.

"It's fixed. Everyone's safe."

"Thank goodness." His posture relaxes. "Great work, Addy. It's nice of you to give Angel a break, and it's a relief to know I can trust you to do a good job."

"Thanks Sam."

"How did things go with Simone?"

"Okay. Actually, it went better than I expected."

"Yeah?" He guides me around in front of him so we're face-to-face and rests his hands on my lower back, pulling me close. "Tell me about it."

"She let me in."

He frowns thoughtfully. "Wow."

"Yeah. I didn't learn anything earth-shattering. Not yet anyway. But I know there's something there. I'll find it."

He lifts one side of his mouth into a crooked grin. "I know you will."

I warm at his confidence in me. "Sam?"

"Hmm."

"Can I talk to you about Mikhail?"

His eyes harden. "There's nothing to talk about."

"I'm not going to try to change your mind," I insist. "I know he's in there for three months. I won't fight you on that."

He looks wary. "Then what?"

"You said you were going to have Angel dig around in his head, find out his secrets. What if it doesn't have to come to that? What if we don't have to give him an ultimatum? There are much nicer ways to get information without leaving a damaged relationship behind."

"You think he'll tell us?" he says derisively.

"Maybe," I venture, "if the right person asks."

"No." I feel his arms and chest grow rigid. "Absolutely not. What kind of a man would I be if I let you in there with him? After what he tried to do to you?"

"I don't have to be alone. You could come with me." He's shaking his head adamantly back and forth. "But he trusts me!" I object.

"I'm sorry. It's out of the question."

I stare hard at Sam's chest and fight back tears. I can feel him watching me but I won't meet his gaze. After a moment he relaxes and his arms around me soften.

"Addy," his face is close to mine. "I don't want you be unhappy. But I need you to be safe. Can you understand that?"

I nod shortly.

"Addy," he says my name again, quietly in my ear. His grip around me tightens, bringing me closer to him until we're pressed together.

The heat begins again, like it did the first time he held me. It starts underneath his hands where they rest on my back and follows the trail they make as one slides up over my shoulder blades, the other around my waist. My own hands move on their own accord, following some deep instinct, as if they already know the steps to the dance. They press into him, up over his chest to his neck, one reaching higher into his hair as I pull him down toward me.

His mouth burns and melts into mine. All my anguish over Mikhail evaporates in the heat of the embrace. He's gentle with me, not rough or urgent, the way the imposter Sam had been. We kiss slowly and the places behind my knees tingle and weaken. After a while he pulls away and rests his cheek on mine, running his fingers through my hair.

I don't want it to be over. I want more of him. When I look in his eyes, they burn with the same feeling, the same heat and intensity that pulls at my gut. But then I feel another Walker approaching Logistics and we both hear footsteps in the hall. I try to clear away the lightheaded feeling I always get when I'm close to Sam as Angel walks in.

"Everything go well?" Sam asks.

"Like clockwork," Angel chirps, smiling.

"Excellent. Where are Ember and Crank?"

"They decided to relieve the others. It was nearly their shift anyway. Addy," Angel turns to me, "thank you for covering for me. I've been enjoying the time off."

"I'm happy to help you. You deserve it."

"Actually," her expression serious, "I've been spending a lot of time with my mother."

Harmony's mention of her mother is unexpected. As far as I know, she's never mentioned anything relating to her life outside of Chaos.

"That's good, Angel." Sam smiles warmly.

Angel looks uncomfortable all of a sudden. She's having a hard time looking us in the eyes.

"Is everything all right?" I ask. She studies the hem of her shirt intently. The last time I saw her fidget this way was right before she asked me to help with Simone. She must need help with something but is afraid to ask for it.

"What can we do, Angel?" I question, trying to make it easier for her.

"Well, you see, it's my mom."

"Is she okay?" Sam asks abruptly.

"Oh yes! She's fine. It's just…" She looks back and forth between the two of us. "She's kind of strapped for money."

"Angel," Sam says, "you can take as much from the Walker account as you need. If anyone's earned it, you certainly have."

She seems to relax a little. "It's just the two of us, you know? My mom and me. And… we've managed to get by on our own so far, but lately things have been really hard. She doesn't know anything about Chaos and I don't want her to find out. I don't have a clue how to handle this whole thing. I could really use your help."

"Sure Angel," Sam assures her. "Whatever you need."

CHAPTER 50

"IDAHO?" EMBER ASKS, her green eyes burning with curiosity.

"Idaho," I confirm.

"Really?"

"Why do you look so disappointed?"

She goes back to rummaging through my closet. She's been helping me pack since we woke up top-side.

"I don't know." Her voice is muffled behind the closet door. "I guess I thought it would be some place more exciting."

I laugh at this.

"Well," she says defensively, "it's always been some big mystery. No one ever knew where she was from. I guess my imagination got the better of me."

"She needed privacy. She's only a kid."

Ember comes back out with a couple tops and bottoms. Folding them nicely into my duffel bag on the end of my bed, she asks, "And it has to be *now*?"

"Yeah. She seemed pretty insistent about it. I guess they really need the money."

"Huh. And she wants you and Sam to bring it to her?"

"It makes sense. It's not like she can hand it over to her mom. Besides, she wants us to visit. From what it sounds like, she doesn't have too many friends. You know how consuming this way of life can be."

"Won't it be weird when two adult strangers show up at a child's house and claim they're her friends?"

"We already got it settled. We don't even have to lie about it. We're going as representatives from the Walker Foundation. We'll say that someone anonymously nominated them for a donation and we're there to determine how much assistance is needed."

I zip the duffel bag closed and swing it over my shoulder. "Ooohhh. Clever."

"You about ready, Addy?" Sam calls from the foyer.

"Coming!"

Ember looks bewildered. "Well, it must be pretty important. I can't ever remember Boss taking time off work."

I'm beginning to think that perhaps Ember's feelings were hurt that she wasn't asked to come along. Angel specifically asked for just Sam and me to come. She thought any more than that would be suspicious.

I put my hands on Ember's shoulders. "When Angel asks you to come, you come. Even if that means taking off work."

"I guess you're right. Anyway, I'm glad she'll be taken care of, her and her mom."

"Me too." We grin at each other before she hugs me good-bye.

"Come back soon."

"You won't even know I'm gone."

✺

The flight from LAX to the Boise airport takes only a few hours. After grabbing a rental car and throwing our luggage in the back, Sam and I head east to the town of Caldwell. It doesn't take long to get there, and once in town we stop and order lunch from a drive-through fast-food chain. Sam punches Angel's address into the car's GPS while we eat.

"Look at that." He points to the highlighted route on the display. "We're only a few miles away."

"I thought we were close by. I can feel her."

I ball up my trash and chug the rest of my soda.

"I'm ready when you are."

Sam grins at me. "Let's go make someone rich."

We drive a short distance then turn into a neighborhood of modest houses. I smile through the open window as the breeze hits my face. The weather is pleasantly warm and the sky's full of fluffy white clouds. It would be impossible to be grumpy on a day like this.

The light blue home we pull up in front of is small and old but looks well cared for. While the grass in the yard is yellow and brown, the bushes along the front walk are neatly trimmed. The sidewalk and driveway look swept and there's a quaint little bench on the front porch.

As we stand on the welcome mat, I give myself a once-over. I smooth out my plum-colored button-up shirt and tuck the ends into my dark slacks. I wore my best clothes hoping to make myself appear older and more professional. Sam's dressed similarly in gray slacks and a pale blue dress shirt. He looks tough, like a detective on a crime show. He sees me scrutinizing him.

"What?" He smiles a bit self-consciously.

"Do you think we look convincing?" I ask.

"Don't stress, Addy. It won't matter what we look like once it's clear we're offering money. We could be wearing clown suits for all that matters." He reaches up and presses the doorbell.

"And you'd still look like a cop." I grin at him.

"Ha. Probably more so."

The door opens.

"There you are!" A woman with slightly graying hair stands in the open doorway. She's covered from head to toe in scars.

"Faye?" Sam and I say in unison.

"We've been waiting for you. Come on in." Faye winks at the two of us conspiratorially. We step inside the foyer and follow her into a small but tidy sitting room. On a couch with an outdated floral pattern sits a petite woman, hands clasped in her lap.

Her clothing looks worn and faded and hangs off her small frame as though it's two or three sizes too big. Her mousy brown hair is pinned back away from her face revealing big violet eyes. Her expression is haunted. She seems shaken, as though recovering from shock.

"Mrs. Tanner, this is Sam and Adelaide." We reach across the coffee table and take turns shaking hands.

"Pleasure," she mumbles absently. "Please, sit."

We sit next to Faye on an adjacent sofa.

"I've already spoken with Mrs. Tanner—"

"Cadence, please," Angel's mother interjects numbly.

"Yes, of course," Faye continues. "I've informed her of why we're here and how the Walker Foundation intends to help."

"Wonderful," Sam replies. He's hiding his confusion and surprise better than I am. "Looks like you've done our work for us," he says amiably.

"I've spent some time visiting with Mrs.—excuse me— with Cadence and her daughter, Harmony, and I'm confident they're the perfect candidates for our charity."

"That's happy news," Sam answers. "Congratulations, ma'am."

Mrs. Tanner's trembling hand floats to her face, touching her mouth, then her cheek.

"Oh, goodness. This can't be real." She looks from face to face, as if waiting for one of us to crack and tell her it's all a cruel joke. When our eyes meet, I smile encouragingly at her.

"It's real, ma'am," I assure her. "From what we hear, you and your daughter are two very special people, and you deserve whatever help we can give you."

This seems to be too much for her. She buries her face in her hands, her shoulders shaking with quiet sobs. Faye reaches across the table and rubs her shoulder comfortingly.

"There, there now. It's all right. Take as long as you need, dove." Faye turns toward Sam and me and says quietly,

"Perhaps you two would like to spend some time visiting with Harmony. I've got a few more details to hammer out with her mum and it may be a while."

"That's a great idea," Sam says softly. "Where can we find her?"

"Down at the end of the hall there, on the right. It's the door with 'princess' on it."

As Sam and I walk down the hall, I whisper to him, "Did you know Faye would be here?"

"I had no idea." He looks as puzzled as I feel. "Angel must have asked her to come a few days ago before she ever mentioned it to us." We stop outside the door with big pink letters spelling out the word "princess."

"A few days ago?"

"It had to have been. Faye would've needed more time to get here from London."

"That's so strange." My hand's resting on the door knob. "Why Faye?"

Sam shrugs his shoulders.

"And why not mention it to us?"

"I don't know, Addy. Let's go find out." I push open the door.

What I find waiting for us on the other side is the last thing in the world I would have ever expected to see.

CHAPTER 51

THE WALLS OF the bedroom are a light pink. A white dresser is in one corner of the room and a purple, oversized bean bag is in another. Against the back wall is a bed. It's much like one you would see in a hospital, the head slightly raised to a comfortable angle. Chairs sit on either side for visiting. Light from a nearby window falls directly onto the bed, illuminating the small form lying on top of the white sheets.

Automatically, I start to back away to leave, embarrassed that I've stumbled into the wrong room.

Please stay.

I freeze where I am, unable to look back at the still figure lying on the bed. Sam peers around me in confusion.

Please.

Though I recognize Angel's voice in my head, the child I glimpsed on the bed couldn't possibly be her. It just couldn't be.

"Oh,... Angel." Sam's hand falls heavily on my shoulder. He must have seen what I saw.

With great reluctance I turn back toward the room.

Come sit with me.

I'm shaking now, tears already blurring my vision. I blink them away as I walk toward an empty chair next to the body on the bed. We sit, one of us on each side, in the silent room.

The child in front of me is severely disabled. Her arms and legs are pulled in close to her body. Her knees are bent and her legs are crossed. They are so tightly pressed together that they appear welded to one another. Her toes are pointed up toward her shins at an uncomfortable looking angle. Her arms are in the same state, held stiffly against herself, hands curled inward.

The strain of this rigid position is evident all over her body. Her skin's pulled firmly across flexed muscles and bulging tendons. An expression of agony looks to be permanently engraved on her face. Though the features there are slightly skewed, the eyes that stare back out at me are undoubtedly Angel's.

My composure breaks. I drop my head next to her and weep. "I didn't know. Angel, I'm sorry. I didn't know."

Don't be sad, Addy. I'm not sad. There's no need for that.

Sam reaches out and softly places a hand on Angel's shoulder. "What is this Angel? Are you sick?"

Suddenly hope soars through me. I sit up straight and lay my hands over Angel's twisted frame. I close my eyes and prepare to heal her.

STOP.

The command echoes through my mind like a gunshot. I have no choice but to obey.

"What? Angel! Let me fix you."

I don't need to be fixed. This is who I was meant to be. This is the way I was made.

"The way you were made? You mean you've always been like this? I don't understand. How is this possible? You aren't like this in Chaos."

Since the moment I arrived there, my body in that plane of existence has been whole and unburdened. I can't imagine being asked to except the call to Chaos and not be provided a vessel best able to serve the realm's needs.

"But your body here never changed? How cruel is that?"

Her earnest eyes look back at me. *It was overwhelming kindness to grant me an able body there, even if only for a few short years.*

"But I'm sure *this* body can be healed!" I shake my head in disbelief. "Haven't you tried?"

I can feel her hesitation.

Once. A long time ago, when I first came to Chaos and discovered my abilities.

"And what? You couldn't do it? Maybe if we work together—"

No Addy. I could have healed myself then. In fact, I was going to. But when I began, it felt so wrong I had to stop. To heal my body, to change what was given to me, felt like a mistake, like sacrilege. I couldn't do it.

I look at her, confused.

"How could it be wrong?"

I know in my heart this is how I'm supposed to be. This trial is mine to live. I don't know why it's this way, but I've accepted it.

"But you must be in pain. At least let me make you comfortable."

No. The pain is mine to bear.

My frustration turns to bitterness. "Then why am I here? Why is Faye here, if not to heal you?"

I needed you to see this. I needed you to be able to hold this image of me in your mind so you can explain it to the other Walkers. I'm sorry, Addy. I'd do it myself and spare you this burden, but I can't bear all the questions. I can't bear to live through their good-byes.

My heart is a stone in my chest—hard and cold and heavy. I stare unbelieving into Angel's eyes.

"No," I whisper.

"What do you mean 'good-byes'?" Sam asks, grief making his voice thick.

I'm tired.

"No," I repeat.

I've been tired. For many years. I've held on desperately, terrified of leaving Chaos without someone like me, to do what only I can do. And then you came, Addy.

"Don't." I'm angry now. "Don't make this my fault."

I'm trying to thank you. I'm hurting, Adelaide. I've been in constant pain my entire life… and I'm so tired.

"So you're going to die because of me?" I'm sobbing uncontrollably. "You can't. Please Angel! I can't do this

without you. I'm... I'm not ready. I'm not strong enough."
I look to Sam desperately. "Tell her, Sam. Tell her she can't leave."

There are tears standing in his eyes as he looks back at me. "That's beyond me, Addy. I'm so sorry." He reaches out to grab my hand, but I pull away from him, feeling betrayed. "We can't make that decision for her, for anybody."

"You're not thinking clearly," I tell Angel. "I'll heal you and you'll see. You'll understand then." But I know as I say the words how wrong they are. A sick feeling comes over me as I picture myself healing Angel's body against her will.

"You'll do no such thing." A stern voice comes from the doorway. I turn to see Faye step into the room and close the door behind her. "Harmony has the right to choose her own path. I was hoping it wouldn't come to this, but if you try to heal her body, I'll block you in every way I can."

"So that's why you're here," I say accusingly. "To keep me from preventing the death of a child."

Faye's eyes narrow. She is livid. "And you would hold her here? Unnaturally? You would prolong her suffering? Adelaide Shepherd, shame on you." The indignation in her voice and expression weakens me. I'm crushed by the weight of her words. When she sees how she's wounded me, her demeanor softens.

"Can't you feel it, dove? Can't you feel her pain?"

I close my eyes and mentally reach for Angel. It takes me only a moment of searching before I once again come up against the wall in her mind. Only this time she allows me through. Like a flood, the pain rushes in. I can feel it in every inch of her body. It's crippling. Muscles burn with a dull ache. Bones scream out in protest against the constant rigor of the body. This is what she feels all the time? How is she able to withstand it?

Not only has Angel hidden her pain from all of us, but tucked behind her wall I find more sources of misery. I see through her eyes. I witness what she has endured every single day. Her mother's weary, tired eyes as she cares for her. The strain on her face as she lifts Angel in and out of bed, in and out of her wheelchair. How the constant, around-the-clock attention drains her, physically and emotionally. The overheard conversations on the phone with debt collectors inquiring after overdue medical bills. The crying she hears through the walls at night. And on top of it all, the immense effort of hanging on, of willing her body to live one more day. And then one more.

It's too much.

Dismayed I realize I have to let her go.

Do you see now?

"Yes. I'm sorry. It was selfish to ask you to stay." I know to let her die would be a mercy, but it doesn't make the pain of losing her any less intense. Sam reaches for my hand again and this time I hold on tightly.

You must help the others. They won't understand. Show them what you've seen.

"Wait. Now? Are you leaving right now?" I ask, startled, as the reality of it sinks in.

Soon. I'd like a few more hours with my mother. The money

she's getting will relieve most of her stress. I'd like to see the joy it gives her before I go.

Sam wipes tears on his sleeve and tries to smile through his grief. "I'll miss you, sweetheart." His voice trips over the last words. He leans forward and kisses Angel on the cheek.

Sam. You can hear the smile in her voice. *I love you, brother.*

Sam only nods, unable to speak.

Faye steps closer and leans down to kiss Angel's hair. "Sleep in peace, my dear."

It's been so long since I slept, I'm looking forward to it. Thank you, Faye.

Sam stands and walks to the door. I can't believe this is good-bye. I can't believe I'll never see this perfect, beautiful, smiling child again. Angel responds to my desperate thoughts.

I won't be far, Addy. I'm only going to another realm. A fourth realm. And somehow... I have a feeling it will be the best one yet.

I force my legs to stand and lean down and kiss her porcelain cheek.

"I'll see you there someday," I whisper into her ear.

Though I weigh a thousand pounds, I somehow make it to the door. Sam wipes my tears away as best he can. I turn from the doorway and look upon my precious friend one last time. I don't know for certain, maybe it's only the light from the window playing across her face, but for a moment

I imagine I see her pained expression relax and a peaceful smile rest on her lips.

꙳

Later that night, I lay in my hotel room in downtown Boise, wrapped tightly in Sam's arms. When the time comes, it's marked by an absence of warmth, a sudden emptiness. I can feel the exact moment when a piece of my heart leaves this world forever. To realms unknown.

CHAPTER 52

THE NEXT FEW days are dark and difficult. We gathered the Walkers together and Sam told them of our trip to Idaho and what transpired there. The news was met with stunned silence. It was Simone who finally broke the quiet with a sound of pure heartache. Her grief made it real for the others.

Amidst the pain were questions. Why? How? Couldn't she have been helped? The only way to answer was to show them what I saw. To make them feel as though they were there with me, standing witness. I replayed the scene in the Walkers' minds, and I left out nothing. The knowledge that Angel was no longer suffering seemed to be the only comfort any of us could cling to.

The Walker Foundation paid for Harmony Tanner's funeral. It was a small event. Very few people attended, only Cadence Tanner and her brother, who had flown in from Washington, and a local pastor who read a few verses from the Bible and said some kind words. There was, however, a small group of strangers there as well, a dozen or so, more representatives from the charitable foundation who came to pay their respects.

All of the bills had been paid, all of the debt cleared. Cadence Tanner would receive a monthly stipend for as long as she lived. She would always be cared for and unknowingly looked after by those whose lives had been touched by her daughter. A large sum of money was donated in Harmony's name to fund research into further understanding and treating her disorder.

After the graveyard service, Sam and I approach Mrs. Tanner to offer our condolences. She's standing in front of an easel where an oil painting rests, a wreath of fresh daisies encircling it. She addresses us without looking away.

"It's funny. I have no idea where this came from but I'm convinced it's from an angel." She's smiling wistfully as tears stream down her cheeks. "You know, I used to dream sometimes... when things got really difficult." She turns to smile at us.

"In my dreams, Harmony was a healthy little girl. She would run and play and laugh. Oh, her laugh was like wind chimes!" She pauses a moment, overcome with emotion. Sam and I stand at her side, viewing the painting I had made for Cadence. It's of Angel, the way she always appeared in Chaos. She's on a swing that hangs from a tree in a field of flowers. She's leaning back, bare feet rising up to meet the sky as her white sundress trails behind her. Her hair dances around her face and her sweet smile is infectious. Her eyes are both wise and innocent, the way they were in life.

Angel's mom clears her throat. "The painting was left

here for me. No note or anything. I don't know how anyone could have known this, but this is exactly how she looked to me in those dreams. This is how I imagine her now, in heaven."

∽

"Sam, someone needs to tell Mikhail. He should know."

"I wanted to talk to you about that." Sam pushes back from his desk in Logistics and motions to an empty chair next to him. I sit down and cross my arms, ready for an argument. He must see the determination on my face because he speaks mildly, to defuse the tension.

"Are you meeting with Simone soon?"

"Are you changing the subject?" I challenge him.

He sighs. "No Addy. I'm just curious how things are going, what your plans are for the night, if you're still having a hard time with Angel's passing. That's what boyfriends do. We worry."

I can tell he's trying to soften me up by using the word "boyfriend." I'd be ashamed to admit it worked if it weren't for the sincerity in his expression. He's genuinely concerned for me and I can't blame him after the week we've had.

Things have been beyond stressful without Angel. I'd already been performing all her duties when she was here, but knowing that she isn't around anymore to catch me if I slip up is terrifying. I guess I always thought she would be here for me to fall back on if I needed her. Now I'm completely on my own.

It's up to me to constantly monitor all of Chaos for

weak spots, new tears, new Walkers approaching, current Walkers in distress, injuries that may need to be healed, and maintain the wardings and seals around the entrances of the Calms. And all of these things must be done simultaneously. Not to mention I'm the only one who can assess new Walkers for potential abilities.

And that hasn't been going very well for me. My time with Simone has been anything but productive. Angel's death has hit her even harder than the rest of us, plunging her into a deep depression. When we're together, she's moody and distracted, often dissolving into tears, putting an early end to our sessions.

"I'm sorry, Sam. I don't mean to be confrontational."

"I get it." He nods in understanding. "You're stressed. Unload on me. That's what I'm here for."

"I'm supposed to meet Simone in—" I check my watch, "twenty minutes. I think things are getting better. She hasn't had a crying fit in a few days. That's promising at least."

"Well, keep it up. She's been devastated. I think the way she's treated right now, when she's most vulnerable, can have a huge impact on how she acts toward us in the future."

I nod gravely, thinking of the old snarky Simone compared with her newly humbled self. "She does seem to have lost a bit of her sting, hasn't she?"

"It's strange how losing a loved one can change you." He agrees. "It completely flips your view of the world and your outlook on life."

"Let's hope for the better then."

"So," he grins, lightening the mood, "I spoke with Crank earlier."

"Oh man." I groan. "Don't get me started!"

"You're on your fourth Big Bike?" he smirks, incredulous.

My cheeks burn hot with embarrassment. Crank's been working in his shop night and day for the past week, trying to build me my very own Big Bike. The only trouble is I can't seem to stay on it.

I totaled the first model within seconds, mistaking the gas for the brake. I wrecked the second and third because of a few miscalculations in judgment on my part. Ember teases that it looks like Jana's bad-driving gene runs in the family. But in my own defense, driving a massive, awkward motorcycle is nothing like driving a car.

"Yeah, he swears this new one will be completely crash-proof. He's probably putting giant training wheels on it as we speak," I grumble.

Sam chortles. "Which means you may last a whole five minutes." I glare at him petulantly.

"So, about Mikhail." I bring the conversation back to where we began.

Sam breathes out a long puff of air. "Yes. I guess it can't be avoided any longer."

"He needs to know about Angel. Like it or not, Sam, he's a member of this family and he deserves to know."

"I agree with you." His easy acceptance surprises me.

"So you'll tell him?"

"In three months, when his sentence is up."

"What? Come on, that's not fair."

"He wasn't *fair* to you, Addy. He wasn't *fair* to any of us when he lied to us, betrayed our trust, and refused to share his abilities. He doesn't get to have fair."

"And what's going to happen in three months? Angel isn't here anymore. I'm the only one left who can breach his mind and find out his secrets. Do you expect me to do that?"

Sam runs his hands through his hair back and forth, rubbing his head as he thinks. "I don't know. I can't stand the thought of you anywhere near him."

"Well, I won't do it," I say stubbornly. "I promised myself from the start that I would never forcefully take anything from any of you. That includes Mikhail. I won't invade his privacy."

Now the challenge is in his eyes. "Even if it means protecting us from him?"

"It won't ever come to that. He isn't dangerous."

Sam shakes his head in disbelief. "I can't understand how you can think that. You're an intelligent person. How can you not see that he can't be trusted? How can you say he isn't dangerous?"

I don't know how to explain my gut feeling to him in any way that he'll understand.

"I know," I say with conviction. "I just know, Sam."

His eyes look sad. "Knowing something, and wishing something, are two very different things."

Round and round we go. We always come back to the same conclusion. I believe in Mikhail. Sam doesn't.

"I'll just have to prove it to you."

He looks alarmed. "What does that mean?" he asks, panic in his voice.

"In three months, when Mikhail's time is up, I'll speak with him. I won't force him to tell me his secrets because I won't have to. You'll see."

"I haven't decided yet if I'm going to let you speak to him."

"Then I'll call for a vote." His jaw muscles tighten as he clenches his teeth. "It's my right."

His gaze never wavers. I'm afraid I'll crack beneath it.

"I'm sorry," I state. "But he's not the monster you think he is. Yes, he made a mistake. A terrible one. But no one's unredeemable." I turn and leave before I lose my nerve completely.

❧

I can feel Simone scrutinizing me as I sit on her bed and stare into space. I'm still stewing over the argument with Sam from moments before. Simone's heartbreak over Angel tends to be contagious, so I hold on to my anger to avoid the sadness.

"You're moody today," she accuses me. "Is it *that* time of the month?"

While reproachful, this is a mild insult compared with her old attitude, and I take it almost gratefully.

"Boss and I had a disagreement."

"What else is new? You two fight like an old married couple."

I continue to simmer.

"Let me guess. You want to talk to Mikhail and he won't let you." I look at her suspiciously. Could she have overheard us? I don't remember feeling her presence anywhere near Logistics just now.

"You're very perceptive," I tell her guardedly.

"Oh please, you've been whining about it for ages."

Puzzled and defensive, I raise my voice. "What? No I haven't."

"I don't know why he doesn't let you. Mikhail's putty in your hands. He'd jump off a bridge for you if you asked." She sounds bitter when she says this, almost jealous. It reminds me of Tori and how ugly she can be when she isn't the center of attention.

"So you actually agree with me?"

"Just this time," she clarifies. "Mikhail's one tough cookie to crack. He's hard and cold and strong-willed. But when it comes to you, my friend, he's helpless. You're his biggest weakness."

"Did you call me 'friend'?" I ask in mock disbelief.

"What? No. Of course not—" She continues to ramble on about how we are definitely *not* friends when it hits me.

I hold up my hand to stop her. "Wait. Wait. Wait. What did you say?"

"I said," she enunciates each word clearly, as if speaking to a child, "MY.FRIENDS.ARE.HOT.UNLIKE. YO—"

"No, no, not that. About me and Mikhail?"

She frowns at me in confusion. "That he'd do anything for you? Sheesh, Addy, do you want me to announce it to the world? And you think I'm pathetic?"

"You said I was his weakness."

"Uh. Yeah. It's obvious." She looks at me like I'm clueless. Excited now, I scoot closer and face her.

"Simone, do you remember what one of the first things you ever said to me was?"

She shrugs vaguely. "It probably wasn't very pleasant," she admits. I know she remembers, word for word, and thankfully so do I.

"All night I'd been terrified that Angel would evaluate me and I'd find out I was useless. And then, one of the first things you said to me was I could end up not being able to do anything at all."

She looks a little sick. "Do you want me to apologize? Look, I know I was a total bi—"

"No," I interrupt. "I mean yes, you were, but that's not the point. And then later, when Mikhail saved me from that Greater Shade at my art show, I was miserable because I totally flaked out and could've gotten a lot of people killed. I hated that I had to be rescued, that I couldn't defend myself. And then you stopped me in the hall and voiced all of my fears out loud."

"So I'm really good at hurting people's feelings. Last time I checked, that wasn't a superpower if that's what you're getting at."

I can remember at least a dozen other instances when Simone's words have cut right through someone, exposing their rawest nerves. My suspicion turns to certainty. I know I'm right. I grin now, unable to hold back my discovery. "But it *is* a superpower, Simone. An amazing one." I can see her trying to hide her hope. I can feel her pushing it back down inside her, too afraid to let herself feel it.

"Simone. You can determine someone's worst fears. You can sense their weaknesses."

CHAPTER 53

"Do you have any idea how useful this ability can be?" I ask Simone as she stares numbly into space.

"Hey!" I whistle and wave my hand in front of her face. "Earth to Simone! Do you read me?"

She blinks a few times and looks at me. "Do you really think it's true?"

"I do, and I think we should test it out. Have you ever been in a fight?" I ask, surprised that I don't know the answer.

"No." She looks embarrassed and ashamed. "I went out into Chaos once, for field training. It didn't go well."

"Maybe things will be different now. Since you know what you can do, maybe it'll be easier to fight."

Fear creeps into her eyes and she shakes her head back and forth. "I can't. I can't do that again."

I try not to show my disappointment. We've all been counting on the benefit another fighter could bring us out in the field. I try to make her see how vital her role could be.

"If you come out with me into Chaos on a mission and the Elder Shade attacks—" The blood drains from her face at the thought of it. "Simone, you could see his weakness, his fears. It could tell us how to destroy him."

I let the gravity of my words sink in for a few moments.

"But what if I can't do it? What if you're wrong about me? I don't think we can survive another encounter with that demon. No. I'll get someone killed."

I sigh inwardly. Just when I thought I had the answer, it slips away from me. But then I have an idea. If Simone won't budge, if she refuses to go to the Elder Shade, maybe I can bring the Elder Shade to her.

"I want to try something," I say excitedly, my hope renewed. In response to the nervous look on her face, I guarantee her, "You don't have to do much for this. Just observe. Now, close your eyes."

I reach out and attach myself to Simone's mind.

"I'm going to show you everything I have on this Elder Shade. What he looks like, sounds like, feels like. Every-thing. Even most of what I saw in his mind." I decide to try and spare her the worst parts. "I'm not going to lie to you. This will be very disturbing, but you'll be safe. And if there is a chance this will help us defeat him, it'll be worth it."

I sense her apprehension but can feel her struggle to squash it down with her desire to prove herself.

"Here goes."

I show Simone, in perfect detail, all of my memories of the Elder Shade. Her mind instinctively recoils from the very first sight of him, but I don't let her escape from it. I make her experience all of the same feelings and thoughts I went through. It's essential if she's going to have a complete idea as to who and what this monster is.

I feel the wave of nausea that hits her as she sees the Shade's flesh for the first time. She whimpers when she feels his cold fingers wrap around her throat as I did that night. I share her pain as we endure the screaming migraine his presence created in my mind. And lastly, I feel her triumph at the panic and dismay I caused the Shade when I discovered his memories and desires.

When it's over, I withdraw and find Simone looking at me as though it were for the first time. She's visibly shaken, but I'm surprised to see a deep respect in her gaze. "I can't believe you *lived* that. That was the most horrible thing I've ever experienced."

"I'm sorry." I give her a minute to recover then ask, "Did it work? Where you able to get a sense of him?"

"Yes." She shivers. "Ugh, that was so disgusting." She's still pale so I give her some time.

Finally she continues, "You were right, Addy. I could see his fears as plain as day. It was so easy."

"What were they?"

"There weren't many—only a few, in fact. For one, he's afraid of failure."

"Makes sense, I guess. Who isn't?"

"No," she shakes her head. "He's not afraid of disappointing anyone. He's afraid of what the Circle of Elders will do to him if he fails."

I picture the council of demons inside the top cavern, their ancient evil dripping from their very pores. I imagine whatever punishments they have in store for those who fail them are extremely unpleasant.

"But more than that, more than anything, Addy, he fears *you.*"

"No," I insist, "that can't be right."

"I'm telling you," she grabs my face in her hands and looks directly into my eyes, "you are his biggest weakness."

"But I can't be!" I say, exasperated. "I've tried everything I know. I can't beat him."

"I don't know what to tell you." She drops her hands in her lap. "Other than thank you." She smiles self-consciously. "You didn't give up on me, just like you said. I owe you one."

"Really? Because I know how you could repay me."

She laughs out loud and the sound is remarkable. "Well, that didn't take long."

"Do you think you could keep this from everyone? Just for a little while?"

"Keep what? My ability?"

"No, of course not. That's important and you should get to share that with everyone. Could you just not tell them that last part about the Shade? You can tell them he's afraid to fail if you like, but…"

"You don't need the added pressure," she finishes for me.

"Does that make me an awful person? Asking you to lie to everyone for me?"

She laughs again. "You're asking *me* about being awful?" She sighs dramatically. "Maaaan, I've got a lot of awful to make up for. Anyway, I'm sure they'll understand in the end."

I chew my lip nervously. Simone sees me and continues,

"And if you're worried about Boss, don't be. He'd probably forgive you for cold-blooded murder. I know I said you were Mikhail's weakness, but I'm going to let you in on a little secret," she leans forward and whispers, "you're Sam's weakness too."

"Oh?" I try to look surprised but she sees right through me. Her expression falls flat.

"You already knew."

"Um. I had an inkling."

A steely glint flashes in her eyes, and I remember what Ember said about Simone having a crush on Sam.

"So, you two are together or something?" She looks dangerous. We were finally starting to get along and now she's going to be right back to hating me. She reads my hesitation and nervous expression to mean "yes." *Here it comes.*

But she doesn't explode. She merely slumps forward, defeated, her face that of a child's whose favorite toy's been taken away.

"Figures," she pouts.

I reach out and awkwardly pat her knee. The look she gives me stops me in my tracks. Not wanting to push my luck with her any further, I decide it's the perfect time to leave and slide down off her bed.

"Well, I should probably go. I've got a lot of things to think about."

"Don't hurt yourself." She's sarcastic but I can hear playfulness in her voice too. All is well.

As I'm leaving, something occurs to me. "Hey, Simone?" I turn around. "What are my weaknesses?"

She cracks a sideways grin and asks, "How much time do you have?"

"Hardy har har. Seriously though." Her face turns thoughtful as she examines me. For a moment I'm intensely embarrassed, as though I'm standing naked in front of her.

"Hmmm," she muses. "You have a few of them, though they aren't all that serious. I'd say the one that could get you into the most trouble would be your failure to act on your instincts."

"Huh," I say, confused. My thoughts immediately turn to Mikhail. "I thought I was doing a good job of that."

"I didn't say you weren't. Only that it could be very hazardous for you and everyone around you if you ever stop."

CHAPTER 54

WE NEED A lift. We're overworked, downhearted, and dispirited. Like a runner at the starting blocks, poised in the "set" position, muscles taut, adrenaline pulsing, waiting for that familiar, resonating CRACK of the starter's gun, we're all on edge. Every time I feel that tugging sensation in the back of my mind, I know that somewhere out in Chaos, the threads of reality are beginning to come loose.

It's the same every time. Drop everything. Rush to Chaos. Get to the weak spot as quickly as possible and pray the Elder Shade doesn't get there first. The stress of constantly maintaining that high level of readiness has been taking its toll on the Walkers.

When they aren't scrambling around trying to seal up tears, they're slaughtering Lesser Shades by the dozens. Our theory is kill them all now so that none are left to defend the Elder Shade when the time comes.

Everyone's been pulling their own weight. The Walkers who normally stay in the Calms, like Ben and Faye, have been out fighting and risking their lives. Even Simone has found the courage to step out into Chaos, and her confidence grows with each new venture.

The unending labor and its ill effects have turned my friends gloomy and irritable. Some are outright cranky. On my own shoulders I carry not only the stress the others feel, but also the additional weight of guilt and frustration because I can't go out into Chaos and personally help them. The last thing we need is for me to draw the attention of the Elder Shade directly to a weak spot. That's what we're trying to avoid.

So now I sit in the passenger seat of my car. Ember and Crank bicker in the back seat, and next to them, staring darkly out the side window, is a brooding Lang-hao. The tension in the car has grown over the last twenty minutes and everyone's irritable mood has brought it to a breaking point.

"Enough you two! Please." Sam grips the steering wheel so tightly his knuckles turn white. The light up ahead turns yellow and he brakes harder than necessary, as if to emphasize his rebuke. "Remember, this is supposed to be a fun trip."

Crank grips the back of Sam's seat and pulls himself forward. "Well, maybe it would help if you told us where we're going. At least tell us how much longer we're going to be in this car. I hate not knowing!"

"It's a surprise. Trust me—you'll be happy once we're there. Which will be any minute if you'd please let me drive in peace."

I see the effort Sam's putting into maintaining his calm.

He's been playing referee lately as he seems to be the only Walker unaffected by the stress of our plight. He senses me watching him and turns to look at me. I smile as cheerfully as I can. The tightness in his shoulders seems to ease and I feel his agitation start to abate. I love that I'm able have this effect on him. It makes me feel useful and needed.

Sam turns into a parking lot along the side of a large, low brown building. Once parked, everyone pours out of the car, eager for some space and curious to see where we are.

"No way," Ember says, brightening instantly. "I should've known."

"What? What?" Crank bounces in place.

"We're at the animal shelter. Look." She points to a sign that reads "Los Angeles Animal Services."

"Awesome!" Lang cheers in a complete reversal from his previous mood.

"I get to pick!" Crank shouts and darts off toward the door.

"Oh, no way!" Ember yells as she and Lang take off, pushing and pulling each other out of the way. Crank's almost to the door when Lang throws his arm out toward him, hand clutching the open air. Lang's telekinesis abruptly stops Crank although his arms and legs remain in motion, cartwheeling around as he tries to gain momentum. The effect is comical. He looks like he belongs in a Wile E. Coyote and Road Runner cartoon.

"Lang, that's not fair you cheat!" He shouts over his shoulder.

"Lang!" Sam barks.

Lang releases Crank from his telekinetic grip, and the three of them reach the door at the same time, each fighting to be the first in, creating a struggling tangle of arms and legs and grunts of effort.

Despite the embarrassing display, Sam chuckles quietly. It's a comforting sound and one I don't hear too often anymore. He slips his arm around my shoulders, and I press into him as we walk through the parking lot.

"This was a really smart idea."

He nods. "We needed something, anything really, to boost morale. I've never seen things this bad before. I've never seen everyone so down." His sigh is heavy. I can feel it pass through his chest.

"This will help a bit. Besides," I say, "I can't see this going on much longer. It's been nearly four weeks since our last confrontation with the Elder Shade. He's under a lot of pressure to get his mission accomplished. I don't think he's going to delay much more. He's too afraid of the Circle and what they'll do to him."

"I know." We stop outside the door. "But we aren't ready for him." The lines at the corners of his eyes deepen as he scrunches his face up in thought. I feel the concern he hides so well, tugging at him under the surface, threatening to pull him down.

"Well, there's nothing we can do right now, so let's forget about it." I step back and take his hand, towing him toward the door. "Today's a happy day. Let's try to enjoy it."

❧

Caesar. Our newest addition to the family and mascot of L.A. base is a golden-brown bully mix named Caesar. After walking the kennels for half an hour, fighting over which dog was best, Caesar found us. He was coming back from a checkup with the shelter's veterinarian and when he saw the five of us huddled together discussing our options, he pulled free of his leash and charged.

At first it was alarming to see a tough, muscle-strapped dog barreling toward us with his multi-fanged jaws agape, but as he got closer, what first looked like a ferocious snarl turned out to be a very toothy grin. When he reached us, he began to do the strangest thing I've ever seen a dog do.

He danced. Or more like wiggled. His feet lifted and shuffled, nails tapping the smooth concrete floor. His cheeks were pulled back in a decidedly human smile, tongue hanging out the side of his mouth, while his crooked tail whipped around violently behind him.

The arguing stopped as everyone fell head over heels in love with Caesar. I've never had much experience with dogs (Jana was allergic so we could never own one), but this seemed to be the happiest dog on Earth. When the lady whose leash he had slipped caught up to us, she laughed with us and said he was called "Caesar the people pleaser." We had to have him.

We spend the rest of the day at a pet store buying him everything a dog could need, each of us determined to make him the most spoiled animal alive.

Once home, Sam has time for only a quick dinner before he has to start his night shift. After we eat and he changes into his uniform, I walk with him to the door while he straps on his sidearm.

"There was laughter in the house tonight, Sam."

Sam's grin is evidence he's pleased with his efforts to boost morale.

"Yeah, it's a nice change, isn't it?"

"Most certainly. Maybe we should suggest London Base get their own mascot."

Stepping outside into the warm night, the air feels dewy, and I'm struck by the scent of brine rolling off the ocean a few miles away. I close my eyes and smile into the breeze, thinking I'll never get tired of that smell.

"What do you have planned for tonight in Chaos? More Chronicling?"

Because I've had so much spare time lately, I've taken to updating the *Chronicles*. There's so much to record now with all the new information about the Circle of Elders and the Nether Realm. And who better to record it than the one who witnessed it straight from the enemy's mind?

"Yep. I'm nearly finished. I'll be in the library all night." I feel a twinge of guilt in the pit of my stomach.

"Okay, well, have a good night, Addy. I'll see you in the morning." He leans down and kisses me soundly. I nearly lose myself in the moment, feeling like I could dissolve into him. He breaks the spell when he pulls away, but I'm consoled by the fact he seems as reluctant to part as I am.

I watch his truck pull through the gates and wave into the darkness, not sure if he sees me. Sam trusts me more than he trusts anyone else, and I lied straight to his face. I will not be spending my time in the library tonight. I feel horrible, as if I've betrayed him. As I walk to my room to get ready for Chaos, I push down my feelings of shame and mentally steel myself for the night ahead and for what has to be done.

◈

I open my eyes to total darkness. There are no windows in Major Calm and when the lights are off, shadows swallow my room. I lie still and forcefully steady my breathing.

Breathe in.

Breathe out.

Slowly.

I try to take advantage of the warm, comforting effect Major Calm has on me.

I'm nervous about tonight and even a little frightened, despite the determination I feel about my decision. When I'm satisfied that my heart isn't going to beat out of my chest, I spread my awareness out in search of my comrades.

I can feel Lang-hao and Crank outside the Calm, their minds preoccupied with rooting out Lesser Shades. In the training wing Kira's trying to teach Ember swordplay. Everyone else's presence feels foggy, indicating they're top-side.

If I'm going to do this, I need to do it now, so I get out of bed quickly before I can change my mind. I walk through the empty halls and the vacant common room. It's a true test of the strength of my resolve as I press forward, each step heavier than the last.

Before long I reach my destination. I'm standing outside the heavy steel door to Inner Silence. I reach out, trying to feel anything on the other side of the door, but there's only the emptiness I've come to associate with Mikhail.

I picture his face in my mind: his square jaw covered in stubble, his closely cropped dark hair. And his eyes. Those eyes that are the same color as this steel door in front of me. Those eyes that have shown vulnerability, warmth, and concern.

And anger.

And loathing.

I shiver involuntarily as the kind, shy Mikhail in my mind shifts to the violent, raging Mikhail from that night in my room. Which Mikhail waits for me behind this door? Is this the right thing to do—go in there for answers?

I search within myself for the hundredth time and again the answer is the same. Under the fear and doubt, my instincts tell me as strongly as ever I mustn't abandon Mikhail. I don't know why or how I know, but I'm certain Mikhail will play an integral part in helping us defeat the Elder Shade.

I know the others would never agree with me. I know they would try and stop me if they could. The suspicions they've always harbored for Mikhail have finally escalated into fear and disgust—perhaps even hatred for some of them. I know Sam's basically written him off completely. Simone, who's always reserved her strongest venom for Mikhail, now blames him for any and all of our current troubles.

It's ironic that if it weren't for Simone and her ability

to sense weaknesses, I wouldn't be standing here right now, willing to give him a second chance. She said my biggest weakness would be my failure to act on my instincts and that could be very dangerous. So here I am, acting on my instincts.

Refusing to delay any longer, I close my eyes, lift my arms with my palms facing out toward the door, and focus my mind.

Three wards. Three different unbindings that must be performed simultaneously. I think back to the night Angel, Mel, and I secured the portal and recall with exactness the stitches and seals we used to do so. Now I must reverse them.

I do my best to divide my attention into three separate trains of thought. It's a bit like trying to pat your head, rub your stomach, and hop on one foot all at once, but as the bindings begin to loosen, I'm surprised the task isn't more difficult.

When the last protective threads are severed, I grip the large round hatch door handle and heave to the right. The sound of metal bolts slinking out of their sockets resonates through the empty hallway. Before hauling the door back, I remind myself to guard my heart and expect the worst. The damage he's already done to me is great, and I must protect myself from further harm, emotionally and maybe even physically. At this point, I just don't know.

Taking one last, deep breath, I open the prison door and slip inside.

CHAPTER 55

THE SMALL GREY room is lit by a single fluorescent light running along the center of the ceiling. Even though nothing about the room has changed since the last time I saw it—the metal table and chair are still bolted to the floor and the steel bed juts out from the wall to the right—a visceral sense of gloom now hangs in the air. I shut the door behind me, careful not to turn my back on the still form lying on the bed.

Facing the wall and away from me, Mikhail lies unmoving. Broad shoulders taper down into a strong back and thick waist. I can barely perceive his chest gently rising and falling beneath a navy blue shirt. Unable to "read" Mikhail, there's no way to know whether he's really topside or feigning sleep.

I move toward the chair and unthinkingly try to pull it across the room to his bedside then feel foolish when the bolts hold it firmly in place. I reluctantly kneel instead on the hard concrete next to the bed, feeling vulnerable on the floor.

"Mikhail?" I whisper so I don't startle him. He doesn't move.

"Mikhail," I say, louder now. Nothing. Not even a twitch.

I reach up slowly, watching my hand tremble as I lightly place my fingers on his shoulder.

"Do not touch me."

So he *is* awake. His voice isn't aggressive and he hasn't tried to harm me yet, so I take this as a good sign and press on.

I draw my hand back and self-consciously clasp it to the other in my lap. "I need to speak with you."

Silence again.

"It's really important."

"You should not be here," he says haltingly, his voice is quiet but thick with fervor. "Please leave."

"Mikhail,…" I search for words, distraught that there's no easy way to say what's next. "Mikhail, Angel has died." The words hang there in the silence, heavy, like the executioner's axe poised to drop. I'm waiting for a reaction—an outburst of some kind—anything, but the only change is a slight difference in his breathing. I'm beginning to wonder how long the silence will last when he finally speaks, so quietly I can barely hear him.

"How?" He breathes the word out like a sigh, but he still refuses to turn and face me, so I can't see what emotions might be playing on his face or in his eyes.

"She was sick. All along. She hid it from everyone. She was tired and had to let go."

His response comes quickly this time. "You could not

heal her?" Though his tone is more curious than accusatory, the words still sting.

"I—I could have, but I didn't. It isn't what she wanted."

More silence.

"Does the boss know that you are here?"

"Mikhail," I urge, not wanting to be led down that road. "Angel wanted the other Walkers to understand why she had to let go."

"You must leave. He will kill me if he finds you here."

"Will you let me show you?" I reach up again, intending to rest a comforting hand on his arm. "It was her wish—"

"Do not touch me!" Mikhail shouts. Faster than should be possible, he sits up and whirls around to face me, legs swinging over the side of the bed. Instead of the anger I expect to see on his face, he wears only a mask of fear.

Startled, I jerk backwards, landing hard on my back and elbows. When he sees how he's frightened me, his shoulders fall limp and he drops his face into his hands.

"Adelaide, how can you come here? How can you even look at me after what I did to you?"

"What you did," I say, willing my voice not to quiver, "was wrong and terrible. But it's not who you are."

"You're wrong." He shakes his head back and forth, laughing darkly. "You're wrong, Addy. It is *exactly* who I am. Why can't you see this when all the others can? I was always exactly who they thought I was."

"I don't accept that. It's not true."

Finally he lifts his head and looks me in the eyes, his

features sagging. The lower half of his face is peppered in shaggy scruff. His lids hang heavy over haunted eyes.

"You don't know. You don't know *anything* about me," his voice is quiet and dark. "If you did, you would not be here. You would not say these things to me."

"Then explain yourself," I say sternly.

"What is the point?" He lays his head back against the wall behind him and closes his eyes. "Leave me be."

"The point is that after what you did, after how you betrayed me... all of us... don't you think you owe me an explanation!"

He doesn't react. In fact, he's so still and unresponsive he looks as though he's carved in granite.

"Enough of this. You can't do this anymore. You don't get to shut down or run away, not after what you've done. Your behavior has done nothing but push everyone away. You have no one to blame for the suspicions the others have about you but yourself."

The muscles in his jaw tighten. "This I know."

"Then do something about it. Be accountable for your actions."

"Do you want me to say 'I'm sorry'?" He barely opens his eyes and stares at me from under weighted lids.

"I just want—"

"Because I am," he interrupts. "Addy, there is nothing I could ever do or say that could make up for how badly I hurt you." His chest heaves with emotion and I can see he's struggling to contain his anguish.

I'm also fighting to keep control. A few tears escape and

as they roll down my face, Mikhail lifts a hand as though to wipe them away. He stops, his hand suspended in the air, then pulls it back and balls it into a tight fist on his lap. He glares down at it, perhaps to avoid seeing me cry.

I wipe my wet face on my sleeve and scoot closer to the bed.

"Mikhail… brother, you're my kin. I feel connected to you all the way down to my bones." I lightly rest my hand over his clenched fist and am relieved when he doesn't pull away from me. I nearly choke on my next words. "I forgive you."

His body is shaking. Little splashes of water fall from his face and onto my hand.

"Please, drop your defenses for me. Let me in. Whatever you're hiding, whatever you're afraid of, you have to know it won't change how I feel about you. You think I don't know you, but I do. You have a good heart. You're a good man. Whatever you don't want me to know about you, I promise it isn't as bad as you think. You're family and nothing can change that."

"I will show, then." Dread laces his words. "And you will see."

Finally! Triumph and relief wash over me. "Thank you." Before he can change his mind, I lift my hands and place them over his temples. I close my eyes and eagerly send my consciousness out toward him and wait for him to lower the wall between us, praying he actually does.

After a brief pause and a heavy sigh, his iron-clad barrier begins to dissipate from around him. For the first time,

I'm able to read his frequency. It stirs in me the unlikely mixture of comfort and a kind of stark gravity. Slowly I begin to move into his mind.

Once fully contained within, I'm swiftly inundated with powerful, almost overwhelming stimuli—sights, sounds, feelings, smells. It's similar to the way the Elder Shade bombarded me with those awful images. They're rapid and ceaseless, though this time there's no malice behind it. These images are Mikhail's memories. He's telling me a story. His story.

CHAPTER 56

FEAR HITS ME first.

Hide.

Run.

Don't be discovered.

I see through Mikhail's eyes as he lies on a dusty linoleum floor in a large dark and deserted building. Under his head is a balled up jacket and he shivers from the cold. Scattered around him are the remains of a makeshift camp—empty tin cans and a plastic half-gallon jug of water.

The image jumps now to a darkened alley. Mikhail's pressed up against a dumpster, knees drawn in close, and I hear through his ears as a man and woman scream at each other from one of the apartments nearby. A rat, fur blackened and greasy, crawls across the toe of his shoe.

Again and again, similar scenes play out: Mikhail squatting in abandoned and condemned buildings, sometimes in the wilderness, other times right on the street. In each memory I feel his desperation. He avoids public places, crowds—anywhere someone might see his face and recognize him.

His memories shift dramatically. I get the sense we're moving backwards, as though he's showing me his story in reverse.

Now he lies—naked, wet, and cold—on a slick tiled floor, trying to shield his body from the kicks and blows of others standing around him. The shouts and jeers are in another language, Russian most likely. Hot water from running showers creates a steam that swirls and obscures the faces of his attackers. I wonder why he isn't fighting back. Why does he feel so afraid and helpless? Why can't he fade into the shadows and escape?

The next memory moves backwards still. A barred prison door slams shut, the echo reverberating around in his mind. Keys jingle and heavy footsteps sound off down a cement corridor as Mikhail sits on a metal bed, much like the one here in Inner Silence, only this is a *real* prison cell. It's one of many down a long walkway of cells, each filled with a prisoner clad in faded blue jean coveralls.

I realize this must have been before he received the call to Chaos. This had to have been before he had his powers. He was unable to fight back or escape.

A quick flash of blinding light erases this scene and is replaced by Mikhail standing against a wall, holding a black sign in front of him with a name on it. Mikhail Novikov. Another flash and he's standing in profile against the same wall holding the same sign. What? Mikhail's last name is Kozlow. Isn't it?

Another flash reveals a different man, taller and broader than Mikhail, but he stands against the same wall holding a sign with a different name. Andrei Novikov. This man's face is wide and ruined by acne scars. His lips are thick, his nose flat and crooked. But the eyes that stare blankly back are steel gray and familiar. This is Mikhail's father. Then another flash reveals this same man in profile.

These are booking photos. Mug shots.

Another flash shows another man, closer in age to Mikhail but slightly older. He's short and thick. His small eyes, dark and sunken, glare back at the camera in defiance. His name card reads Nikolai Novikov. Mikhail's brother. Then another flash reveals an older man. Oleg Novikov. Uncle. And then a younger man, Grigori Novikov. Cousin. Each man bears a distinct resemblance to Mikhail in one way or another. Each is being booked into prison.

The next memory is of Mikhail, handcuffed and being pulled from a police car and dragged through a crowd of excited media representatives.

Photographer's cameras flash endlessly, blinding and disorienting Mikhail. Everything is spinning. Police push back against the crowd as microphones are crammed into Mikhail's face. Reporters fire rapid questions at him in another language. I begin to recognize a common phrase being repeated among the shouts. "Novikov Bratva."

The next memory is dramatically different from the last. A younger version of Mikhail, perhaps eighteen or so, sits on a bed in a small, one-room cabin. In his arms lies an older woman. Mikhail leans over her motionless body and weeps.

He clutches her desperately to him, but her body feels cold. His grief overwhelms me and threatens to bury me.

Earlier memories of this woman flood my consciousness. She's at the small stove in the corner of the cabin stirring a pot of food. She hums and sways, absently brushing grey hair back from her face when it falls from her loosely wound bun. A rich aroma coming from whatever she's cooking fills the cabin.

"Misha," she calls softly in a sing-song voice. She turns and smiles warmly at a fourteen-year-old Mikhail as he sets the small wooden table for two. She's the most beautiful woman he's ever known. The love he feels for her is deep and reverent. She's clearly his entire world.

We move backwards again. An even younger Mikhail, perhaps ten or so, is climbing boulders in the woods a ways from the cabin. The woman from the last memory runs frantically toward him, tripping on roots and rocks. The look of panic on her face frightens Mikhail terribly. She picks him up and runs back to the cabin, locking them both inside. She's angry now and yells at him in words I can't understand. She turns and nervously looks behind curtains and out windows as she whispers what sounds like a prayer.

We go further back.

A small boy lies comfortably in a big soft bed. It's nighttime and his eyes are closed but he's not sleeping. He listens to the man and woman yelling in the other room. He's scared. There are other loud sounds—glass breaks and shatters, doors slam. He hears a woman sobbing and pleading.

The noise stopped long ago, but the little boy can't sleep.

His bedroom door opens quietly and a woman comes in. It's dark but he can still recognize her. She has a cut on her eyebrow and a bruise forming on her mouth. She puts a finger to her swollen lips and he nods. She gestures for him to follow her and together, hand in hand, they tiptoe through a large, exquisite home, down a curving marble staircase, through a spacious kitchen, out the back door, and into a waiting taxi cab. He stares through the car window as they drive away from the mansion he's always known as home and prays he never sees it again.

The memories that come next are less clear. They're jumbled images. Men coming in and out of his home. Meetings held in his dad's office. Heavy smoke from cigarettes and cigars. Loud laughter. Angry shouts. Money exchanging hands. Duffle bags full of guns. Big, heavy packages wrapped in brown paper. Sometimes people show up covered in blood. Sometimes people he knows leave and never come back.

One memory stands out clear and horrible: A man goes into his father's office. His father shouts and screams angry things for a long time. Then other men go in and bring out the first man, but they have to carry him. He's bloody and still and looks like he's sleeping.

His older brother and cousin play with toy guns and chase him around the house. They push him down and shoot him dead, and he has to lie there for hours until they say he can get up again. Then they start over.

There's only one more. The last memory Mikhail shows me, the very earliest memory he has from his life, is being rocked, wrapped warm and safe in the arms of the woman—his mother—as she sings him Russian lullabies. Everything is so clear—her deep soft voice, the way she smells, the softness of her cheek as he lays his small hand on it, the feel of her lips as she kisses his face.

And then nothing. The images stop. The story is over. What's left in Mikhail's mind now are his current thoughts and feelings—a mixture of despair, grief, shame, self-loathing, and hopelessness.

I withdraw myself from Mikhail's mind and return to my own. I get up and sit next to him on the bed. Wrapping my arms around him, I pull him in close. He resists me at first but finally relents and falls into my arms. He's racked with silent sobs as he cries into my shoulder.

He fights to gain control of himself, and after a few minutes he quiets down enough to speak.

"So you see?" he says without lifting his face from my shoulder.

"There is darkness in me. In my veins. There always has been. I can't escape it. My mother—" the mention of his mother threatens to steal his composure but he pushes through it.

"My mother, she tried to save me from that life. There was so much goodness in her. She thought, if she could steal me away, raise me far from everyone, far from my father's reach, then maybe his wickedness would not touch me. But she was wrong. I was always going to be this way. Even her goodness could not keep the darkness away. I am Novikov.

I always have been. I always will be. This evil that is in my blood, it cannot be stopped."

I begin to understand. Mysterious Mikhail. He lurks in shadows, avoids eye contact, and lacks any social skills. A lifetime of hiding has formed his behaviors. His mother took him and raised him in complete seclusion, terrified of being hunted down by her criminal husband. Little Mikhail never learned to play with other children. He never had any friends, never any companions besides his mother. He never learned socially acceptable behavior.

His mother must have drilled the necessity for secrecy into him: *Hide your face from the people, the crowds, the police that might see the resemblance to the leading members of the Novikov Bratva. Never let anyone know you. Never let anyone in. If captured, you will be punished for the crimes of your father, of your uncle and brother and cousin. The blood of their victims will be just as red on your hands.*

"Mikhail, that's not you," I insist. "And that's not your family. You have a new family now. We're your family."

He pulls away from me and stares ahead, seemingly unable to bring himself to look at me. "Please do not try to make me feel better. I know what I am and I deserve punishment. I deserve your scorn, not your kindness."

"But you haven't done anything even close to the crimes your family has committed. You've spent the last few years fighting evil, protecting the world from disaster! You're the good guy, Mikhail."

"You do not understand." He swallows thickly, visibly willing himself to continue. "When my mother died, I had nothing. I had nowhere to go. So I go to my father's house. He welcomed me with open arms, his long-lost son return to him. I was to be heir, along with my brother, to his... business."

His face sours as though the word is poison in his mouth. "It was then that the police came. I may not have taken part in my father's crimes, but it would have only been a matter of time before I was as corrupt as the rest of them."

"You don't know that. You weren't raised that way. You were different from them."

He waves away my assurances. "After all my mother had done to protect me from that life, I returned to it the first chance I had. I was weak. I always was and I knew it from the start. I have lived my whole life knowing that one day my father's world would catch up to me. One day, the tainted Novikov blood in my veins would awaken and I would show the world that I am just as wicked as him. And I was right. Look what I did. To the one person who was kind to me. I am a monster."

"What kind of a monster saves lives? What kind of a monster feels sorrow and shame? No Mikhail, real monsters are unrepentant. They don't understand regret. You are not a monster, Mikhail. You are just... human."

The look in his eyes says he wants desperately to believe me. Behind the anguish is a spark. A brief flicker. Is it hope?

"Listen." I grab his face and force him to look at me. "I'm going to tell you something and it may be the most important thing you'll ever hear, so listen well." When I'm certain he understands my grave earnestness, I continue.

"First, I discovered another ability within Simone. She's able to detect a person's biggest weakness. She told me that if I didn't follow my instincts, it could be the downfall of us all. That's my weakness. She also told me that this Elder Shade we've been fighting, his biggest weakness is *me*."

"Then you will defeat him," Mikhail says with conviction. "Everyone knows this."

I shake my head back and forth. "No. I've been thinking, Mikhail. I've had so much time to do nothing but think and I'm sure I finally know the answer." I can feel apprehension grow within him, as though he dreads what I'll say.

"It isn't me, Mikhail. It's you. It's always been you."

I see confusion on his face. Then pure disbelief. "You are wrong. You said Simone knows he fears you most."

"He fears me because I'm the only Realmwalker who believes in *you*. He must know that without me to steer you in the right direction, he's invincible."

"No." He pulls away from me. "No, nooo." He moans and curls up, head between his hands, into a defensive ball. I know he's feared my words would lead to this all along. "Do not ask me, Adelaide. You are wrong."

"But I'm not wrong. Simone's ability tells me I have to follow my instincts and all my instincts point me to you. I don't know how you're supposed to do it. I don't know why you're the key to his undoing, but I know without a doubt that *you* are the answer."

I feel his fear and dread rising, choking him, overtaking him. "Please Addy," he whispers, "you do not know what you ask."

I get the feeling he already knows what he must do, that he's always known. Why has he run from this?

If he can't find faith within himself, I must do what I can to give him all of mine.

"This whole time I thought it was all about me," I chuckle, embarrassed at my pride. "I thought I could swoop in and save the day. I alone could kill the big bad wolf. I'd be everyone's hero." The shame of my arrogance flushes my cheeks and I press cold fingers against them.

"I've been so stupid. I've been blinded by my pride, by my eagerness to prove myself. This isn't my story, Mikhail. It never was. It's your story. You're the hero. I'm only the trusty sidekick who gets you to realize it."

His head is still in his hands. I pray he's listening to me. What I say next I say directly into his mind so there's no hiding from it.

I know in my heart that you can do this. It doesn't matter what anyone else thinks, Mikhail. It doesn't even matter what YOU think. I have faith in you. I believe in you. And when the time comes, I know you'll do the right thing.

With nothing left to say, I get up and leave Inner Silence. I shut the heavy door behind me, replace the wardings, and with renewed hope head to the solace of the library to try and sort through everything that just happened and what my next step should be.

CHAPTER 57

I'M CLEANING THE last of the breakfast dishes when the sound of the front door opening and closing tightens the knot in my stomach. Ember and Crank left after breakfast to take Caesar to the dog beach, and judging from the loud bass reverberating from the upstairs music room, Lang's buried in his element.

It will be just Sam and I, and he'll want to know how my night went. I don't think I'll be able to lie to him again.

"Morning." A smiling Sam drops his keys on the countertop and pulls me into a hug. I squirm and maneuver, trying not to get soapy water on his uniform, but he doesn't seem to care.

"Morning." I smile back and kiss his cheek, already having a hard time looking directly at him. "There's leftovers in the fridge. Hashbrowns should still be crispy."

"Mmmm. Sounds great, thanks."

He eats and I fire off a string of questions about how his night went while I finish drying the dishes. By the time he swallows his last bite of toast, he's beginning to look suspicious.

"Are you okay, Addy?" He studies me through narrowed lids. "You seem... agitated."

I thought I had been doing an okay job at playing cool but Sam knows me too well. I drop down into the chair across from him and stare at my hands in front of me on the breakfast table, nervously picking at my fingernails.

Sam reaches across the table and places his warm, heavy hands on mine. "Should I be worried?"

I have to tell him. I don't want to because I know he'll be mad, but keeping things from him—lying to him—is worse.

"I lied to you, Sam," I say quietly. I look up to see his reaction. He's still watching me with ease, a casual smile on his face, unconcerned with what I'm about to say.

"Well, whatever it is, I'm sure you had a good reason. Tell me about it and we'll work it out." His voice is kind, which makes me feel so much worse. His confidence in me, his belief that I would never do anything to betray him, has frozen the words in my throat.

I take a few deep breaths.

"Sam, I went to Inner Silence last night."

Confusion settles into his expression.

"Um... okay?"

"No, I went *into* Inner Silence last night. I spoke with Mikhail. I had to—"

Abruptly, Sam pulls his hands from mine. He sits back in his chair and looks at me sideways.

"But," he shakes his head adamantly, "but you couldn't have. The wardings... not without help anyway."

"I didn't need any help," I say, looking down at my hands. I'm beginning to wish I could shrink. Just shrink smaller and smaller until I'm out of sight. "I did it on my own," I whisper.

Sam stands up quickly, startling me, his chair nearly falling backwards.

"I know. I shouldn't have lied to you. I'm sorry." I insist fervently.

"What were you thinking?" he whispers. I've never seen Sam this way. I expected yelling. Anger. This quiet intensity is worse.

"I'm sorry I lied, Sam, but I'm not sorry I went."

Inhaling deeply, he puts his hands on his head and turns his back to me.

"I asked you to let me see him. I told you over and over that we need him—that we can't let him rot in there while we try and defeat this Elder Shade without him. Because we can't. It's not possible. I'm more certain of this than I've ever been of anything in my life. It's *him*, Sam."

I'm not sure he's even listening to me. His hands are on his hips now and he's staring at the floor, refusing to face me.

"I tried to do it the right way, but you wouldn't believe me. You wouldn't listen! I didn't have any other choice."

He doesn't say anything.

"Say something, please."

Finally, he turns to face me. *My* Sam is gone. Now I'm

looking at Boss. There's no trace of emotion on his face. He's in full business mode.

"You should know, Adelaide," he says, his voice remaining coldly neutral, "I will need to tell the other Walkers what you have done. You've broken laws. There's a very real chance that you could receive punishment for this."

"What?" I whisper in stunned disbelief. I hadn't even considered this. "You mean, like," I can hardly say it, "Inner Silence?"

He clenches his jaw.

"Why did you do this? I can't understand it. What was the point?"

It takes my mind a second to shift from the possibility of being imprisoned to realizing he asked me a question.

"I had to talk to him. To ask him to kill the Elder Shade. To tell him about Angel, and Simone, and what we found out."

My thoughts are swirling around in my head and coming out as a stream of jumbled words. This isn't how this was supposed to go. I was going to tell him everything in a way he could understand. He'd be mad at first, but once I explained the situation, he'd forgive me. Like he always does. I never expected him to shut me out this way. I thought we were too close for that.

He walks back to the table and leans on his hands on the back of a chair. The muscles in his forearms bulge and his fingers strain as he clutches the chair tightly. He lowers his head and asks quietly, "Did he... did he touch you?"

"No! Not at all. He wasn't—"

"I've heard all I need to know." He turns and starts walking away.

"Wait, Sam!"

"I'm going to Chaos. You can expect a summons later to be formally questioned about your actions. There will be a vote after your hearing."

"Sam please. Hear me out. There are things you need to know!" I plead with him, desperation creeping into my voice.

Before walking out of the kitchen, he turns back. I finally see the anger I've been expecting. "I suggest you don't break any more of our laws in the meantime."

CHAPTER 58

IT'S THREE IN the morning. I've put off going to Chaos as long as I can. I've taken a shower, dried my hair, painted my nails, and finished a novel I've been reading. I'm out of ways to procrastinate. I've managed to avoid everyone all day, so I have no idea what it will be like in Chaos. Will everyone be there waiting for me? Will the trial start as soon as I get there? I don't know how I'm going to face them.

I picture Ember's reaction when she finds out I broke a law. Will she feel as betrayed as Sam? Will Mel? And Crank? I can't bear the thought of losing their trust. Will anyone agree with what I did? Will anyone stand up for me? Or is their anger for Mikhail too strong?

I can't hide here any longer. After all, I told Mikhail he should stop hiding from his problems—that he should be accountable. That's what I need to do. I need to follow my own advice, go face my peers, and accept my punishment. It's the only honorable thing left to do.

Taking one last, nervous breath, I close my eyes and sink through the darkness into Chaos.

≪

When I open my eyes, I'm relieved to see I'm alone in my room. I half expected to find Ember, or perhaps another Walker, pacing the floor, waiting for me to wake up so they could demand an explanation.

Instead, the room's quiet and dark, except for a small desk lamp I left on the night before. I dress in the dim light, listening for any voices in the hallway. When I hear nothing, curiosity gets the better of me and I use my abilities and reach out.

Intending to locate everyone and test their moods, I'm surprised to find only two other frequencies within Major Calm. Timothy, ever eager for an excuse to work with weapons, is in a practice room with Simone, trying to help her master her chosen piece.

After testing out a wide variety of weapons from our armory, Simone surprised everyone by taking a strong liking to the spear. At first I thought it was a joke. How could a spear be a practical weapon against Shades? And then I saw her use it. She has a knack for it, and after a few days of demolishing practice targets, all questions of its legitimacy vanished.

Neither Simone nor Timothy is reading alarmed or upset. Could they truly not know? I push further out, leaving the Calm and entering Chaos. I find Ember and Crank currently in the midst of a tussle with a handful of Lesser

Shades. Though their guard is up, their awareness heightened, they don't feel overly concerned, and I'm confident they can handle the fight. I don't get the sense that either of them is particularly distraught about anything.

Sam spent all of yesterday in Chaos. Didn't he tell anyone? Breaking the rules is obviously a big deal to him. How had he not found the time to do something about it? I'm at a loss as to what should I do now.

Should I wait around and see what happens, or go ahead and tell everyone so they hear it from me? If I tell them myself, maybe I can get ahead of this. Then again, I don't think I can stomach disappointing anyone else tonight. In the end, I decide to wait and let Sam handle it his way.

The only real thing I can do to help the others now is to keep up with my training so I'm ready when it's time to face the Elder Shade. Anyway, the idea of beating a punching bag to pulp is enticing right now.

After changing, I make a point to say "hi" to Tim and Simone before finding a room of my own to practice in. I choose the practice room equipped with a row of hanging punching bags on the right and padded, body-shaped posts lining the left. This room, like all the others, has a media panel on the wall by the door. I select some upbeat music and slide the volume bar over until the sound is almost too much to stand.

Bouncing to the music, I go to work on the nearest heavy bag. I start with some easy shots, light punches to help warm up my muscles and joints. I'm gloveless, so I expect

I'll have some damaged knuckles to clean up throughout my workout.

I bounce and jab and circle and punch. The progress I've made with my combat skills pleases me. It's strange to see myself now, to compare myself with the soft, weak, carefree girl I was a few months ago. If I hadn't experienced this transformation firsthand, I wouldn't have believed someone could grow so much in so little time. Of course, I did have the benefit of my "extra" abilities to aid in the process, so maybe it isn't a fair assessment.

I push myself, throwing hard punches, focusing on speed and accuracy. My pulse quickens as my heartbeat thumps in my ears. Sweat pulls loose strands of hair from my ponytail and sticks them to my face and neck. My breathing comes faster and my face feels hot from the exertion. I resist the urge to heal my stressed body and instead try to enjoy the ache and burn in my muscles, the stitch in my lungs as they yearn for more oxygen.

The rhythmic blows become a dance. Right left. Right left. Hook. Cross. Left. Uppercut.

All the while I circle. Breathe through my nose. Move my feet. It's hypnotic and I lose myself in the trance, surrender to the spell of it, letting go of all thoughts and concerns, becoming numb. I'm not sure how much time has passed when I'm grabbed suddenly from behind.

"Addy, stop."

"Wha—?" I breathe out trying to get my bearings. I was pulled so abruptly from my workout that the quick shift of momentum throws me off balance. Stumbling, I nearly fall to the ground, but Sam catches me and holds me up.

"Stop! What are you doing?"

I look up at him, brows furrowing in confusion. Can't he see I'm exercising?

"What do you mean?" I manage to say through gasping breaths.

He grabs my wrists and shoves my hands in front of my face. "Look at yourself!"

Now I see what he means. The flesh on my hands is in tatters. Blood seeps freely down my wrists and forearms. The swinging punching bag behind Sam is stained red on all sides and a small puddle is forming on the floor beneath it.

"Fix it," he barks, clearly disturbed.

"Yeah, of course." I pull my wrists free of him and turn away. I send the message to my body to heal the damage. It takes less than a minute. I wipe off as much blood as I can onto my sweats and turn back to face him. "See, no big deal."

"No big deal?" he sounds incredulous. He breathes out through clenched teeth and looks down at the blood smeared on his hands.

"I just got too into it. I won't do it again." I indicate the mess I made of the equipment. "I should clean this up. It'll only take a minute or two then I'll head to the briefing room." My stomach bottoms out as I think of what's coming.

"What? What's in the briefing room?"

"The trial. Isn't that why you're here? My summons?"

"Oh... uh, no Addy," he says, avoiding my eyes. He

looks uneasy, maybe even a little embarrassed. "Listen, I'm not going to report what happened."

"You're not?" This revelation startles me. I take a tentative step, bringing me closer to him. Has he forgiven me? When he doesn't move away, I reach for his hand. As I lace my fingers through his, he finally meets my gaze.

He shakes his head, almost imperceptibly.

"Why not?"

"Everyone's stressed out as it is. I've been struggling to keep their spirits up and hashing this out right now would be really bad for everyone. It would pull us apart. We need unity right now more than ever."

Nothing he's said hints at forgiveness. Then I realize he isn't canceling the hearing, only postponing it. But he's holding my hand, so…

"Are we…" I feel my eyes begin to burn. "Are we still…"

He pulls me into an embrace, and I push my face into his chest as my composure breaks.

"I don't know what we are, Addy," he mumbles. "I only know that the last twenty-four hours have been torture."

"I'm so sorry, Sam. Hurting you, it was never something I wanted."

"I know that. I do." He squeezes the back of my neck. "But I'm having a hard time with *myself*. I don't believe in what you're doing. I don't agree with it. I can't support it in any way. But I need you. I don't want to be without you. Ever."

"I was so worried I'd lost you. I thought I'd messed up so bad you'd never forgive me."

"You were worried? Imagine how I felt when you told me you were in a locked room with Mikhail. Alone."

"I know. I feel awful. It's just... I wish you could project yourself into other people's minds the way I can. Then you'd know what I know. If you could feel how certain I am about this, you'd understand why I had to do it."

He leans back to look at me. "I understand you felt compelled—perhaps so much you couldn't resist. And I feel bad I didn't have your back. I admit I didn't even want to understand. I hear the name 'Mikhail' and my defenses automatically go up. If I'd known you were *that* determined, I'd have helped you find another way."

"Really?"

He nods and runs his thumb across my cheek.

"I shouldn't have put you in a position like that, where you felt you had no other option but to lie to me. We're a team, Addy. We need to work together, not against each other."

I ease up onto my toes to reach his mouth. He kisses me back and his passion, his intensity, equals mine.

"Addy," he whispers between kisses, "Addy, I love you."

I whisper back, "I love you too, Sam." I clasp his face in my hands. "I love you."

CHAPTER 59

IT STARTS WITH that gentle plucking at the back of my mind. A mild sensation. I nearly dismiss it as that nagging feeling you get sometimes when you know you've forgotten something.

I had just sent Mom off to "AZ" after a long and much-needed week together, and things had been looking up for the Walkers lately. The number of Lesser Shades was dwindling and there had been only a couple encounters with Greater Shades. They'd all been dispatched with relative ease, none even coming close to being as formidable as the Elder Shade. No one had even seen him since that last battle in the rainforest. There had been talk that maybe he abandoned Chaos. Maybe having failed, he returned to the Nether Realm to face judgment from the Circle of Elders.

Regardless of the talk, I never believed that. I've been in his head. I know the terror he feels for the Circle. The power they have over him is complete.

No, he's out there. Perhaps he's biding his time, waiting

for us to drop our guard. My gut tells me this is exactly what he wants. And I'm worried it may be working.

"How do you DO that?!" Timothy asks from over my shoulder. I'm working on my latest art piece, a charcoal sketch of my grandmother as she was in a black-and-white photo taken in the sixties. Her hair's pulled back from her face and she's wearing heavy cat eyeliner and looking like a true diva.

"Don't bother her, you'll mess her up," Simone chides Timothy. The two of them are here at L.A. base on "vacation." To everyone's surprise, they've been spending a lot of time together. Timothy himself remains the most astonished of all.

Also surprising, Simone hasn't changed her appearance in quite a while. She's still the same delicate strawberry-blonde water nymph she was a few weeks ago. Maybe she's finally okay with herself, and maybe Timothy has something to do with that.

They're all gussied up for a night on the town and asking if I'd like to go dancing with them. While I'm thrilled they seem to be enjoying themselves, their lax attitude makes me nervous. This kind of carelessness—going out and partying—is exactly what we should be guarding against. But seeing Simone so cheerful and, well, *kind* stops me from voicing my concerns.

"Sorry guys, I hate to be a stick in the mud, but I think I'll hang out here tonight. Have a good time though!"

The gentle plucking sensation I nearly dismissed earlier has grown into a steady tug.

"Uhhh, guys?" I call after them before they can get too far.

Simone pokes her head back into my doorway. "Please do not say what I think you're going to say."

"Sorry Simone, weak spot."

"Damn it all to the Nether Realm!" She stomps her foot like a child. "I spent the last hour getting ready."

From behind Simone Timothy holds up two fingers and mouths the words "two hours." He puts a hand on her arm. "Let's take care of it quick so we can still go out tonight."

They hurry back down the hall, I assume to find the nearest bed. As I'm about to send out a mental alert and the location of the weak spot to every Realmwalker, things quickly go from bad to worse. That steady tug is now an urgent alarm.

Realmwalkers, I send it out forcefully to ensure I have everyone's full attention. *We have a weak spot. You'll find it here, in this area. I show them where I mean. It's deteriorating much faster than it should. You'll most likely find a Ripper there working on it. Good luck and happy hunting.*

I'm convinced the others have understood my urgency when I sense them start to pass, one by one, into Chaos. I lie on my bed and stare at the ceiling. I always go to Major Calm when this happens, to be nearby and on hand just in case. When I feel the last of them leave this realm, I close my eyes and join them.

⁓

"We need a sealer on site now. Kira, you're the fastest. Go.

Lang, you watch her back. We'll head that way as soon as we're equipped and ready." Lang and Kira turn on their heels and run toward the garage.

We're in the armory getting outfitted. Sam continues to instruct the remaining Walkers while he selects his usual handguns from the arsenal. I try to make myself useful by helping some of the others fit into their armored body suits and distributing gear.

"I'm ready to go now, Boss," Faye tells Sam. "There really should be a healer out there."

Sam puts a hand on her shoulder affectionately. "Not alone." He looks around the group. His eyes skip over the faces of my friends, and he's disappointed when he doesn't find the one he's looking for. Sam must be starting to realize how much we all rely on Mikhail's skills. Our eyes meet briefly. He knows I saw him looking for the Russian.

"Ember, Crank. You two ready?"

"Yes sir," Crank says.

"Got my weapons right here, sir!" Ember grins as she holds up her hands.

"Go with Faye. I want a situation report as soon as possible," he says, tapping the com unit on his ear.

"Got it!" Ember calls behind her as they leave.

After everyone's geared up, I walk with them to the garage and marvel at their composure. My nerves are always a rattled mess until the tear is fixed and everyone's back safe and sound.

As I reach the bottom of the stairs leading into the

garage, I'm suddenly overcome by the level of intensity coming from one of the Walker's "frequencies."

"Whoa," I breathe out, reaching out to Sam for stability.

"What is it?" he asks, concerned.

"It's Kira. She's in some kind of trouble."

Sam touches his earpiece. "Kira, what's your status?"

Silence.

"Kira, respond."

When she doesn't answer, he looks to me. "Tell me what's going on out there."

I squeeze my eyes closed and send my full awareness toward Kira. What I find fills me with dread.

There, right outside the quickly eroding fabric between Chaos and the Nether Realm, is a void of darkness. A black stain. A malignancy so filled with evil that it can be caused by only one thing. I rapidly retreat to my own mind and open my eyes. The remaining Walkers are circled around me, waiting anxiously for my answer. The silence is thick, heavy with anxious anticipation.

"It's him," I whisper.

"All right, everyone," Sam says, galvanizing us into action. "You all know how important this is," he shouts as they hustle to the bikes. "If we fail tonight, Chaos will fall. We must protect Earth Realm no matter the cost." He looks at each of us gravely. "To the very end." His eyes settle on mine. "To the very last of us."

There are no shouts of assent this time. No cheers of encouragement. The atmosphere is quiet and grave as each of the Realmwalkers mounts their bikes for what, in their minds, may be the very last time.

The Walkers rev their bikes and begin to pass through the threshold to Chaos.

"Addy, go grab your body armor!" Sam shouts at me over the roar of engines. "I'll wait for you here."

"There's no time. I don't need it anyway!"

Sam considers for a second then nods and holds his hand out to me. "Come on!"

I stare at his outstretched hand for a second. Then another. I take a step backwards towards the stairs.

"Addy NO! There isn't time."

"I have to." I yell over the noise to be heard. "We can't do this without him. Go, they need you. I'll catch up!"

"Damn it, Addy!"

I turn and dash up the stairs before he can stop me.

CHAPTER 60

OUTSIDE THE DOOR to Inner Silence, I unbind the wards. My mind is in so many different places already, observing and worrying, that this simple task is much more difficult than it was the first time.

Will Mikhail listen? Will he be willing to help? This is my last chance to get through to him.

When the wards are gone and the last metal bolt clinks from its socket, I heave open the prison door and hurry inside.

"Mikhail!" I shout, nearly breathless.

He looks at me, startled, from where he sits on the edge of the bed, his chin in his hands.

"Mikhail, it's happening. Right now. We have to go!" I motion for him to follow me. Instead he looks horrified and backs farther onto the bed.

"I cannot, Addy. You are wrong about me. If all of you cannot stop him, there is no way I can. I am no better than any of you."

A hot rage floods through me. I run at him and grab the front of his shirt in my fist.

"Damn it, Mikhail. There's no time! They could be dying out there!"

I've startled him, but he's still not moving.

"You listen to me." I push my face close to his. "You can either sit here and hide while the rest of us fight to defend our home—our families," I scream at him, "while we give all we have to protect Earth Realm from being torn apart by evil, while we battle to the last one of us," my vision swims in angry tears, "or you can do what you're meant to do and stand with us. You're the only one who can do this and you know it! I can see it in your eyes, Mikhail! You already know what to do. Why the hell won't you help us?"

"It will change me, Addy. You cannot understand. I will be ruined. Darkened." The sheer terror in his eyes alarms me. "I would be better off dead."

"If you stay here any longer, you will be. We all will be."

I see the conflict raging within him, but I can't wait around for him to make up his mind. I'm out of time. If I want to be able to help my friends, I must leave now.

"What's it going to be, Mikhail? Will you let us all die? Or will you do what only you can? Will you be the man I know you can be?" Before I turn to leave, I try one last time to get through to him.

"Think of your mother, Mikhail. Do you think she risked her life for you, shielded you from your father's wickedness, kept you as far away from darkness as she could, only to have you give in to it right when it matters most?"

I whirl around and run as fast as my legs can carry me through the empty halls. I clamor down the stairs to the garage, taking them two at a time, praying I got through to Mikhail.

Once I reach the garage, I can't believe what I find. A very anxious Sam waits on an idling Big Bike. I'm overwhelmed with gratitude. This show of support for me must have been so difficult for him, knowing how badly he's needed by the others.

We know each other so well now that all it takes is a glance for him to see how much it means to me. In that moment, all is understood between us. Without wasting another second, I climb onto the back of his Big Bike.

"What happened? Is he coming?"

"I don't know. I hope so."

He nods and faces forward. "Hold on, Addy. We'll be going fast."

I reach my arms around his torso and squeeze him tight. Sam switches gears and the Big Bike rises up from the ground then we're off and climbing into a cloudless, brightly lit sky. I look down and find a spanning, powder-white beach to the left and a calm ocean to my right. I could almost mistake this place for the beaches along the California coast if the washed-out colors didn't give it away. Behind us, the entrance to Major Calm is marked by the dark opening of a massive rocky grotto.

I can feel the Walkers far ahead of us. Their moods are a frenzied mixture of distress and fear and exertion and, in some, even pain. I think of the ones that are hurting. I can't stop my mind from seeing them in the worst possible ways.

Awful images, scenarios of them dying play out over and over in my head.

Sam, I send directly to him, *if this doesn't turn out the way we hope—*

"Stop Addy." He interrupts. "We can't think like that."

He's right, of course. We need to stay positive. Still…

I lay my head on his shoulder and feel his warmth. I move my hands up his chest until they rest over his heart. I can feel it thumping through his whole chest.

I love you, Sam.

He takes one hand off the bike and rests it on mine. After a few seconds with nothing but the sound of wind in my ears, he responds.

"Love you, Addy."

I wish those words carried less weight, had less finality behind them. This can't be the last time he tells me that. It can't be.

As we get closer to the battle, I'm able to get a clearer image of what's happening. It seems we were right to have been weeding out as many of the Lesser Shades as possible. It feels as though the entire Shade population of Chaos is there fighting, and they're still managing to overwhelm the Walkers. I can't imagine how awful it would be if we'd been less vigilant.

I can feel the Elder Shade's presence strongest of all. His evil carries a uniqueness I've grown familiar to. What's unfamiliar to me, though, is the feeling I'm getting from the tear site.

I can feel the threads being swiftly unwound by the

Elder Shade, and I can feel them being repaired just as quickly by Kira and Mel. This I expected. What surprises me is that, as the barrier between the realms warps and flexes, I can feel something just behind it.

An enormous pressure is building up on that side. The burgeoning barrier stretches out, threatening to burst open, making Kira and Mel's job all the more difficult. From the tear seeps a coldness that rivals any to be found in Earth Realm. It permeates down into the marrow of my bones, filling me with its icy chill, pulling my soul into despair.

The worst part is that I know what's causing it. Behind that tear awaits every dark and creeping thing, every monster from every fable. Very soon, there will be enough hate, rage, and bloodlust to fill an entire realm. I can feel them—their yearning, their hunger. I know that among them, the Circle wait impatiently. Perhaps they wait at the front of the line.

"There they are!" Sam calls over his shoulder. I lean around him and can just make out the group ahead. The sounds of battle ring through the air. Bellows and roars. Gunfire and explosions. A grenade goes off, sending a vast pillar of sand into the air.

"Drop me by the Elder. I have to help the sealers!"

"Okay Addy. But please," he squeezes my hand, "be careful."

As we approach, I quickly scan the area to get an idea as to what we're up against. The actual tear site is in the water, right above the surface and about twenty feet from the shore. The Elder Shade is waist deep in the ocean, his gnarled arms stretched out in front of him. His head is down as he concentrates on his task.

Kira and Mel are about ten feet away from him, one on each side. It takes all their focus to keep the tear from bursting, and the waves tug and pull at them as they work.

The other Walkers are all over the beach. The splashes of black Shade blood are a striking contrast to the white sand. Most are doing what they can to keep the Lesser Shades away from the sealers, but a few Walkers, including Timothy and Lang, are directing their efforts toward the Elder.

Timothy lobs another grenade at him, but as it explodes, sending water in all directions, it's clear that he's once again protected by an unbreakable barrier. Through it all, he never moves. He doesn't falter even a little, and he never turns his attention from the tear.

We're almost to him now.

"Are you ready?" Sam shouts.

CHAPTER 61

"HELL YEAH!" RIGHT before Sam and I are directly over the Elder Shade, he turns the bike sharply as he stops, causing the back wheel to swing around. I use the momentum to launch from the side of the bike out toward the tear. I'm quickly gauging where and how I will land in the water as I glide high over the Elder Shade's head.

Time slows.

I'm looking down at the Elder from far above when his head snaps up. His gaze finds me and I'm immediately wrapped in his icy grip. He pulls his arm back from the tear sight and raises it up over his head toward me.

Time catches up.

He snatches me from my fall with the strength of his mind, the force of it giving me whiplash, and I hang in midair.

I stare into his hollow eyes and watch as his ragged, slick mouth becomes a grin. He's happy to see me. He throws his arm back sending me shooting out over the beach with such speed I barely have time to save myself. Just before

I'm slammed into the ground, I send force out the ends of my extended arms. It slows me down enough that I tumble roughly into the sand.

"Stay down!" I hear to my right. I drop from hands and knees to my stomach as fire blazes out over me. I bury my face in the sand and throw my arms over my head. Though I can feel the flames lick over my back and arms, I'm left unsinged.

With my face in the sand, I feel the ground shake as the combat goes on around us. The sizzling I hear to my left is the burning carcass of an unrecognizable Lesser Shade.

I turn my head around and find Ember wearing a smug grin. She makes her hand into a pretend pistol and blows actual smoke from the tip of her finger. I smile back at her but before I can thank her, the sand by her feet begins to quiver.

"Ember! Look out!" A flat, disk-like Shade resembling a crab claws its way out of the sand. It stands taller than our heads, snapping its pincers at us as it dances back and forth on spindly legs.

Ember waves me on, shouting over the noise. "I've got this. You go do what you gotta do!"

I charge down the beach, kicking up sand behind me. I have to dive and dodge around the clashing Shades and Walkers. I'm about thirty feet from the water's edge when I trip over something large. Sprawling out on my stomach, I turn reflexively, expecting the thing that tripped me to attack now that I'm down. What I find instead is worse.

Lang-hao is lying on his side in the sand. Two barbed

quills, each the size of my arm, have impaled him through the stomach and chest. He's gasping for breath but his lungs won't work properly. Blood flows from his wounds and out his mouth.

So much blood.

I scramble on my hands and knees through the sand until I'm by his side.

"It's okay, Lang. I can fix this." My hands move franticly over him. His eyes roll back and he goes limp. "Stay here! Lang!" He's lost too much blood to stay conscious. He's hurt so badly I don't know where to start. I look around frantically for Faye. I find her at the water's edge healing Simone, who looks to be in misery.

I'm on my own.

"Okay, I can fix this. I can fix this," I whisper repeatedly.

I send out energy and, using the skill that Lang himself taught me, rip the quills from his body. With my hands over his chest my mind commands his body to repair the injury. I push the process harder, faster than I ever have before. I'm so afraid he'll bleed out before I can fix him. I watch as his muscles spread across the open wounds of his torso, reaching for each other and knitting together. Soon the flesh follows the same pattern. Once I know the worst is over, I order the body to begin creating new blood to replace the amount he lost.

An explosion behind me sends sand into my back so forcefully it tears into my clothing and cuts my skin. My ears ring from the blast. The world in front of me tilts and sways in my sight. I'm dizzy from the battle raging around me.

I look toward the ocean and the tear site and see Kira and Mel struggling to keep up with the Elder Shade. He's too strong and too fast. They're losing strength and it won't be long before they fall. I need to get to them.

Lang is recovering but his heartbeat is still weak and I'm afraid to leave him. I look at Faye across the beach. Simone, better now, helps the healer to her feet among the waves.

Faye. She looks up and our eyes meet. The scars on her face stand out vivid white even at this distance.

She nods to show she understands.

But right then, a great black aquatic tentacle bursts out of the ocean behind Faye. She dodges to the left but isn't quick enough. The slippery arm snakes itself around her mid-section. Simone's blood-chilling scream fills the air as Faye is lifted high into the air.

"Faye!" I yell, leaping up and running to her. As she hovers in the air, our eyes meet and a sick feeling settles into my chest.

Faster than lightning, the arm cracks downward, slamming Faye hard onto the surf.

"No!" My shout is a strangled cry.

The sea Shade raises Faye into the air again. I'm almost to her.

SLAM.

Before Faye can be lifted off the ground for a third time, Sam reaches her and dives onto the slick arm, pinning it to the ground. I arrive and push my mind into the arm of the Shade. I rip apart the flesh until the arm is severed from its body.

More twisting tentacles stretch up out of the churning waves, feeling, groping their way toward us. Sam works to untangle Faye while I sever the monster's other arms. One after another they come—three, four, now six. I pull apart limb after limb, littering the beach with writhing, oozing black ropes until there are no more.

"Addy," Sam croaks, leaning protectively over Faye, "she needs you."

I fall to the ground next to my friend's broken body. Her eyes are closed and she's very still.

"Is she—" Sam starts but can't bring himself to ask.

I lift my hands over her body, intending to send my mind out toward her, when she opens her eyes. She's in excruciating pain. I quickly shut off the pain sensors in her brain and her relief is instantaneous.

"Don't you worry, Faye." I try to reassure her, but she knows as well as I do how grave her injuries are.

Someone shouts for help somewhere up the beach and Sam jumps to his feet but hesitates.

"Go! I'm fine here."

When I look back down at Faye, she's looking behind me, her eyes wide. I spin, ready to fend off another Shade, but there's nothing there. Looking back at Faye, I find she no longer looks surprised. Her expression is peaceful and filled with a sweet kind of longing.

I return my hands to their place above her, but she uses what little strength she has left to push them away.

"Faye? What—"

"Shhh, don't Addy," she whispers through cracked lips, still peering over my shoulder. "Don't waste time."

"Faye NO! It's not too late." We both know I'm lying.

"Please Addy,…" she smiles serenely, "let me go to him."

Again I turn around and find nothing behind me. She's hallucinating. She thinks she's seeing her dead husband.

She whispers something but I can't make out the words. Again I try to heal her and again she stops me.

"Faye. Please. I have to *try*," I beg her, sobbing. I can see she's determined but I can't bear to say good-bye. We need her. She's like a mother to all of us.

Her eyelids flutter and a tear rolls down the side of her face. With her last breath she utters, "Allen… my Allen."

And then it happens.

The tear rips wide open, making an audible CRACK that resonates deep within me. The cold that had been slowly seeping from the tear site now readily flows out onto the beach, spreading invisible tendrils that reach into me and wrap around my heart, turning it to ice in my chest.

Like a dam bursting, Shades of all sizes, Lesser and Greater alike, pour from the Nether Realm and into the ocean. They slink and slither, dash and fly in all directions. The water, as if reacting to the very nature of the demons, churns violently. A murky blackness spreads out from the opening, tainting the ocean, turning it into a viscous, oily broth.

Leaving Faye's body behind, I rush to the tear site.

The Elder Shade, having accomplished his task, turns and joins the melee on the sand. Behind him, knee deep in the water and facing the tear, I'm surprised to see Crank. I'm surprised because he looks excited—no *giddy*—as he flexes his hands eagerly.

"This is *my* show now!" He throws his arms out wide and I watch, stunned, as the ocean responds to his command. The tide swells to an incredible height and the sea rushes forward.

Waves come crashing in and around the tear, forcing back the stampede of Shades. Crank's tiny frame is dwarfed by the massive waves his awesome power is commanding. He's single handedly holding off the armies of hell. I pray he can hold out long enough for us to reseal the tear.

I search for the two sealers, fearing the worst, but then I feel their auras. I find them in the water still, fighting against the currents of the now-crippling tide. I didn't see them before because they're covered in the black sludge that has bled from the Nether Realm, camouflaging them against the murky waters.

They're weak. Mel loses her footing and is pulled beneath the waves. Before she can be washed away, I grasp for her with my mind. Holding her tightly within the grip of my power, I drag her up to the shallows where she can breathe.

While I have her, I send strength through her body and rejuvenate her exhausted mind. Refreshed and feeling new, she plants her feet firmly in the sand and resumes her work on the tear. When I'm confident she can stand on her own, I repeat the process within Kira.

With the opposing forces of the charging Shades

pushing back against the furious ocean, the hole between our realms continues to take the brunt of the abuse. It rips and tatters, becoming larger by the second. It will take all three of us working together to fix it.

At the back of my mind, I feel a familiar life force flicker and weaken. A woman screams and at the same time, Timothy's light, his aura, blinks out of existence.

I can't wait another second or more will die, more lights will extinguish.

Running through the sand and surf, I mimic Sam's ability to utilize my muscles to their full capacity to get me to the portal sooner. I throw my thoughts out, feeling with invisible hands, tracing the edges of the tear. I begin stitching. It's slow at first, but then Mel and Kira find the place I'm working on and join their efforts with mine.

With the strength of our combined abilities, the bottom of the tear begins to weave together. I push harder, force the fabric to meet and mend, placing bonding wards on the seam along the way so it can't be re-opened.

It's working. The once gaping rift is now halfway closed. The Shades in the Nether Realm turn frantic. Desperate to get through the opening before it closes, they jockey for the front of the herd. Obsidian tusks, horns, claws, tentacles, and feelers protrude from the hole as the mass of dark bodies beyond roils and churns.

We are two-thirds of the way done when the ocean suddenly stops its deluge. An unseen force plucks up Crank and tosses him like a rag doll out over the ocean.

"I've got you, Crank!" Lang shouts, and I spin to see my

friend, very much alive, face pinched in concentration as he reaches out for Crank.

The Elder Shade, maybe sensing his work was being undone, has returned. Crank's efforts posed the greatest threat, so he attacked him first, but soon he will turn his attention to Mel and Kira and me.

Lang catches Crank in the air and begins to pull him back to his post. In the few seconds he's been gone, dozens of Shades have spilled out through the hole.

The Elder Shade turns toward Lang with his arms outstretched, intending to stop him from helping Crank. I know I have only a second to intervene.

HEY!

I send my thoughts out to the Elder Shade. For a minute it works. His gaze flicks in my direction.

I have to distract him. I have to keep him off the others long enough for them to do their job. But the Elder turns and takes another step toward Lang.

You were wrong about us, you stupid, worthless pawn!

His steps falter slightly.

You thought we couldn't do it, but look at us!

I use false bravado to try and provoke his pride.

It works. He turns toward me.

YOUR PATHETIC ATTEMPT WILL NOT SUC-CEED. YOU ARE NOT THE ONE AND THE ONE HAS FAILED YOU.

The one? Does he mean Mikhail? As a last ditch effort I close my eyes and feel for Mikhail's frequency. He isn't here. He hasn't come to help us. I can't feel any trace of him within Chaos at all. Feeling my despair, the Elder coughs out a wet laugh.

HIS FAILURE IS YOUR DOOM.

I move backwards, circling around him, maneuvering him away from the others. I need only keep him talking a little while longer. But the Elder Shade has something more than talking in mind.

His laughter grows louder and louder until it fills me. It bounces off the walls inside my head, blocking out everything else. I can no longer move of my own accord. My back and neck stiffen, forcing my head back, and my feet leave the ground. A sharp burning begins to spread across my abdomen.

What is that? What's happening? I sink within myself, traveling through my body until I reach the area that's aching. I go even deeper, all the way to the cellular level, and am horrified at what I find. My cells, my flesh and muscles and sinews and bones are unbinding. They are coming apart! I am coming apart. The Elder Shade is unraveling me the same way he did the fabric of reality.

CHAPTER 62

I ACT SWIFTLY, furiously mending my insides, countering the undoing he works inside me. I'm vaguely aware of the other Walkers battling around me. I think I hear Sam shout my name but I'm unsure. Healing myself has become my main priority, commanding all my attention. Anything else is a distraction.

Though my body is healing, it isn't fast enough. The burning begins to spread up and across my chest, down into my thighs. The affected area is becoming too large. I can't keep up with it. The worst part is the pain. If I quit healing for even a second to tell my brain to stop the pain, I'll be torn to pieces.

Blasts, one after another, rain down around us, sending sand and pieces of Lesser Shades flying through the air. And the Elder's assault never wavers.

My shoulders begin to burn, followed quickly by my legs. Everything's on fire. I heal and I heal but I can't keep up. I'm in over my head and losing what little ground I have.

I can't stop shrieks of agony from escaping my throat. It feels as though my whole body is screaming with me.

Visions come unbidden to my mind. My mother. My sister. Sam, Ember, everyone I love. Everyone I'm failing. I see Angel. The little girl radiates a joy that is almost palpable. I see Faye. She's young and beautiful. Her skin is flawless, free of scars. She's under the arm of a handsome man who smiles down at her lovingly.

I see my father clearest of all. He looks just as I remember him. His kind smile and warm eyes send peace throughout me.

My body is beyond pain now. I'm numb from head to toe, but still I try. Still I work feverishly, concentrating on keeping my vital organs intact. I hold out as long as I can because every second the Elder spends on me is a second given to the others.

My father is reaching for me. He's so clear, so close. His love wraps around me like a safe blanket. Everything I remembered about him floods through me, filling my senses. His sparkling green eyes, the way he smells, how it feels to fall into his arms. Suddenly I'm afraid I'll disappoint him.

I've failed, Dad. I've failed everyone.

But all I feel from him is love and acceptance. He's here. He wants to comfort me. All I have to do is let go and I'll be with him. It seems such an easy thing and I wonder why I've been fighting it so hard.

I forget why I'm resisting. I forget all my worries. I'm ready to let go.

The image of my father, hand extended toward me, dissolves as my eyes are forced open.

The Elder Shade, mere feet away, stares into my eyes.

He knows I'm seconds away from dying.

LOOK AT ME AS YOU DIE.

So he will rob me not only of my life, but of the last bit of peace I so desperately cling to.

No. I won't let go. I refuse to give up. If I die, I die fighting.

He begins to fade from sight as my vision blackens.

I'm losing consciousness.

Before he disappears completely, he snaps backward, his tall frame bent in an unnatural angle. His hold on me is broken and I fall to the sand, landing on my side. My body is so unhinged I'm unable to move. The Elder stumbles backwards, writhing and twisting in a macabre dance.

With renewed hope I continue to repair the damage he's done to me. The Shade seems to be in pain. For the first time, I sense fear in him—fear for his life. Something is attacking him. Somehow, someone has gotten past his defenses. As soon as my neck is healed enough, I turn my head around, looking for the source of the attack. The only action left on the beach is at the tear site. Every remaining Walker stands defending Crank, Mel, and Kira.

Twisting back I watch as the Elder's flesh stretches and expands. He looks as though he'll burst. His head rolls around in agony. He claws at his chest and falls hard to his knees.

Where is this coming from? What's happening?

Right now, it doesn't matter. I must take advantage of his condition. I've healed the life-sustaining organs within me enough now to shift my full attention his way. Reaching a weakened arm out from where I lay in the sand, I put all of my strength behind a shockwave of pure energy directed at his chest.

Sand blasts up and out all around him but he's unaffected. How is he still untouchable? I try sending fire. A ribbon of flames swirls up around him, but his flesh refuses to burn.

An awful bellow comes from the Shade as his ribcage swells outward and sucks back in. His stomach bulges grotesquely out to one side. The Shade arches violently back as an arm, a black sludge-covered arm, erupts from his chest. And then another. They push and pull on the ribcage from the inside, ripping the wound open, spilling the Shade's insides out onto the sand.

The Elder Shade wraps his arms around himself, trying to keep everything in, but he's growing weak and can no longer hold onto his defenses. As his shield—the only thing holding him together—drops, what's left of him explodes, sending black mist and greasy clumps of ichor showering down upon the beach.

Kneeling in the sand amid the blood rain is the Shade that burst from the Elder's chest. This one is smaller than the Elder and oddly humanoid. But now I can feel him. It isn't another Shade—it's Mikhail! He's drenched in the blood of the Elder Shade and is badly shaken. I feel his body slip into shock as he falls forward onto his chest.

CHAPTER 63

I TRY TO get up, try to run to him, but I fall back down, too weak to stand.

The coldness emanating from the breach ceases. My eyes travel to the tear site and find it sealed. Kira is putting the final strengthening wards on it now.

The ocean is back to its own natural pull and swell. The few remaining Lesser Shades turn and flee. Simone spears a gorilla-like Lesser Shade straight through its neck before it can escape.

I scan who's left standing among the Walkers. They stare about them with identical expressions of stunned disbelief as they look around the carnage-strewn beach and find no Elder Shade.

Help Mikhail! I project to all of them, then retreat back into myself to finish healing. I can't help Mikhail or anyone else in this condition. Lying in the sand, covered in blood both red and black, I've never been more exhausted. As badly as I want to quit—to close my eyes and fade into a peaceful rest, I know I don't have that luxury. There are others that will need to be healed, damages that will need to be tallied, losses that will need to be counted.

Dizziness overwhelms me as the scene around Mikhail swirls unfocused in my vision. Mikhail is a black blob, covered head to toe in the Elder Shade's thick blood. He's distressed—panicked even—trying desperately to wipe the sludge from his skin. He manages only to spread it around.

Though the Shade is dead and gone, a heavy sense of malevolence hangs in the air, and it seems to be emanating from the Elder's remains that are now clinging stubbornly, unnaturally, to Mikhail's flesh. The others, unable to feel the evil that lingers, stare in worried confusion at Mikhail as he becomes more and more hysterical, trying to rid himself of the cloying filth.

He tears his shirt from his body and picks up handfuls of sand to rub into his skin but to no avail. The greasy blood seems to be seeping into his very pores. Mikhail lets out an agonized groan that becomes a frustrated shout before he collapses, retching into the sand.

I try to speed up my self-healing, but I don't have the strength to go any faster. I can't even project my thoughts any more. I want to scream at the others, "Help him!" but I can't do anything but sew myself back together. Can't they see his despair? Can't they feel him suffocating?

Sam reaches me and kneels by my side. "Addy, tell me you're all right."

I stretch an arm out and point to Mikhail.

"Help him," I croak. I look up into Sam's face, pleading with my eyes. He looks back and forth between the two of us, clearly reluctant to leave me. After what seems like for-ever, he gives me a determined nod and stands quickly.

Reaching Mikhail, Sam bends and threads his arms around his chest and tries to lift him. His skin is so slick with the greasy Shade blood it's difficult to keep a grip on him. Sam's efforts to help Mikhail rally the others. They rush forward as one, each grabbing limbs, offering support. Together they carry the despondent Walker to the ocean's edge where they lower him gently into the waters.

They encircle him so completely it's difficult for me to see what's happening. Comforted with the thought that he's no longer alone, I close my eyes and shut out all out-ward distractions.

I travel the length of my body, starting at my head and ending with my toes. Along the way I pull joints together, mend sinews and ligaments, patch together broken veins, strengthen layers of muscle and flesh. Once finished, I make a second trip, this time healing my outermost layers of skins that have been broken down and left raw and bleeding. The damage is so extensive that I marvel I survived at all.

Feeling worn out but more or less in one piece, I manage to get to my feet. I walk toward the huddle of Walkers gath-ered in the shallows of the ocean. What I see when I arrive both shocks me and warms my heart at the same time.

The Realmwalkers have gathered around Mikhail and have used the ocean's waters to wash the Elder Shade's blood from his body with their own hands. Every last one of them is scooping up handfuls of the sea and rinsing every inch of Mikhail.

Kira and Ember are working on his arms. Ben and Mel are cleaning his back and chest. Simone works in earnest to remove the sludge from his short hair. The feeling of darkness that had lingered with the Elder's viscous remains has faded completely, and the atmosphere is now one of weary excitement and joy. Everyone's helping— Sam and Mel and Crank and Timothy.

Timothy? He's alive? Happiness surges through me, but before I can allow myself real relief, I need to be sure that Mikhail's okay. Gently jostling the others out of my way, I squeeze between the ranks and kneel in the water in front of Mikhail.

Looking at his blood-smeared face, I see his expression has changed from one of agony to one of wonder. He looks around at the others in complete bewilderment. I clasp his face in my hands and make him look at me. His eyes are wide and when he looks at me, I'm not sure he even sees me.

Using the water at my knees, I begin washing the grime off his face, the whole while muttering assurances to him.

"You did it, Mikhail. You did it. It's over now. Everything's okay. You're okay. It's all over."

"It really is over, isn't it?" Mel asks beside me. Everyone glances around, looking into each other's faces. They fight back nervous, tentative smiles, as if they're too afraid to hope.

"Yes," I say firmly. "Mikhail has killed the Elder Shade. The tear's been sealed shut. It's really over," I confirm to my friends, putting to rest their fears and doubts. I can feel the relief wash over everyone, but I know it will be short lived. As if reading my mind, Sam speaks to the group.

"We've had a victory here today, but it's come with a price." I can feel his internal struggle to keep his grief from his words. Immediately everyone looks around. Even Mikhail seems to be taking a mental tally of the Walkers standing around him.

Small gasps can be heard from a few of them, but it's Ben who whispers, "Faye."

Sam nods grimly. "Addy helped her pass peacefully. She wasn't in any pain." This does little to comfort the group. No one speaks; the sadness is too thick. The only sounds are the ocean's waves behind us and the quiet sobs of my friends.

It's Mikhail's bold voice that finally breaks the silence, surprising everyone.

"We must honor her brave sacrifice." I look into his eyes and see clarity. Whatever shock he has been through, the stupor has finally lifted. His face is tear-streaked, but his voice is thick with fervor.

"We will not leave her here to lie with the carcasses of these foul beasts."

CHAPTER 64

IT WASN'T THE kind of farewell we would have envisioned for one as beloved as Faye Devon, but given the state
of the bone-weary, battle-worn Walkers, it was the best we
could do. We stood and formed a circle, arms across each
other's shoulders, around Faye's burial site. We had carried
her far away from the war zone and found a place close to
the entrance to Major Calm.

With a gentle breeze coming in off the surf, we each took
turns sharing our fondest memories of Faye. It was difficult to
face such a deep loss in the wake of a victory, but the time we
spent there saying our good-byes was cathartic and something
we couldn't have done without.

After the last of us speaks, we walk quietly together back
to the shelter of the grotto. I scan the group, noting how some
walk hand in hand, others arm in arm, each supporting and
comforting one another. I'm filled with pride and gratitude
to be counted among these great men and women. Once safe
inside the garage of Major Calm, I wait until the last of us
passes through the doorway.

"All right, everyone," I announce. "I know you're all tired, but no one leaves until they've been given the 'okay' from Doc Shepherd. So form up a line, the worst of you first, please."

"Are you sure you can manage?" Sam asks quietly in my ear. I nod and smile reassuringly at him. The Walkers are all in fairly decent shape considering the fight we just had. The injuries are relatively minor, the worst being a dislocated collarbone and some broken ribs.

When Tim shuffles up to take his place in front of me, I stretch up and hug him tightly around the neck.

"You were dead. I felt it. I felt you die!"

He pats my back gently until I release him.

"I was," he says. Smirking comically, he jerks his head at Simone who's clinging to his arm. "But this one wouldn't have it."

I'm not the only one staring in astonishment at Simone.

"She gave me CPR. Wouldn't give up on me." His voice is teasing, but his face is filled with tenderness as he looks at her. "She didn't stop until my heart was beating again."

Simone's cheeks flush pink as she feels everyone's eyes on her. "It's not that big of a deal," she says dismissively. When everyone continues to stare at her, she gets defensive. "Sheesh, people, I'm not completely useless. I know things, okay? I played a doctor once in a movie."

This earns a laugh from everyone, lightening the mood considerably. Embarrassed and seemingly eager to get the attention off of her, Simone says, "Besides, I'm not the hero here. Mikhail is."

"Yeah Mikhail!" Crank pipes up. "What happened, man? How did you *do* it?!"

"Wait," Kira interrupts, "how did you even get there? I mean, from Inner Silence and all?"

Others start to talk simultaneously, each asking what happened and how. Mikhail seems overwhelmed with the attention and unsure how to respond. It takes Sam intervening to quiet everyone down.

"All right, all right, everyone. Give him some space. Let him explain."

Mikhail looks shyly around at the others, looking uncertain of himself. When our eyes meet, I give him my best smile and the tension melts off him.

"It was Adelaide," he says, still looking at me.

I shake my head adamantly but he continues.

"I couldn't have done it without her. She believed in me."

"What?" Someone voices their confusion.

Sam interjects, "Addy's believed for some time now that it was never her who was meant to stop the Elder Shade, but Mikhail."

Everyone looks at me with confusion, disbelief, even hurt. Ember seems most injured. Stepping closer to me, she asks, "Why didn't you say anything?"

"I tried." I say exasperated. "No one would listen! You were all so…" I look to Mikhail, not wanting to hurt his feelings, but the look on his face tells me he understands.

"No one wanted to hear about Mikhail. I knew none of you would believe me." Their confusion and disbelief turn to shame as many of the Walkers avoid eye contact with both me and Mikhail.

"She tried to tell me," Sam says, shouldering the bulk of the shame upon himself. "I shot her down and left her with no other option but to act without me or my help."

"I see now," says Mel. "That's why the Elder Shade was so intent on destroying you, Addy. He must have known somehow that even though it was Mikhail that could destroy him, he'd never have been able to do it without you."

Realization dawns clearly on the others' faces.

"Okay, that makes sense now, but that still doesn't explain how Mikhail was able to get out of Inner Silence," Kira insists gently.

"I snuck into Inner Silence. On my own." This alarms the others, so I take a second for the surprise to sink in. "I thought I'd be able to open the doors on my own and I was right."

They are obviously scandalized, so I plead, "I know. I'm so sorry. It was wrong of me to go behind your backs—"

"Stop." Ben's normally gentle voice is angry. I stare back at him, stunned by his demeanor.

"Don't you dare apologize for doing what you felt you had to. Addy," he looks at me intently, "if you hadn't released Mikhail, we'd all be dead now. Do not apologize for that."

Next to me, Ember quietly nods her head in agreement. She reaches out and takes my hand firmly, to show her support.

"So now we know how you got out," Simone muses. Tilting her head to the side, she looks calculatingly at Mikhail. "But how did you do it? How did you kill that thing?"

"Yeah, I mean," Crank motions wildly with his hands, "he was like, untouchable man!"

"From the outside," I clarify.

"What—"Timothy starts but then stops abruptly, understanding dawning on him he looks at Mikhail in disbelief.

It takes a little while for the other Walkers to all catch up, but when they do, they share matching looks of shock. Mikhail squirms visibly under their scrutiny.

Breaking the silence, he explains simply, "I am a shadow traveler. I move through darkness."

"Mikhail," Kira steps forward and places a hand on his shoulder. "Were you really inside that thing?" She looks afraid of his answer.

He lowers his head as if in shame and nods. "It was the only way."

"Thank you." Kira's look of fear is now one of marvel and respect. "Thank you for doing that for us."

Others chime in now.

"Thank you, Mikhail."

"Yes, thank you."

"It must have been awful."

I've been finely tuned to Mikhail's state of being since he destroyed the Elder Shade, and I've felt as he's gone through shock, fear, exhaustion, bewilderment, and unease at all the focused attention. He's managed to keep all of this under the surface, but now the outpouring of gratitude from the Walkers and the feeling of finally being needed and accepted threatens to overwhelm him.

Fortunately, I have a deeply intuitive boyfriend who also

happens to be our caring leader, and all it takes is one meaningful look from me for him to understand.

"Okay Walkers. Listen up." Sam effectively draws everyone's attention away from Mikhail, and he continues, "Each one of you performed amazing feats tonight. I couldn't be more proud of any of you." I can feel the pride pulsing through each of my comrades at these words.

"It feels as though this war had been a long time coming. All the hard work, the long hours that each of you put into preparation, whether it was thinning the ranks of Shades or putting in extra training time to keep in the very best form, it all paid off. If any one of you had given even one less ounce of effort, I'm not sure we would have succeeded. Congratulations are in order for *all* of you tonight. I think it's safe to say you've all earned some much needed rest. Go sleep, relax, celebrate. You've just saved the world."

The next few days are a welcomed vacation spent recuperating. Each of us has our own way of getting ourselves back into a normal routine. Simone's idea of therapy is to visit all the world's most elite shopping destinations. Poor Timothy gets dragged from Beverly Hills to Madison Avenue, then on to Milan and Paris. I'm sure it isn't his ideal way to spend the time, but he never complains; his affection for Simone runs too deep.

Ben and Mel quietly take care of affairs with the Devon family. They ensure that Faye's funeral expenses are covered by

The Walker Foundation and issue a generous donation to the hospital where she had dedicated her life top-side.

Ember, Crank, and Lang-hao eagerly take on the responsibility of throwing the largest, most extravagant celebration party probably ever thrown. All the Walkers, their families, and friends are flown to New York City to party on the roof of a downtown skyscraper. Lang-hao insists on live music while Ember insists on live exotic animals. No one was eaten, though it was a night to remember.

Kira has taken an interest in Mikhail lately. She works with him daily to help bring him out of his shell. I'm not sure if she's driven by the guilt she feels for the way she previously treated him, the gratitude for his part in saving the world, or whether she genuinely likes him. It's difficult to tell, but she seems to be making progress. Mikhail smiles more now than he ever has before. It warms my heart to see the others engage him, embrace him.

Still, in the darkest places of my mind, I can't fight off the nagging feeling that he isn't as okay as he lets on. I was only inside the mind of the Elder Shade for a very short time, and it was the worst experience of my life. I can't imagine what it must have been like for Mikhail.

The words he once spoke to me, his fears that night in Inner Silence, still haunt me.

It will change me, Addy. I will be ruined. Darkened.

I can't know if those words were merely unfounded fears of self-doubt or if maybe they meant something I truly could not understand.

Despite losing Angel and Faye, we're healing. I feel as

though our emotional scars have only made us stronger and brought us each closer together. I still struggle at times to fill the roles they left behind, but I continue to try and it gets easier every day.

Sam and I spend every moment together. He's my reward. To have the love of a man as strong and good as Sam is more than I deserve.

It's strange to look backward from here. That person I was that first night I fell into Chaos is a complete stranger to me. Since that night, I've faced death countless times. I've met with pure evil and come away victorious. I've suffered devastating losses but learned that tragedy shapes us, for better or for worse. I've grown strong and confident. I've come to understand that the deep love of true friendship is the most valuable thing in life. I've learned that everyone deserves a chance at redemption, and most importantly, I've learned to always have faith in myself, against all odds.

I look at who I am now, at what I've become, and I hope it is something worthy of admiration. I hope that when I finally come face to face with my father again, that he will wear an expression of pride. I will forever hold this secret wish deep within my heart. But for now, I'm done looking backward.

I'm unsure of our future. Everything's peaceful now—blissful even. But if there's one thing that Chaos has taught me, it's to enjoy the peace while you have it and to always be ready for the unexpected.

LOGAN

I LIE ON my side, legs curled up, cradling my mangled hands to my chest. I know I should be frightened. I should be terrified. But all I feel is sadness. I'm going to die tonight.

The snow nearly covers me. A loud crack and groan in the distance can only be one of the many trees around me surrendering to the weight of the storm. My vision is flooded with white. White ground, white-covered trees and bushes. The very air is filled with white sheets of angry snow.

I don't see any of it though. I close my eyes, and all I see is a pair of rich brown eyes framed by long, delicate lashes.

Jessica.

I can't believe this is how it will end. After everything I've lived through. After all I've survived! Only to die in my sleep? From some nightmare?

The sorrow seeps from my heart and fills my entire chest until I'm struggling for breath. This pain drowns out all others. My wrists, which feel broken, and my throbbing hands and knees are nothing compared to the heartbreak that's crippling me.

The trees around me continue to crack and groan. I don't care. All I can think about is that when I die tonight, no one will know. No one will be there to find my body. No one will come looking for me. And all I will have to look back on is a wasted life of delinquency and crime.

Maybe it's best I die tonight. Maybe this is nature's way of stopping me from becoming something worse than I already am. A true monster. Maybe I even agree.

But Jessica.

An earth-shaking explosion to my right sends snow and dirt and branches raining down on me until I'm covered and there's nothing left but darkness. The deafening ring in my ears blocks out all other sounds, but the ground trembles and shakes beneath me. Maybe it will open up and swallow me whole.

This is it. Any second now.

As a life of anger and hatred flashes before my eyes, I see hundreds of stupid choices I've made. I see dozens of people I've wronged, cheated, robbed. I see others who have tried to reach out and help me and I've only pushed them away. I see nothing that I can be proud of. This is the legacy I leave behind.

But of all the things I've done to regret, the one that hurts the most, the one that's the source of my current agony, is that Jessica will never know how I feel about her. She'll never know that when I imagine myself happy, I imagine I'm with her. She won't know that I hate the person I am because someone like me can never deserve someone like her. And she'll never know that of all the people I've ever met, she's the only one who has made me want to change.

The earth is still again. Why haven't I died yet? The ringing in my ears is fading and I can hear something. What is that? It sounds like voices. I can't make out the words but it sounds like voices yelling. Something steps on my leg and I jerk reflexively. A muffled voice shouts with excitement.

So I'm to be caught and tortured. This is more fitting, I guess. The snow covering my face begins to shift and the darkness starts to fall away. Words become clearer and I'm able to make out different voices now.

The blinding white of the snowstorm breaks through and temporarily steals my vision. When my eyes adjust, I'm met with a very confusing sight.

Standing over me is a young girl, my age. Her dark hair is covered in white flakes of snow, and her cheeks are rosy from the cold. The warmth of her smile starkly contrasts with our freezing surroundings.

"There you are!" She grins and kneels down beside me.

"How is he?" Another girl, one with fiery red hair blowing wildly in the wind from the storm, appears over her shoulder.

"Not bad. Suffering from shock though."

The brown-haired girl gently wraps her hands around my wrists, and at the same time a third person joins us. A man holding guns at his sides backs himself against our small huddle and faces out. I'm not sure what he's searching for, but it's obvious he's scanning the area for something. His alert posture suggests it can't be good.

"Look at me," the brunette says kindly. As soon as our eyes meet, I know I'm safe. I swallow a sob of relief. I'm not going to die. Maybe I'll even get to see Jessica again. I don't know how I know it, but these three people will protect me or die trying.

"What's your name?" She releases my wrists and places her hands over my ears.

"Logan." The ringing stops completely, and she moves her hands to my knees.

"Feeling better now, Logan? Do you think you can stand?"

The man with the guns tenses. "We've got inbound."

"I can stand," I say, awestruck as I support myself on the wrists that were broken only moments ago. "How did you do that?"

The two girls each throw one of my arms over their shoulders and guide me through the snow-laden foliage. I hear something crashing through the woods behind us.

"I'll tell you all about it soon," she assures me. "We're almost to the clearing where the bikes are. A little bit farther and we'll be home free."

After stumbling a few more times over broken limbs and roots hiding under the snow, we come to the edge of a large clearing.

The redhead inhales sharply. "Uh Addy, I don't know about 'home free.'"

I look out ahead to see what they're all staring at, and in the middle of the clearing is what can only be the bikes she had referenced—except they're surrounded by a small army of the most horrifying creatures I could've ever imagined.

The beasts glisten with oily black flesh that stands out sharp against the pure snow. They nuzzle and nudge each other, eagerly pawing at the earth. Some circle the sky above the rest while some slither and crawl through the legs of others. The coldness that fills my heart at the sight of them has nothing to do with the weather.

The man touches something in his ear. "Walkers. Looks like we could use some backup after all."

That's when the first one sees us.

The air fills with shrieks and shouts and angry bellows, and the ground shakes so violently I'm having a hard time keeping my feet. The three strangers take a protective stance in front of me, but not before I see the herd of demons stampeding in our direction. It looks like I might not make it after all.

Don't worry, Logan. You'll make it through this just fine.

The girl with the brown hair—Addy, I think they called her—turns and winks at me. A warmth, bone deep, spreads through out me. I hear her voice in my head again.

This is what we do. This is who we are. You're one of us now. Let me be the first to say, Logan, welcome to Chaos.

About The Author

CM FENN GREW up in Mesa, AZ. Along with being a wife and mother she is a proud veteran of the US Air Force and is currently a full time writer.

When CM was a child she surrounded herself with fascinating friends and lived wild adventures every day. No matter they all existed within her mind. As an adult, she's finding what a joy it can be to set all these mind musings free onto pages for other like minded dreamers to explore.

When she's not writing you can usually find her spending time with her kids, going to concerts, spoiling her dogs, or if she's really lucky, sneaking some gaming time into her busy life.

Follow me on Twitter: @CMFennWrites
Like Chaos on Facebook:
Chaos – The Realmwalker Chronicles #1
Find us on Goodreads: Chaos
(The Realmwalker Chronicles #1)
Visit my website: www.therealmwalkerchronicles.com